PENG

HOUSE
at the
EDGE
of the
WOODS

ABOUT THE AUTHOR

Rachel Hancox read Medicine and Social and
Political Science at Cambridge, qualified as a doctor three
months after getting married, and has juggled her family,
her career and a passion for writing ever since.

She worked in Paediatrics and Public Health for
twenty years, writing short stories alongside NHS policy
reports, and drafting novels during successive
bouts of maternity leave.

She loves singing, cooking, gardening and pottery, and
has five children, three dogs and a cat. As someone once
said, she thrives on chaos. She lives in Oxford with her
husband and youngest children.

ALSO BY RACHEL HANCOX

The Shadow Child

The
HOUSE
at the
EDGE
of the
WOODS

Rachel Hancox

PENGUIN BOOKS

PENGUIN BOOKS

UK | USA | Canada | Ireland | Australia
India | New Zealand | South Africa

Penguin Books is part of the Penguin Random House group of companies
whose addresses can be found at global.penguinrandomhouse.com

Published in Penguin Books 2024

001

Set in 9.25/12.5pt Sabon LT Std
Typeset by Jouve (UK), Milton Keynes
Printed and bound in Great Britain by Clays Ltd, Elcograf S.p.A.

The authorised representative in the EEA is Penguin Random House Ireland,
Morrison Chambers, 32 Nassau Street, Dublin D02 YH68

A CIP catalogue record for this book is available from the British Library

ISBN: 978-1-529-16034-5

www.greenpenguin.co.uk

MIX
Paper | Supporting
responsible forestry
FSC® C018179

Penguin Random House is committed to a
sustainable future for our business, our readers
and our planet. This book is made from Forest
Stewardship Council® certified paper.

For Jo and Charlotte and Camilla

Prologue

AUGUST 1993

The roads are empty. It's four o'clock on Sunday afternoon and no one else is heading home yet. Everyone else is making the most of the last weekend of the summer holidays: enjoying beaches, barbecues, glasses of wine in the garden. Kirsty feels a flash of regret, but it's gone almost at once. She's glad that they left early; glad that she made a stand. It feels good to be driving down a deserted motorway with the sun glazing the tarmac and a heat haze blurring the horizon. It's almost as though she's driving through empty space: through a universe filled with possibility.

'Look.' She turns to Ben, hunched down in the back seat. 'Can you see out the front? It looks as if we're floating above the road.'

Ben leans forward. 'Like a hovercraft,' he says.

'Yes.' Kirsty smiles. He's not her son for nothing.

'Why does it?' he asks.

'It's the hot air,' Kirsty says. 'The heat coming off the road.'

But it's not just that, she thinks. It's the lightness inside her, lifting them up. The thought of what she's put behind her, and of what lies ahead: the rush of relief and excitement. That's how aeroplanes fly – because of the rush of air over the top of their wings. You can hardly believe that would be enough, but it is.

She catches sight of Ben in the mirror, watching her, and she feels a surge of love. Her big little boy. Her tiny giant.

'Where shall we fly on the hot air?' she asks. 'Where would you like to go?'

He screws up his face. 'To Africa,' he says. 'Or maybe Antarctica.'

Kirsty laughs. 'Those are very different places.'

'Or the Amazon,' Ben says.

'I'd like that too,' she says. She hesitates then – but she won't tell him where she's thinking of taking him. Not yet. She knows the questions he'll ask and she needs to be ready to answer them. But the thought of it squirms up through her body now, a tingle of pleasure travelling all the way to her fingertips. She mustn't count any chickens, she keeps telling herself. She mustn't let her hopes run away with her. She's been so careful all this time, so cautious: she's built herself up into a person who can cope with the reality of life. But she's ready now – today – to grasp her life in her hands. To make it what she wants it to be. She's ready to move forwards.

As if it's heard her thoughts, the car stumbles just then. Stutters, then picks itself up. All right, old car, Kirsty thinks. Perhaps there was something wrong with it after all? Only another ten miles, she tells it. You can do it.

'The Amazon, then,' she says to Ben. 'But home for tea first, maybe?'

And then the car stutters again, more violently. The jerk throws Ben forwards against his seatbelt and Kirsty brakes.

'Sorry about that,' she says. 'Are you OK?'

Ben nods.

'We'll go more slowly for the last bit,' she says. 'Come on, car. Keep going.'

But the car won't listen. There's another jerk, more violent than the last one. Kirsty slows to thirty, then twenty. Maybe they can keep going like this, if—

'Whoa,' she says. 'OK. We'd better stop. What a pain. I'm sorry, Ben. I don't think we'll be going to the Amazon today.'

'Will we get home?' he asks, as they come to a halt on the hard shoulder.

'Definitely.' She turns, smiles at him. 'We just need a bit of help.'

There's no sign of civilisation anywhere nearby: the motorway runs through woodland just here. Beside the hard shoulder there's a ditch, a fence, then nothing but trees. She should have been looking out for an emergency phone, once the car started playing up, but she wasn't. She unbuckles her seatbelt, looks again at Ben. What should she do? She doesn't like to leave him, but she has no idea how far she'll have to walk, and he's tired.

'Will you sit tight, Ben?' she asks. 'I'm going to leave you to look after the car.'

'OK.'

'You'll be all right.' It's half-question, half-assurance. She purses her lips, wondering whether it would be better to take him with her. Whether it would be better for them both to wait in the car. But no one has passed them since they stopped except a single lorry, going too fast, that made the car shudder. Damn it, she thinks. Damn it. But she'll find a phone. It'll be all right.

'Don't get out,' she says. 'And when I've gone, push this knob down, OK? That'll lock the door.'

Ben nods. He doesn't look worried: that's a relief. He trusts her.

'You're a good boy,' she says. 'I won't be long.'

She opens the door and climbs out on to the hard shoulder.

PART ONE

I

It was Ben's height that struck Rebecca first. She was five foot nine, so men didn't often seem tall to her, but Ben did. He had a big head too – big even for his body, with a square jaw and heavy cheekbones. Something about his size made him seem vulnerable, as though he didn't quite fit in the world other people inhabit.

Her friend Carol introduced them, doing her duty as hostess at a house-warming party: 'Rebecca, meet Ben.' Then she raised one eyebrow and said, 'Rebecca's into travel.'

'Not really,' Rebecca protested. She was working for a travel agent then; that was what Carol meant. Not that she'd been trekking in the rainforest. It made her feel a little foolish. 'How do you know Carol?' she asked.

'I don't.'

Rebecca laughed, but Ben's expression didn't change. He looked at her gravely, as if he was trying to work something out. Rebecca could hear the things other women might say now, the edge of flirtation – *Did you just walk in off the street, then?* – but she didn't say them. She could already tell that Ben wasn't a man to play games with.

'Her brother went to my school,' Ben said. 'I met him at Sainsbury's last week and he invited me.'

Rebecca was thirty-three, and she hadn't had a boyfriend for two years. Since her mother died she hadn't minded being single – it had been a relief, almost, to give up the effort – but it seemed to her suddenly that encounters like this mattered, at her stage in life.

7

It was as if she'd reached the point she'd been rehearsing for all this time. So she stuck with Ben, applied herself to the conversation. He liked animals, she discovered. When he was a little boy he'd had an imaginary alphabet of pets, from axolotl to zebu.

'Not zebra?' she asked, and he fixed those serious eyes on her again.

'Zebra's what everyone else would choose,' he said.

'Like aardvark,' Rebecca said, and he smiled suddenly. And that seemed to establish something between them, like an invisible filament forming in a test tube.

'Getting on well with Ben, I see,' said Carol, when Rebecca passed her on the way to the loo. 'Strong and silent, eh? Deep waters. And you know about his background?'

'No?'

'Oh, you should ask him. His mum was murdered. Attacked when their car broke down on the motorway. You might remember, it was all over the news. He was in the car. He was only seven.'

Ben and Rebecca left the party soon after that and went on to an Indian restaurant nearby. She couldn't remember later which of them had suggested it. Over supper he told her his story himself, unprompted, and the way he told it made her feel it wasn't something he did lightly. She was a little drunk by then, but her whole mind was on Ben, on what he was saying and how his words made her feel.

She did remember the murder. She must have been ten or eleven at the time, a few years older than Ben. Kirsty Swarbrick's death was top of the news for weeks, but it was the child's involvement – Ben's – that made such a splash in the media. That and the fact that it happened on an ordinary Sunday afternoon in August.

'My mother went for help,' Ben said. 'She told me to sit tight.'

He looked straight at her, watching her face. Rebecca felt a prickle of imaginary pain, and she realised she'd let her hair fall back from the scar above her right eye. It wasn't the exposure that unnerved her so much as forgetting that automatic gesture of self-protection. She saw Ben's eyes flick to the scar and away again, and

8

she felt a flutter of warmth and release – something like what her father would call grace. Her wound was on the outside, but Ben understood it. He knew what it meant.

'There was a man in a white car,' he said. 'He parked a bit behind us. I saw him in the mirror, getting out of his car. I thought he was going to help. I waited for him to come and talk to me, but he didn't. Then I looked again and his car had gone. A policeman stopped eventually, but there was no sign of the man. They never found out who he was.' He hesitated, but only for a second. 'My mother's body was found in the woods beside the motorway.'

'I can't imagine what it must have been like,' Rebecca said. 'You must have been terrified, waiting all that time for her.'

'I remember sitting in the car,' Ben said. 'I remember the smell of it, and the heat, and not daring to open a window.'

Rebecca recalled, with a flutter of guilt, how she'd pictured that scene herself, at the time. Lying awake at night, she'd scared herself in that delicious way by imagining herself in the car, waiting and waiting. Her mother lying dead in a tangle of woodland.

'What happened to you?' she asked. 'Did your father bring you up?'

Ben shook his head. 'I never knew him. My mum was eighteen when she had me. My grandparents weren't much older than some kids' parents. They looked after me.'

Eighteen, Rebecca thought. So Kirsty had only been twenty-five when she died.

'I must have got my height from my dad, though,' Ben said. 'My mother was barely five foot. When I was a little boy I used to look at tall men sometimes and think, I wonder if that's him.'

Rebecca looked back at him, but she didn't smile. She'd already worked out that smiling meant something special, with Ben.

'But I was OK,' he said. 'My grandparents lived in the country-side, near Warwick. That's where we were coming from that day – we'd been to visit them. I liked living there. I'd like to live in the country again one day.'

When they'd finished eating they walked back to Rebecca's flat and went to bed. It was unlike anything Rebecca had experienced before, the weight of this big man on top of her and the little boy wrapped in her arms. He made her feel safe and needed, and more like herself than she'd ever been before.

She saw Ben every evening that week, and at the end of it he asked her to marry him. A whirlwind romance, Carol said, when she told her. Rebecca enjoyed her surprise, and the feeling of doing something people didn't expect. Of not turning out to be quite who they thought she was.

It's the only hasty decision she's ever made, and she's never regretted it. Six years later, they're still happy. They were made for each other: that's what she tells herself every time she feels that little twinge of surprise at waking up next to him; that little frisson of unease when she drives past a patch of woodland on the motorway.

2

Perched on her scaffolding tower, Rebecca's attention is focused on the ceiling above her and the gradual spread of colour across it. But she enjoys the small shock when, from time to time, she looks down into the great hall beneath: the way the world is inverted, the tiled floor curving away from her like a chequerboard sky. It pleases her to think that she shares this perspective on the world with Michelangelo and Tiepolo, who must have squatted like this, on platforms thirty feet above the ground, to paint their ceiling frescoes. She likes to imagine them mixing their colours, or leaning back to consider the angle of an arm, as they unfolded their masterpieces across the vaults of Vatican chapels and Venetian palaces.

This commission is Rebecca's big break, and she's determined to make a success of it. Marchboys House is a Georgian mansion deep in the Warwickshire countryside, and everything about it is on a grand scale, from the landscaped park, ringed by woodland, to the lofty hall she has been employed to decorate. It must have had murals aplenty in its heyday: it's easy to picture an eighteenth-century Cupid aiming his arrows across the broad span of this ceiling. But Marchboys was almost destroyed by a fire a few years ago, and there's nothing left of the original decoration. The house is being meticulously restored by the new owner, a wealthy businessman called Pieter Blake. Her client, Rebecca thinks, remembering the businesslike concision of their initial negotiations.

'You haven't been doing this long,' he said.

'Three years.' Rebecca smiled, hoping to convey confidence. 'I retrained. I'd always wanted to be an artist.' She hesitated – but Pieter didn't seem to require any more explanation. He's a direct person, no-nonsense. He reminds Rebecca of a shark: that same sense of restless power. The same sleek lines.

'I like what I've seen of your work,' he said. 'But this would be the biggest project you've undertaken?'

'Yes,' Rebecca admitted. 'But size isn't really an issue. It's just a question of time.'

Pieter nodded. If he had any idea of the technical challenges of painting a domed ceiling, he gave no sign of it. Perhaps, Rebecca thought, he was used to trusting in other people's expertise.

'When would you be able to start?' he asked.

He grew up in Hong Kong, he told her that day. Rebecca was surprised, not just by the fact but by him sharing it. She decided it was a deliberate strategy, to give the impression that she was in his confidence. But it made him, somehow, less accessible rather than more. It set a boundary: here is what you can know about me.

The ceiling is a wedding present for Pieter's fiancée, Freya. She's an actress – a famous one, apparently, although Rebecca hadn't heard of her. Pieter wants the painting finished during the three months she's away filming in New Zealand.

Rebecca's touched by the idea of a surprise gift on such a grand scale. It's hard to imagine living in a house like this, with its countless rooms and echoing spaces, but sometimes she tries to picture herself coming down that curving staircase each morning and glancing up at her mural, framing the scene with its own particular magic – because instead of classical myths or Bible stories, Pieter wants her to paint fairy tales on the ceiling. He's given her a book of stories to draw on, and Rebecca is entranced by them. She rarely read fairy tales as a child; they fell, along with drawing and painting, into the category of the trivial and the fanciful that was disparaged by her mother. Her hobbies were chosen for her: piano lessons and Guides and the church youth group. Being let loose on this expanse of white plaster is strangely thrilling. Her days are spent in the company of giants and dragons, and at night her dreams inhabit castles and forests and magic gardens.

Rebecca tilts her head back now to inspect the tree whose branches have been unfurling beside a dusty road. Then she finds a pencil and sketches in little birds, two or three and then a dozen more, perching among the foliage. Swallows, perhaps, returning from their winter sojourn in Africa, or larks and nightingales to serenade her through the solitary hours on her scaffolding tower. They don't belong to any of the stories she's been using, but there's bound to be one with birds in. She could ask Ben – but Ben isn't interested in fairy tales. She hoped he might like the book Pieter gave her, but he barely glanced at it when she brought it home. Perhaps he thinks it's childish. Or perhaps he didn't grow up with fairy tales either.

Sunlight fills the hall all day through the tall windows along the façade, and when it starts to fade there's a monumental chandelier with three dozen light bulbs and long ropes of glass crystals. It's useful to see what the ceiling will look like by its dazzling artificial light, but daylight is better for painting, and dusk comes early in January. Rebecca usually continues for a couple of hours after the chandelier is lit, but tonight she's ready to stop a bit earlier. She keeps a drum of water on the platform to wash her brushes and a supply of rags to dry them. Climbing down, she stretches her limbs and her back, then looks up for the last time to appraise the day's progress. Far above, the painting has edged a few feet further across the ceiling, but there's still a long way to go.

Ben's in the kitchen when she gets home. He likes cooking, especially when he can use produce from the garden: he grows vegetables and fruit, and keeps hens and bees. Herb bushes – rosemary, thyme, sage and bay – flank the little path from the gate to the front door, perfuming their homecoming each evening, even in the depths of winter.

They bought this house a month before their wedding. Ben had some money in the bank – money given by well-wishers to a fund launched after his mother died. His nest-egg, he called it. He'd always imagined, Rebecca realised, that it would be enough to buy the house of his dreams, but even with the mortgage they could raise between them there wasn't much they could afford. When he saw this cottage, though, Ben's eyes lit up. A tumbledown two-up, two-down in a village ten miles from Banbury without a shop or a church wasn't what Rebecca had had in mind, but she could see at once that it was exactly what Ben wanted. He even loved its name, None-go-bye – though whether he thought it suggested isolation or constant companionship Rebecca wasn't sure, and didn't ask.

There was no proper kitchen when they moved in, just a wood-burning stove and a cracked Belfast sink, but there were – there are – apple trees and beehives in the garden. The motorway runs close by, and Rebecca was afraid that would upset Ben, but once you're inside you can hardly hear it, and when the wind blows the other way it becomes a distant rushing sound you could almost mistake for a river.

'Hello,' she calls, as she comes through the front door. 'That smells good.'

'Curry,' Ben replies. 'Rogan josh.' He's never forgotten their first date in the Royal Balti: curry is their leitmotif.

'Delicious.' Rebecca puts her arms around him. He smells of soap and earth and frying onions, and his beard brushes her forehead when she leans into him. 'Have I got time for a shower?' she asks. 'I reek of paint.'

'If you want,' he says. 'I haven't put the rice on yet.'

Rebecca kisses him and slips up the narrow staircase that reminds her of doll's houses and secret passages. The treads creak as she reaches the landing. There's no light here, but she knows this space intimately, the three doors all within an arm's length: their bedroom overlooking the garden; the box room where Rebecca draws; the bathroom Ben plumbed in himself. The tub came from a scrapyard: the enamel is chipped, but it's deep and solid, and Ben installed a shower head over it. Rebecca sheds her clothes and steps in, drenching herself briefly to rinse away the traces of Marchboys House. Home, she thinks. It feels good to be home.

*

She has Ben to thank, really, for her new career. For the fact that the pipe dream she barely acknowledged for so long has come true. Ben wanted to learn about bee-keeping, so he could repopulate the old hives in the garden, and there was a course at the adult education centre in Banbury on Tuesday evenings. But they'd only been married a year, and Ben felt bad about leaving her alone for an evening every week.

'You could come too,' he said. 'They do lots of other classes.'

If the painting class had been on a different evening, life might not have taken the same turn. But it wasn't – and Rebecca confessed that she'd always wanted to paint. When she was a child, her godmother once took her to an art gallery and sent her home with a little watercolour set and a newly kindled passion, but her mother didn't approve. 'Don't waste your time on that,' she said, her face folding into familiar lines of disappointment. 'You don't have any talent for it, Rebecca.'

The adult Rebecca marvels sometimes that she took her mother's words so much to heart. But children are impressionable, and it became a self-fulfilling prophecy: she abandoned the watercolour set, and gave up art lessons at school as soon as she could. Even at thirty-four self-doubt might well have triumphed over temptation if Ben hadn't been so keen for her to join him. But the class in Banbury was a revelation, and the instructor had no truck with the idea that it might be too late to start – nor with the idea that painting was something you could dabble in casually. By the third week, she was lingering behind Rebecca's stool. She offered challenge rather than praise, but it was clear that encouragement was implicit. By the end of term, the others were gazing enviously at Rebecca's canvases, and she began to feel a cautious pride in her work.

Ben's bee-keeping course finished at Christmas, but Rebecca didn't want to stop. So Ben signed up for furniture restoration, and then, in the summer, vegetable gardening. Their lives, Rebecca thinks now, were transformed by the adult education centre. Their house, their garden, her career. After a year, Rebecca's teacher suggested a City and Guilds course, and soon after that she passed on a small commission: an imaginary garden seen through a *trompe l'oeil* window in someone's dark living room.

Rebecca was astonished, at the beginning, that people were prepared to pay her to adorn their houses and shops and restaurants, but they were. More and more plain walls were transformed by her brush into landscapes and city streets, secret rooms and fantastic scenes. Leaving the travel agency to paint full-time was a big step, but it has paid off. Last year she earned almost the same as Ben.

But Ben's salary, with a local plumbing firm, is steadier, and he likes it that way. Ben likes routine and repetition. Every evening he dips his head under the lintel of the cottage like a cuckoo squeezing into a thrush's nest, and the dogs bound up to meet him: two German shepherds with heavy tails called Ada and Bertha who have the run of their quarter acre of garden during the day. They have a good life, Rebecca thinks. And so does she. She has her work, the run of her imagination. And her evenings with Ben.

'I killed one of the pullets,' Ben says, as he serves up the curry. 'Everything's home-grown except the rice and the spices.'

'It's delicious.' Rebecca smiles to conceal her squeamishness over the chicken. 'Could we grow spices?'

'We ought to try,' Ben says. 'Oh, and I spoke to a man over in Essex who's getting rid of a couple of hives. I'm going to see him at the weekend.'

Rebecca is pleased by this news: not just because Ben has been wanting more hives, more bees, but because it means they won't be going to Hove this weekend.

It was clear to Rebecca the first time they met that she was never going to win Ben's grandparents' hearts – nor they hers. She was relieved when they moved to a flat near the seafront in Hove soon after she and Ben got married; having to drive down now and then was much better than having them ten miles away and being under the constant threat of their dropping in. When Terry died suddenly, three years ago, Rebecca was sure Maureen would move back closer to Ben, but so far she's stayed put. The visits to the south coast have been more frequent, though. And although it was Terry's relentless teasing that Rebecca particularly disliked, she finds Maureen almost as difficult to get on with – or to understand.

Maureen dotes on Ben, but her only daughter is never spoken of in the reverential terms Rebecca expected. Kirsty's photograph sits on the mantelpiece at Hove, the same wide-eyed, hopeful-looking girl Rebecca remembers from the news stories. But her parents' recollections paint a different picture: Kirsty's behaviour as a tantrum-prone toddler, a challenging child, an infuriating teenager, is recalled with a mixture of exasperation and satisfaction that Rebecca has always found perplexing. It's hard to tell whether the exasperation (or the satisfaction, for that matter) relates to her indomitable spirit or to its premature quashing.

They must have mourned her, Rebecca tells herself. They must have asked themselves endlessly what happened, as any parents would. Perhaps it's simply that grief is a private thing, and Rebecca has never been regarded as part of the family. And perhaps she shouldn't take the hostility too personally, she thinks now. Perhaps no woman was ever going to have their blessing to marry Ben, especially a vicar's daughter halfway to middle age, tall and angular and too plain, too shy, to carry it off with any flair.

'That looks wonderful,' she says, as Ben produces an apple crumble from the oven.

'I put star anise in it,' Ben says. 'Like they did on *Bake Off*. It makes a change from cinnamon, I suppose. Do you want cream or ice cream?'

Rebecca grins. 'There's some Häagen-Dazs,' she says. 'I'll get it.'

Watching Ben fill their tiny kitchen with food is a pleasure she'll never tire of, she thinks, as she fetches the ice cream from the freezer. She takes her turn at cooking, but she's never enjoyed it the way Ben does: it reminds her too much of the martyred hours her mother spent producing dull meals, and of the days when even that was beyond her.

After supper they wash up together, Ben splashing hot water and suds and Rebecca drying and putting away. The dogs shuffle around them amiably, their tails measuring out the narrow span of the kitchen.

'Shall we take the kites out this weekend?' Ben asks, as he hands her a glass to dry.

'I thought you were going to see the new hives?'

'That won't take all weekend,' he says. 'There's Sunday too.'

Rebecca doesn't reply. Kite-flying could mean one of the hills near here where other enthusiasts gather, but she suspects, glancing at Ben's face, that it means the beach. That it means Hove, after all. Ada settles in her basket with a heavy sigh, her eyes fixed on Rebecca.

'Only if you want to,' Ben says.

Rebecca knows there's no twist to this phrase. Ben says exactly what he means: it's one of the things she loves most about him. But she knows which answer he's hoping for.

'Of course I do,' she says. 'You know I love flying the kites.'

'Great.' He smiles at her. 'There's supposed to be a good wind, this weekend.'

As far as Rebecca can judge, Ben's childhood was even more limited than hers. The Guides and piano lessons feel like rich pickings by comparison with the Disney films that accounted for most of his entertainment. She likes to think he's making up for it now, though, with the vegetable garden and the bee-keeping and the dogs. Kite-flying is his latest passion: Rebecca bought him a manta ray for Christmas, a huge thing with streamers and long wings.

She smiles. Perhaps there should be a kite on the ceiling at Marchboys, she thinks. One of those giant dragon kites you see in Chinese festivals. Perhaps Princess Elvira could fly one from the window of her tower room.

3

Rebecca shuffles her drawings into a neat stack before tapping on Pieter's door. She's a little nervous: this is the first time he's asked to see her since she started at Marchboys. He appeared in the hall the previous afternoon to suggest incorporating their faces – his and Freya's – in the mural, and Rebecca has come up with several ideas. Representations of the cardinal virtues were popular in the cinque-cento, she's going to tell him. Or perhaps he'd like to be the woodcutter, with Freya as Red Riding Hood?

Pieter's study is enormous. There's a pair of black leather sofas, a wide mahogany desk and a fireplace with a bas-relief frieze above it. The windows look out towards the belt of woodland that sur-rounds the house, hemming it in like a dark fringe around the green sweep of parkland. Pieter taps on the desk, and Rebecca spreads the sketches across it.

'I like what you're doing,' he says, before she can speak. 'I like it very much. The style is just right.'

'Thank you.' His words bring a thrill of relief. Not just his words: there's something about his voice, the weight of assurance it carries, that makes his approval feel compelling.

'I don't want you to rush it,' he continues. 'I can see it's a big job. I've got more sense of that now.'

'I'm on schedule,' Rebecca says, 'if that's what you mean.'

Pieter picks up one of the sketches, then puts it down again. 'How would you feel about extending the project?' he asks.

'Perhaps a frieze going up the main staircase. And the pillars in the entrance hall – what about marbling? Can you do that?'

Rebecca has a fleeting image of the house covered in paint, with trees and sky and flowers spreading everywhere until there's no bare plaster left, like a tattoo enthusiast whose body is entirely inked over.

'I could,' she says. 'I'd have to . . .' She thinks fast. There are other clients in the pipeline, but none more important than Pieter Blake. 'It would mean moving things around,' she says, 'but I'm sure I could.'

Pieter nods: a precise gesture. Everything about him is efficient, Rebecca thinks. Effective. Economical.

'Let's start with the pillars,' he says. Then he surprises her again. 'Have lunch with me tomorrow. There's someone I'd like you to meet.'

As she fills in the stonework on a turreted castle the next morning, Rebecca realises she's being watched. She looks down to see a small girl standing in the hall.

'Hello.'

'Hi.' The child swings her leg, as though practising something halfway between a ballet step and a free kick.

'You must be . . .' Rebecca knows Pieter's been married before, but he's never mentioned a daughter.

The child narrows her eyes, inspecting the ceiling.

'Emily?' Pieter appears behind her. Rebecca can see the likeness, now they're together: Emily has his dark hair and high cheekbones. 'What do you think of the painting?' he asks.

'It's not finished.'

'It's a big job,' he says. 'Rebecca's only been here a few weeks.' Then he smiles up at Rebecca. 'Are you ready to stop for lunch?'

Rebecca leaves her painting smock on the tower. She's worn a dress today, but she wishes she hadn't. It's too old and shabby to pass muster: it would have been better not to have made an effort at all than to have made an inadequate one.

*

Emily, it turns out, is the person Pieter wanted her to meet. Rebecca isn't sure whether to be flattered: possibly he just wanted to share the burden of entertaining her. Emily's school has an INSET day, he explains, and her grandmother is working. Her mother isn't mentioned.

'What do you like doing, Emily?' Rebecca asks.

She's trying to work out how old she is. Seven or eight, perhaps. She seems a very definite child. Out of the corner of her eye Rebecca can see Pieter watching her.

'Just ordinary things,' Emily says. She has a heavy fringe, and a way of retreating under it that's a little unsettling. Rebecca wonders what sort of fairy tale she might put Emily in, if her father asked.

'Oh, come on.' Pieter smiles at his daughter. 'You like doing lots of things.'

Rebecca is beginning to wonder whether she should have offered to help with the food when the door opens and Pieter's assistant, Sam, appears with a tray. Rebecca looks down at the table when her plate is set in front of her. She's never been in a private house where servants brought the lunch before.

'Thanks, Sam,' says Pieter, as he leaves. Rebecca glances at his back, ashamed of not meeting his eye. She waits a moment, but Emily starts eating straight away. She tackles the sauté potatoes first, Rebecca notices.

'Good?' Pieter asks, and Emily nods.

'I like chips better, but these are OK,' she says, and Pieter laughs.

Rebecca still isn't sure what she's doing here. Clients often treat her as a friend, even a confidante, but Pieter strikes her as someone who guards his privacy carefully. Perhaps she's too insignificant to matter, Rebecca thinks. She feels a prick of disappointment, and dismisses it crossly.

'Where do you live?' Emily asks her, midway through her pile of potatoes.

'Not far from here,' Rebecca says. 'About an hour away, in a little house with a long garden.'

Emily considers this. 'Have you got pets?' she asks.

'We have bees and chickens and two dogs.'

Pieter looks up at the mention of bees – or perhaps at the 'we' – but it's the dogs Emily latches on to.

'I want a dog. Granny won't let me and Dad won't either.'

Rebecca smiles carefully. No reference to her mother again, she notices. 'Dogs are a big responsibility,' she says.

'I haven't got any brothers or sisters,' Emily insists, 'so I ought to have a dog.'

'Don't lobby Rebecca,' Pieter says. 'There's nothing she can do.'

He grins at Rebecca then, as if he's pleased with his feisty child, or perhaps with his management of her. Rebecca smiles back. She should stop overthinking this invitation, she tells herself. Why shouldn't Pieter decide to be friendly?

While Ben drives to Essex on Saturday afternoon, Rebecca goes to visit her father, but she makes sure she's back in plenty of time to welcome the new hives. She knows Ben will appreciate that: for a prosaic man, he has an almost mystical attitude to his bees.

While she's waiting, she fetches potatoes and onions from Ben's store and makes a start on supper. It's definitely her turn. Cottage pie, she thinks. That always feels appropriate for None-go-bye.

Some vestiges of the kitchen's original state are still visible, but not many. They've installed a new oven and a new sink and a row of oak-fronted units, and the rustic dresser has been filled with Rebecca's grandmother's Royal Doulton tea set. Now and then Ben buys her a piece of china as a gift, something with flowers on it like the tea set, and the accumulation has given the dresser a cheerfully chaotic look that spills over into the rest of the house. When they first moved in they furnished it with cast-offs and junk-shop purchases, and they've never got round to changing anything. But it's cosy, their little nest. There are bright colours, soft cushions. It feels more like home than anywhere Rebecca has ever lived.

As she scrubs the earth off the potatoes, she wonders, not for the first time, what her mother would have made of None-go-bye, and of Ben. Sometimes her mother's judgements surprised her. But not often.

No one, it seems to Rebecca, starts off by thinking their childhood is strange, and it took her a long time to notice – and longer to mind – that other people's lives weren't like theirs. Her mother was ill as far back as she can remember, and multiple sclerosis was just as much a part of their family as the Church was. It wasn't so much a physical constraint (her mother was in remission more often than not) as a psychological one: it defined the limits of what was possible; what was permissible. Her mother mustn't be upset, and certainly couldn't be flouted. When Rebecca had her accident, she was the only child in the ward whose mother didn't stay overnight, although she understood clearly enough that there was more than one reason for that.

Then there was the experience of being the vicar's daughter at the primary school where her father came in every week to take assembly: a stooped, prematurely aged figure whose soft voice was less suited to the school hall than the doorways and corners in which the two of them conducted their conversations at home. Her father understood what it all meant for Rebecca; that was the subtext of those quiet exchanges. But even today – even now that her mother has been dead for eight years – it's impossible to imagine discussing any of it openly.

She and her father are never short of things to say to each other, though. He liked hearing about Marchboys House today, about the painting and Pieter and the lunch with Emily. He loves children, despite his awkwardness with them. Tipping the pale chunks of potato into a pan, Rebecca thinks that she is more fond of her father than she can explain; certainly than she could explain to him.

Ben is back later than she expects, and by the time she hears his car, the cottage pie is in the oven. Rebecca rinses her hands under the tap and goes out to meet him. Ben the bee-man, carrying a white hive up the garden path, ready to receive a new swarm in the spring.

*

23

On Sunday morning, they drive down to Hove. Ben's grandmother has made her famous stew for lunch, and covered the little table with a lacy Sunday cloth. The flat is arranged around the sliver of sea view: they eat beside the window, the sky grey and blustery beyond.

'Lovely,' Ben says, after the first mouthful. *Ben's favourite*, Maureen says, every time she serves it. There's garlic bread as well as potatoes: her boy has always needed feeding up.

'Your mum didn't like stew,' Maureen says. 'She never ate her food. Too many sweets, I reckon. She got 'em cheap from Woolworths.'

Ben doesn't reply, but Maureen is content to conduct this sort of dialogue on her own. Sometimes Rebecca wonders what Ben makes of these references to his mother; whether his silence implies agreement or resentment. How much does he remember of her? she wonders. Or have his memories been overwritten by his grandparents' account? He never speaks about Kirsty. Never since that first night they spent together.

'Wild as a hare,' says Maureen.

In the photograph on the mantelpiece, Kirsty doesn't look wild. She looks ordinary.

4

Emily is at Marchboys again the following Wednesday, and in the middle of the morning Pieter appears in the hall.

'Rebecca,' he calls up to her, 'could I ask a favour? I have to go out this afternoon. Could I ask – I know it will hold you up, but Emily has promised to be good.'

Emily is practising handstands against the wall; Rebecca glances anxiously at the marble floor.

'She's ill,' Pieter says, without irony. 'Off school.'

Rebecca has no experience with children, but she doesn't want Pieter to guess that. Perhaps, she thinks, he planned the lunch so he could ask her to babysit later. If that's true, she doesn't mind. She's rather flattered.

'Of course,' she says.

Emily has walked her feet down the wall into a bridge. She tilts her head round, upside down, to grin at them both.

'I could do flips on your bars,' she says. 'Or I could show you the best climbing trees.'

It would be nice to explore the grounds, Rebecca thinks. She hasn't dared to venture beyond the drive so far. 'We could take a sketchbook,' she says. 'Maybe I could put your favourite tree in the painting?'

'Thank you,' Pieter says. 'I'm very grateful.'

He raises an eyebrow, hinting at complications. Rebecca smiles, pleased to be in his confidence. Almost.

*

It's tempting to ask questions, once she and Emily are left alone, but Rebecca cautions herself against it. She recognises enough in Emily – an only child from an unusual family – not to underestimate her.

They set off towards the woodland, Emily halting every few steps to attempt another handstand. It's a fine day: one of those crisp, blue-skied days that late January sometimes produces. The grass is pale green and the naked trees splendid, waiting for their leaves to return.

'I'm glad we can be outside today,' Rebecca says.

'Look!' says Emily. 'That was a good one.' She looks up to check Rebecca is watching. 'What's that scar on your face?' she asks.

Rebecca's hand flies up. Adults never ask that question. 'Just something I got when I was little,' she says.

'How old?'

'About your age, actually.' Younger, she corrects herself. Somehow she has never settled on telling the story straight. She waits for the next question, but Emily has moved on. *I fell out of a tree*, she was going to say.

'Can you paint dogs?' Emily asks. 'Could you put my friend's dog in the picture? He's a collie.'

'Yes, I could do that.'

Emily flips upside down again, and for a moment she's a different creature, something with two white tentacles waving triumphantly in the air and tendrils of dark hair brushing the spring grass.

'Did your parents divorce?' she asks, when she's upright again.

'No,' says Rebecca.

'Mine did. When I was a baby.'

'That's sad.'

'Then my mum died. She was ill and then she died. That's why I live with Granny.' She looks at Rebecca again. 'How did you get your scar, then?'

'I fell out of a tree,' Rebecca says, without a blink. But that *then* at the end of Emily's sentence catches her attention. What does she mean? Does she associate divorce with scars? She must feel the loss of her mother, Rebecca thinks. Another child with a tragedy behind her. But Emily is regarding her serenely.

'I like climbing Daddy's trees,' she says. 'They've been here for centuries, Daddy says.'

Rebecca feels uneasy, suddenly, about looking after this child. She doesn't want her to climb anything. But that, she thinks, was what her mother always wanted: to stop her doing things. Unbidden, her fingers reach for the light ridge of her scar. She was always told it was her defiance that was to blame, but she knows that's not true.

Emily has got a few yards ahead of her, proceeding in a sort of gallop, but now she circles back, holding the reins of an invisible horse.

'Dad likes you, doesn't he?' she says.

Rebecca is caught off guard: her heart trips, then recovers. 'He likes my work, I hope,' she says carefully.

'He wouldn't let me play with you if he didn't like you,' Emily says. 'He doesn't like many people.'

Rebecca laughs, partly with relief.

'Have you got children?' Emily asks, on her next circle round.

'No,' Rebecca admits, her mind spinning from the rapid turns of the conversation. 'But if I did, I'd want one just like you.'

But if she hopes this sentiment will have an impact on Emily, she's disappointed. Emily gallops on towards the edge of the woods, and it's not clear she's even heard what Rebecca said.

The noise that wakes Rebecca that night is familiar: a sound like a baby crying. She sits up in bed. Beside her, Ben thrashes, sweat damp and pungent on his body.

'Ben,' she says, 'darling Ben, it's all right.' She leans over to stroke his cheek. 'I'm here. It's all right.'

There's a sort of moan then; a sigh of relief and exhaustion.

'A nightmare,' Rebecca says. 'Was it the old one?'

'Yes,' he says. He rolls towards her. 'I'm sorry,' he says. 'I'm sorry I woke you.'

'Shh,' she says. 'Don't worry. It's all over now.'

'Yes,' he murmurs.

'Do you want to tell me about it?'

There's a pause before he speaks. 'I was running through the forest,' he says. 'Someone was chasing me.'

It's always the same words, the same scene.

'Poor Ben,' she says. 'You're safe now. Everything's all right.'

His skin feels clammy over the bulk of his jaw. In the dark he looks vanquished, like a slain giant, but his breathing has settled. Rebecca spreads and closes her fingers, feeling the resistance of his flesh, the prickle of his stubble, the slow warmth of him.

'Ben,' she says, barely aloud. Oh, Ben.

For a while she lies beside him while he twitches and grabs at the sheet with little muttered exclamations, slipping back into sleep. Then, as the clock edges towards five, she slides out of bed and goes down to the kitchen, where the dogs lift their heads to greet her.

Ben's nightmares wax and wane. There was a time, not long into their marriage, when they came almost every night. Since then there have been more good periods than bad, but each time Rebecca thinks they might be gone for good she's disappointed.

She has racked her brain for clues about what triggers them, but she's never found any pattern. She's sure a therapist could help, or even a sleep counsellor, but she's never dared to suggest it. And the nightmares are over quickly enough. Afterwards, sometimes half-asleep, he repeats those same words: the forest, and someone chasing him. Just like a fairy tale, Rebecca thinks, as she carries a cup of tea back upstairs with her. She found an article once that said running through a forest means loneliness and fear. Ben's not lonely or afraid now, but perhaps the little boy inside him still is. Perhaps there's danger in the shadows of the trees, and no one to rescue him.

He opens his eyes when she climbs back into bed. 'Is that tea?' he asks.

'Do you want some? I thought you were asleep.'

'No, it's all right.'

She takes his hand. 'Do you want to talk?'

Ben shifts on the pillow. 'You talk,' he says. 'Tell me about your painting.'

'About the stories, you mean?'

'No, tell me about him. About Pieter Blake.'

'I don't know much about him,' Rebecca says. 'He's – rich. He works hard.' She's aware of choosing her words carefully, and she's not sure why. 'He's very particular about the painting. He knows what he wants.'

'Do you talk to him a lot?'

'Not as much as some clients. He's very busy.'

There's a little silence then. It's not unusual for Rebecca to talk about her clients, but something about this feels strange. Uncomfortable, even. Is that because it's the middle of the night, or because she's been drawn in more than she's acknowledged by Marchboys House? But keeping things from Ben would be more uncomfortable.

'He's got a daughter,' she says. 'She doesn't live with him, but she's there sometimes.' Rebecca takes a sip of her tea. 'She's a funny child,' she says. 'She says funny things.'

'Like what?'

'Oh, I don't know.' *Dad likes you, doesn't he?* No, not that. 'She asks lots of questions. She asked if we had any pets, and I told her about Ada and Bertha, and that you keep bees.'

There's another silence, and Rebecca feels the conversation drifting away. They could still get another hour's sleep before the alarm, she thinks. She puts her teacup on the bedside table and starts to slide back down under the covers.

'Does she live with her mother?' Ben asks.

Rebecca's heart flutters. 'With her grandparents,' she says. 'Her mother died. She was ill.' Her mind is full of that afternoon with Emily now, the bright chatter and the undercurrent of danger. Was that her imagination? she wonders. The effect of all those fairy tales?

When Ben starts speaking again it startles her.

'It was very dark in the forest,' he says. 'There were trees all around. I couldn't see the sky through the branches. I had to keep running, but I didn't know why. I didn't know who was chasing me.'

Rebecca is back with him now, a strange hot tide of feeling washing through her. 'I love you,' she says. 'I love you, Ben.'

She kisses his cheek gently and he murmurs. She can't make out the words, but he lifts his hand and strokes her hair gently. So gently, for a man of his size. And then he runs his fingers down her back, and she arches towards him and feels pleasure and anticipation coursing through her.

Rebecca's sexual experience was limited, for a 33-year-old bride. Her first boyfriends were of the chaste, church-youth-group variety, and when she got to university celibacy proved harder to throw off than she'd imagined. At last, in her final year, a fellow History student came back to her room after a party and deflowered her, breathlessly and thrillingly – and, to her delight, stayed around for more. They moved to London together, got jobs, felt like grown-ups. He was, she was sure, the love of her life, but six months later he fell in love with someone else. Her mother had never liked him, but Rebecca's heart was broken.

After that there was a long barren spell, interspersed with the odd mirage – men her friends introduced her to, men she met through a dating agency, and one man who came into the travel agency where she was working to book a holiday for two, then came back a week later to tell Rebecca his girlfriend had dumped him and to ask if she'd go to Budapest with him instead. The travel agency's rules of etiquette didn't anticipate this eventuality, so Rebecca agreed. The weekend included more imaginative sex than she'd previously encountered, but she couldn't see the relationship continuing back home, and it didn't. By then her mother was dying, and Rebecca spent several months enduring her mother's disappointment about her single state while her own disappointment was locked firmly away. A couple of the church-youth-group boyfriends reappeared – one a vicar now, the other a gambler, but no less dull.

And then there was Carol's party: then there was Ben. Ben was more solid, more real than anyone Rebecca had met for years. He was tall enough to tower over her, considerate enough to count as a miracle, and he loved her. Almost at once he loved her, and declared it without a qualm. What he'd recognised in her, Rebecca wasn't sure: she'd stopped believing in her own good qualities by then. But she found herself moulding to him in a way so natural it felt as though she was rediscovering her true self. And she remembered, with Ben, that sex could be a source of pleasure rather than anxiety.

Sex with Ben is still as straightforward as it was that first night. He likes her body, and he handles it with the same deliberate care he employs with his bees and his bantams. He likes to fall asleep holding her hand, or resting his head in the arch of her neck: he makes Rebecca feel wanted, competent, whole. After six years they still have more sex than most couples, if she's to believe the articles she sees from time to time. It is, for her, an affirmation – proof that they belong together, their long legs latched around each other and Ben's breath soft in her hair. They don't speak much, during or afterwards, and she likes that too. Budapest man liked to debrief, to make suggestions for next time. Silence is very much better, she thinks, even if it's a silence in which questions are stilled rather than answered.

5

Pieter is abroad on business the next week. He's left instructions for Rebecca to be given a key, Sam tells her, when he opens the front door on Monday morning. She can let herself in and out from now on. Being presented with the key to the house gives Rebecca a little frisson: in the fairy-tale land that fills her mind, it seems to hold a special significance. She imagines opening new doors, discovering hidden places, even though she knows she won't go further than the hall.

The painting progresses well that week. Rebecca likes the idea of Pieter being surprised, when he gets back, by how much she's done, and that spurs her on. A giant beanstalk curls its branches across the ceiling, and a thatched cottage appears among its roots. The forest spreads further across the dome in one direction, the ocean in another. By Thursday afternoon, a dozen new figures have been sketched in, including Pieter and Freya. They're the narrators, she's decided. Or perhaps the audience. She's placed them at the apex of the dome, where God would be in a Florentine church. She just needs to make sure they're big enough to be seen clearly, but not so big that they spoil the balance of the composition. Towards the end of the day, she climbs down to have a look from the floor.

Rebecca goes up and down the tower several times a day, and has never faltered. But her mind is so engrossed in the painting, in imagining Pieter and Freya looking out of it, that when she hears a shout, her first thought is that their painted faces have come to life. For a split second she imagines them coming down the ladder after her, followed by the servants from the castle and the sailors from the little boats and the wolves and bears from the forest, and that idea is so marvellous and so terrifying that she loses her footing and slithers down the last ten feet, landing in a crumpled heap on the tiled floor.

It all happens so quickly that she can't quite believe it at first. For what feels like a long time she doesn't move, and she keeps her eyes closed for fear of what she might see when she opens them. Not wolves and bears, but blood, or smashed limbs. Perhaps this numb darkness is death – except that surely you should not, if you're dead, be able to wonder about it.

And then there's a voice. 'Rebecca?'

It can't be Ben, she thinks. Unless she's not where she thought she was, or more time has passed than she has realised.

'It's Pieter,' the voice says. 'Are you hurt?'

Pieter. Of course. It must have been Pieter's voice that startled her, as she climbed down the ladder.

'My ankle,' she says.

She doesn't know how she knew that her ankle was hurt, but she's right. When she tries to move it, there's a sharp stab of pain. Her eyes are open now, and she can see Pieter kneeling beside her. He hasn't shaved and his face looks rougher, but also softer, than usual.

'How far did you fall?' he asks.

'I don't know. I was nearly down, I think.' The wolves hadn't reached the platform yet, she almost says, but she stops herself. She must look woozy, though, because Pieter is looking at her anxiously.

'Shall I call an ambulance?' he asks.

'Wait.' It's odd, thinks one part of her brain, that her main concern is not to overreact; not to overplay her injuries. She tries her other limbs one by one. Nothing broken, she thinks, except perhaps that ankle, but there'll be plenty of bruises, and her head is throbbing. Did she hit it, or is it just the shock? She feels a skittering in her chest like a belated rush of fear, and the sudden press of tears.

'My ankle hurts,' she says, and then she reaches a hand to her forehead and winces. 'I'll have a bruise there too, I think.'

'I'll call my doctor,' Pieter says. The resolution in his voice is a relief. Yes, she needs someone else to make a decision, Rebecca thinks. She can't be expected to do that.

The doctor – a private doctor, Rebecca surmises, from the speed of his response and the cut of his suit – arrives within fifteen minutes. He is very thorough, and Pieter watches closely, asking questions.

'A sprain,' he pronounces, 'and possible concussion. No need to go to hospital, but someone should keep an eye on her tonight.'

'My husband,' Rebecca says. 'He'll keep an eye on me.'

But when she phones Ben, he doesn't pick up. He's on call tonight, she remembers. She tries to explain that he must be dealing with an emergency, but she can hear her words tripping each other up.

'She can stay here,' Pieter says, and the doctor nods. 'Jenny Piper could come in. My housekeeper. She used to be a nurse.'

Rebecca wants to protest, but the adrenaline has sapped away now and she feels frail and tearful. It might be hours before Ben could get here. And there's a strange pleasure in falling in with what these powerful men are suggesting. So she nods, murmurs thanks, and Pieter smiles. It's the first time he's smiled all evening, and tears rise again in Rebecca's eyes.

A bedroom is prepared and a meal bespoken. Scrambled egg and smoked salmon is the proper thing for an invalid, Pieter says. Rebecca keeps saying thank you, and yes please, and things happen exactly as Pieter dictates. The curtains are drawn in the bedroom she's taken to, but Rebecca guesses that it looks out over the front of the house. She must be close to her ceiling, she thinks. Or perhaps she's got everything the wrong way round.

Sometime later, when she's finished eating, there's a knock on the door and Pieter appears in the doorway. 'Are you feeling better?' he asks.

'Yes,' Rebecca says. 'Thank you. Thank you for everything.'

Pieter lifts a hand dismissively. 'You're better off here, if your husband's on call.'

Rebecca waits for him to retreat again, to shut the door behind him, but he doesn't. He stays in the doorway, looking uncharacteristically irresolute, as though he feels he ought to make conversation but can't think how to.

'What does he do, your husband?' he asks, after a moment or two.

'He's a heating engineer,' Rebecca says. Pieter doesn't answer, and Rebecca feels a flush rising in her cheeks. Pieter would call Ben a plumber, she thinks. 'He's a very practical person,' she hears herself saying. 'He can turn his hand to almost anything. He grows most of our vegetables, and he keeps bees.'

'You mentioned the bees before.'

'Did I?' She told Emily about the bees, Rebecca thinks, at that lunch. She feels flustered, but Pieter smiles.

'He sounds an interesting man,' he says.

Rebecca nods. She should stop, she tells herself, but she wants to explain Ben to Pieter now. She wants to do him justice. 'He had – something awful happened to him when he was very young,' she says. 'His mother was killed. He was sitting in the car. They'd broken down.'

Pieter's expression shifts a little. As if he was in a board meeting, Rebecca thinks, picking up a fact that might be worth noting. 'An accident?' he asks. 'Someone drove into them?'

Rebecca shakes her head, then wishes she hadn't: it feels as though something is loose inside it. 'She was murdered.'

'Really?' Pieter looks straight at her now, his attention engaged. 'What a terrible thing.'

'Ben saw a man,' Rebecca says. 'He stopped just behind them in a white car. Ben thought he was going to help. The police never found him, but they think he was the murderer.'

Her heart is beating fast: she's never talked about Kirsty's death to a stranger before, and she's not sure why she's done it now. Not just to explain Ben to Pieter, she thinks. Perhaps as an offering, something to repay Pieter's hospitality? But it's not her story to tell, and perhaps telling it will make Pieter think worse of her, not better.

Oh, she's so tired now. She's done in by the shock and the pain and the strangeness of the situation; by the wash of shame and embarrassment that seems to pulse through her blood vessels into her damaged flesh and flowering bruises.

Perhaps sensing some of this, Pieter raises a hand. 'I should leave you in peace,' he says. 'Jenny will sleep next door. She'll check on you now and then through the night.'

'Thank you,' Rebecca says. She wants to say it's not necessary, that inconvenience, but she knows there's no point. And she knows his departure is tactful; it reinforces her sense that she's made a fool of herself, telling him about Kirsty.

When he's gone, she reaches for her phone and tries Ben's number, but it goes to voicemail again. She leaves another message, trying to sound calm and reassuring, but she can hear her conversation with Pieter echoing in her head, and she hopes against hope that Ben won't be able to hear it too. And then she turns off the phone, and the light beside the bed, and lets sleep come to her.

In the morning, the doctor returns to check on Rebecca. Her ankle is swollen, but he bandages it and gives her a pair of crutches so she can keep the weight off it.

'Look out for dizziness or nausea,' he says, and then he raises an eyebrow. 'I don't suppose you'll fancy scaling that scaffolding for a while anyway, but you'd best keep off it until the ankle's better.'

Pieter suggests she stays in bed, but Rebecca demurs. She brought in her marbling equipment earlier in the week, and she tells him she can make a start on the pillars from the ground. She could do it sitting down, even.

'If you're sure,' Pieter says, but he looks pleased. He doesn't like wasted time, Rebecca thinks, especially not when he's paying for it. And she's keen to re-establish herself as a competent professional; to put the previous evening behind her.

When she hobbles back into the hall, the painting astonishes her. There it is, extending its reach across the broad ceiling, every brushstroke made by her. She stands for a moment, amazed by the colours, the shapes, the life of it.

'It's coming on, isn't it?' Pieter says.

She hadn't realised he was standing behind her: she turns, catching another smile. A smile of satisfaction and pleasure elicited by her work. She blushes.

'I've done a lot this week,' she says.

Pieter points at the dome. 'Is that us at the top? Me and Freya?'

She was coming down to inspect those figures, Rebecca remembers, when she fell. 'Yes,' she says.

'Like God,' says Pieter, and she nods – but he's turned away already.

'Let Sam know if you need anything,' he says.

Rebecca likes marbling. She likes the combination of skill and accident in the line-making, the swiftness and patience of the work as the layers are built up, creating the illusion of depth. Transforming a plain white surface into something that looks for all the world as though it has been carved from a block of stone.

She's chosen a green marble effect called *vert de mer*. The process involves multiple stages, so she moves from pillar to pillar, letting each layer of paint dry, then honing the fine detail of the finish with one of the special brushes and tools she keeps for this purpose. A swan's feather to trace the finest lines; a badger-hair brush to blur the colours. The hours pass rapidly as the pillars turn from white to mottled green, then acquire veins and fault lines and dappled structure. At lunchtime Sam brings her a sandwich and a glass of orange juice and she sits, her head swirling a little from *trompe l'oeil* and, perhaps, from the after-effects of her fall. She doesn't look up much, that day. She leaves the half-finished stories floating above her to themselves.

Ben comes to collect her towards the end of the afternoon. Pieter doesn't appear, and Rebecca is glad of that. She opens the door herself, and at the sight of Ben she feels everything shift and settle inside her as though it's finding its place again.

'I'm so pleased to see you,' she says. 'Thank you for coming.'

Ben frowns, noticing her crutches. 'I should have come last night,' he says.

'You couldn't,' Rebecca says. 'You had to work. I was fine. They looked after me.'

Ben nods, but he looks anxious. There are bruises all the way up her left leg, a graze across the side of her chest. She needs to keep them hidden, Rebecca thinks. They'll worry Ben.

'Do you want to see the painting?' she asks. 'It's not nearly finished, of course, but . . .'

She steps back from the door to let him into the hall, bracing herself for his reaction. Ben's opinion matters to her.

'You've done all this?' he says, and she laughs.

'Do you like it?'

His eyes flick to the pillars, then back up to the dome. Rebecca is conscious of the areas of white that still remain, and of the sketchiness of some sections: woodland and sea and fields blocked in roughly, waiting to be animated.

'Of course I do,' he says, 'it's such an achievement' – and Rebecca almost laughs again. Trust Ben to admire the technical challenge, she thinks, not the artistry. She slips an arm inside his elbow and leans against him. The image of herself sitting up in bed and talking to Pieter filters into her mind, but she banishes it.

'Is the little girl here?' Ben asks. 'The daughter?'

'Not today.' Rebecca would have liked Ben to meet Emily, but maybe it's just as well. 'Let's go home,' she says. 'I'm ready for the weekend.'

'What shall we do about your car?' he asks, when they come out into the driveway.

'Pieter's going to get someone to drive it home for us,' Rebecca says. Sam brought her that message with a cup of tea, an hour or two ago.

'That's nice of him.'

Ben helps her into the front of the van, passing the crutches in after her. As they drive away from the house, Rebecca wonders how long it will be before she can drive again, and how she'll get to Marchboys meanwhile – but she doesn't need to think about that tonight. She can't wait to be back at None-go-bye now, to see the dogs and the garden. It feels as if she's been away much longer than two days. There's a whole weekend ahead, she thinks. They can—

'Where did you sleep?' Ben asks, breaking into her thoughts.

'Last night? she asks. 'In one of the spare bedrooms. There must be dozens.'

They're driving through the village now: Rebecca looks out at the church and the row of shops along the high street. Ben's question and her answer float in her head, a loose strand of dialogue that she can't make sense of. Neither of them says anything for a while, and then Ben speaks again.

'Do you like him?'

'Like who? Pieter?' Rebecca's heart quickens. It's not like Ben to ask so many questions. There's a sudden fluster in her head, a weight of something like guilt in her belly. Ben doesn't know about the conversation last night, she tells herself. That's not what this is about. But what *is* it about, then? Is he jealous, or just curious? She casts around for an answer that will satisfy him.

'He's very rich,' she says. But that sounds odder than she intended, and Ben frowns.

'You said that before,' he says.

Rebecca tries again. 'I mean – he's not like us. He's used to having people to do things for him. He called a private doctor to come and see me last night.'

Ben nods. 'But you like him?' he asks again.

'I don't *dis*like him,' Rebecca says – and then she stops. She feels a little alarmed now, as much by the answers she might give as by Ben's questions. She reaches for honesty, and almost finds it.

'I suppose I'm intrigued by him,' she says. 'I've never met anyone like him before.' She swallows quickly to steady her voice. 'I'm flattered that he chose me for this job, and I'm glad he's pleased with what I'm doing. And he was very kind last night. I was grateful. I was worried about being a nuisance.'

39

RACHEL HANCOX

That's all true, she thinks. Perhaps more truth than she needed to tell. She leans back against the headrest and closes her eyes.

Ben looks at her, his expression suddenly different. 'Are you in pain?' he asks.

'I'm tired,' she says. 'I've got a bit of a headache.' And then she manages a smile. 'But I'm very glad to be back with you.'

And that's the truth too, she thinks. That, surely, is the most important truth, the one she needs to hold on to. Nothing else – nothing else – matters.

6

Rebecca feels worse rather than better the next morning, her whole body stiff and painful. The memory of the fall and what followed feels like a bad dream she can't get out of her head. But she and Ben have a quiet day; a nice day. Ben gets on with jobs in the garden, and Rebecca sits on the little patio by the back door, wrapped in a blanket, and reads. Beyond the apple trees and the greenhouse the new beehives are just visible, and in the foreground the dogs romp like children.

From time to time she notices Ben watching her. Does he look anxious? she wonders. Suspicious, even? Or is that her imagination?

She thinks back to that peculiar exchange in the car yesterday evening, and to her conversation with Pieter the night before, and she tells herself there's no connection between those two things. If Ben's anxious, it's because of the accident; because he wasn't there to rescue her. It upset him, that's all. But for a few minutes she can't concentrate on her book. It's as if it's not just her body that's been shaken up, she thinks. It's as if the world – her world – has been set askew by her fall, as it might be in a fairy tale. As if unexpected things might happen now.

'I said we'd go to Hove tomorrow,' Ben says, at supper time. 'But maybe we shouldn't, if you need to rest.'

Rebecca looks up. *Again?* she thinks, but doesn't say. *So soon?*

'Grandma wants me to help her clear out some stuff,' Ben says.

41

Rebecca really can't face Hove tomorrow. She was hoping for another day just like today. But Ben won't want to let his grandmother down: Maureen doesn't like to be disappointed.

'Why don't you go?' she says. 'I should probably take things easy, but she'd love to see you on your own for once.' She sounds to herself like someone speaking an unconvincing line of dialogue, but Ben looks pleased.

'If you're sure,' he says.

Rebecca's not sure at all, but she can't say that. So she smiles, nods again.

Ben hesitates for a moment, looking at her. 'I'll leave the dogs here with you,' he says. 'They can keep you company.'

Ben brings her a cup of tea before he leaves, and Rebecca agrees that she'll stay put and rest her ankle. Maybe if she does that it'll be better by tomorrow, she thinks. She hates the thought of this dragging on, keeping her away from the ceiling.

After he's gone, she reaches, on a whim, for the thriller on Ben's bedside table. It's worse than she expected: a bloodthirsty story told in brutal, choppy prose. Such unlikely reading material for gentle Ben. Are all boys, she wonders, coaxed into reading by blood and terror? Or is there another reason Ben's drawn to this kind of thing?

There's a clutch in her stomach as her thoughts flit to Kirsty again, to her violent death, but there's a different inflection this time. It's really very odd, she thinks, that she and Ben haven't spoken about his mother's death since the evening they met. She assumed then that it would become something they'd share, but the horrors of Ben's past have recurred only obliquely, in his nightmares and in the brusque allusions of his grandparents. If that conversation with Pieter unnerved her, she thinks now, perhaps it's partly because she saw things, that evening, through the eyes of an outsider. Saw how strange it would seem to Pieter that the subject is never discussed.

Has she been wrong to suppress the questions she'd have liked to ask all this time? She's conscious, suddenly, of a sharp curiosity about what happened on that August afternoon. About the mystery that squats, unresolved, in the centre of their lives. It strikes her anew how frightening it must have been for Ben. How disturbing. How much it squeezed his childhood – his whole life – out of shape. Perhaps she has never seen that entirely clearly because her own childhood was odd too. Perhaps that's why Ben was drawn to her, why they've fitted together so well – but perhaps it hasn't been the best thing for him.

Sitting in bed, her body bruised and tender, she lets the details of Kirsty's death play out in her mind. She thinks about Ben waiting in the car while his mother went for help; about the other car that pulled up behind them and the man who got out of it. She thinks about the shadowy father figure who's never mentioned; who seems hardly to feature in Ben's imagination. And then she remembers something else from that first evening they met. *When I was a little boy*, Ben said, *I used to look at tall men sometimes and think, I wonder if that's him*. She remembers that that touched her almost more than anything else: the thought of Ben going through the world looking out for his father.

But an idea occurs to her now, an idea so shocking that it makes her heart stop for a second.

What if Ben saw the man who got out of the white car that day more clearly than he's admitted? What if he saw a tall man – perhaps even someone he'd seen before? Someone he had every reason to believe would help them?

Is it possible that he's known all along who strangled his mother and left her lying limp and lifeless in the woods? That he's kept that fact secret all this time – secret even from his wife?

Outside the window, a squirrel leaps on to a branch of the cherry tree, knocking it sharply against the glass, and Rebecca jumps. It's a mad idea, she tells herself. Whatever strangers might think – Pieter, or anyone else – the trauma of Ben's childhood is not as big a deal as it might seem. Ben's a steady person, and they have a normal life: they have jobs, a house, the dogs. Look, she tells herself: all around her are the trappings of their shared world. The wardrobe with her clothes on one side and Ben's on the other, and on the chest of drawers the photographs of their wedding, and of Ada and Bertha as bright-eyed puppies. She knows him intimately, the good, kind man she's married to.

She gets up now and makes her way downstairs. In the kitchen the dogs greet her rapturously. She opens the back door for them, but they don't want to go out; they insinuate themselves around her legs as she makes herself cheese on toast and finds the remains of last night's apple tart. Brunch, she thinks. Ben doesn't like meals to be conflated, but when he's not here she can please herself.

But that thought provokes another lurch of uncertainty: a return of the feeling that a gaping hole might open up at any moment in the centre of her life.

What would it feel like, she wonders, to have told such a life-changing lie? To live with a secret that grew with you – that got bigger and bigger as your understanding of life developed – but which you had to keep hidden because there was never a moment when telling the truth was possible?

It's just a hypothetical question, she tells herself, but her heart's racing now, fear and doubt coursing through her body. She longs to hear Ben's car pulling up outside so she can push away this phantom husband whose placid exterior masks darker shadows than anyone has ever guessed, but he won't be back for hours yet. For the first time she dreads the idea of being alone at None-go-bye. She eats the cheese on toast, makes herself a cup of coffee she doesn't want to drink, then shoos the dogs outside and stands in the garden for a while, watching them play. She needs a fairy godmother, she thinks, with a magic wand that can set everything straight again.

Ben comes through the front door on the dot of six, just as he promised. Rebecca goes to the door to meet him; to kiss him.

'Hello,' he says. 'How are you feeling?'

'Good,' says Rebecca. 'Better.' And it's true. Her homespun husband is home, with his canvas jacket and green tartan shirt, bringing a gust of sea air into the house. She can feel her body softening, her mind cleaving to the familiar comfort of his presence. 'Did you have a good day?'

'Not bad,' he says.

'I'm sorry I didn't come,' Rebecca says, 'but I've rested a lot.'

He nods, turns away to hang up his jacket.

'Ben—' she begins. *I missed you today*, she means to say, *I love you*, but the words hold themselves back. They're true, she thinks, but she feels a qualm about speaking them. She doesn't want to protest too much. To tempt fate. 'I've made a quiche,' she says instead.

They go up to bed early that night. While Ben's brushing his teeth, Rebecca glances again at the thriller on his side of the bed and feels a little shudder as she remembers the train of thought it set off earlier. She doesn't like to think of him reading that stuff. Perhaps she should read him a fairy tale from the book Pieter gave her? She's noticed him looking at the book once or twice, but when she started telling him, this evening, about a scene she's painting on the ceiling, a miniature child an old couple find in their garden, he didn't seem interested.

In any case, Ben has something else in mind tonight. Rebecca senses it as soon as he climbs in beside her – a weight of expectation and excitement. She's apprehensive about her bruises, but she chases her reluctance away as he reaches an arm towards her.

'I love you, Rebecca,' he says. 'I love you so much.'

He presses himself on her with less diffidence than usual, less gentleness. Rebecca doesn't resist, but she doesn't like it – not just because of the bruises, but because she wonders what's brought on this urgency. Surely not just a day apart? He can't have guessed what's been going through her mind today, she tells herself. He can't, surely, have sensed the wild suspicions she's given houseroom to.

And then, just before he comes, she lifts her arm, and Ben sees the chain of bruises running up it. His eyes widen as he gasps and grimaces and collapses on her chest, and she yelps, tears starting in her eyes.

'I've hurt you,' he says, pushing himself up now and looking down at her with a mixture of tenderness and accusation. 'Why didn't you say you were so bruised?'

'I didn't want to worry you,' she says. He's shivering: partly from the shock of the timing, she thinks, from a kind of post-coital dislocation, but she knows it's not just that. 'They're only bruises,' she says. 'They'll be gone soon.'

'I don't like you being hurt,' he says.

'I know.' Rebecca's close to tears now, exhausted and disheartened. Pain pulses through her body, and out of nowhere she feels a shot of fear – about what Ben might do, what he might be capable of – but that's so shocking and so terrible that it shuts off the tears and the self-pity. Closing her eyes, she winds herself around his chest and lays her head on his shoulder.

'It's all right,' she murmurs. 'I'll be better soon.' He sighs, a deep troubled sigh, and she repeats the words gently, patiently, like a mantra, until his eyes shut and his breath quietens and a longer, slower sigh signals his descent, at last, into sleep.

7

Pieter has evidently forgotten his promise to deliver Rebecca's car home, so Ben arranges to start work late on Monday morning so he can take her to Marchboys first.

On the way there, Rebecca talks about a programme she heard on the radio about hedgehogs. Looking out at the familiar landscape, she feels a wave of chagrin. She was a little mad yesterday, she thinks; she let herself slip into fairy-tale land. Perhaps it was the painkillers Pieter's doctor gave her, or the aftershocks from the fall. But it's a new day today, a new week. Things can go back to normal.

She stays on the ground that morning, continuing the marbling of the pillars and taking stock of the ceiling from beneath. Her eye is drawn, as she hoped, to the key images: the beanstalk, the river, the dragon; the misty mountains which are still no more than sketched outlines. She's pleased with the way the river meanders around the dome in a loose spiral, and with how the dragon's lair is taking shape – the glint of treasure in the cave behind her and the edges of the woods scorched by her fiery breath.

The dragon comes from the story of the moon princess. A tiny girl who has been adopted by an elderly couple disappears, and her bloodstained clothes are found in the dragon's cave. The villagers have always been afraid of the dragon and are glad to have an excuse to kill it. But it turns out the dragon had tried to protect the child from the wolf who was the real culprit, and that it had been protecting the village for years too.

Rebecca loves the idea of the dragon as an unsung hero, and the poignancy of it being so misunderstood. She's curious, too, about the old man and the old woman – about whether their motives were as straightforward as they might seem. Did they give the child a home, or abduct her? Should they have protected her better, or given her more liberty to learn about the world? The story isn't black and white, she thinks; the deeper you look, the more fascinating it is. Perhaps she'll give it more space on the ceiling. She's already painted the little girl curled in her silvery, moon-like nest: perhaps she might be seen climbing an apple tree – a sop to Emily – or riding a harvest mouse along the ridge of the cottage's thatched roof? But she won't allow the wolf to see her, Rebecca decides. She has the brush in her hand: she can control what happens next.

That evening she leaves Marchboys earlier than usual and drives herself carefully home. By the next morning her ankle feels almost back to normal. She's been lucky, she thinks. As she climbs the ladder for the first time since she fell off it, she feels a surge of elation, as though she's overcome something much greater than a sprain.

It's good to be close to her ceiling again. She spends a little time on the moon princess's cottage, and then she turns her attention to the castle where Princess Elvira is shut up in a tower with her faithful dog Arkady. That's another story she likes: the toad prince who isn't what he seems, and the well-intentioned father who imprisons his daughter to save her from the plague. She can't escape from parents and children at the moment, Rebecca thinks. Fairy tales are full of them, good parents and bad. The best parents often die young: there's a thought to ponder. But the children are all innocent. They are always the heroes of their stories.

Pieter's at home today. Rebecca hears him talking to Sam, and his familiar clipped footsteps going up and down the corridors. She half-expects him to appear in the hall and ask how she is, but he doesn't, and she tells herself she's relieved. She tries not to think about him, to lose herself in her painting.

But as the day goes on a worry seeds itself in her mind. It occurs to her that she never thanked him properly for his kindness the other night. Should she have done that? Brought him a gift, even – a pot of honey, perhaps? She has no idea; no sense of whether it was a trifle for Pieter or an inconvenience he endured graciously. *It's never wrong to say thank you*, her mother used to say. Maybe, she decides, her mother is right in this instance. And she needs to maintain an ordinary relationship with her client: she can't avoid him.

And so, before she leaves that evening, she steels herself to knock on the study door.

'Come!' Pieter calls.

Rebecca opens the door a little way and puts her head round. 'I just wanted to say thank you again,' she says. Pieter is sitting at his desk, but he swivels round to face her, his expression distracted. 'For looking after me when I fell,' Rebecca explains.

'Oh!' Pieter laughs, as though all that happened weeks ago, and was long forgotten. 'It was nothing. I'm glad you've made a full recovery.'

Rebecca nods, and starts to withdraw.

'Come in,' he says. 'Unless you're in a hurry?'

Rebecca hesitates. She ought to refuse, to say she needs to get home, but she finds herself going into the study, shutting the door behind her as Pieter directs.

'Would you like some tea?' he asks. 'I could get Sam to bring some.'

'No, thank you.' Rebecca brings a Thermos with her every day – but more to the point, she doesn't want Sam bringing her another tray; doesn't want him thinking that she's crossed some sort of boundary.

'I've been doing some reading,' Pieter says, when she's settled on one of the sofas by the fireplace, 'about the story you told me.' He smiles. 'About the murder.'

'Oh.'

'It's very interesting.' Pieter raises his eyebrows as though he assumes Rebecca must have done the same – read everything she could find about what happened to her husband.

'I only know what Ben's told me,' she says.

Pieter shrugs. 'Most of what's known came from Ben,' he says. Rebecca flinches slightly, hearing Pieter speak Ben's name. 'He was the only witness.'

'Yes.' Rebecca gives a little smile that she hopes might draw this conversation to a close, but Pieter isn't deterred.

'There are some curious facts,' he says. 'The white car, for instance. It parked behind them, according to Ben. But if you spotted a car on the hard shoulder and decided to stop, you'd be more likely to pull up in front of it, wouldn't you, by the time you'd come to a halt?'

Something turns in Rebecca's stomach. She remembers her flight of fancy at the weekend, the mad idea that Ben had known the man who'd stopped.

'Possibly,' she says.

'Unless, I suppose, it was a particularly flat, straight stretch of motorway, and you could see the car from a long way off.'

Rebecca shifts in her chair. She wishes fervently that she'd never mentioned Kirsty to Pieter. But he's looking at her keenly, almost as though he thinks she might have something to hide. He's her employer, she reminds herself: he's a man people do things for.

'Maybe the man in the white car saw Kirsty walking along the hard shoulder,' she says. *Kirsty*: she needn't have used her name. Although Pieter must know it, of course.

'Walking back the way they'd come?' Pieter asks.

Rebecca nods. 'Perhaps she'd seen an emergency phone box while they were slowing down.'

'She wouldn't have had a mobile phone, of course, in 1993.'

'No.'

'So she was walking back along the hard shoulder, and the man in the white car stopped. And then he lured her, or manhandled her, over the fence beside the motorway? Into the woods?'

'I suppose so.' That's what must have happened, Rebecca thinks. Somehow she has never considered that part of it.

'And Ben didn't see anything?'

'If they were behind him, he couldn't have seen very easily,' she says.

'But he saw the car stop. He saw the man get out. And then he stopped watching?'

Rebecca is torn, now, between reluctance and curiosity. Curiosity which she's kept shut away, but which it seems she can't suppress any longer. 'If the man saw Kirsty walking and then stopped,' she says, 'he'd have parked between where Ben was sitting in the car and where she was by then. So he'd have had to walk away from Ben to catch up with Kirsty.'

'Yes.' Pieter nods. 'That makes sense. The car would have been between them.'

Rebecca flushes, pleased to have solved the puzzle. She shifts again, preparing to get up – but Pieter still hasn't finished.

'It's possible, of course, that the white car was following them,' he says. 'That the driver was someone Kirsty knew.'

Rebecca's heart skips and races. She waits for him to say: *Someone Ben recognised.* But he doesn't.

'The other thing that seems strange to me,' he says instead, 'is that she left Ben in the car.'

'Why is that strange? He was safer there.'

'But someone could have taken him from the car,' Pieter says. 'Or he could have got bored of waiting and wandered out on to the hard shoulder alone. I'd have kept the child with me.'

Rebecca stares at him. She can't quite believe she's having this conversation, but part of her doesn't want it to stop now. Part of her knows she's just as interested as Pieter.

'I suppose people don't always think straight in an emergency,' she says.

'True,' he says – but she can see he's not convinced. Perhaps Pieter Blake thinks straight all the time. Especially in an emergency. Perhaps that's what's made him rich.

There's a pause.

'I should go,' Rebecca says. 'I'm still – it's a long drive.'

'Of course,' Pieter says. But he doesn't move, and Rebecca stays where she is too. 'He was seven?' he asks. 'Ben was seven?'

'Yes. A big boy for seven, though.'

'Grown up, you mean?'

'Tall, too. He looked older. He's always ... His mother must have thought she could trust him to stay put.'

Pieter nods again. And then he gives one of his rare smiles.

'I've kept you,' he says. 'I'm sorry. You should get on your way.'

8

Rebecca arrives back just after Ben that evening. At first she doesn't realise he's still in his van: she parks behind it, tucked off the road in the layby they treat as a private parking space, and it's a shock when the driver's door opens. For a moment she thinks the person getting out is a stranger – that Ben must have left the van unlocked and someone was planning to steal it, and now possibly to attack her – but then he turns, and she recognises his outline, the way he moves. She gets out of her car, covering that momentary flash of fear with a cheerful greeting. Covering, too, the uncomfortable feelings that Pieter's questions have left her with.

'How was your day?' he asks. The same question as always. And the same answer.

'All right. How was yours?'

And then it occurs to her that perhaps Ben hasn't just arrived home. That he's been waiting in the van, wondering where she was. 'I'm sorry I'm late,' she says. 'Pieter wanted to talk to me. I couldn't get away.'

She's not sure whether Ben's heard her. He stops, just as they get to the front door. 'I've got some boxes to bring in,' he says.

'Boxes?' She turns, looks at him. Is something amiss, or is she imagining it again? She mustn't make too much of things, she tells herself. The uncomfortable feelings are in her head, not his.

'Things Grandma's cleared out,' Ben says. 'I said I'd take them for her.'

'Do you want a hand? How many are there?'

But he shakes his head. 'They're heavy. You go on in.'

The dogs are waiting outside the back door, eager for their supper. They watch expectantly while she fills their bowls. Rebecca loves the dogs, but she hates feeding them: the smell of their food, and the haste with which they eat it, turns her stomach.

'Good girls,' she says, covering her distaste with a cheerful, sing-song tone. 'Have you had a nice day? The sun's been shining, hasn't it?'

And then another thought hits her. Not even a thought: something like a sudden draught, catching her off guard. A momentary yearning to be back at Marchboys House, sitting in Pieter's study. Talking on easy terms, not hamstrung by shyness and inhibition; daring, perhaps, to ask him a question or two about his life. The wish is gone in a moment, but it leaves a shadow. A tingle. She mustn't let Ben sense it, she tells herself. She must push it away, forget it.

She can hear Ben going to and fro across the tiny hall now, setting the boxes down in the sitting room. Rebecca reaches for affection, but instead, to her dismay, there's a flash of irritation – with Maureen for making Ben go all that way to collect her rubbish, and with Ben for not taking it straight to the dump. She breathes out carefully, steadying herself. She's tired again, on edge.

She turns towards the fridge, finds the remains of last night's curry. She didn't think she was hungry, but she is. Healing her body – keeping herself going – is tiring. Thinking so much. She busies herself with saucepans, and when Ben comes into the kitchen everything's on its way.

'I'd have done that,' he says.

'No need.' Rebecca smiles. 'Boxes all in?'

'Yes.' He stands in the doorway, looking at her. 'I'll lay the table,' he says.

She should have added some stock to the curry, she thinks, when they're sitting down. It's rather dry. But Ben doesn't seem to mind. He's halfway through his plateful already. Rebecca watches him, thinking how strange it is that you can know someone else so intimately and still not have any idea what's going on in their head sometimes.

'What's in your grandma's boxes?' she asks.

'I don't know. She'd packed them up already.'

'Do we need to sort through them?'

'I think there's some of my stuff,' he says. 'From my old room.'

'Oh.' Of course, Rebecca thinks. Not just rubbish. 'Shall we have a look after supper?'

'Not tonight,' Ben says. 'I'm tired.'

Rebecca nods. 'No rush.'

She feels guilty, now, for her irritation – and for that conversation with Pieter earlier. For her disloyalty. She wants to blame Pieter: all that money and power, she thinks, has made him careless of other people's feelings; other people's stories. But it's her fault too, she knows that. A wave of regret washes through her, and then a rush of tenderness: the same feeling she had when she first met Ben, when he told her about his alphabet of animals. *Zebra's what everyone else would choose*, she hears him saying. And he chose her, didn't he?

The boxes are stacked against the wall in the sitting room, seven or eight of them, and when they settle down to watch television after supper Rebecca imagines the contents of Ben's childhood packed inside. Books, maybe; toys. Top Trumps cards. She imagines him at eight or nine, playing football in the school playground, taller and broader than all the other boys. And then she imagines him at four and five and six, when Kirsty was still alive. Will there be things from that part of his life? Would his grandmother have kept them?

She feels a powerful urge just then to ask Ben about his mother, and a kindling of hope that the boxes might provide a catalyst for that. It's almost as though the first seven years of his life have been blanked out, she thinks, and that can't be a good thing. And Kirsty's life has been squeezed out of sight too. Poor Kirsty: the most interesting thing about her is that last half hour. Certainly to strangers.

*

55

Ben has to leave early the next morning: his first job is almost an hour away, and he needs to call in at the yard first to pick up some stuff. He creeps out as quietly as he can, but quiet creeping isn't Ben's strong point, and Rebecca always finds it hard to go back to sleep once she's been disturbed. She waits until she hears the van pull away, then she throws back the covers. She might as well set off early too. The fall has put her behind schedule: that and the addition of the pillars. Thank goodness, she thinks, that Pieter's idea of continuing the mural up the stairs hasn't been mentioned again.

But when she gets downstairs, her momentum slows. The dogs are so pleased to see her, and the kitchen is so peaceful. She could allow herself a leisurely breakfast and still be at Marchboys earlier than usual. The memory of last night lingers still: the happy way it ended. The nature programme they watched, and then, seizing some thread of sentiment, her suggestion that she might read Ben the Elvira and Arkady story. *I was painting a story today that I thought you'd like*, she said. And he did: she was so pleased about that. He loved the idea of the devoted dog who was a prince all along. He saw himself in the story, Rebecca thinks, smiling, as she waits for the kettle to boil.

She takes toast and tea through to the sitting room and drags one of Maureen's boxes over to use as a table. The dogs climb up beside her, and she feeds them her crusts. 'Special treat,' she says. 'Don't tell Ben.'

And then, on impulse, she moves the empty plate to the floor and lifts the flap of the box. It would be useful, she thinks, to have an idea what's inside them. She'll have a quick peek, and then she'll go to work.

The first box contains a bag of gloves and hats, mothy and stale-smelling, and beneath them a bundle of old maps. Ben has never mentioned holidays in Wales or Devon. Did Terry and Maureen travel more before Ben moved in with them? Rebecca wonders. Did they take Kirsty to the seaside? These can all go to the dump, anyway. She puts them back and folds the lid down again.

But now she's started she's tempted to open another. There's no harm, she tells herself. Ben need never know.

The second box contains more old clothes and a mishmash of other things: chipped Pyrex dishes, an old-fashioned alarm clock with a cracked face. But in the next one, a stack of children's books catch Rebecca's attention. Enid Blyton, Noel Streatfeild, Nina Bawden. They don't seem like the sort of books Ben would have read. She opens *Ballet Shoes* – and sure enough, in looping, childish writing on the title page is the name Kirsty Swarbrick.

Rebecca's heart jolts. She flicks through the first few pages – and then she has the strangest feeling. The sudden sense that Kirsty is in the room with her. Kirsty looking exactly as she does in the photo on the mantelpiece in Hove, a smiling girl faded to sepia, her hair sun-kissed and her freckles blurred.

In Rebecca's mind, Kirsty takes the book from her hand and settles cross-legged on the floor to read. For a moment Rebecca hardly breathes. Kirsty's not there – Rebecca knows she's not there – but she feels close enough to touch. Close enough to talk to. *Who are you?* Rebecca wants to ask. *What happened to you?* All that talk of Kirsty being difficult and wayward doesn't sit easily with *Five Children and It* or the Narnia books. Some of them have been bought second-hand; they have *5p* pencilled on the inside cover. Rebecca can't imagine Maureen buying books for her daughter at jumble sales. Did Kirsty buy them herself, perhaps, with her pocket money?

And then Rebecca opens *The Peppermint Pig*, and her head fills with a sound like a fire alarm. The pages of the book have been removed, and in their place there's a notebook the same size as the battered paperback cover. The title page has been left in situ, so anyone who happened to pick it up would have to turn another page to discover its secret: the fact that it contains the diary of Kirsty Swarbrick, aged fourteen.

Rebecca shuts the book, her heart pounding. She should put it back, she tells herself. She shouldn't read it. But Kirsty has been sitting with her, just there on the rug. It's almost as though she wanted

Rebecca to find the diary. And it's better, surely, than knowing only what Maureen and Terry have said about her: only what everyone in the country read in the newspapers for a fortnight after she died.

For a few more moments Rebecca stares at the book, and then she opens it again and reads the first entry.

January 1st, 1982. Age: 14 and 2 months. Height: 5'1". Weight: 7 stone 4. Eyes green, hair brown with a bit of ginger, bra size 32A. Best friend: Jackie Downey. Favourite subject: RE, because everyone fancies Mr Tollitt, specially since the lesson on Buddhist monks when he looked so sad and serious and Lisa swore there were tears in his eyes. Now in RE everyone tries to get him to cry again, but you have to listen a bit to think of ways to do that, and none of us are ever going to forget the Buddhists' begging bowls or the Five Pillars of Islam, are we?

Back to the point. Highlights of last year: Charles and Di's wedding, painting my room Apricot Glow, getting a job in Woolworths on Saturdays with Jackie. A fiver a week and a staff discount too! Favourite product: Maybelline Kissing Potion. Cherry Smash for me and Bubble Gum for Jackie. Also those mood lips that change colour depending on how you feel, or they're meant to anyway. They're meant to tell whether you're in love, but imagine if they really did? Better to stick to Kissing Potion, I reckon, and have a laugh about whether boys would like Mighty Mint or whether it would taste like toothpaste.

Best Christmas present: new jeans, even though it took me HOURS to take in the legs. They're really tight round the calves now, so it's hard to get them on, but they look perfect. Worst Christmas present: Rubik's Cube. Mum and Dad were a year behind, as usual, and what made them think I wanted a Rubik's Cube anyway?! I could've got one in Woolies if I had.

Favourite films of the year: Raiders of the Lost Ark (Jackie), Chariots of Fire (me). Jackie likes to pretend she's a tomboy, up for an adventure, but actually she just fancies Harrison Ford. Jackie says, so what, that's better than fancying God so much you'd give up an Olympic medal, but the point is they all got their gold medals anyway in Chariots of Fire. And I DON'T fancy God, even for Mr Tollitt. Jackie was bored by the time I'd explained all that, though. But we agree about our favourite single: 'Tainted Love' by Soft Cell. I LOVE that song! I don't know if I want to run away, not really, but it makes me feel cool and sort of powerful to think I could if I wanted to. I love the kind of 'chink chink' sound that could be a door slamming shut behind you.

Things I HATE: being called Titch, specially by boys like Kenny and Simon who are really lame and only do it to make themselves look cool. Jackie says they fancy me secretly, but everyone knows all the boys fancy Jackie. Not that I'd want Kenny or Simon to fancy me anyway, but if they ever take any notice of me it's just so they can get noticed by Jackie. Jackie says my boobs have really come on this year, but a Titch with big boobs is still a joke. A Titch with gingery hair and a face you hardly notice, next to Jackie with her blonde curls and her lips she swears are naturally red.

I know Jackie hasn't done it yet, but no one else knows that and so everyone looks at her, trying to seem like they're not looking, when she says casual things about getting a lift home from youth club with Mick, who left school last year, and parking the car in a layby on the way. I know Jackie's too scared of her dad to do anything really, but I wish I had the guts to pretend I had. I wish I could say sarky things about Kenny or Simon having a chipolata in their pants. Even my mum makes jokes about how no one will ever want a scrawny little thing like me. She was a scrawny little thing too, until she got to be a fat one instead, but she got my dad somehow. But sometimes I look at my mum and dad and I think, is that what it's all about, fancying a boy, catching a boy? Is that where it gets you? I look at the two of them eating ham and chips, with nothing to say to each other except sarky remarks about me, and I wonder what the point of it is – Maybelline Kissing Potion and all the rest. Whether any of us, even Jackie, will end up with Harrison Ford instead of our dads.

OK, then – hopes for this year. 1982. I don't know! That's my trouble: I don't even know what to hope for. I know I'd like to be different from the Kirsty Swarbrick everyone knows, but I don't know how.

Rebecca shuts the book again. There's plenty more – most of the pages are filled with Kirsty's curly handwriting – but it's too painful to read on. Rebecca feels like a voyeur, knowing what Kirsty couldn't know when she wrote it: that she'd be dead barely a decade later, achieving fame in a different way from any she could possibly have imagined.

But Rebecca feels something else too, something unexpected: a powerful affinity with this child, this young woman, with her touching honesty and surprising insights. She'd have liked to be friends with Kirsty, she thinks. Next to her, Kirsty would have been the daring one, the one everyone noticed. Rebecca didn't have lipstick at fourteen, or a Saturday job at Woolworths.

She sits for a moment, trying to picture Jackie Downey and Mr Tollitt the RE teacher. Maureen and Terry eating ham and chips, and Kirsty hoping her life would turn out better than theirs.

It wasn't much to hope for, Rebecca thinks. But did hubris get the better of Kirsty, even so? Did those girlish hopes and dreams lead her, somehow, to that terrible moment by the side of the motorway? Or was she just horribly, tragically unlucky?

9

For the rest of that week, Kirsty's voice fills Rebecca's head. *Maybelline Kissing Potion*, she thinks, as she paints the red lips of Princess Elvira and the brown eyes of her faithful hound Arkady. And she wonders, as she strings bunting from tree to tree for Elvira's birthday ball, what Kirsty made of the souring of Charles and Di's fairy tale. Did it confirm her suspicion that romance was an illusion? Or did she still think she might find it if she looked further afield, in the world beyond her parents and Woolworths? Did she try, inspired by Soft Cell? *I don't know if I want to run away, not really, but it makes me feel cool and sort of powerful to think I could . . .*

Perhaps there are more diaries, Rebecca thinks, buried in those boxes. Volumes for 1983 and 1984, or perhaps even later. Might they explain how sweet, scrawny, hopeful Kirsty ended up pregnant at seventeen and dead at twenty-five? Might they provide some clue, even, to the long-hidden secret of who Ben's father was?

The boxes stay where Ben stacked them, but every evening Rebecca glances into the sitting room, afraid that he might decide to take the whole lot to the dump before they've looked through them together. Before she's worked out what to do about the diary. She ought to show it to him, she knows that – but those six years of silence are hard to break. He might be upset that she looked in the boxes without him. And what might he feel about glimpsing his mother as a teenager? About the fact that her diary must have been in the house all the time he was growing up? Every time she starts thinking about it, Rebecca feels paralysed. She's never been any good at things like this: at broaching difficult subjects. She, too, was brought up to push things out of sight, not to find ways to examine them.

Perhaps, she decides, she should put the diary somewhere safe for now, just in case. But what if there are more volumes to be found? She can't bear the idea of them being thrown out. She needs to find an opportunity to search through the rest of the boxes, she decides. But Ben gets home before her every evening for the rest of the week, and they leave at the same time in the mornings. And the idea of slipping downstairs in the middle of the night feels too underhand. Kirsty was Ben's mother, after all. The secrets her diaries might hold are Ben's secrets.

All that week Rebecca works hard on the ceiling. The pillars are finished now, and they look wonderful, as though they're part of the fairy-tale kingdom that's spreading across the dome: part of a palace that has thrown open its doors on to a landscape of magic and beauty. She finishes the dragon too, painting in her tail, scale by barbed scale, and wisps of smoke curling from her nostrils. And then she moves on, sketching in more figures, more scenes.

The biggest difficulty with a project like this is paying attention at the same time to the fine detail and to the scope of the whole piece. As she paints the tiny sails of the flotilla of boats, Rebecca frets about whether the waves are lifelike enough, the boats' prows tilted at the right angle – but when she sits back to trace their course upriver, she worries about the size of the different elements, and whether the perspective will work properly from the floor. She'd love to ask Pieter what he thinks, but she dreads speaking to him again. The discomfort of their last conversation has been complicated by the discovery of Kirsty's diary, and the guilty knowledge that she longs more and more powerfully to know what happened to her.

But she's comforted by the thought that Pieter's mind probably moved on to other things as soon as she shut the study door behind her that evening. His life is so busy; that flare of interest in Kirsty was surely just a passing whim. And Rebecca, too, will soon be forgotten. Perhaps Pieter has lost interest not just in her but in the mural, she starts to think, as the days pass and there's no sign of him. Perched up on the scaffolding, her neck aching from being lifted towards the ceiling for hour after hour, she begins to see the whole thing as a childish conceit, something no serious person could really want in their house. Perhaps he'll paint over it once she's gone, she thinks. Part of her enjoys letting this idea take hold. She remembers the same feeling from her childhood: the pleasurable pain of imagining the worst.

Meanwhile, she paints more and more furiously, as though she wants to get the charade over with. Colour spreads to fill the outlines she's sketched: she adds a flock of sheep on the slopes of the mountain range, a shoal of dolphins off the rocky coast, an arrowhead of migrating geese over the sea. She immerses herself in the landscape until it's as if she's not the painter any more, but an anonymous figure looking across the bay to the glittering city, observing the comings and goings of sailors and shepherds, princesses and dragons and giants. A traveller in an antique land, she thinks. Or perhaps she lives here now: perhaps she's made all this entirely for herself.

And then, towards the end of Thursday morning, Pieter appears suddenly beneath the scaffolding.

'Things have come on,' he calls up. 'You've been working hard this week.'

Rebecca's heart jumps. She can't find her voice for a moment, and when she does it sounds faint and tentative. 'I hope you like it,' she says.

But Pieter is already speaking again. 'I've got a photographer coming tomorrow. To take pictures of the ceiling.'

Rebecca is taken aback. 'Tomorrow? But it's not nearly finished.'

'There'll be plenty of photographs once it's finished,' Pieter says, 'but this stage will be lost by then. The process. The scaffolding. The story unfolding.'

Rebecca is silenced again. So much for losing interest in the project, she thinks. 'I suppose so.' She forces a smile, forces herself to hold on to her composure. 'Maybe I could use some of the images on my website, if you wouldn't mind.'

Pieter opens his hands in a *there you are* gesture. He's pleased, Rebecca thinks. And that pleases her too, despite herself.

Rebecca is well placed to witness the photographer's arrival the following morning: she hears a car approaching, the slam of a door. She imagines him standing in front of the house for a moment, taking in its proportions, and then there's a jangling sound, a bit like a collection of tin cans on a rope. She's never heard the front doorbell before: people seem to arrive silently at Marchboys House, admitted by some secret code. It's as if this visit is deliberately stagey.

She moves carefully towards the ladder. After her fall, she's been more wary about the descent; she likes to take her time. She's halfway down when the door opens, caught in the visitor's gaze as his eyes lift to the ceiling.

'Wow!' he says. 'What a sight!'

He cranes his neck, taking in six weeks of Rebecca's work in five seconds. His expression makes Rebecca's stomach squirm pleasurably. And then he turns to Pieter, holding out a hand. 'Clive Pettit,' he says. 'Nice to meet you.'

Rebecca, with her painter's eye, is fascinated by him. He's short, plump, bristling with energy.

'This is Rebecca Swarbrick,' Pieter says, as she reaches the bottom of the ladder. 'The master painter.'

'I've googled you,' says Clive, 'but I wasn't prepared for this. It must be extraordinary, painting up there all day.'

'Yes.' Rebecca hesitates, battling a sudden flood of shyness. 'It feels different as the picture grows,' she says. 'At the beginning there was nothing but white plaster all around me, which was weirdly disorientating. It felt as though the floor was the ceiling. I used to look out and wonder why the doors were hung in mid-air.'

She stops again, afraid she sounds ridiculous, but the photographer nods. He deals in images too, she reminds herself.

'Fascinating,' he says. 'I can just imagine that.'

Pieter is looking at her too, one eyebrow raised. Rebecca looks down at the floor, as if to remind herself which way up the room is. She waits for Pieter to say something about the ceiling, about his original conception of it, but instead he turns his eyes back to the dome, and Clive Pettit does the same. And then just when Rebecca is gathering herself to point out – what: the dragon, perhaps? – Pieter claps his hands together.

'Let's eat,' he says. 'We can talk over lunch.'

Rebecca hadn't expected the lunch. She'd imagined the photographer's visit taking half an hour at most, but Pieter seems determined to make an occasion of it. Clive Pettit, she discovers, is something of a celebrity. His pictures have been in all the glossy magazines. Pieter must be paying him a fortune, she thinks.

'It's very clever,' Clive's saying now, 'the new and the old. Easy to go too far one way or the other.'

He's going to photograph other parts of the house too, and the grounds, and Rebecca assumes at first this comment must be about the renovation project as a whole, but his eyes turn to her, waiting for a response.

'Thank you,' she says.

'Can we go up on the scaffolding after lunch?' he asks. 'I'd love to get some close-ups.'

Pieter climbs the ladder too in the end, and he and Clive sit and watch while Rebecca mixes yellow paint for a row of sunflowers. She's used to being observed, but not at such close quarters, and the scrutiny of these two men is disconcerting. She can sense the male pheromones that fill the space around them. Confidence, competition, curiosity.

'I want these to pick up the gold in the dragon's hoard,' she hears herself saying. 'There isn't much yellow in the composition so far, so it needs to be a similar shade.'

They watch as she loads the brush with paint and touches it to the plaster, drawing it across the surface to shape a petal, and then

65

another, and another. Pieter's attention seems to her even more intent than Clive's, although she resists the temptation to turn her head to confirm this impression. Clive's presence sharpens Pieter's interest in her, she thinks. He's a businessman: he pays attention to what other people are interested in.

She has to work quickly to make sure the texture of the paint is consistent: it dries fast on this porous surface. As she's drawn into the familiar routine of transferring colour from her palette to the ceiling above her, she's conscious of the occasional click of Clive's camera, the creaks as he shifts position to get a better angle. It must be almost ten minutes before the sunflowers are finished and she plunges her brush into a jug of water, and it seems suddenly extraordinary that these men – these busy, impatient, important men – have sat and watched her for all that time. It reminds her of the city lawyers who salved their souls by coming to her father's church on Sunday mornings.

'You use water-based paint,' says Clive, as she rinses the brush.

'It's a kind of vinyl gouache,' Rebecca says. 'It's easy to work with, and it's waterproof when it dries.' She flushes a little, as she often does when she hears herself speaking with authority. 'And matt, which is important for murals, since you have to be able to look at them from different angles without reflection.'

Clive nods. 'And how did you prepare the surface?' he asks.

Rebecca glances at Pieter. 'The plaster was renewed before I started, then sealed with a mist coat of white emulsion. That's a good base to paint on.'

Clive tips back his head to look across the breadth of the ceiling.

'It's quite a task, tackling something this big,' he says. 'You must have to plan very carefully.'

Rebecca smiles. 'Up to a point,' she says. 'There are mural artists who plan meticulously, and they'll tell you you can't do it any other way. But I like to leave a bit to chance. I've done plenty of sketches, of course, and plans for each segment – it's tricky to work on a domed surface, quite apart from the fact that ceilings are harder than walls anyway, because they occupy a different plane to—' She breaks off, grimacing apologetically. 'Sorry, I don't mean to . . .'

'No, no: carry on.' Clive raises an eyebrow in encouragement. 'You've got a captive audience.'

'Well,' Rebecca says, bashfulness vying now with an eagerness to talk about her project. 'The thing about ceilings is that you don't normally look at them, and when you do, it can be from any direction. That's the first challenge: there's no right way up, so it has to work from multiple perspectives. And the second challenge is that it occupies a different realm. With a wall, you're creating something that becomes part of the room. You can use *trompe l'oeil* to introduce objects, or decorative details, or a view beyond the room – and when you're in that space, when you pass through it, they're there with you. A ceiling mural is always up above, where there's not meant to be anything except – sky. It's a different sort of illusion.'

She pauses. She's rehearsed some of these ideas in her head, but she's never strung them together before. It's strange, hearing her voice echoing across the dome, where there's normally nothing but silence. To her surprise, she finds she's enjoying herself.

'With a ceiling as high as this there's lots of scope for playing with perspective,' she says. 'You can make things come closer, or recede away. And with the curve, the dome, the perspective shifts all the time – while you're painting it, even. You have to keep stopping, checking. It plays tricks on you.'

'Fascinating,' says Clive. He moves a few inches, peers over the edge of the platform. 'Being up here all the time must be a challenge too. And painting upside down. I take my hat off to you.'

When they've gone, their gravitas undone a little by the awkward business of scrambling down the ladder, Rebecca sits back on her heels for a few moments. Well, she thinks. But the thought stops there, a sentence barely launched. Across the span of the ceiling, she can almost see the dozens of pairs of eyes she's painted, peering out at her. Wondering, she thinks, what all those words meant.

10

Rebecca doesn't see Clive Pettit again until the end of the afternoon. She's begun to wonder whether he's already gone, wafted out through the mysterious portal that admits other visitors, when she hears footsteps approaching, and then Pieter speaking. She can't hear what he's saying but he sounds energetic, excited. The visit has been a success, she thinks. She imagines them walking up Pieter's lime avenue, admiring the gargoyles on his folly, and she hopes her painting hasn't been eclipsed by them.

The footsteps come into the hall, then pause.

'Goodbye, Rebecca,' Clive calls up. 'I've so enjoyed meeting you.'

Rebecca leans over the edge of the platform. There's a moment of dizziness in which the two men look like pieces on a chessboard, waiting for her to move them across the chequered floor.

'You too,' she says.

Clive and Pieter shake hands, and the door opens and shuts. Rebecca waits, her brush in her hand. The mural seems to wait too – the flotilla paused midstream, Arkady's ears pricked, the dragon alert to the presence of a stranger.

'That went well,' Pieter says. Is he addressing her? Rebecca glances down, and sees that he is. He has his hands on his hips – a stance of satisfaction but also, Rebecca thinks, of irresolution. 'Can I come back up?' he asks. 'Do you mind? Does it disturb you?'

Rebecca is reminded suddenly of occasions at home, at the vicarage, when her father would put his head round her door late at night, after an evening working on a sermon or visiting a parishioner. *Can I come in?* She feels an ache, a yearning, that transfers itself somehow to Pieter.

'Not at all,' she says.

Pieter grasps the ladder. 'To tell you the truth, I don't have much of a head for heights,' he says. 'I surprised myself, earlier.'

'A chance to survey your domain from above,' Rebecca says, but he makes a sound that's half-groan, half-laugh.

'I'm not sure I dare look down,' he says.

Rebecca laughs too. She can't help herself: the idea of Pieter being afraid of anything is too ridiculous to imagine. But then she remembers his solicitude after she fell, and she thinks perhaps he understood better than she imagined how shaken she was. Perhaps it wasn't just about covering his back, the care he took that evening.

'Look up instead,' she says. 'Imagine you're climbing the beanstalk.'

Pieter manages a chuckle, hands gripping the rails tightly. 'Does that mean there's a giant waiting for me?' he asks. 'Or a goose that lays golden eggs?'

'Perhaps both.' It's Rebecca's turn to feel giddy, not from vertigo but from the hint of flirtation in this exchange. Careful, she thinks, offering a hand to help him over the top on to the platform. But she can't help being pleased. Flattered. Pieter squats down, holding firmly to one of the bars.

'I see what you mean about being disorientated,' he says. 'Seeing the floor as a ceiling.'

Rebecca follows his eyes as they sweep slowly across the dome, and she remembers her fantasy about him painting over it. She's a fool, she thinks. For one thing, Pieter is a man who knows his own mind. He wouldn't change it so easily. He wouldn't waste the money he's invested in the project, either.

'You've done a fantastic job,' he says now, as though her uncertainty has communicated itself. 'Clive was very impressed. He said he's never seen anything like it.'

'Did he like the rest of the work too?' Rebecca asks.

Pieter smiles. 'I think he liked the ceiling best,' he says. 'The world has plenty of lime avenues, after all. But he was impressed by the philosophy, I think. The remaking of the place for the twenty-first century.'

'I'd like to see it all,' Rebecca says, before she can stop herself. She's never seen the formal gardens, or the folly, which are on the other side of the house from where she walked with Emily.

Pieter looks pleased. 'Of course – you must,' he says. 'I should have suggested that.'

'One day,' she says. She picks up her brush again, eager to show him she's not wasting any time.

'Has your husband seen the ceiling?' Pieter asks, after a minute or two.

'He saw it when he came to pick me up after I fell.' Rebecca takes a breath. 'I've been talking for weeks about the stories – the ones from the book you gave me – but I don't think it made much sense to him until he saw the ceiling.'

'He's lucky to have you,' Pieter says. 'Someone so steady, so intuitive. After the trauma of his childhood.'

Rebecca blushes. 'That's kind of you,' she says. 'Ben's a steady person himself, actually. A rock.' And then she indicates a section of the mural with her brush. 'What do you think about having another castle on the far side of the mountains? Would it make that area feel too crowded?'

But Pieter isn't interested in the painting any more. It occurs to Rebecca suddenly that he always meant to turn the conversation back to Ben. To Kirsty.

'You said Ben was big for his age,' he says. 'As a child.'

'He still is,' Rebecca says reluctantly. 'A gentle giant.'

'A gentle giant,' Pieter says, as though he's turning the words over in his mind. 'Was he always gentle?' he asks. 'Was he a gentle child?'

'I think so,' Rebecca says. Is Pieter sizing Ben up as a rival? she wonders wildly. Surely not. 'His grandparents adored him,' she says. 'They seem to have been fonder of him than of his mother.'

Once again she pulls herself up, but once again it's too late.

'Interesting,' Pieter says. 'The teenage pregnancy, I suppose – did they disapprove of that?'

Rebecca has the Kirsty of the diary in her head now; she feels protective of her. 'I don't know,' she says. 'They've always ...' Pieter's looking at her with a voracious sort of interest which it's almost impossible to resist. What the hell, she thinks. She can speak out for Kirsty. 'They've never had anything good to say about her,' she says. 'I've always found that strange.'

'It would have been natural to spoil Ben,' Pieter says. 'Given what had happened.'

A thought strikes Rebecca just then. Might Pieter have told Clive Pettit who she is – who Ben is? Might he have seen that as an irresistible hook for Clive's interest?

'I shouldn't talk about it.' She sounds prim now, but that's too bad. 'It's not my business, really.' *Certainly not yours*: she can't say that, but Pieter might infer it.

'I understand,' he says, but his expression doesn't change. He doesn't take his eyes off her face. 'There's something I haven't told you,' he says. 'I haven't been entirely straight with you about my interest in Kirsty's death.'

Rebecca stares at him. 'What do you mean?'

For a moment Pieter waits, perhaps choosing his words, and Rebecca can feel her heart thumping.

'There's a connection,' he says, 'with Marchboys House. A slim one, I grant you, but ... The name is very old: it goes back to the twelfth century. It means "the house at the edge of the woods". March means "at the edge" or "on the borders" in Anglo-Norman, and Boys, of course, is the French *bois*. The original manor house was on the edge of a vast forest, one of the king's prime hunting grounds. And that forest extended from here, from our remaining bit of woodland, as far as the wooded area where Kirsty was found.' Pieter lifts an eyebrow. 'So in a sense – at a stretch – she was killed on my land.'

'I see.' So he feels he has a legitimate interest in Kirsty's death,

Rebecca thinks. Presumably he's used to thinking like that – to assessing his sphere of influence. And it explains things. She feels a tinge of relief.

But when Pieter speaks again his voice is different. 'This is a mad thought,' he says. 'You'll have to forgive me, but I've been turning it over in my head, and I have to say it now.'

'What?'

'No one else saw that white car,' Pieter says. 'No one saw anything, apart from a couple of motorists who half-remembered a broken-down car.' He hesitates. 'Ben was a big boy, a strong boy for seven. His mother was very slight. Perhaps he panicked when the car broke down. Perhaps he was frightened. Angry.'

Rebecca feels suddenly cold. 'What are you saying?'

'It's not impossible,' Pieter says. 'It wouldn't even be his fault, really. A boy of seven, confused and upset.'

'What are you saying?' she asks again, with more edge to her voice.

Pieter looks at her steadily. 'I'm saying perhaps he hit out. Perhaps he killed his mother. Perhaps that's the answer to the mystery.' He shrugs. 'Perhaps he doesn't even remember what he did.'

'He stayed in the car,' Rebecca says. 'He didn't get out until the police stopped to see what was going on.'

'Maybe that's what he remembers,' Pieter says. 'Maybe he's suppressed what really happened.'

'No.' Rebecca shakes her head violently. 'No, no, no. You're mad.' But even as she's speaking, she knows he's not. She knows it could be true. She's seen photographs of Ben, not long after his mother's death. He'd have had the strength, certainly.

'I'm sorry,' Pieter says. 'I've upset you. Offended you.'

Rebecca doesn't trust herself to speak.

'I shouldn't have said anything,' Pieter says. He looks abashed, the smooth line of his jaw flushed in a way that makes him seem unfamiliarly raw and human. 'I just – I'm always looking for the answer no one else has thought of. It's a bad habit – in some circumstances, at least. Forgive me.'

'It's fine,' Rebecca says.

But it's not fine. Nothing's fine. She wants to cry; she's dangerously close to it, and she's afraid that Pieter can see it in her face. For a moment she thinks that if she leaned forwards an inch or two, if she allowed her distress and confusion to show, he might touch her; might even kiss her. She digs her fingernails into her palm.

'I should be getting home,' she says. It's only a quarter to five, but she's worked long hours this week. She's done enough.

'I *have* offended you,' Pieter says. 'I'm sorry. Please forget what I said.' He hesitates. 'I'm very grateful, Rebecca, for everything you've put into this project. I hope it'll be worth it. I hope it'll launch your career.'

'Thank you.' Rebecca can't bear the humility in his voice now. 'I'm grateful to you too, for the opportunity.'

It feels odd to be speaking so formally when they are so close together, perched beneath the dome of the great ceiling with the river and the mountains, the dragon's lair and the castle and the beanstalk all within touching distance. Perhaps Pieter can read her mind, because he reaches out a hand now towards the sunflowers Rebecca painted earlier.

'You could almost pick them,' he says. 'I'd like to have them in a vase. Such a splash of colour.'

Rebecca looks at them too: at the brazen yellow and the dark stippled centres, the artful freshness that comes from painting them so fast, the petals dropped into place with a flick of the brush. They'll hardly be visible from the floor, she thinks. Just a patch of gold to catch the eye.

The journey home seems to take longer than usual. It feels as though every section of road has been stretched, the distances distorted. The world has warped, Rebecca thinks. It won't stay the same for long enough to let her get her bearings.

Ben's already home when she arrives, playing in the garden with the dogs. Rebecca comes through the house and stands by the back door. Next to Ben, Ada and Bertha don't look so big; they could be puppies, cavorting around a small boy. It looks like a set piece from an advertisement: the dogs barking joyfully, the apple trees and the beehives, perhaps a bottle of wine in the fridge. Rebecca badly wants to believe in this scene, the start-of-the-weekend cheer of it. She wants to put everything else out of her head, especially Pieter's dismaying suggestion and her own dismaying response, up on the platform under the painted dome.

'Hello!' she calls, and Ben turns.

And then there's a moment, just a moment, when she sees a shadow in his face, a haggardness and sorrow and anger she's never seen before. And although she's sure it's just her imagination, it's enough, that fraction of a second, to send another tumult of conflicting emotions tumbling through her, so that she doesn't know whether to run towards her husband or away from him.

Ben her rock; her gentle giant.

Ben who never talks about his mother.

'Good day?' she asks, the effort to steady her voice surely obvious.

'It was fine,' he says. He's pocketed the ball now; the dogs watch him, tongues lolling, squatting on their haunches. 'Did the photographer come?'

'Yes,' she says. She pauses, takes a deep breath, smiles. 'He spent the whole afternoon there.'

'Did he like the painting?'

'I think so, yes. He climbed up on the scaffolding so he could see it up close.'

Why does she feel as if she's pretending – as if she's performing a role for someone who's watching to see how well she can sustain it? It's as if neither of them is quite real; neither of them is quite who they seem. Ben looks at her for a moment, and she has no idea, none at all, what he's thinking.

There *is* a bottle of wine in the fridge, and Rebecca drinks a lot of it that evening. They find a pizza in the freezer, and Ben has a few cans of beer. They say things to each other, normal things, but Rebecca can't escape the feeling that they're slipping in and out of another sort of evening where things are quite different, and after a while she's not sure which is the reality and which is the fiction cooked up by her mind.

'So was Pieter pleased with the photographer's visit?' Ben asks, when the last piece of pizza has gone.

'He was very pleased,' Rebecca says. She tries to meet Ben's gaze, but Pieter's voice drifts into her head, saying, *I'm always looking for the answer no one else has thought of,* and she shuts her eyes to try to silence it. 'The pictures might be printed in a magazine,' she hears herself saying – and then Pieter's voice again: *Ben was a big boy, a strong boy for seven ... Perhaps he doesn't even remember what he did.*

Pieter's wrong, she thinks. She mustn't listen. Mustn't let him poison her mind. She hauls herself back with a concerted effort. 'I wish he'd waited until the mural was finished,' she says, 'but he wanted some photos of the work in progress.'

She looks at Ben then, and he nods, but there's a little frown between his eyes. She forces a laugh, and pushes her wine glass away. It's not her doing these things, though. It's someone with a suspicious mind. Someone with something to hide. 'I've had too much wine,' she says, and Ben looks back at her steadily.

'Shall we find something to watch?' he asks, and she nods.

There's a new film on Netflix about an Australian family living out in the bush. As the story unfolds, Rebecca can feel the wine smudging the edges of her mind and a sort of dreaming calm coming over her. Images from the television mingle with images from the mural: the daughter of the bush family becomes the hapless Elvira; an eagle circling over the forest could almost be the moon princess's dragon, her wings spread proud and mighty. Rebecca glances at Ben, his face catching the light from the wide prairie sky.

Perhaps, she thinks suddenly, life is only complicated if you choose to let it be. If you fill your mind with fairy tales, colouring the plain surface of the world with the grotesque and the unexpected; if you let strangers redraw the boundaries of your world in ways that make no sense at all in the cold light of day. Surely she can choose to go back to the old familiar version of their cosy None-go-bye life? Perhaps what happened thirty years ago doesn't matter: childhood was a dark place for them both, but the children they once were are a long way away now. Like figures you might glimpse in the corner of a painting, slipping out of sight between the trees.

As this seductive idea settles in her mind, Rebecca feels a lightening of her spirits – but it only lasts for a moment or two. Only until she remembers Kirsty – *eyes green, hair brown with a bit of ginger* – who was killed in broad daylight, by person or persons unknown. Kirsty surely deserves to be wondered about; to be attended to. She can't be allowed to slip out of sight by the side of the motorway, in the yellowing newspaper cuttings and the casual deprecation of her parents.

Rebecca glances across the room at the stack of boxes. Ben might easily decide to get rid of them this weekend. The wheedling voice in her head has one more go: would that be such a calamity? Isn't it enough that Rebecca has read that first diary entry; that Kirsty's voice has been heard?

She knows it's not. She just doesn't know what to do about it.

11

Rebecca wakes to a painful throbbing in her head. Too much wine, she thinks. The bloom of February sunshine around the edges of the curtains feels like a reproach, but as she blinks herself awake, there's a sudden dousing of relief: it's marmalade day, she remembers. One of her favourite days of the year. It's still early, not yet eight, but she drags herself out of bed and limps to the shower.

Ben's still asleep when she sets off. She leaves a note on the table in case he's forgotten where she's going, and a clean cup beside the teapot.

At the front door she hesitates, and then she darts back into the sitting room. *The Peppermint Pig* is exactly where she left it, wedged down the side of the box. She slips it into her pocket, then folds the flaps of cardboard carefully back in place. This needn't be a moment of decision, she tells herself. She can put it back later. She just needs to keep it safe for now.

Marmalade has always been the domain of Rebecca and her father. Ben doesn't approve of buying foreign fruit, but Rebecca is grateful that he's happy to leave the Seville oranges to them: this tradition goes back a long way.

When she was a child, her parents made marmalade together every February, in the lull between Candlemas and Lent. Rebecca can still picture them sitting at the kitchen table, their voices low and companionable: her father asking, *Is this all right? Is this about the size?* and her mother's tone a little less sharp, a little less irritable

77

than usual. A whole day when nothing else happened, and the house was filled with the smell of simmering oranges.

The ritual was – is – one of the very few their family sustained: an activity that was consistent with the vicarage way of life but exceptional, almost inexplicable, in its joyfulness. It made Rebecca feel, for one day a year, as if they were the kind of family she wanted them to be. The Christmassy bustle and smell of it, as a child, was always more intensely pleasurable than Christmas itself, when meals were squeezed into the gaps between church services and present-opening was a thing to be dreaded, with no one to supply the excitement or the gratitude but her.

When Rebecca was old enough, she was allowed to help – *my apprentice*, her father called her – and she remembers vividly the pleasure of being admitted to her parents' shared sense of purpose, and her pride as she stuck labels carefully on to the rows of jars. It seems to her still an optimistic thing to do, and a bountiful one. They make more marmalade every year, she and her father, than either of them can possibly eat, but the lion's share was always given away anyway: to the WI sale, the church bazaar, the Harvest Festival. These days her father passes it on to the women who used to preside over those occasions, and now preach and baptise and bury instead.

Rebecca's father still lives in the 1970s semi in Chesham that her parents moved to when he retired. This house has taken on the same look as every vicarage they ever occupied. It gives the same impression of well-intentioned homeliness: not the kind of homeliness that's actually comfortable to live in, but a veneer of it, despite the shabbiness of everything, which is supposed to make people feel welcome. Or perhaps, Rebecca thinks, her eyes ranging over the ugly ornaments and disconsolate curtains, to make them glad to return to their own homes.

'I've bought organic oranges,' she says, setting the box down on the table. 'I don't know if it'll make any difference to the flavour.'

'To the moral flavour, at least,' says her father, and she smiles.

Although the ritual is time-honoured, it's not set in stone. A couple of years ago they started boiling the oranges first, to soften them, before scooping out the flesh and chopping the skins. One year they added a few grapefruit and lemons to the mix. But the truth is that, even after all this time, they are not as expert as they ought to be: they still find it hard to judge the setting point, so some years the marmalade turns out so dark it's almost caramelised, and other years it's pale gold and rather runny. So there's variety enough, they've agreed, without altering the ingredients.

'I would have got the pan down,' her father says, 'but you would have scolded me.'

'Quite right.' Rebecca drags a chair across and climbs up to retrieve the preserving pan from one of the high cupboards. Her father rinses the oranges, and a few moments later they're immersed in boiling water, the gas turned up high beneath them.

One advantage of this method is that it provides an interval, early on, that they can use for other jobs, and for lunch. When they've got the pan safely to a simmer, Rebecca rummages in her bag. She splashed out a bit this morning at the farm shop where she stopped to buy the oranges.

'I've brought some nice soup,' she says. 'Do you want to eat now, or . . .'

Looking up, she catches her father's eye, and is momentarily floored by his expression, revealed before he can hide it. Patience, good humour, and a reluctance to be a nuisance: an expression she recognises so intimately that it's almost as though it's written into her DNA.

'I've been doing some sorting out,' he says. 'I've found some photograph albums. I thought we could look through them together.'

'Of course.' Rebecca thinks of the boxes from Hove sitting at None-go-bye, the coincidence of that – and then she wonders, with a spasm of ice in her chest, why her father has been clearing things out.

There's a small stack of albums waiting in the sitting room.

Strangely unwieldy objects, Rebecca thinks, to be the repository of memory. She opens the first one on the coffee table.

'Goodness! Look at me!'

Her father smiles, his face relaxing. Rebecca is three or four in these photographs, her hair in two short plaits.

'I'd forgotten we had so many photographs,' he says. 'All that time and trouble putting them in albums, and then you never think to look at them.'

'I'm glad you've got them out,' Rebecca says. 'Oh, I remember that dress . . .'

The photographs feel safer than Rebecca feared: she doesn't remember many of the events they record, and the childhood contained in their pages somehow doesn't evoke the one she looks back on with such mixed emotions. It looks like a very ordinary upbringing, with birthdays and holidays and bicycles. Perhaps it was, she thinks. Perhaps it's her memory which has distorted it, adding shadows and twists that were never there? She turns the pages, smiling and exclaiming, her father happy beside her.

Afterwards, while the oranges cool in a colander, Rebecca heats the soup and they sit at the table to eat it.

'How is Ben?' her father asks.

'Fine,' she says, with barely a tremor. 'He sends his love.'

There are many things she and her father have never said to each other about her husband, her marriage. She's conscious now of how much she'd like to talk to him – about Kirsty's diaries, certainly, and perhaps about Pieter's questions too – but she feels a great reluctance to broach any of it. The day is sacred, she thinks, and so is her father. She can tell him only the truth, and at the moment the truth is more complicated, more infused with doubt and fantasy, than she can easily explain.

They establish a rhythm for chopping the oranges: Rebecca cuts them in half and scoops the flesh into the pan, and her father slices the empty shells. Rebecca's eyes flick, now and then, from her part of the operation to his, and she feels, each time, a sharp tug of affection for his large knuckled hands, his frown of concentration. Despite her upbringing, she is not a believer, but she often wishes that she could share in what matters most to him. And just now, she thinks, it would surely make a difference. It would provide a compass to navigate by.

'Are these up to scratch?' he asks, noticing her watching him, and Rebecca hears him speaking the same words to her mother.

'Perfect,' she says. 'They're a nice bright orange, aren't they? The marmalade should be a good colour this year.'

'Amber,' her father says. 'Your mother loved amber. I gave her a necklace once, when we were engaged. I wonder what happened to it. It should have come to you.'

Rebecca doesn't remember the amber necklace. Her mother rarely wore jewellery, but perhaps she had a streak of worldly desire after all. She never gave any sign of it – but she never gave any sign of being fulfilled by what she had, either. For a moment Rebecca's mind turns to her scar, to the day she never thinks about, but she drags it away.

'Do you remember the canal at Chattington?' her father asks – and she's struck by the way his thoughts have kept pace with hers.

'Why did we walk there?' she asks. 'There must have been prettier places we could have gone.'

'You liked the ducks,' he says.

'Did I?'

'And the swans,' her father says. 'There was a family of swans near the railway bridge.'

'Perhaps I should put a swan in my painting,' Rebecca says. 'There are lots of birds, but no swans.'

It's almost four o'clock by the time the marmalade is bottled. Twenty-four jars, and a sheet of labels to stick on when they've cooled. They do look like amber, Rebecca thinks: like ancient resin with the fossils of long-dead creatures suspended within them.

'A good day's work,' says her father.

'A very good batch,' Rebecca agrees.

And then she realises, with a clutch of panic, that it's almost time for her to go home. In a moment her father will fetch her coat from the hook in the hall, a small courtesy he never forgets. But he doesn't, not yet.

'Cup of tea?' he asks instead.

'OK. Thank you.'

He hesitates. 'There are things on your mind,' he says.

Rebecca's face tightens. 'I don't want to . . .'

Her father puts a hand on her arm. 'My dear,' he says, 'I have so few uses these days. Please let me help.'

And then, before she can stop herself, Rebecca is crying. She presses a hand over her eyes in a futile attempt to halt the tears, makes a small gasping sound of agitation and apology, and her father pulls her into a bear hug. He's so gaunt, and the gesture is so rare, that the strangeness of it shocks her out of her convulsion of weeping.

'I'm sorry,' she manages to say. 'I don't usually cry.'

'No,' he says, 'but you can.'

For a few moments she clings to him, to the feeling of being held tight, and then she pulls back. 'Dad,' she says, 'are you all right? I've had this feeling all day . . .'

'Sit,' he says. 'Let me put the kettle on.'

'I'll put the kettle on,' she says. 'I can do that. But . . .'

'It's nothing serious,' he says. 'I was going to tell you, Rebecca, but . . .'

'What?' she says. 'What's the matter?'

'My prostate,' he says, and she can hear the slight shock of the word in his intonation. 'A very small cancer. Slow-growing. It's not going to kill me.'

'Cancer?' Rebecca sits down heavily, the kettle forgotten. How could he have gone to hospital appointments, had tests, and not told her? Shock and fear make her voice shrill. 'So you've got to have an operation? Chemo?'

He shakes his head. 'At my age the treatment is likely to do more harm than good, apparently. I'm on what they call active surveillance.' He pulls out the chair next to her and lowers himself on to it. 'I'm sorry, Rebecca. I should have told you sooner. I wanted to know what I was dealing with first.'

'I would have come with you to the hospital,' she says.

'I know you would.' He smiles. 'But you have plenty to think about.'

'None of it more important than you,' she says, and she means it. 'Next time, will you . . .'

He nods. 'I promise.'

Rebecca looks at him for another moment, and then she pushes herself up. 'Tea,' she says.

While she busies herself with the kettle and the teapot, she can feel her heart thudding in her chest as she digests her father's news. Illness frightens her because of her mother, she thinks; because it upturned everything when she was young. And this illness has made her indestructible father mortal. This cancer might not kill him, but something will, sooner or later. The concerns she brought with her this morning feel so thoroughly eclipsed that she's embarrassed, now, to remember how much they preoccupied her.

'Thank you,' her father says, when she sets the pot down on the table. They drink out of mugs these days: a small shared act of heresy. 'I'm afraid there's no cake.'

'I brought biscuits,' Rebecca says, remembering, and she gets up to rifle in her tote bag. They are expensive biscuits, chocolate-covered gingers.

'What a treat,' her father says. 'Thank you.'

'You're really all right?' Rebecca asks. 'You're not just saying that to . . .'

'I'm perfectly all right.' He puts a hand over hers. 'Tell me what's on your mind, Rebecca. You didn't come here this morning worrying about me.'

'No,' she admits, 'but I . . .' She remembers the canal, their walks, and feels tears rising again. He has a place in her life that no one else can fill, she thinks; his wisdom is a resource she will never replace. And that thought tips her, at last, over the edge.

'It's Ben,' she says. 'And his mother. Her murder.'

Her father doesn't flinch. 'A terrible tragedy,' he says. 'A terrible thing to happen to a child.'

Rebecca isn't sure whether he means Ben or Kirsty. Perhaps he's thinking of them both.

'Pieter—' she begins. 'My employer, Pieter Blake, started asking about the case.'

Her father raises his eyebrows. 'Does it worry him?' he asks. 'Your connection to it?'

'No, no; nothing like that. He's just – curious. He read up about it, all the newspaper reports. He's interested in the details.'

'I see.'

'You remember,' Rebecca says, 'that Ben said he'd seen a car, a white car that stopped near them?' Her father nods. 'Pieter – well, actually, I'd been wondering too, as it happens, whether Ben knew more than he told the police. Whether he recognised the man in the car. Whether he's suppressed it all these years, or – kept a secret.'

Her father is very still. There is a special quality to his listening, Rebecca thinks. It's as if her words are allowed to bloom, to develop, instead of shrinking into absurdity. As if anything that's said to him has a solidity which is, in itself, ineffably reassuring.

'That might be so,' he says. 'I dare say the skill with which children are interviewed has progressed in the last thirty years. The care given to them afterwards too.'

Rebecca nods. She thinks of Maureen and Terry; of seven-year-old Ben with his big, solemn eyes. And then she thinks of Pieter, up on the scaffolding tower.

'Pieter wondered –' she begins '– I'm sure this is completely absurd, but I haven't been able to stop thinking about it.' She stops, swallows. Can she really say this out loud? Hand it over to her father for serious consideration? 'He wondered if Ben could have killed his mother,' she says, in a rush. 'Ben was big for his age, strong, and Kirsty was small and slight, and . . .'

She's weeping again now, with shame, and despair. What kind of woman imagines her husband might be a murderer? What kind of woman is married to a man for six years and doesn't think of it?

'My poor Rebecca,' her father says. 'What a terrible thing to carry with you.'

'It's ridiculous,' she says, through her tears. 'I know it is.'

'Why so?'

She shrugs hopelessly. 'Ben wouldn't hurt anyone,' she says. 'He's the gentlest man.' But is she sure that's true? 'It just makes me feel – I keep thinking maybe I don't really know him. Maybe I've never known anything about him. None of the important things. Our life – we skate over the surface. There are things we never say.'

Her father takes a sip of tea.

'Doubt is the most human emotion,' he says. 'How can any of us really be sure of another person when we have only our own senses to rely on?'

'But . . .' Rebecca bites her lip. 'Do you think a child could do something like that and become a normal adult?' she asks. 'Someone steady and reliable and – safe?' She hesitates. 'Theoretically speaking, I mean.'

'I believe everyone is capable of redemption,' he says.

'And the sin of a child . . .'

'Is a complex business,' her father says. 'Theologically. And in other ways.'

Rebecca feels suddenly sick. 'I don't believe it,' she says. 'I don't believe he could have done it. It's a horrific thing to suggest. I can't believe I let myself . . .'

Her father takes her hand. 'An experience like that – the loss of his mother in such violent circumstances – leaves terrible scars. You know that. You knew it when you married Ben. It will always make things difficult, for both of you. But your love – that is an instrument of redemption, Rebecca. Perhaps it might help to see it that way round.'

'Maybe,' she says. She swallows. 'I'm sorry. I shouldn't have . . .'

He puts a hand on her head now, a blessing. 'You're a good person, Rebecca. A strong person.'

'Not as good as you. Nor as strong.' She thinks, then, of the things he has had to bear; the crucible in which his love for her mother was tested, year after year. She thinks of the cruelty her mother was capable of, and the scars she bears herself. Life is complicated, she thinks again. Love is complicated. But perhaps loving someone thoroughly, whole-heartedly, can heal you too. 'Thank you,' she says. She leans forwards to kiss him, and he holds her still for a moment.

'I wish I could resolve this for you,' he says. 'I wish I could tell you what happened thirty years ago: I can see how much that would help you both. But you have always known that it's unlikely you will ever know the whole truth. That you may have to live with that for the rest of your lives.'

Until the next life, Rebecca thinks, when everything is known, and everyone made whole and perfect. She wishes, deeply wishes, she could believe that.

12

Ben is unloading the dogs from the back of his van when Rebecca gets home. The three of them have a fresh, windswept look that lifts her spirits.

'Been for a walk?' she asks.

'Yes. I found a great place for the kites.' Ben smiles as he slams the door. 'Somewhere I found on the internet. Lots of people recommended it.'

'And did they fly well?'

'Yes.'

There's a tiny hesitation that snags at Rebecca's attention for a moment. There's probably a long story he doesn't think she'll be interested in, she thinks; some technical detail about currents and lines.

'The marmalade came out well this year,' Rebecca says – and then, because it's the kind of thing you tell your husband, the kind of thing you can't not share, she says, 'My father's been diagnosed with prostate cancer. But it's a slow-growing tumour, apparently. They're not going to treat it.'

'OK.' Ben looks at her for a moment. 'I'm sorry.'

She shakes her head. 'He told me not to worry.'

They're still standing in the lane, outside the garden gate, and this feels suddenly to Rebecca like an important moment: a chance to change something, perhaps; to choose where they go next. She has no idea whether Ben feels it too, but she holds out a hand and he takes it, and then he pushes open the gate with his other hand

and the dogs rush through and pull them both up the path, and they laugh. And then, on the doorstep, when he's unleashed the dogs, he kisses her.

'Oh, Ben,' she says.

His hand's in her hair; she's always loved the feel of it, the way it's big enough to cup the back of her head. 'What is it?' he asks.

'Nothing,' she says. 'Nothing. I've had things on my mind, that's all. I've been a bit distracted.'

'Your painting,' he says, and she shrugs.

'That and other things.'

For a moment his hand stops. 'What other things?'

She can't bear that note of disquiet in his voice. 'Nothing important,' she says. 'Nothing we need to worry about.' She knows that that's not entirely true. She's not sure she can make the things that have been worrying her unimportant again. She's not sure, either, that she's capable of the fierce, redemptive love her father commended to her. But she can try. She can do her best.

She can feel Kirsty's diary in her coat pocket still, and as she stands there, close enough to hear Ben's heartbeat, her father's last words come back to her. He's right, she thinks: knowing the truth about Kirsty's death would solve all this. Her doubts about Ben, which feel so shameful, but also so hard to dismiss. And perhaps more than that: perhaps his nightmares, and whatever shadows lie beneath the reserve that has always seemed so much a part of him.

And isn't it possible, she thinks, that the answer to that terrible question might, after all, be within their grasp? Mightn't the diary hold some clue? The killer could be someone Kirsty knew: a boyfriend, perhaps. Someone she got embroiled with.

Especially if there are more volumes, might they not lead them towards the truth?

The first thing, Rebecca thinks, as she tips pasta into a pan, is to tell Ben about the diary. That shouldn't be so difficult, but somehow it is. How can she admit to having found his mother's diary – having read some of it – and kept it from him? Would it be better to put it back, then, and stage another discovery? But she's hopeless at pretending, and it seems wrong to conceal deceit with more deceit. And then she wonders whether it might be better if she read the rest of the diary first, even searched the remaining boxes for other volumes, so she knows what there is to find out. So she's prepared. But is it Ben she's concerned to protect, or herself? What is it she thinks she might discover if she reads on? She feels suddenly dizzy, overwhelmed by the enormity of the situation.

She won't say anything tonight, she decides. They're both tired, and she needs to think. Perhaps they might go out for the day tomorrow, and the right moment, the right mood, might present itself.

Sunday morning dawns bright and sunny, and Rebecca wakes to the childlike joy of an empty day, followed almost instantly by the recollection of what's riding on it. Of what she's hoping for. Ben's still asleep, and she slips downstairs and makes breakfast, then carries it up to him on a tray.

'Shall we go somewhere today?' she asks, as she dips a soldier of toast into her egg. They're Ben's chickens' eggs; the yolk is a deep gold. 'What about that stone circle we keep meaning to visit?'

'Abberbury?'

'Yes. It's not far, is it? The weather's going to be nice.'

Rebecca feels a stab of what feels almost like deception – but it's just a day out, she tells herself. They haven't had a day out together for ages, unless you count Hove.

The stone circle is harder to find than Rebecca expected, but at last she spots the stones, jutting above the skyline on the slight rise of a hill. Cows are grazing among them, and a row of oak trees stand a little way off, like respectful courtiers.

They park on the verge and unload the dogs. There are several other people there: a small boy is trying to climb one of the flatter stones while his parents remonstrate with him, and on the far side of the circle, an elderly man reads a guidebook entry to his wife.

Four thousand years, Rebecca hears; *fifty metres*; *five tonnes*. Three teenage girls sit cross-legged in the middle of the circle, discussing its role in some cult fantasy film they've all seen.

'Have you always liked places like this?' Ben asks, as they set off to walk round the perimeter.

'I suppose I have,' she says, a little surprised. Both by the question and by her answer, she thinks. 'It's like stepping into history, isn't it?'

'It's something and nothing,' Ben says. 'They're just stones, if you look at it one way.'

Rebecca laughs.

'Impressive stones, though.' Ben pats the one they're passing and grins at her.

Just then the three teenagers get to their feet and join hands, and a moment later they're spinning around, the sun catching their bright hair. As the spinning gets faster and their shrieks echo between the stones – *Oh my God, Jade, I'm gonna fall over* – there's a lurch, a slip, in Rebecca's head. They could be Kirsty and Jackie and Lisa, she thinks, fourteen years old again and dancing on the grass. Who knows what tricks time can manage inside a Neolithic circle? She shakes her head, shakes off that thought, but she feels the weight, then, of what she needs to say to Ben. Might this be the moment? She feels a momentum rising inside her, words forming in her head – but before she can speak there's a buzzing sound, and Ben frowns and reaches into his pocket.

Rebecca looks at him: Ben doesn't usually have his phone on, unless he's on call. He stares at it for a moment, then types a reply.

'What is it?' His grandmother, Rebecca's thinking. But she would ring, not text.

'Work,' he says. 'Jules is on this weekend, but he's ill. Stuart's been covering, but he's got a family thing later so they want me to do the evening.'

'Oh.' Rebecca digests this. 'Should we go?' she asks.

'I'm not taking over until four,' he says. 'It's been quiet, Stuart says. But we should probably get home by then.'

Rebecca nods. They're almost back where they started now.

'Shall we get some lunch?' Ben asks. 'We passed a pub on the way that looked OK.'

There's nothing to stop her mentioning the diary at lunch, but she doesn't. Partly because she's reluctant to start the conversation when he might be called away, Rebecca thinks. But it's not just that. It's also that she's rather ashamed, as they sit in the pub with plates of fish and chips in front of them, about the muddle she's got herself into. That she can't decide on the right tone to take; can't work out how Ben will react. *It's something and nothing,* she hears Ben saying. Perhaps that's the truth of all this.

They're both quiet on the way home, and an odd sense of limbo hangs over the rest of the afternoon. Neither of them can settle to anything. And at ten o'clock, just when they've begun to think there's not going to be a call this evening, that they're safe to go to bed, Ben's phone buzzes. Five minutes later he kisses her goodbye and heads off into the night.

When Rebecca arrives at Marchboys the following morning, she's aware at once that something's wrong. There are two police cars in the drive, and the front door is wide open. She pulls up a little way from the house, wondering what to do. For a moment she considers driving away again – whatever's going on, it's clearly not her business – but that might look odd, she tells herself. So she parks in her usual place and gets out.

Pieter's assistant Sam is standing just inside the front door.

'What's happened?' Rebecca asks him.

'Emily's disappeared,' he says. 'Pieter's daughter.'

'Disappeared?' Rebecca echoes. 'When? How?'

'From her grandmother's house,' Sam says. 'She wasn't in her bedroom this morning.'

'Oh, God.' Rebecca feels sick. Little Emily: she remembers her upside down in the meadow, her legs waving like a sea anemone. 'When was she last seen?'

'Last night, when she went to bed. There's no sign of a break-in, but her window was open.'

'So they think she's been abducted?'

'Either that or run away. Pieter's frantic.' Sam looks calmer than she'd have expected. Perhaps that's his role: the anchor for the floundering ship. 'They've spotted an intruder on the CCTV here, over the weekend,' he says. 'They're wondering whether it might be connected.'

'Was Emily here this weekend, then?'

Sam shakes his head. 'No, but she's often here. If anyone was watching her, planning something, they'd know that. They could have been scouting around.'

'God.' Rebecca hesitates. 'Did they break in, the intruder?'

'No – just walked around the house, looking up at the windows, brazen as you like. If you were planning to kidnap Pieter's daughter, if you knew what he was worth, you'd guess he had CCTV cameras, wouldn't you?'

'I suppose so.'

'They caught him on the camera by the gate too. A man with a beard, driving a Transit van. Two big dogs in the front seat.'

A great rush of wind fills Rebecca's head.

'Yesterday?' she asks, and Sam shakes his head. 'Saturday,' he says. 'Saturday afternoon.'

For a moment Rebecca can't speak; can't even think. She remembers Ben unloading the dogs from the van on Saturday evening, saying, *I found a great place for the kites*. She remembers that slight hesitation when she asked him a question, and the way he protested too much, perhaps, about where he'd been. *Somewhere I found on the internet. Lots of people recommended it.* She thinks of the doubts she's wrestled with these past few days. Of the emergency last night, and the fact that Ben wasn't supposed to be on call.

It might not be him on the CCTV. Or it might be him, and there might be an innocent explanation. But somehow she knows it will be, and she fears there isn't.

The scaffolding tower is standing in the hall, exactly as she left

THE HOUSE AT THE EDGE OF THE WOODS

it. Rebecca longs to climb back up the ladder – to murmur some platitudes to Sam and retreat into her fairy-tale world. If she had an hour or two with the dragon and the moon princess and the faithful Arkady, she could think things through calmly. She could absorb herself in stippling in the leaves on the trees in the great forest while she works out what to do.

But she knows already what she has to do. And she knows that if she doesn't do it now, straight away, they'll wonder why. They'll work out soon enough that it's Ben on the CCTV, and then she'll look guilty too. Pieter will remember her saying, *You're mad*, dismissing his warnings. They'll assume she's covering up for Ben, and that will only make things worse for him.

Even so, her mind wrestles with alternatives. She could drive away now, and find Ben before the police do. She could make him tell her the truth. But Rebecca's seen enough crime dramas to imagine the worst. What if he's got Emily hidden somewhere, and she makes him panic?

A wave of dizziness sweeps through her. Surely, surely, none of this can be happening – but she has to believe that it is. It's not just in her head now; not just a fairy tale. When she and Ben walked around the stone circle yesterday with the dogs – when they ate their fish and chips at the pub – was Ben's mind full of violence, all that time? She ought to be asking why – why on earth Ben would steal a child from her bed; why he'd hurt her – but the answer to that question is waiting before it can even be thought. Because, somehow, Ben has an inkling of what Pieter suspects. Because perhaps, inconceivably, it's true.

'Can I see the CCTV?' she asks, before her mind can run on any further. 'I'm just wondering . . .'

Sam looks at her sharply. 'Have you seen someone hanging around?' he asks.

'No.' This is her last chance, Rebecca thinks. She could drive to her father's. She could ask him what to do. But she can't do that; she knows she can't. 'I'm just wondering whether it's someone I know.'

*

93

The police officer Sam takes her to has a brutal look, nothing like the complex, humane characters who populate TV dramas. But he doesn't ask many questions, when Sam explains that Rebecca's been working here, and that she thinks she might recognise the man on the CCTV footage. He leads her into a part of the house she's never seen before, to a small room with a bank of screens. And a moment later the central screen fills with an image of Ben – beyond a shadow of a doubt Ben – walking round the perimeter of Marchboys House.

'Hold on,' the policeman says. 'There's another camera round the back. I'll just—'

'There's no need,' Rebecca says. 'I know who that is. It's my husband, Ben Swarbrick.'

And then she has to sit down, because it's a terrible thing to give your husband up to the police. It's a terrible thing to start believing that he might have committed murder.

PART TWO

PART TWO

13

Ben is listening out for Rebecca's car, but he notices the headlights first, a glow in the glass above the front door that grows rapidly brighter as she approaches. He hears the engine stop, hears her slam the car door, and then her footsteps coming up the garden path with a sort of click, the way they sound when she walks briskly. And then she's inside, and she's smiling and her cheeks are round and shiny and smooth and he can tell she's had a good day.

'How was it?' he asks, even so. 'Did it go well?'

She shakes her head – not to say no, but as if she needs to clear something, settle something, before she speaks.

'It was amazing,' she says. 'It's a wonderful house. A wonderful project. It's going to be a huge challenge, but it'll be fun, I hope.' Then she pulls a face; the face that says *yikes* and *we're in this together* and *I'm glad I've got you*. 'I hope I'm up to it,' she says. 'I've never done anything like this before. It's an enormous space, and the ceiling's domed. The whole surface is curved. And he's got high standards, Pieter. He's very rich. He could have employed anyone.'

'That's great,' Ben says. 'I'm so pleased.'

And he is. He's proud of her, delighted for her. But he feels something else, too, at the edge of everything: a tiny flicker of unease about Rebecca working in a huge house owned by a rich man, so far from their world. He wishes, just for a moment, that Pieter Blake *had* chosen someone else. But he knows that's unreasonable. Rebecca's been so excited about this. It's her big chance.

She's looking at him now. 'Is everything OK, Ben?' she asks. 'Has something happened?'

'No,' he says. 'Nothing at all.' Ada rubs her face against his leg, and he bends down to stroke her. 'So you're going to take the job?' he asks.

'Do you think I shouldn't?' She cocks her head: not exactly teasing him, but not serious, either. How could she not take it? *It could make my career*, she said last night. 'Do you think I'm not up to it?'

'Of course I don't.' He takes a step towards her and puts his arms around her. 'I'm so proud,' he says. 'You'll do a wonderful job.'

To Ben, Rebecca is a miracle. When he was younger, and used to imagine himself married, it was always to someone like her: someone kind and cheerful, who'd smile when he came into the room and liked the same things that he liked. Part of him doubted that he'd ever meet anyone like that, but another part always believed he would. That the world had someone waiting for him.

And when he first saw Rebecca, at the party Conor West invited him to, it was as if he recognised her from his own future. He'd never much liked parties, and he wasn't sure why he'd agreed to come to this one, except that he'd been flattered that Conor had seemed pleased when they ran into each other at Sainsbury's. But when Conor's sister introduced him to Rebecca, he'd understood. This was why he was here. For this person, this woman, with her dark hair and her round eyes that looked up at him in a way that was neither shy nor bold, but careful and gentle. He was so overwhelmed to find himself talking to her that he was almost struck dumb. He worried, then, that she'd walk away again and find someone else to talk to, but she didn't.

After a few minutes, maybe not even that long, he felt something taking root inside him. Love at first sight. And amazingly, Rebecca seemed to feel it too. It wasn't his childish fantasy, it was real: a living thing that grew and flourished as the months passed, its leaves unfurling and its branches reaching up towards the light. Ben had never had a girlfriend before, not one who'd lasted for more than an evening or two, but it turned out that he didn't need any practice runs. All he'd needed was to meet Rebecca. He thinks, sometimes, about that moment in Sainsbury's – how, if he hadn't been looking for spaghetti, he might have missed Conor, and never been invited to the party. How the universe nudges things into place, sometimes, to make sure you don't miss your step.

It was a strange time, that summer. It's easy to tell the story now, Ben thinks, so it sounds as though things had already begun to fall into place for him: there was his new job at Fortescue's, and the one-bedroom flat he was renting with the extra money. He'd been excited about both those things. He'd felt like a proper grown-up at last.

But in reality, it was more complicated than he'd expected. The job had been pretty tough at first: they were big on customer service at Fortescue's, and although Ben was polite, his shyness counted against him. People sometimes thought he was surly, and the boss didn't like that. And although he'd never really liked house-sharing, having to live with other people's mess and noise, he was lonely in the new flat.

What was worse, the loneliness left space for things he'd managed to keep out of sight for a long time. When he sat down on his new sofa to watch television, he remembered sitting on his own in a corner of the playground. When he turned off the light at night, he remembered lying in his bed at Grandma and Grandpa's house, certain that he'd never get used to living there. Being a grown-up – having a flat and a van and colleagues who said, *Morning, Ben*, and included him in their jokes – meant you weren't supposed to have those sorts of feelings any more. But it turned out the person he was left with when he came home to the flat wasn't the *Morning, Ben* man. The person inside him who crept out when no one else was around didn't really believe in the grown-up Ben. Even the green Fortescue's sweatshirts felt a bit like a school uniform some mornings.

And then one night, not long after he moved in, he dreamed about his mother.

They were on a bus together, he and his mum, and they'd been somewhere nice, somewhere like a zoo or a fair, and he was feeling happy. She'd bought him sweets, and she held his hand all the way home. But when the bus stopped outside their flat, she said she wasn't coming in with him. *You'll be OK, won't you?* she said. *You're a big boy, you can look after yourself.* But Ben wasn't OK. He couldn't get the key into the lock on the front door, and the person who opened it for him at last told him he was a nuisance. And then he was angry: angry with the person at the door, and with his mum, and with himself for letting her walk away. He was so angry that he woke up shouting and thrashing under the duvet.

The dream left him wide awake, so he got up to make a cup of tea. And then, while the kettle was boiling, he heard his mother's voice. *This is a nice place*, she said. *I can see you'll be happy here.* She spoke very clearly, and when he glanced over his shoulder he could almost see her, in the shadow of the door frame. But then the kettle clicked off and he shook his head and told himself to stop being stupid: he was awake now and she wasn't here, was she? It was just him, grown-up Ben.

But his mother kept coming back after that. She'd turn up first thing in the morning or last thing at night, or right in the middle of a Sunday when he was least expecting it. The new flat wasn't much like the place where they'd lived when he was little, but something about the cramped rooms and the white walls began to feel famil-iar. Hearing his mother in the next room; the mixture of happiness and uncertainty. And the strange feeling that she was sometimes a long way away, even when she was right there eating breakfast with him, or tying his shoelaces, or tucking him up in bed.

He didn't believe in ghosts, but he began to think about what it might mean if he did. There'd be things he'd want to ask her, he thought. Not just about that day, the last day, but other things too. There were some questions that were always at the back of his mind, and others that hovered just out of reach. Was that why she'd come? Why his subconscious had conjured her up?

As the summer went on, his mother's presence troubled him

more and more. It began to affect his work: he made a couple of mistakes, failed to listen when a customer asked him a question. He started to worry that he might lose his job.

And then he met Conor in Sainsbury's that day, and Conor invited him to the party.

Perhaps he wouldn't have gone if he hadn't been grateful to have an evening out of the flat: that thought occurred to him towards the end of the evening. Was it chance, then, or fate? Perhaps his mother had come back to make sure he went? Perhaps the dead version of her understood things – understood him – better than she had when she was alive.

In any case, after he met Rebecca, things changed. After that it was the grown-up Ben who seemed real again – more real than he ever had. When he met customers, he imagined he was talking to Rebecca, and he found he could smile and chat in just the way the boss liked. When he sat on the sofa, or turned off his bedside light, Rebecca was there beside him. And his mother didn't appear again.

He knew it was wrong to be relieved. He knew the story he told himself about his mother drifting away because she could see he was happy with Rebecca wasn't true. But she was dead; she'd always been dead. It was better not to have her lurking at the edge of his vision. The questions he might have asked her lingered for a while, and then they, too, drifted out of sight. He'd never be able to ask them, he told himself, so it was better not to think about them.

He never told Rebecca about the months when his mother spoke to him in the silence of the flat. The first night he and Rebecca met, he told her the story of his mother's death, and that was enough. Rebecca understood what it meant, and she didn't ask about it again. They could get on with their lives, plan their wedding, look for somewhere new to live.

When they moved into None-go-bye, he felt he'd arrived in the place he'd always wanted to be. That first spring, he dug over the garden and built a little potting shed. That summer, they lived on their first crop of runner beans and tomatoes, a glut of their own creation. And that autumn, they found Ada and Bertha in a rescue centre and brought them home.

Meanwhile, Ben's probation at Fortescue's finished and he was given a modest pay rise. He signed up for a bee-keeping course at the adult education centre, and Rebecca came along to do a painting class, which turned out to be a wonderful thing for her, the start of a new career. The following spring, Ben acquired his first swarm of bees. He loved the idea of the garden buzzing all summer with their own little tribe of honeybees; of Rebecca painting under the apple trees with the dogs at her feet. Their own miniature Eden, he thought.

But by the time summer came, the nightmares had begun.

It's always the same nightmare. And although he recognises it now, although he knows what it is as soon as it starts, he can never escape until it's played itself out. Sometimes it leaves him alone for weeks at a time, sometimes for months – but every time he thinks it's gone for good, it catches him out. It reminds him that the past is still there: that the grown-up Ben isn't entirely who he seems.

14

Rebecca's been at Marchboys House for a couple of weeks now, and things have settled into a familiar rhythm. She gets back later than usual in the evenings because it's a long drive, almost an hour, but otherwise it's been just like her doing any other job. She comes home tired and cheerful, covered in paint, bringing with her the smell of someone else's house. She talks about the scaffolding tower they've built for her and how strange it feels to perch on top of it all day, and about the huge pots of paint she's ordered to cover the ceiling: more paint than she's ever used before.

Ben talks about his work too. He's been partnered with a new recruit for the next few weeks, charged with helping him learn the ropes, and he takes that responsibility very seriously, modelling the perfect Fortescue's manner with customers and taking extra care over every job. He likes having someone to work with: the time passes more quickly, and there are more stories to repeat at the end of the day, anecdotes Jamie has told him and little details about customers and their houses that he might not have noticed on his own.

At home, he decides to try some recipes from a new Indian cookery book Rebecca gave him for Christmas. Rebecca has always loved curry, and Ben likes mixing up the spices, experimenting with the blend. At the weekend he checks on his bees, still deep in their winter slumber, and sorts through the packets of seed in the shed – it's not long now until he can start planting this year's vegetables. He and Rebecca start talking about booking a holiday for the summer: there's a website they've used before that lists dog-friendly cottages. They're thinking about Scotland this year. Ada and Bertha would love that, Ben thinks. He imagines them running across beaches, up mountain paths between banks of heather.

And then one evening Rebecca brings something home from Marchboys. A book Ben knows; a book he recognises immediately, even though it's years since he's seen it, and which turns his heart, his stomach, upside down.

Their special book, his mother used to call it. It had little black and white pictures in the corners of the pages, and the stories weren't the usual fairy tales like 'Sleeping Beauty' and 'Red Riding Hood'. They were stories other children didn't know.

When Rebecca puts the book down casually on the kitchen table, Ben stares at the cover for a long moment, and then he looks away. But when she picks it up again to make space for their supper plates, he can't help saying something.

'What's that?' he asks.

She holds it out to him, nonchalant. 'It's a children's book,' she says. 'Fairy tales. Pieter gave it to me because he wants me to use some of the stories in it for the ceiling.'

'Oh.'

Ben's struggling to get things straight. It's pure chance, he tells himself, that she's been given that particular book. It's for her work; for the painting. But he can't think of it as a coincidence, somehow. He can't help feeling it means something. Rebecca's looking at him curiously now, but he doesn't want to explain: instead he turns back to the stove to check the rice. Best to put it out of his mind, he thinks.

But that's difficult, because Rebecca wants to talk about the book. About the stories. Over supper, she tells him about the things she's painting, and when he doesn't respond she thinks it's because he doesn't know the stories.

'I didn't read fairy tales when I was little, either,' she says. 'I had a book of Bible stories with beautiful pictures, but it wasn't the same thing.' She smiles at him. 'I could read some of them to you.

That might be helpful for me, actually. They're meant to be read aloud. It might be fun too.'

Ben doesn't reply. He pours them each another glass of wine, and just then the dogs start barking at something in the garden, and he gets up to call them in, and the moment passes. Rebecca won't ask again, he tells himself. It's not like her to press things. But all evening, even while they're watching an episode of *Blue Planet*, the little pictures from the fairy-tale book flicker across his mind's eye like a black and white cartoon.

His mother's voice starts as a whisper, like something at the edge of the room. But even though he tries hard to concentrate on the television, it grows gradually louder and louder until it fills his head, and there's no room for any other thoughts. And then he shuts his eyes and he's back there, back in the cramped little flat, in his familiar little-boy's bedroom.

His mother's sitting on his bed, and she's got the book in her hand, the one with the nice pictures and the long words he doesn't really understand, although he likes the sound of them – and when she reads to him, it doesn't matter anyway, because it's as if the story's really happening, as if they're both inside the book. Ben loves that feeling.

'Did your mummy read you this story?' he asks, when she turns the page, and she laughs, although he doesn't know why it's a funny question.

'No,' she says, 'I read them to myself. Well, my godmother read them to me at first. She gave me the book.'

'Who's your godmother?' he asks.

'She's dead now. A long time ago.'

'Why did she die?'

His mother shrugs her shoulders. 'People do,' she says. 'Everyone dies eventually.'

'But not you,' he says.

'Even me, one day.'

He feels something clutching at him then. 'Not you,' he says again. 'You can't die. I need you.'

She ruffles his hair: he likes it when she does that. 'I won't die for a long time. Not until you're grown up, OK?'

One of the stories in the book is called 'The Magic Mirror', and it's about a boy whose mother dies, but he gets a magic mirror so he can see her and talk to her every night. Ben doesn't like that story, even though it has a happy ending. Not all the stories in the book have a happy ending: that makes it a grown-up book, his mum says. But he's glad she's reading him a happy story tonight.

He's not sleepy yet when she finishes reading, and he doesn't want her to turn the light off and leave him alone. She doesn't seem to be in a hurry either, tonight. She's holding the book, looking at it. On the cover, there's a picture of a forest, with a path going through the middle and two people walking along it between the tall trees. Ben likes that picture. It's them, he thinks. Him and his mum.

'Did you keep the book all this time so you could read it to me?' he asks.

She shakes her head. 'No, I bought this one for you.'

Ben's disappointed. He wanted it to be the same book she had when she was little. 'What happened to the one you had?' he asks.

'I gave it to someone.'

'Who?'

'No one you know.' She's put the book down now, and she's pulling up his covers, getting ready to tuck him in.

'Was it my dad?' he asks, although he knows she doesn't like him mentioning his dad. She gets her tired voice then, and that makes Ben sad. His dad was gone before he was born, she always says. *Is he dead?* Ben asked once, and she shook her head. *I don't know*, she said. There are other questions Ben longs to ask: *Does he know about me? Didn't he want me?* It's hard to stop those questions coming out. He has to take a deep breath and hold them tight inside himself. He often thinks about his dad when they're reading the stories in this book, especially the one about the old man who finds a tiny little girl in the garden, and tonight he thinks again that maybe there's a magical story about him and his mum and dad. Maybe his dad turned into a tree like Arkady, who was a dog who was really a prince. Or maybe he died fighting a giant, to save Ben and his mum.

He looks at his mum now. She still hasn't answered, and he plucks up his courage to ask again.

'Was it my dad you gave the book to?'

'No,' she says. 'Not your dad.'

She doesn't say anything more, but she doesn't sound tired or cross this time. She sounds almost as if Ben's said something nice, but he knows it isn't what he's said that's nice, but what it's made her think about, and Ben's worried, suddenly. Not worried-about-her-dying worried, but the other kind. The worry that there's someone else she loves more than him. He always thought it was his dad, but maybe it's someone else, and that feels worse, because then the other person has nothing to do with him. Even if they're from long ago, before he was born, they might come back. Or part of his mum might be left there with them. The part of her that sometimes isn't here with him.

'I wish you didn't give the old book away,' he says.

'But this one's just the same,' she says. 'And I got it specially for you. I had to look for it.'

She smiles at him then, but he can't tell whether she means it. He thinks maybe she got the book to remind her of the person she gave the old one to.

When she turns off the light and shuts his door, he takes the book off his bedside table and holds it for a bit, looking at the picture on the front with the forest and the tall trees and the people walking. But it feels scary now it's dark in his room, so he puts the book under his pillow and shuts his eyes.

15

The next weekend, Ben goes to collect the new hives he's taking off a man in Essex who's giving up on bee-keeping. He'd have liked Rebecca to go with him, but she's gone to see her father – and driving himself there and back gives him a chance to think. To think about his bees and the new hives and the garden, and about Rebecca too.

His grandma thought no one could ever be good enough for him, but Ben knows that Rebecca is more than he deserves. He doesn't ever forget that. But thinking about Rebecca feels a bit more complicated than usual at the moment, because of Pieter Blake and Marchboys House and the fairy-tale book. He can feel things getting tangled, the way they used to sometimes before he met Rebecca.

Pieter Blake must have had the same book as his mum when he was little, Ben has decided. He's probably about the same age as she'd be now, so that makes sense. Obviously if Pieter wanted fairy tales on his ceiling he'd think of his old book, and if he wanted Rebecca to paint those particular stories he'd give her a copy. It all sounds straightforward when Ben sets it out like that, but he still can't help feeling uneasy about it. And seeing the book again has made him think about his mother, and about the person she gave her copy to, and he'd rather not do that.

He's glad they're going to Hove tomorrow. Life always feels less complicated when they're with his grandma. She has a way of keeping things in their place that Ben has always found reassuring, even though he knows most things aren't as simple as she likes to make out. Politics, the price of things, the past: they're all swept away with a shake of her head and a click of her tongue. *No point bothering about things you can't change*, she says – and according to her, most things in the world fall into that category.

Ben smiles now, thinking about Grandma. She's incorrigible, Rebecca said once, in a rare moment of annoyance, and she's right. Of course she is. But he likes having Grandma in his life. He likes going down there and eating her stew and letting her put his childhood back into the box she made to hold it, all those years ago.

It *is* stew for lunch that Sunday, and afterwards they fly the kite Rebecca gave him for Christmas, the giant manta-ray one. He loves watching it soar over the beach, and he loves seeing Rebecca enjoying it too, her face open and smiling. He knows she finds Grandma tricky: she's always been possessive, and Rebecca wasn't what she expected. Rebecca doesn't get her jokes. He ought to mind that they don't really get on, Ben thinks, but he doesn't. It means he doesn't have to share them with each other: he can have each of them entirely to himself.

When he finds himself on his own with Grandma on the way back from the beach, he considers telling her about the things that have been on his mind, but he knows she'd laugh at him. *You're catching her ways*, she'd say, *with all that worriting*. Worriting is a waste of time, in her book, and she's always scoffed at people who have time to waste. Though what she does with her time these days, Ben has no idea.

'You're OK, though, Grandma?' he says, as they make their way along the seafront.

'What d'you mean? D'you mean am I about to follow your grandad into my grave?'

'No, of course I don't mean that. I mean ...' Ben frowns, but before he can finish the sentence she's taken the lead from him.

'Are *you* OK, is what I want to know,' she says. 'With Rebecca hanging around this millionaire?'

'She's not hanging around him, Grandma. She's doing a job for him.'

'Money turns women's heads,' she says. 'You'd better watch it, Ben.'

Ben shakes his head. 'Not Rebecca's,' he says. 'Don't you worry about that.'

And the funny thing is, the conversation makes him feel better. Maybe it's because Grandma has always said things like that about Rebecca, and he's always laughed at her. Or because he wonders, now, if that *is* all he's been worried about, and putting it so bluntly makes it sound ridiculous. It makes him feel there's nothing to worry about after all.

He has a fleeting glimpse then, in his mind's eye, of the kite dipping and twisting high above their heads, its long tail looping across the sky as though it was writing a secret message. The kite's a sort of miracle too, he thinks. It can't fly on its own, but as long as he holds on tight to the strings it can dance in that great open space like a free spirit.

16

He's in a forest with his mother, and they're both running as fast as they can. It's very dark, and there are wolves and crows calling through the trees and brambles catching at his ankles. He's frightened, very frightened, even though he knows his mother's just behind him. He's carrying something, a sword or an axe with a heavy handle, but he doesn't know where it came from or what he's supposed to do with it. He keeps trying to throw it away, but his hand stays clenched stubbornly around the handle.

He can't remember what they're running away from, or whether it's just the kind of forest where you have to keep running. When he glances over his shoulder, his mother's there, but he can't see her clearly because the trees are very tall and it's dark beneath them. She's wearing something white and flowing, like a nightie, but that's wrong because she was wearing jeans and a T-shirt. He remembers that. A blue and white striped T-shirt. But perhaps that was another time, another place?

And then there's a cry, and when he turns round his mother's not there any more. He searches frantically among the trees, shouting her name. When at last he finds her, lying under a tree, he can see that she's dead. Her head's been cut off, and there's blood everywhere. He looks at the axe in his hands, and he sees that it's covered in blood now. So he drops it and he runs, runs, runs, tripping and stumbling over the tree roots, but he can't get away from the place. However fast he runs, he never even gets to the edge of the little glade. His screams fill the air, the whole forest, so loud that even the wolves are silenced.

'Ben!'

His mother's calling him, but he knows she's dead: he saw her lying there. He wants to keep running, but his legs have turned to mud and he can't move.

'It's all right, Ben. I'm here.'

Her arms are around him now, her hand stroking his face, and relief rushes through him. But it's not his mother; it's Rebecca. And then there's a great swirling wind in his head, and it blows up the dead leaves from the forest floor and sets the crows shrieking, and he moans in fear, because after all he's only seven.

'Was it the old nightmare?' Rebecca asks, and he opens his eyes at last.

'Yes,' he says. It's dark in the bedroom, but he can see the outline of the window and he can feel the duvet around him. And Rebecca, holding him. 'I'm sorry,' he says. 'I'm sorry I woke you.'

'Shh,' she says. 'Don't worry. It's all over now.'

'Yes,' he says.

'Do you want to tell me about it?'

He shakes his head – but he needs to tell her. He needs to tell her the right story.

'I was running through the forest,' he says. 'Someone was chasing me.' He shivers, even though it's warm under the duvet.

'Poor Ben,' Rebecca says. 'You're safe now. Everything's all right.'

'Yes,' he says again.

But everything's not all right. It's been months since the last nightmare, and he really thought it might not come back this time.

He wants – part of him wants – to go back and finish the dream, so he can make sure he's a long way from the axe and the tree where his mother's lying. He wants to know it's going to end, even though it never does. He lies very still, and he doesn't move when he hears Rebecca climbing out of bed. He waits, but sleep doesn't come. He can hear Rebecca downstairs, moving quietly around the kitchen, and then he follows her footsteps back up the stairs. When he opens his eyes she's climbing back into bed, holding a cup.

'Is that tea?' he asks.

'Do you want some? I thought you were asleep.'

'No, it's all right.'

But the nightmare is still there. There's a hum of danger in his mind, a buzz of adrenaline in his veins.

Rebecca hesitates a moment. 'Do you want to talk?'

'You talk,' he says. 'Tell me about your painting.'

He doesn't know why he asked that, but it's too late now.

'About the stories, you mean?' she asks.

But that's too much – and also somehow not enough. 'No, tell me about him,' he says. 'About Pieter Blake.'

'I don't know much about him,' Rebecca says. 'He's rich. He works hard. And he's very particular about the painting: he knows what he wants.'

'Do you talk to him a lot?' Ben asks.

'Not as much as some clients. He's very busy.' She hesitates. 'He's got a daughter,' she says. 'She doesn't live with him, but she's there sometimes.' This is a surprise: it doesn't fit with Ben's idea of Pieter Blake. 'She's a funny child,' Rebecca says. 'She says funny things.'

'Like what?'

'Oh, I don't know. She asks lots of questions. She asked if we had any pets, and I told her about Ada and Bertha, and the bees.'

Ben digests this. He doesn't like the idea of Rebecca talking to Pieter's daughter, and maybe to Pieter, about their life. But he's told Jamie, the lad who's working with him, about the dogs. It's the same thing, he tells himself.

'Does she live with her mother?' he asks.

Rebecca looks at him quickly, as though she doesn't want to make too much of it. 'With her grandparents,' she says. 'Her mother died. She was ill.'

There's a long silence then, and in it Ben can feel things shifting, the earth lifting and fracturing. He tries to hold on to the present – the bedroom, the duvet, Rebecca's voice – but in the half-dark he feels himself tumbling back into the shadows of those giant trees. And then he hears himself talking again.

'It was very dark in the forest,' he says. 'There were trees all around. I couldn't see the sky through the branches. I had to keep running, but I didn't know why. I didn't know who was chasing me.'

One day, he thinks, he'll slip up. He'll mention his mother, or the axe. Is that why the nightmare keeps coming back? Because he's so frightened of what it means?

'I love you,' Rebecca says, and she kisses his cheek. 'I love you, Ben.'

For another few moments he lies still, with her arms wrapped around him and her hair against his face. And then suddenly he wants very badly to make love to her. He wants the comfort of it, the reassurance. The reminder that he's not a little boy any more. He touches her hair, her back, and he feels her tense and soften, and then there's nothing in his mind but her.

17

The nightmare fades from view again after that night, as it always does, but Pieter's daughter lodges in Ben's mind. He imagines her running loose in a huge old house with lots of empty rooms, like a child from a book. A child whose mother is dead and who lives with her grandparents, just like he did. It's no surprise he's curious about her, he thinks, even though their lives could hardly be more different. What would it have been like if he'd had a wealthy father he could go and stay with after his mother died?

He'd like to know the little girl's name, but Rebecca didn't mention it. He could ask, of course, but Rebecca might think that was odd. Maybe there'll be something on the internet, though, if her dad's that rich. So in his lunch break one day, when Jamie's on a training course, Ben tries Google. He doesn't find the child's name anywhere: he hardly finds any mention of her, in fact. But he finds out other things. Things that surprise him.

Pieter Blake was born in Hong Kong but educated in England, he reads on Wikipedia. He went to a school Ben has vaguely heard of and then to Birmingham University, and he made his first million by the age of twenty-seven. Not quite like a dotcom prodigy, but still. There's a lot of detail about Pieter's business interests which Ben skims over, but he spots a brief reference to the house in Warwickshire, as well as flats Pieter owns in Kensington and Hong Kong. There's nothing on Wikipedia about his wife: Ben has to dig a bit further, typing in *Pieter Blake wife*, before he finds any mention of her.

And when he does, he has to read it twice.

The marriage only lasted a couple of years, and Sally Blake died a few months after they were divorced, when their daughter was still a baby. That much tallies with what Rebecca told him. But surely – *she was ill*, isn't that what Rebecca said? What the child told her? Ben searches for another article in case this one is wrong, but every account is the same. There was an accident; a tragic accident. Sally Blake fell from a fourth-floor hotel balcony in Spain.

Ben lets his phone drop for a moment. Could Rebecca know that? he wonders. Could she have lied to him? Surely not. And surely the little girl wouldn't lie, either. But why would her father not tell her the truth about something so important? Why say her mother was ill? Ben feels shaky now. Pieter Blake was staying in the same hotel, the articles say, even though they were divorced. That detail is enough to goad Ben into opening the search page again. There must, he thinks, be more information somewhere. And there is. Below the articles from financial journals, the respectful profiles in glossy magazines, he finds a series of sensational tabloid headlines. Ben's not interested in gossip, as a rule, but he clicks on one, and then another. And another.

At first he feels a ghoulish sort of fascination. Several of the pieces are about the women Pieter's been associated with since his wife's death, and although Ben's not well up on celebrities, doesn't watch the TV programmes they feature in, even he has heard of a couple of them. The articles are mostly the usual kiss-and-tell stuff, but a couple are more unsavoury. *Rich List businessman Pieter Blake is known for his ruthless deal-making* ... Ben stops. Rich List? What does that mean? Tens of millions? Hundreds? *Now sources close to him allege there's a darker side to Mr Won't-take-no-for-an-answer*, the piece continues, airing the claims of a former employee. *Jilly Jones spills the beans on Bullying Blake*, the next headline announces. *Pieter was cruel and controlling, the former* Date Me *star claims in the wake of their split* ...

Then he comes upon the articles which suggest there might have been more to Sally Blake's death than an accident. The claim that

Pieter was there when she fell is repeated. Drugs and alcohol are mentioned, but also the fact that Pieter and Sally were engaged in a bitter custody battle for their baby daughter.

None of the articles contain anything more than speculation and circumstantial detail, but by now Ben's fascination has turned to alarm. Is Rebecca safe, he wonders, working for this man? Does she have any idea what his reputation is like? And why on earth would a multimillionaire employ someone like Rebecca to paint a mural for him when he could have some fancy-pants interior designer from London? How did he even hear about Rebecca?

It's possible, Ben reasons, that Pieter asked one of his minions to find someone unknown, someone less likely to blab about him. There was a piece in the paper about the mural Rebecca did last year for the hospital in Banbury; they might have found that. Maybe they were looking for someone local, and even though Banbury's not exactly close to Marchboys, it's in the next county.

But what if there's something more sinister to it than that? What if, for some reason, Pieter has set his sights on Rebecca? Maybe it's a game that amuses him: finding someone ordinary and straightforward, then flattering them into falling for him. The kind of thing they might make into a Netflix miniseries. Ben remembers the spring in Rebecca's step that evening after she first met Pieter; he thinks about his grandma's warning, and the uneasiness he's found so hard to dismiss.

And then he shakes his head. No, that's nonsense. Rebecca is everything he ever dreamed of, but a man like Pieter Blake, who dates A-list celebrities, wouldn't look twice at her. He's engaged, too, to Freya Malone. Her picture's in several of those tabloid articles, a glamorous 25-year-old in a bikini on a yacht. What could Pieter want with Rebecca if he's got someone like that?

Ben flicks off his phone, crumples his crisp packet into a ball and climbs down from the van. That kind of tabloid coverage is often overhyped, he tells himself, perhaps more fiction than fact. He won't mention it to Rebecca: he doesn't want her to laugh at him.

But he'll find an opportunity to ask her a bit more about Pieter, he decides. Probe a little. And now he'd better get a move on: he's got a boiler service after this job, and he's supposed to be there by two.

Ben works hard for the next half hour to get the new taps connected up to the customer's bath. Gold mixer taps: not that much of an indulgence, really, but people are always pleased with them, and they look good in this bathroom with its elegant blue and white tiles. He fixes the panelling back on the side of the bath and cleans up meticulously. The boss is scrupulous about that.

But while he's driving to his next appointment, Pieter's daughter drifts back into his mind. The image of the little girl running around in that big empty house feels different now he knows more about her father. Rebecca's description made her sound more ordinary than you'd expect, even though she hasn't had an ordinary life at all. She must, Ben thinks, remember almost nothing about her mother. Would it be easier, though, not remembering anything? Not having scraps of the past lurking in your head, or being haunted by questions no one knows the answers to?

He grunts, tightening his grip on the steering wheel. Don't go there, he tells himself. Stay here, with the van and the uniform and the bag of tools. He turns off the main road on to the lane that leads to the next customer's house. He's been here before: a square 1950s villa with draughty windows and old-fashioned furniture.

'It's Ben, isn't it?' the lady says, when she opens the door. 'Nice to see you again.'

Ben smiles. Customers don't usually remember his name, and he was with a colleague last time. See, he tells himself: he has a proper grown-up life. He just has to hang on tight to every bit of it.

'It's nice to see you too,' he says. 'How've you been keeping?'

She makes him a cup of tea, and even remembers how he takes it. 'My husband was the same,' she says. 'Sweet enough with just the one sugar, he used to say.'

Ben smiles again. 'Let's have a look at this boiler, then.'

*

Ben doesn't like being on call overnight, but it's one of the pillars of Fortescue's customer service. The people who pay for their services pay for peace of mind, the boss likes to say, and lots of them sign up for the emergency cover package. Every employee does two nights a month and three or four weekends a year. The weekends are often busy, but it's unusual to get called out overnight in the middle of the week.

But this particular duty night, towards the end of that week, is different. There's a call at five, when he's just left the job he's been at all day – and he hasn't even got to that customer yet when there's another call, another urgent job to go on to straight afterwards. He tries to ring Rebecca, but she doesn't pick up. She'll be driving, he thinks. She'll be on her way home. He leaves her a message, explaining about the call-outs, and asks her to ring him when she gets in.

He has his phone on silent while he's dealing with the leaking pipe at the first customer's house, but he glances at it once or twice, and he sees the missed call from Rebecca and the voicemail notification. He smiles, imagining her at home with the dogs. There's some of last night's pie left: he hopes she's found it. He'll call her back when he's finished here. The next job sounds like a quick one, and three calls in a night would be unheard of. He should be home by ten thirty at the latest.

He waits until he's back in the van before he listens to Rebecca's message. Two messages, in fact. He feels a quiver of anxiety when he notices the second one, but only a quiver. He selects the first message and presses play, and her voice fills the cab.

Hello Ben, it's me. You're not to worry, but I've had an accident. I fell off the scaffolding, not from very high, but I've hurt my ankle, and I hit my head too. I'm OK, though; I'll be fine. They're being very kind here. Pieter's called his private doctor. I'll let you know what he says.

Ben's heart is thumping now. He curses himself for not listening to the message sooner. He wants to ring Rebecca back straight away, but he forces himself to play the other message first, in case she's at a hospital or something. He'll ring the boss, he thinks, tell him his wife's had an accident. Someone else can go out to the second customer.

Rebecca's voice sounds more quavery this time, even though she clearly wants to reassure him.

Hello darling, I'm sorry to miss you again. Everything's fine. The doctor says it's just a sprain. But they think I should stay here overnight in case I have concussion. Pieter's housekeeper used to be a nurse, and she can keep an eye on me.

There's a pause then, and Ben has a sudden vision of Pieter Blake standing over Rebecca while she talks. Is she really all right? he wonders, panic rising inside him. Why aren't they taking her to a hospital?

I think it's the best thing, Rebecca says. *I'm very tired, and I don't expect you could get here for a while. Don't worry about me. I'll speak to you tomorrow, my love.*

Ben touches the call-back symbol, but Rebecca's phone goes straight to voicemail. Either it's run out of battery or she's turned it off. It's only just after nine o'clock. Could she be asleep already?

He shuts his eyes. *Everything's fine*, he hears her say. *Don't worry. I'll speak to you tomorrow.* But what if she has one of those brain haemorrhages you can't spot at first? What if Pieter Blake – Mr Won't-take-no-for-an-answer – decides to check on her himself in the middle of the night?

He must go and get her, he decides. He can't risk it. He types Marchboys House into the satnav, and watches the route wiggling across the screen.

But then he stops himself. By the time he gets there it would be almost ten thirty. The whole house might be asleep by then. He can hardly insist Rebecca needs to go to hospital when a doctor has said she doesn't, and she might be embarrassed by him turning up in the middle of the night. Angry, even. And even if the boss is OK with it, someone else will have to go and deal with the next call, and the customer's been waiting several hours already because the last job took longer than he expected.

He clenches one fist inside the other, the way he does when he needs to settle something with himself. No, he's not being sensible. Much better to get on with his work and leave Rebecca to the ex-nurse and the private doctor. Surely she'll be safe in their hands? He sends her a text message she can read when she wakes up, and then he puts the next customer's address into the satnav.

He still feels queasy about it in the morning, though. He doesn't like the feeling of being out of the loop. An image comes into his head of Rebecca in a four-poster bed and Pieter bringing her break-fast on a tray: Rebecca's laughing and smiling, and wondering what she's doing married to Ben. He knows that's nonsense, but the fact that she's spent the night at Pieter's house – the fact that she's hurt, and Ben hasn't been there to look after her – makes his stomach clench.

He rings Rebecca's number again before he sets off for work, but her phone's still going to voicemail. He records a message, then deletes it. Better to text her, he thinks, so she can't miss it. He chooses his words carefully, in case she's with Pieter. *Silly old Ben*, he imagines her saying. *Poor old Ben*. Rebecca's a kind person, a sensible person, but maybe Grandma's right about her head being turned, especially after last night. Princess Diana came to his school once, and even though he couldn't even see her properly, he could feel the magnetic field around her. Famous people, rich people, change the air in the room, he realised then. They make other people behave differently.

As he sets off in the van, he tells himself Rebecca's asleep, that he shouldn't expect her to text back for hours yet. But he hears his phone ping soon after he gets to his first job of the morning, and his heart leaps. Ignoring the boss's rules, he clicks on the notifica-tion straight away.

Lovely to get your messages, the text says. *I'm feeling a bit bruised but I'm fine. Looking forward to seeing you later.*

Ben reads the words several times over, looking for a chink, but he can't find one. He sends another quick message back, and when he has a break he rings her.

'It's so lovely to hear your voice,' she says.

'And yours,' he says. 'You had me worried.'

'I'm sorry.' She doesn't know how worried he was, or what about, and he's glad of that. 'I'm OK, really,' she says. 'I'm going to do a bit of painting on the ground today. I can start the marbling on the pillars.'

'Shouldn't you be resting?' he asks, and he imagines her shaking her head.

'I'd rather be working,' she says. And then she hesitates. 'I probably shouldn't drive, though,' she says. 'At least – I don't feel I want to just yet. Maybe . . .'

'I'll come and get you,' he says.

'Are you sure? I could . . .'

'Of course I'm sure.' He grins, even though she can't see him. 'I'll be finishing around three today,' he says, 'since I was on call last night. I'll be there as soon as I can.'

Marchboys House is even more impressive than Ben expected. It's one of those square, flat-faced houses with rows and rows of windows that you see in costume dramas, and it has grounds that are more like a park than a garden, with oak trees dotted here and there and a ring of woodland beyond. It feels odd to drive up to the front door, and his heart does a sort of leapfrog when Rebecca opens it. He wants to hug her, but he feels too self-conscious. This is the sort of house where he'd normally go to the back door.

'I'm so pleased to see you,' she says. 'Thank you for coming.'

'I should have come last night,' he says, but Rebecca shakes her head.

'You couldn't,' she says. 'You had to work. I was fine. They looked after me.'

He lets his eyes rest on her for a moment, taking in the reality of her. His Rebecca.

'Do you want to see the painting?' she asks. 'It's not nearly finished, of course, but . . .'

That makes his heart tumble too: the thought of the fairy tales, which he hasn't let himself think about recently. But when he steps into the house, he's astonished. The hall's bigger than he imagined, and the ceiling. Rebecca kept telling him it was a huge space, but he wasn't thinking on the right scale. And she's painted so much already. There's an ocean, a forest, a castle. A dragon sits in the entrance to a cave over to the right, and little boats sail towards a port.

'You've done all this?' he says, and Rebecca laughs.

'Do you like it?'

Even the pillars round the edge of the hall are being painted. The top halves are still white, but the bottom halves have been coloured to look like a greenish stone. Ben remembers, then, what Rebecca said on the phone earlier: she must have been doing those today.

'Of course I do,' he says. 'It's such an achievement.' He looks around the hall again, his eyes lingering on the doors and corridors opening off it, leading into the other parts of the house, and his mind slips to those articles on the internet; to the reason he started googling Pieter. 'Is the little girl here?' he asks. 'The daughter?'

'Not today.' Rebecca slides her arm inside his, and Ben feels his heart swell. He's relieved that she's safe, and not too badly hurt, but he feels very proud of her too. Proud of what she's done here. He wants to tell her all that, but he can't find the words for it. For everything he's feeling.

'Let's go home,' Rebecca says. 'I'm ready for the weekend.'

As they come out of the front door, Ben spots Rebecca's blue Corsa, parked just around the corner of the house. 'What shall we do about your car?' he asks.

'Pieter's going to get someone to drive it home for us.'

'That's nice of him,' Ben says.

And it is, of course it is – but the mention of Pieter's name is enough to take the edge off the pleasure of seeing Rebecca. Ben hates the casual way she uses it, as though she's in his world now. And then he can feel everything that's been wound up so tightly inside him today unravelling, and relief and happiness spiralling back into suspicion.

'Where did you sleep?' he asks, as they turn out on to the main road.

Rebecca frowns, as if she's not sure what he means. Ben isn't sure what he means either. He was thinking of that four-poster bed.

'Last night?' she asks. 'In one of the spare bedrooms. There must be dozens.'

Let it go, Ben tells himself. But Pieter's in his head now, in the van with them, and he can't get rid of him. Anyway, he told himself he'd ask Rebecca more about Pieter, didn't he, after he found all that stuff online? He needs to know how he behaves towards Rebecca, whether he's wormed his way into her affections.

'Do you like him?' he asks. He doesn't mean his voice to sound aggressive, but he can tell it does.

'Like who? Pieter?'

He can't see Rebecca's face, but he hears the hesitation, and his heart squeezes tight. He hasn't mistaken that. He sees her mouth moving as she frames her next words.

'He's very rich,' she says at last.

'You said that before.'

'I mean – he's not like us. He's used to having people to do things for him. He called a private doctor to come and see me last night.'

Ben nods. 'But you like him,' he says.

'I don't *dis*like him,' Rebecca says. She sounds uneasy now. Is that because he's asking too many questions, or because she's got a guilty conscience? 'I suppose I'm intrigued by him,' she says. She's choosing her words carefully still – but she always does, he tells himself. She weighs things up, finds just the right way to say them.

'I've never met anyone like him before,' she says now. 'I'm flattered that he chose me for this job, and I'm glad he's pleased with what I'm doing.' She hesitates again. 'And he was very kind last night. I was grateful. I was worried about being a nuisance.'

Ben glances across at her. She's leaning back against the headrest and she's shut her eyes. She looks exhausted, her face sagging under the strain of the last twenty-four hours. He's an idiot, he thinks. What on earth is he doing? She's had a nasty fall, and all he can think about is Pieter Blake. About those stupid articles, and all Pieter's money, which means nothing to Rebecca. He should be ashamed of himself. He takes his left hand off the steering wheel and touches her knee.

'Are you in pain?' he asks.

'I'm tired,' she says. 'I've got a bit of a headache.' She takes a deep breath, sighs it out. 'But I'm very glad to be back with you.'

And that's enough, he thinks. That's more than enough. The road's opening out in front of them now, and Ben presses his foot down on the accelerator and lets the van bowl along between the high hedgerows.

18

Ben's determined to look after Rebecca this weekend. He got things wrong in the car: he let his fears get the better of him, and if Rebecca's upset, thinking badly of him, it's his own fault. It's just stupid, he thinks, to worry that something precious is under threat, and then put it at risk yourself.

They have supper at the pub in the village on Friday evening, and on Saturday Rebecca sits in the garden, wrapped in blankets, while Ben clears the last of the leaves from the lawn. The crocuses are coming up already, speckling the area under the apple trees with yellow and purple. It doesn't take long for spring to arrive, he thinks. For the year to turn back towards the sun. He looks up from time to time and sees Rebecca watching him, and he feels contentment seeping back into his bones.

It's not until the evening that he remembers the phone call from Grandma earlier in the week, asking if they'd go down to Hove again on Sunday. She's doing some clearing out, she said. She wants him to help her.

They don't have to go, he tells Rebecca. It can wait. But she shakes her head.

'Why don't you go?' she says. 'She'd love to see you on your own for once.'

'If you're sure.' He hesitates. He hates the idea of leaving Rebecca, but maybe, if he's needed in Hove, it would be better to go. 'The dogs can stay here with you,' he says. 'They can keep you company.'

*

Ben sets off early on Sunday morning. The roads are clear, the winter sky as colourless as a sheet of glass, and as he heads down the M23 he has the sudden feeling that he's driving into a vacuum. As if he might end up anywhere, or perhaps nowhere: at the edge of the world, where anything could happen.

There's a stab, then, of unexpected joy. That's the kind of thing his mum used to say, he thinks. A little riff of fancy, then a chuckle, a glance at Ben. The two of them in the car, heading off for an adventure. Does he remember that, or has he imagined it? He can't be sure. He tries to hold on to the memory, but it's too elusive to pin down. A feeling, a mood, as much as anything. Her tone of voice, and the smell of the car, condensed into an instant.

But like one of his kites, that sharp fragment of memory trails other things behind it: the questions he never quite asks himself; the things he tries not to think about. He watches them dart and twist across his mind, and when they've gone, when there's just the road ahead and the empty sky, he goes on staring into the space where they were for a long time, trying to make sense of them. He's tempted to pull off the road now and stop for a while – to sit in the car beside the motorway, as he did all those years ago, and let it all come back to him. He has the feeling, suddenly, that that might be possible: that the answers might be waiting, buried somewhere in his mind. For a moment, barely a moment, that thought fills him with hope, but terror is close behind it.

It isn't answers he wants; he knows that. All he's ever really wanted is for things to be simple and straightforward. A simple childhood; a simple marriage. But his life hasn't been simple, and it's no use pretending it has. No use pretending the past doesn't matter. He knows Rebecca would like him to talk about it – he can feel that, every time the nightmare comes back – but he daren't. He daren't let himself say anything, because – he takes a deep breath, facing up to himself – because he's afraid of what might come out. Of what she might think of him. There: that's the truth. The thing he's most frightened of now is losing Rebecca, and that means the other things have to be buried even more deeply. He has to make them stay out of sight.

He grips the steering wheel more tightly, and as the miles pass and the whiteness of the sky turns into a watery blue, he steers his mind carefully back towards today. Towards Hove. At least with Grandma things are simple, he thinks. Almost too simple. And it occurs to him then that that might be part of the problem – part of the reason he's been left with all this muddle and complication, all these scraps of memory that rattle around in his head.

There was a time, just after Grandad died, when things might have taken a different turn, but they never did. Ben had no idea where to begin, and Grandma's never been one for talking. *No point going into all that*, she used to say, if he ever dared to ask about his mother. It was the same for bullies at school, or things Grandad said when he thought Ben wasn't listening. *Keep your head down and ignore it* was her motto. Grandma didn't know how to be gentle, Ben thinks now, but she did her best for him. *My little soldier*, she called him. *My little man.* Every day after school they'd sit at the table together and have tea and biscuits. Custard creams.

On impulse, he stops at the next service station and buys a packet of custard creams. He looks at the bunches of flowers near the door, but he leaves them. Grandma wouldn't understand that, he thinks. She'd wonder what was going on.

If he'd hoped Grandma might be different today because he's come on his own, he'd have been disappointed. But he didn't really hope that. And he's used to behaving in a certain way with her, anyway. He was going to tell her about Rebecca's fall, but he doesn't. He doesn't tell her about googling Pieter Blake either. Grandma reads the *Mail*. She probably knows more about Pieter than Ben does, but he doesn't want to discuss it with her.

It turns out she doesn't want Ben to help her sort things out so much as to take away the things she's already sorted. She's got some boxes from somewhere and she's filled them with stuff she wants to get rid of. Ben recognises some of Grandpa's clothes in one box, and a few things that used to be in his old room at the top of another.

'You can look through it when you get them home if you want,' she says, 'but I wouldn't bother. Most of it's been in the box room since we moved here, and I'm sick of having it around. A load of rubbish I don't need.'

'All right,' Ben says. He wonders what's brought all this on, but he doesn't ask. He carries the boxes down to the van, and then they have a cup of tea and a custard cream.

It's still only three o'clock, but as Ben empties his teacup he thinks of Rebecca on her own at home – thinks of how he wasn't with her on Thursday night when she fell off the scaffolding, and how he promised himself he'd look after her this weekend.

'I should be going, Grandma,' he says. 'The traffic'll only get worse. Sunday evening, you know.'

If she's sorry he's leaving already, she doesn't show it. There's a moment when Ben wishes she would – when he wishes it with such sudden vehemence that he almost wants to say something to upset her, just to see that she can react – but the thought is gone almost before he registers it. He leans down to kiss her, and she smiles briefly, and pats his arm.

'Drive safe,' she says.

And perhaps that's an offering, he thinks. Perhaps that means more than it seems, because she never usually says anything like that. It's an unspoken rule that they never acknowledge the dangers of the road.

Rebecca has made a quiche for supper. It's sitting on the side in the kitchen when he gets home, hot from the oven – and the fairy-tale book is beside it. Rebecca must have been reading it today, Ben thinks. Before he can look away, Rebecca has picked it up.

'I do love these stories,' she says. She's got two cans of beer out of the fridge, and she holds one out to him. 'There's one called "The Moon Princess", about an old couple who find a tiny little girl in a flower in their garden.'

Not a flower, Ben thinks, a currant bush. He takes a sip of the beer.

'One day she disappears,' Rebecca says, 'and everyone thinks a dragon has taken her, so they kill the dragon, but then they find a dead wolf inside the dragon's cave and it turns out the dragon tried to protect the child. And the dragon had been protecting the village too, so it ends badly for everyone.'

Ben nods; tries to smile.

'I'm not sure how I can get all that into the painting,' Rebecca says. 'A miniature child won't be visible from the floor. But I suppose Pieter will know she's there.'

She puts the book down then, but her hand stops, just touching the cover.

'They call the child Quietness,' she says. 'It's a name the old lady has thought of. She has a whole alphabet of names for the children she's never had. It reminded me of your alphabet zoo.'

She looks at him then, and for a second Ben wonders whether she's guessed that he knows the book; whether he's given himself away somehow. And then he's not sure why he hasn't told her, and there's another second when he nearly does – when he can taste the words in his mouth – but he stops himself. Once he starts, he thinks, who knows where it might lead? Better not to risk it. But that moment in the car this morning comes back to him now, the moment when he almost grasped the thread of magic that wove through his mother's life – the thread you hardly ever saw, but which made your breath stop in your throat when you did. He glances at the book again – the book which contains 'The Moon Princess' and 'The Magic Mirror' and 'The Toad Prince', all the stories she used to read him – and then Rebecca turns away to lay the table, and the moment has gone.

After supper, Ben remembers about Rebecca's car. No one has brought it back yet. Perhaps Pieter's forgotten, Rebecca says. Ben's secretly pleased about that.

'I could drop you at Marchboys in the morning,' he says, and Rebecca smiles, as though the idea of a journey with him is something to look forward to. He reaches across the table and takes her hand.

'Shall we go up soon?' he says – and then, in case she thinks he's being too forward – 'I expect you could do with an early night.'

'I am tired,' she admits.

'You go on up,' he says. 'I'll take the dogs out quickly.' And then he grins. The dogs have heard him: they're at the door already, waiting.

Rebecca's in bed when he comes up. She looks very peaceful lying against the pillows, but when he climbs in beside her she lifts her head towards him and he's pleased that she's been thinking the same as him; that she wants the same thing.

'I love you, Rebecca,' he says. 'I love you so much.'

He can't tell at first that something's wrong. He isn't paying attention, maybe – but just before he comes he feels her flinch, and the shock of it courses through him. He pushes himself up so that he can see her face – and then he notices the string of bruises up her arm. There are more on her chest and down her legs; more bruises than he's ever seen on anyone.

'I've hurt you,' he says, aghast. He levers himself off her very carefully, as though she was made of glass. 'Why didn't you say you were so bruised?'

'I didn't want to worry you,' she says. 'They're only bruises. They'll be gone soon.'

'I don't like you being hurt,' he says. He can feel things liquefying inside him. He can't help blaming Pieter for the bruises. Can't help thinking of him in that big house, oblivious to Rebecca's injuries.

'I know.' She rolls towards him, resting her head on his shoulder. 'It's all right,' she says. 'I'll be better soon.'

Ben's heart is racing, but Rebecca lies still beside him, murmuring gently, stroking his face, and gradually he feels his body calming, his pulse slowing. And although he knows he should be worrying about her, not the other way round, he can't hold on to his mind any longer. All the things he's been trying to shuffle into place are slipping out of focus now. It's been a long day. He slides towards sleep, with Rebecca curled up close against him.

19

Ben's grateful that he's got Jamie with him again the following week. He's a good lad, Jamie, a quick learner without being cocky, and always cheerful. He talks about his girlfriend's parents' pug and what a vicious little thing it is; how she wants them to get a dog but he's resisting. Ben talks about Ada and Bertha, and about Rebecca, and he thinks how solid their life sounds, with the cottage and the garden and the bees. He likes seeing it all the way it sounds to Jamie. He doesn't hint at his doubts. But the idea that something's not right keeps creeping back; the sense that the picture he's painting isn't real. It feels almost like someone else's life he's talking about.

On the Tuesday evening, he gets home a bit later than usual. Rebecca would normally be back already, but there's no sign of her car – and as he turns off his engine he's suddenly terrified that she's not coming home. That she's staying at Marchboys House with Pieter Blake. And with his daughter: she might well be part of it, Ben realises. Rebecca's fond of the child, he could tell that, and perhaps Pieter can see that Rebecca would be a better stepmother than Freya Malone.

He ought to go in and deal with the dogs, but instead he sits outside the house in the van, in the dark, and wonders what he'll do if Rebecca never comes back. What his life would mean without her. And although it's only ten minutes until she pulls up behind him, it feels like forever, and it's the strangest feeling, as if he can't tell what's really happening any more. As if she's been away for days, weeks, and what's come home is not the whole of her. They both get out at the same time, and she calls to him as she slams the car door.

'Have you just got back?'

Ben can't see her clearly in the dark, but her voice sounds strange. Perhaps he startled her, he tells himself. 'Just now,' he says.

'How was your day?' she asks.

'All right,' he says. 'How was yours?'

'Good,' she says. 'I've nearly finished marbling the pillars.'

Ben remembers the green stone effect: he imagines it creeping steadily up the pillars like a kind of algae.

'I'm sorry I'm late,' Rebecca says. 'Pieter wanted to talk to me. I couldn't get away.'

Ben's heart thumps. He's not wrong about her tone of voice; he's sure he's not. He stops in the middle of the garden path. It's as if a giant hand is holding him back now, telling him not to follow her into the house. Not to go on pretending that everything's OK.

The stuff he brought back from Hove's still sitting in the van, he remembers. That'll buy him a few minutes, at least.

'I've got some boxes to bring in,' he says.

'Boxes?'

'Things Grandma's cleared out. I said I'd take them for her.'

'Do you want a hand?' Rebecca asks. 'How many are there?'

He shakes his head. 'They're heavy. You go on in.'

While he's carrying the boxes in, he can hear her in the kitchen, feeding the dogs. *Good girls*, she says. *Have you had a nice day? The sun's been shining, hasn't it?* Her voice is full of sunshine too, soft and crooning. Ben's heart is filled with yearning. When he comes into the kitchen, she's picking up the dogs' bowls, ready to rinse them.

'I'd have done that,' he says.

'No need.' She smiles. 'Boxes all in?'

'Yes.' He stands in the doorway, watching her. She's got the remains of last night's curry on the stove, the rice pan ready. The dogs are rubbing against his legs, and the doors are shut tight against the darkness outside.

'I'll lay the table,' he says.

While they're eating, Rebecca asks him about the boxes, about what's in them and whether he needs to sort through them, but Ben can't face doing that tonight. There's a David Attenborough programme on, so they watch that instead. After a few minutes Rebecca puts her hand on his knee and he takes it in his. He doesn't do anything else; doesn't pull her closer. But he can feel the force field between them, the crackle of energy. Perhaps Rebecca can feel it too, because when the programme finishes she squeezes his hand.

'Are you all right, Ben?' she asks. He can't see her expression, but her voice is gentle, careful. 'Is there something on your mind?'

Ben feels suddenly breathless. Perhaps he should tell her the truth, he thinks. Some part of it, at least. But the words tangle themselves in his throat and refuse to come out.

'Not really,' he says. 'Work things, a bit.'

'Do you want to tell me?'

He shakes his head. 'It's nothing,' he lies. 'Just a difficult customer.'

'I'm sorry.'

She looks at him for a moment, and then she says, 'I was painting a story today that I thought you'd like. There's a dog in it who sounds a bit like Ada and Bertha. He belongs to a princess who's shut up in a tower.'

Elvira and Arkady, Ben thinks.

'It reminded me of you, somehow,' Rebecca says. 'Not that you're like a dog, of course, but . . .'

He stays very still then, as her voice trails away. Perhaps, he thinks, the book is more important than he thought. Perhaps . . . 'Why don't you tell me the story?' he asks.

'I don't think I can remember the whole thing.'

'You could read it to me,' he says. He thinks she's hesitating, so he starts to say *not if you don't want to*, but she's already getting up

THE HOUSE AT THE EDGE OF THE WOODS

to fetch the book, and she seems so pleased that the wave of doubt rolls on and away. And then she's back, settling herself beside him.

'It's called "The Toad Prince",' she says. There's a tiny gap, like the space between the title and the first line, and then she launches into it. '*There was once, in a far-off land, a princess called Elvira, who was beautiful and kind and clever. She lived in a castle beside a lake with her mother and father, and her friends the skylarks sang outside her bedroom window each morning while she plaited her long auburn hair.*'

Rebecca reads beautifully. Her voice is warm and low-pitched, and it's as if she can picture the whole scene in her head – which of course she can, Ben thinks, because she's painted it. She's painted the castle with a secret garden high up inside its walls, and the pond where the wicked toad prince appears. After a few minutes, Ben has almost forgotten where he is, and who's reading to him – but at the same time he knows that she is Elvira and he is Arkady, just as she said. Her prince in disguise, always at her side. Rebecca curls in closer to him as the story rolls on, paragraph by familiar paragraph.

When she's finished, they sit in silence for a few moments. The dogs are flat out at their feet, and it's late now, but Ben feels a strange sort of excitement.

'They had their happy ever after,' he says, 'but they didn't realise it.'

'Who did?'

'Arkady and Elvira.'

'After they were turned into trees, you mean? They lived happily ever after with their branches wrapped around each other?'

'Before that,' Ben says. 'The years before that when they were happy together. They should have been grateful for that.'

Grandma's boxes stay where he left them, in a pile in the sitting room. Ben can't bring himself either to look inside them or to take them to the dump. Perhaps it's hearing 'The Toad Prince' again, he thinks. It's brought back something from the past, but it's changed it too – he can't hear his mother's voice reading that story any more. And he doesn't want that to happen to anything else: for things to take root in the present, or to be changed by being looked at. The past is complicated, but he's frightened by the idea of it disappearing.

But even so, since the Toad Prince evening he's had the feeling of being on tenterhooks, waiting for something to happen. He's anxious, afraid, but also, in a strange way, energised. He feels as though he's gearing up for action.

Meanwhile, it's his last week with Jamie, and he's supposed to be letting Jamie take the lead now, making sure he's up to scratch. The customer whose boiler they're servicing this morning reminds him of the one who remembered his name and how he took his tea, but she's brisker. There's no tea today, no chat. She lives alone, this old lady, but there are photos of her family on every wall. Wedding portraits, holiday snaps. Ben thinks about the photos as he watches Jamie starting on the familiar routine. Flue, pilot burner, main burner, heat exchanger.

'OK?' he says. 'Happy with that?' – and Jamie nods and grins. He'll be off on his own next week. He's probably looking forward to that, Ben thinks.

Rebecca's late again that evening. There was supposed to be a photographer coming to Marchboys today, he remembers, to take pictures of the ceiling. Perhaps that's taken longer than she expected. She comes through the house while he's throwing a ball for the dogs in the garden. He doesn't turn round immediately; he lets her call him, so he can hear her voice before he sees her.

'Hello!' she says. 'Good day?'

'It was fine.' He used to like guessing what she'd been painting from the colours spattering her clothes. Yellow, today. Is that the sun, or the gold of a crown? 'Did the photographer come?' he asks.

'Yes.' Rebecca smiles briefly. 'He spent the whole afternoon there.'

'Did he like the painting?'

'I think so, yes. He climbed up on the scaffolding so he could see it up close.'

For a moment longer Ben looks at her, and then he throws the ball once more, watches Ada leap away after it, before they go back into the house.

He's more certain than ever, this evening, that something's wrong. Rebecca looks preoccupied, and she doesn't seem to hear what he's saying half the time. She talks about the photographer, about how the pictures might be printed in a magazine, but her eyes look distant, like his mother's used to sometimes. She drinks a lot too – most of a bottle of wine – which isn't like her, even on a Friday.

After supper they watch a film, but Ben can't concentrate on it. His mind keeps turning things over, teasing at the threads of worry that have knitted themselves into such a tangle over the last few weeks. And as he sits there, feeling Rebecca's body close to him but sensing that her thoughts are a long way away, things start to settle in his head. A pattern starts to appear. It seems clear to him now, incontrovertibly clear, that Pieter Blake is at the centre of everything. That whatever has changed in Rebecca, in their marriage, began with him.

He shouldn't have dismissed those tabloid articles, Ben thinks. Pieter Blake lives in a world where he makes the rules: where he can buy anything, and buy his way out of anything. He might have a glamorous fiancée, but she's on the other side of the world. If it amused him to dally with Rebecca, he wouldn't hesitate. He wouldn't care what damage he was doing, whose happiness he was ruining. He probably pushed his wife off that hotel balcony too.

And then another thought crosses Ben's mind. An even darker thought: one that changes everything.

Perhaps he was right that the fairy-tale book is important. Perhaps there *is* more to it than coincidence. Pieter Blake went to university in Birmingham. He must have lived in the area for several years; the same area Ben's mother grew up in. What if they met? What if Pieter Blake was already that ruthless, charming, icehearted man the tabloids paint so vividly? What if he captivated an innocent girl, then deserted her? What if he was the person who occupied that secret, sorrowful place in his mother's heart? The person she gave her copy of the book to?

Ben can feel an icy clamp around his chest now. Perhaps he's gone mad. Perhaps all this is a crazy fantasy. But he has to know. He has to ask.

Rebecca's going to her father's tomorrow. They're going to make marmalade together, as they do every year. Ben had planned to take the dogs for a long walk, perhaps take the kites if there's enough wind. But he could go up towards Marchboys. He could go to the house and speak to Pieter Blake face to face. He could ask him the questions that are clamouring in his mind now. He could make it clear to him that he's met his match: his nemesis. He could find a way to make him understand.

PART THREE

20

While Rebecca stares at the blurred image of Ben, frozen on the CCTV monitor, she has the impression of things moving at speed around her. A senior police officer appears, and Rebecca confirms that the man on the screen is her husband. They show her images from the gate, and she says yes, that's Ben's van; that's their dogs. She tells them that Ben's been to Marchboys before, to collect her, and she admits that she's talked to Ben about Pieter, and about Emily, just in the way you normally talk about your work when you go home. They ask where she was on Saturday, and where Ben said he'd been.

'He didn't say exactly,' she says. 'He said he'd been to fly his kites. He has several kites; it's a hobby.'

The policeman's look implies that it's a strange hobby for a grown man.

'What about last night?' he asks. 'Sunday night? Where was your husband then?'

Rebecca's stomach clenches. 'We were at home together,' she begins, 'we'd been together all day. But Ben was called out to an emergency in the evening.'

'What time?' the policeman asks.

'Just after ten,' Rebecca says.

'And you heard the call?'

'No,' she admits. 'I was in the bathroom. Ben came through to tell me he had to go and deal with a leaking pipe.'

'Do you know what time he came home again?'

'I heard him come in,' Rebecca says. 'I was asleep, but I woke up when the front door closed. I don't know what time it was.' She hesitates. 'It was quite a long way away, he said. The call-out. He covers a wide area when he's on call.'

'But you can't say exactly when he got back.'

'No.'

'And did you speak to him after he came home? Did you notice anything unusual?'

'No.' Rebecca shakes her head. 'I must have gone back to sleep. But he was there in the morning, in bed beside me.' She halts, remembering something. 'He was there when I woke later in the night too. That was at three o'clock. I checked my phone then, because I wasn't sure if I'd set my alarm.'

The policeman nods. Rebecca watches his face, trying to work out what he's thinking.

'Do you have any children, Mrs Swarbrick?' he asks.

Rebecca is taken aback. 'Just dogs,' she says. 'Two dogs.' But they've seen the dogs, she remembers, on the CCTV footage.

And then, because she wants them to understand, wants them to be gentle, she says, 'You ought to know that my husband had a difficult childhood – his mother was murdered.'

'His mother?' The police officer's face doesn't change. He's trained not to react, Rebecca thinks.

'It was a famous case,' she says. 'Kirsty Swarbrick. Ben was her son. He was in the car when it broke down. When she was killed.' If she explains it properly, she tells herself, they'll understand. But she knows there's no way to explain anything that will change their minds – or the facts.

'Where is your husband now?' the policeman asks.

'At work,' Rebecca says. 'He'll be at work. He'll be out on the road.'

They take the contact details for Fortescue's, the registration number of Ben's van, the address of their cottage.

'We'll need you to make a witness statement, Mrs Swarbrick,' the policeman says. 'We could take you to the station at Hinkworth, if that would be convenient.'

We could take you, Rebecca thinks. In case she makes a run for it, or because they think she's too shaken to drive? She doesn't have the strength to ask.

'OK,' she says. 'That would be fine.'

It's horrible, being in the police station. Rebecca is left alone in a room with grey walls and a single high window. It makes her feel like a criminal. And perhaps that's how the world will see her, she thinks, if it's true that Ben has taken Emily. She'll be one of those women people speculate about. *She must have known, surely? Being married to him all that time. How could you not know?*

She wonders whether they've found Ben yet; whether they've arrested him. Her heart quails when she imagines him being told that Rebecca identified him. She thinks of the eccentric idyll that is None-go-bye and wonders whether all of that is gone for good. She remembers Kirsty's diary, hidden in a drawer beside her bed. If the police search the house, will they find it? Will Ben find out that she took it – that she didn't tell him about it?

But all these thoughts feel like pieces of a fairy tale, no more real than Princess Elvira or the dragon in her cave. Real life must still be there somewhere, Rebecca tells herself. If she walks through the right door – if she opens her eyes from this nightmare – she'll be back where she started this morning. Emily will be at school, and Pieter will be in his office, and nothing will have happened.

But it's the alternative facts – the ones involving the CCTV and Ben's absence last night and the things she told him about Pieter and Emily – that insist on her attention for now. The same questions and the same answers are repeated until Rebecca can hardly tell whether they're true any more, or whether they're just the things she's chosen to say in this strange game. Once or twice she forgets what crisis this is, and imagines that she's in a hospital, not a police station. That someone is undergoing emergency surgery, and she's waiting to hear whether it's been successful.

When the police are happy with her statement, they tell her she's free to go.

'I'd ask you not to go home for the time being, Mrs Swarbrick,' says the officer in charge.

For her own safety, Rebecca wonders, or because None-go-bye is a crime scene? She nods, manages a small smile. 'Of course,' she says.

But where else can she go? What can she do? She has no friends close enough to trust. She longs for her father, but she couldn't face him yet. Besides, her car is at Marchboys, and she can't possibly go back there.

She walks out of the police station, her whole attention focused on staying upright, keeping moving, and turns uphill towards the town centre. When she reaches the high street she goes into a café. It feels odd to do something so ordinary, as though a woman in her position has no right to be among normal, blameless people, but no one looks up. No one notices her.

She orders a toasted cheese sandwich. Her head is still spinning, but she takes a deep breath, sits back in her chair. When her food comes, she eats as slowly as she can manage. She can stay here for an hour, she thinks. She can eke out the day in small portions. Everything will be all right, she tells herself, but she doesn't believe it. She doesn't believe anything will ever be all right again.

She feels a little better for the sandwich, and for managing the business of eating it and paying for it without attracting attention. It occurs to her that she has always been on the edge of society, trying to conceal the fact that she doesn't quite fit in. She was the vicar's daughter; the tallest girl in the class; the student who didn't know what to order in the pub. That's what drew her to Ben, she thinks. He was a kindred spirit, another misfit.

But she won't think about Ben. She won't allow herself to.

Next door to the café there's a charity shop with a couple of pretty dresses in the window. She bought a dress the day her mother died, Rebecca remembers: not a funeral dress but a gorgeous summer frock she wanted too badly to resist. She won't buy a dress today, but perhaps she could find something to read, then sit on a bench for the rest of the afternoon.

The man on the till smiles as she comes in. Rebecca turns towards the bookshelves – and then she sees a woman with a small girl, and her heart stops.

'Emily!' she cries, before she can stop herself. The woman turns to look at her, the child too, and of course it's not Emily, it's nothing like her – but the woman's staring at Rebecca now, and Rebecca realises that she's making a noise, a keening, gurning noise, and she gulps hard.

'I'm sorry,' she tries to say. 'I thought you were . . .'

The woman looks alarmed now, edging her daughter behind her, and the man at the till is looking at Rebecca too.

'Are you all right?' he asks. 'Do you need to sit down?'

Rebecca shakes her head vehemently. 'No,' she says. 'Thank you. I thought – she looks like someone I know.'

There's a murmur of sympathy, perhaps of relief, as the onlookers construct a backstory. Rebecca puts the book she's holding back on the shelf and heads for the door with as much decorum as she can manage.

Outside, she leans against the wall, her heart racing. The café misled her, she thinks. She thought she was OK, but she's not. She's lost. She has no idea what to do with the rest of the day, or with the rest of her life. She stares up and down the high street as if she's hoping for a miracle – and then she sees the church spire rising behind the row of shops opposite, and she hears her father's voice. *Believe in the light*, he says. *Believe in the good*. How can she possibly do that now? What good is there left to her? But the spire draws her across the road, even so. She needed a sign, and there it is.

The church is cold and dark, but the door is open and the interior blessedly empty. Rebecca slides into a pew near the back and rests her head on her hands as though she's praying. Perhaps she is praying, she thinks. Perhaps this is what prayer is: not the empty, pious recitations of her childhood, but this desperate seeking for answers. *Dear God, what has happened to me? Where have I gone wrong?* If she knew how to pray properly, she thinks, she would pray for Emily – and for Kirsty too. For those two ordinary girls whose voices fill her head.

Suddenly she's trembling so violently that she clutches at the back of the pew. How can she reconcile the Ben she knows – kind, eccentric, gentle Ben – with the image she saw on the CCTV this morning? The logic of what's happened is unavoidable, but it makes no sense. And in the face of it, her life makes no sense either. She hasn't cried yet, but she does now. Tears course down her face: tears for herself, as well as for Emily and Kirsty.

And then there's a wave of self-hatred that takes her breath away.

She's at the centre of all this, she realises. She's the connecting piece that links everything together. She brought Ben to March-boys; she talked to him about Pieter and Emily. She allowed Pieter to talk to her about Kirsty, about Ben, and perhaps Ben could see her doubts taking hold. She let her father tell her she was doing good, but perhaps the truth is that she married Ben without proper reflection; that she's never faced up to the responsibility of involving herself in his life. If he has taken Emily, she has driven him to it. She's made him jealous, or suspicious, or . . .

She stands up abruptly, the tremor gone now that she can see things so plainly. She must go back to the police and explain all this to them. She must make them understand her part in Ben's crime, and then share in his punishment.

She hardly glances at the other people on the high street. She passes the charity shop and the café as though they were route markers on her final journey through the normal world. Her heart tumbles with dread and excitement as the police station comes into sight – and then she stops dead. Standing on the pavement outside is Pieter.

21

'Rebecca!'

Pieter steps forward just as Rebecca comes to a halt. She doesn't want to meet his eyes, but she can't avoid it.

'I'm so sorry, Pieter,' she manages to say. 'I'm so terribly sorry.' She means to say more, to admit her guilt, but the words won't come out.

'I've been worried about you,' he says. 'The police said you'd left, but your car's at Marchboys.'

Rebecca stares at him. He's so calm, she thinks – but he's used to crises, she reminds herself. He's not the type to show his feelings. Words form in her head: *I won't need the car. I've come to tell the police . . .*

'Let me give you a lift back,' Pieter says.

This is the last thing she expects. She feels a whirring, a fogging, in her head. 'I don't . . .' she begins. 'I need to speak to the police again.'

Pieter frowns. 'They said they'd finished with you.'

For the first time his self-control falters, and Rebecca can see the strain in his face. She's about to explain that she has more to tell the police, but then she hesitates: she can come back later, she thinks. And it's impossible, somehow, to say no to Pieter, even if the way she nods and smiles fills her with self-loathing.

Pieter's car is low-slung and black, and the engine makes a rich, slurpy noise. A kind of recklessness fills Rebecca: she's down to the last things, she thinks, the last moments of pleasure.

'I want to thank you,' Pieter says, as he pulls out on to the road. 'It was courageous, what you did.'

Once again, Rebecca is astonished. 'I beg your pardon?'

'Identifying your husband,' Pieter says. 'No hesitation, they said. No weighing things up. That was – impressive.' He looks sideways at her, and Rebecca wants to shrink down into the car seat.

'What else could I do?' she says.

It occurs to her that Pieter, too, is not quite in his right mind; that he's forgotten his daughter's life is at stake. Solving the mystery of who took her is hardly the point. But then she realises that he must believe Emily is still alive. He must think Ben will tell them where she is – perhaps that Rebecca will persuade him. And then there's a surge of hope: if she can play a part in saving Emily, would that be enough to counterbalance the mistakes she's made? To redeem herself, just a little?

'It must have been a shock,' Pieter says, 'seeing him on the CCTV footage. Realising . . .' He stops, and Rebecca sees the lines of tension in his face again. 'It's strange,' he says. 'We had all those conversations about Ben, about his mother's death, but it never occurred to me he might do something like this.'

Rebecca blenches at the sound of Ben's name. 'Have the police found him?' she asks.

'I believe so.'

Rebecca wants to ask more questions, but she doesn't. A glimpse of Ben in handcuffs flashes into her mind. Would they let her speak to him? she wonders. But maybe they'd misinterpret her offer, suspect her of wanting to help Ben get off – and it would be better, much better, if he tells them where Emily is of his own accord. Then she remembers how she's reckoned up her part in all this, the blame she shoulders, and she feels dizzy, again, from the helter-skelter of emotions and rationalisations. From the sheer weight of shock that has knocked the ground from under her feet.

Pieter glances at her. 'You look done in,' he says. 'We'll get you something to eat when we get home.'

'No,' Rebecca says. 'Please don't worry. I'll just . . .'

But she can't go home; the police have asked her not to. She'll have to stay in a hotel, she thinks. Or perhaps with her father.

'You should stay at Marchboys tonight,' Pieter says, as though he's read her mind.

'No,' Rebecca says again. 'I couldn't possibly . . .'

'Of course you can.'

Pieter sounds adamant and, despite everything, Rebecca feels a quiver of pleasure which she pushes away as hard as she can. She'll hold fast, she tells herself, whatever he says. She'll leave as soon as they get to Marchboys.

They drive the rest of the way in silence. As they pass through the gate at the end of the drive, Rebecca feels in her handbag for her car keys. She means to be discreet, but Pieter guesses what she's doing.

'No argument,' he says. 'You need something to eat.'

'I had lunch,' Rebecca says – but her voice sounds less resolute than she hoped. Despite herself, she follows Pieter into the house. There's no sign of Sam, or of the housekeeper.

Pieter opens an enormous fridge in the corner of the kitchen. There's not much inside: a box of eggs, some butter, some bread. Rebecca's heart turns over, remembering the night she stayed here after her fall. The supper Sam brought her.

'I could make scrambled egg,' she says, and Pieter nods. If he remembers too, he gives no sign of it.

It's such a relief to do something normal, practical. The eggs are organic, and the yolks remind her of the sunflowers she painted the day Clive Pettit came. Was that only a few days ago? Staring at the swirl of colour in the bowl, it occurs to her that she might never again work on the ceiling.

'It must be frightening to think of all the time you spent with him,' Pieter says.

Rebecca doesn't turn round. She pours the eggs into the pan and starts stirring.

'I was never frightened,' she says, and Pieter makes a little noise of interest, or perhaps of disparagement. *Maybe you should have been*, she imagines him saying. *Maybe that's where you went wrong*.

But instead he asks, 'What was he like to live with?'

Was. Rebecca baulks at that, as she did earlier when Pieter spoke Ben's name. She baulks, too, at the idea of giving up what she has left of Ben: her memories of their life at None-go-bye. But Pieter has a right to ask. He has asked nothing else of her.

'He was always gentle,' she says. She can feel tears rising again now.

'Never lost his temper?' Pieter asks, and she shakes her head, but it's not true. Who never loses their temper? Pieter gives a short laugh. 'Well, they say you can't tell a psychopath when you meet them. Even when you live with them, perhaps.'

Rebecca busies herself ladling the egg on to plates. Is Ben a psychopath? Is that the cold truth?

'You mustn't blame yourself,' Pieter says – and although that's exactly what Rebecca has been doing, she shakes her head again. She's starting to feel uneasy – alarmed, even. Not about Ben, but about Pieter. Surely this isn't a normal reaction for someone in his position? She wonders suddenly whether he'd brought her to Marchboys so he'd got her where he could see her. So he could torment her a little, like a cat playing with a mouse.

When they're sitting down, she casts around for something else to talk about, but there's nothing. They eat in a silence that feels full of hazards. Rebecca feels afraid now, although she couldn't say what of, exactly.

'Ben's mother was eighteen when he was born?' Pieter asks.

Stop, Rebecca thinks. *Please stop*. 'Yes,' she says.

'And she never revealed who the father was?'

'No.'

'So he was brought up by his grandparents?'

Like Emily, Rebecca thinks. She nods.

'Are they still alive?'

'His grandmother is.'

Panic is rising in Rebecca's chest now. Might he imagine this counts as polite conversation? Or is it impossible for him to think about anything else? But who is she to judge what normal behaviour might be, in such abnormal circumstances?

Just then Pieter's mobile phone buzzes, and he snatches it up. Rebecca stands, and takes their empty plates over to the sink.

'Right,' she hears Pieter saying. 'I see. Where? That's confirmed? Yes, I understand. Yes, please do.'

There's silence then. Rebecca wipes the plates with a dishcloth and waits. If she stops what she's doing, she might simply crumple to the floor. Have they found Emily? Is she alive?

'That was the police,' Pieter says at last. 'It seems your husband's alibi stands up.'

'What?' The words echo in Rebecca's head. *Stands up. Stands up.*

'The emergency call-out,' Pieter says. 'It was almost two hours' drive from here, and he was there until two a.m. And you have confirmed that he was back home by three, as I understand it.'

'Yes.'

Pieter nods briefly. 'The police are coming over now,' he says. 'They want to confirm your statement.'

Pieter's manner has changed: he's agitated now. Irritable. He gets up abruptly from the table and opens a cupboard, then pours himself a slug of whisky. He doesn't offer any to Rebecca. Is he more worried about Emily now, Rebecca wonders, or just disconcerted because the narrative he'd constructed has been thrown off? Because his theory about Ben might be wrong?

And then, as the kitchen door shuts behind Pieter, the weight of the news hits Rebecca. Ben has an alibi. He couldn't have taken Emily. He couldn't have done it. Her mind scurries in search of loopholes: could he have got up again, after three o'clock? No; there wouldn't have been time to get to Marchboys and back, to abduct a child, before the alarm went off at six. The implication is clear: Ben is innocent.

Adrenaline races through her, thumping into the corners of her body so that her fingers tingle and her hair stands on end. Ben is innocent. She thinks then about how she blamed herself, earlier;

she remembers how close she came to confessing her part in it all. If she'd gone back into the police station and gabbled about guilt and mitigating circumstances, it might have blown her credibility and undermined Ben's three o'clock alibi. Thank God Pieter appeared before she could do that.

She's still standing by the sink, but suddenly her legs won't hold her any more. She sits down at the table, her whole body trembling.

What has she allowed herself to believe? That Ben, gentle Ben, would steal a child? That he might have killed her? She pictures him now in his bee-keeping outfit, a benevolent alien protecting his swarm, and then again in handcuffs, bewildered and frightened. Unjustly accused.

All the adrenaline has gone now. Every bit of her aches with exhaustion and wretchedness. She longs to get out of here, to drive back to None-go-bye and wait for Ben to come home. But she can't go yet. She must wait for the police and confirm her statement. She must stay calm and make certain of that link in the chain.

After a few moments she gets up again to fill a glass with water. It's started to rain; she watches through the window as the fat drops splatter on the pale stone paving outside. The double glazing is so effective that the scene plays out silently, the rain casting a watery veil across the parkland and the thick band of trees beyond, dissolving them into patches of colour: pale green, dark green, brown and grey.

And then, in the middle of the picture, she spots a splash of blue. Not the sky, but the colour of a piece of sky fallen to earth. It could be a wooden post, except that it's moving. Rebecca stares at it: a human, walking, she thinks. And an instant later she knows who it is.

22

For a long moment Rebecca stands perfectly still, watching the little figure make its way across the expanse of grass. She expects noise to erupt at any minute from elsewhere in the house, but nothing happens. And then it occurs to her that she might be the only person who's noticed. The only person who knows that Emily is alive and well; that she's coming home. Even then she can't move: she needs to be certain, she thinks. She can't raise Pieter's hopes unless she's sure. Every second brings the figure closer – and then there's a sudden skip and a hop, a flailing of short legs, and Rebecca can wait no longer.

'Pieter!' she calls. She rushes out of the kitchen, down the corridor towards Pieter's study. The door to the hall is straight ahead, and there's a moment when she imagines she can see the ceiling beyond it, the great expanse of colour and drama she has created. 'Pieter!' she shouts again, pushing open the door to the study.

'What?' There's an expression on Pieter's face she's never seen before, but she ignores it.

'Look out of the window!' she says. Pieter's study has the same view as the kitchen: he'll be able to see for himself.

Pieter swivels his chair round, but he doesn't stand up. 'Jesus Christ,' he says.

'It's her, isn't it?' Rebecca asks. She's briefly terrified that she's wrong – that Pieter thinks this is some kind of joke.

'Yes, it's her.'

'She's safe,' Rebecca says. He can't take it in, she tells herself. He's in shock. 'She's all right, Pieter.'

'I can see that.'

Rebecca bites her lip. Perhaps she shouldn't say any more. Perhaps she should slip out and leave him to have this moment alone. But she can't help herself: the relief, the joy, is too great. She can express it for him.

'I'm so pleased,' she says. 'What a relief. I really didn't think . . .' Her voice trails away. Pieter has turned to face her again now, and his face is oddly blank, as though he's having to fight hard to control his emotions.

'Where the fuck has she been?' he asks.

Rebecca has never heard him swear before. She stares at him for a moment, then attempts a smile. 'We'll know soon enough,' she says. 'The main thing is she's safe.'

It's only four o'clock, she thinks: only eight hours since her grandmother realised Emily wasn't in her bed. How extraordinary that eight hours can contain so much.

Pieter stands up, and makes for the door. Rebecca hesitates. Perhaps she should go home, she thinks. The police can't need to speak to her now, and she should leave the family to their reunion. But something stops her. Something about Pieter's face reminds her, strangely, of her mother. An impression of pent-up anger ready to burst out. Another aphorism of her father's drops into her head: *people don't always express their love in the usual way.*

She moves over to the window. Emily is only ten yards away now, and Rebecca watches her come to a halt as her father emerges from the house; watches him walk towards her and put his hands on her shoulders. Watches Emily flinch, and guesses what has happened: no abductor; no brush with death. Just a simple story of a child running away. An adventure – a protest, perhaps – that had consequences Emily could never have imagined.

If there had been no CCTV footage, Rebecca thinks, that would surely have been the police's first thought. They would have searched the village, the woods, instead of chasing around the countryside after Ben. She feels her heart drop for the hundredth time that day: she's part of that chain of consequences, she realises. By identifying Ben she took their attention off other possibilities, other leads.

Just then the doorbell rings, the old-fashioned clanging one at the front of the house. Rebecca waits, but there's no sound of footsteps, so she darts out of Pieter's study and across the hall. On the doorstep are two police officers: the senior one she met this morning, and a younger woman. Before they can speak, Rebecca announces the news.

'She's here!' she says. 'Emily's back! She appeared out of the woods, just a few minutes ago.'

She hardly hears what they say, the murmurs of surprise. She steps back from the door so they can follow her into the house, and then something makes her hesitate.

'Wait here a moment,' she says. 'I'll fetch them.'

She finds Pieter and Emily in the kitchen. She calls Pieter's name as she comes down the corridor, but even so it feels as if she's caught him unawares. As she enters the kitchen, he turns to look at her with the same blank expression on his face.

'The police are here,' she says.

'You'd better explain yourself to them, then, young lady.' Pieter's voice is rough. 'Apologise for all the time you've wasted.'

Emily is looking at the floor, her shoulders hunched. Pieter brushes past Rebecca, and Rebecca risks a quick smile at Emily when she lifts her eyes.

'I'm very glad to see you,' she whispers. 'And so is your dad.'

'*He's* not,' Emily says, not troubling to keep her voice down. 'He's furious.' The expression on her face is complicated: there's a trace of defiance, almost of pride, that Rebecca wonders about. There must have been a reason for her to run away. She's certainly got her father's attention now, if that was what she was after.

'He was terribly worried,' Rebecca says. 'We all were. We thought someone had taken you.'

Several things flash through her head: that image of Ben in

handcuffs, and Pieter saying, *What was he like to live with?* Her mother reprimanding her for some small transgression. She should be angry with Emily too, Rebecca thinks, for all the anxiety she's caused, but she can't bring herself to be.

'It's all right,' she says. 'It's just the shock. The main thing is that you're safe.'

And then, because she doesn't want Pieter to suspect her of talking privately to Emily, she takes her hand and leads her through to the hall, where Pieter is greeting the police. His manner is affable again, conveying relief tempered by an edge of exasperation. But when he turns his head and sees Emily standing behind him, the steel comes back into his voice.

'You've got some explaining to do,' he says. 'These people are going to be very interested to hear what you have to say.'

The child's story is much as Rebecca imagined. The female police officer takes the lead, but Emily doesn't need much leading. Her voice is remarkably matter-of-fact as she relates the events of the last twenty-four hours.

'I had an argument with Granny,' she says, in her strange, precocious way. 'I don't usually have arguments with her, but yesterday I did.'

Rebecca remembers her saying, *Granny won't let me have a dog*, and waits to hear where the line was drawn that Emily wanted to cross. But she doesn't say, and no one asks her. Rebecca guesses from the expression on the older policeman's face that the grandmother hasn't mentioned an argument.

'I wasn't *really* cross,' Emily says. 'But I was –' she struggles for a word '– I was frustrated. So I decided to run away. People in books run away. They have adventures. But I didn't know the way to anywhere except Dad's house.'

'Did you climb out of your window?' the woman asks.

Emily looks at her father, as if she's weighing up the question, wondering whether he would be impressed if she had. 'No,' she admits. 'I went out of the back door.'

There's an exchange of glances, then, between the police officers. It occurs to Rebecca that the CCTV footage might not be the only thing that led them to suspect a kidnap: that Pieter's wealth, and perhaps also his persuasive powers, played a part. That they've assumed this precious child was kept safe behind locked doors. Rebecca wonders suddenly whether Emily's disappearance has made it on to the news yet, or whether the whole thing will pass unnoticed by the wider world. And then she feels a searing flash of anger – not at Emily, but at the situation, the police, Pieter's security cameras. It was all for nothing, the agony she's been put through. And Ben: she hardly dares to think about Ben just yet.

Emily is describing, now, how she reached the woods, and what she did when she got there; how good she is at climbing trees. Rebecca looks at Pieter, and it occurs to her that he's very angry. With Emily, no doubt, and with the police for failing to search the woods, but quite possibly with Rebecca, too, because she led the police in the wrong direction. And, perhaps, because she led him to reveal more than he would have liked. Among all the surprises and reversals of the day, the memory of that half hour in the kitchen with Pieter stands out sharply just now. At some point his anger will erupt, Rebecca thinks, and she'd rather not be there to witness it; certainly not to be the target. She stands up.

'I need to go home,' she says. 'Can I ask where my husband is, please?'

It's not quite six o'clock when Rebecca pulls up outside None-go-bye. If she'd had an ordinary day at work, she thinks, this is exactly when she'd have got home. She'd have driven along the same route, parked in the same place. For a moment she wonders whether they could pretend it has been an ordinary day; whether they could tacitly agree to say nothing about what's happened. Her heart thuds as that idea flits across her mind and is dismissed.

Ben's van isn't here yet. Rebecca goes through to the kitchen and opens the back door to let the dogs in, and they nearly knock her off her feet as they rush inside, leaping and barking. Rebecca smiles, turns to follow them – and then she stops.

Ben is standing in the hall. The door is still open behind him, the floodlight in the porch framing him in a bright halo that casts his face into shadow. But even so his expression makes her skin shrink. It's not as simple as anger or sorrow or exhaustion, but all those words race through Rebecca's head as she gazes at him.

'My love.' She takes a step towards him, and he flinches. She feels the gesture like a punch in the chest, but she tries again. 'My poor love. What a terrible thing. What a dreadful day.'

Ben still doesn't speak. His eyes are on her, but it feels as though he's not really seeing her. Even the dogs have dropped back; they're squatting in front of him, tongues lolling. They must be hungry, but they're not barking for their food.

'I haven't fed them yet,' Rebecca says. That, surely, will get through. The dogs' needs can't be ignored. She moves towards the bin where the dog food is kept – and Ben does the same, so that they brush against each other in the middle of the floor. She feels him tense again; feels the hostility in his flesh when it touches hers.

'Oh, Ben,' she says, a small sob in her voice. 'I'm so sorry.'

Because she can see clearly, now, how much is at stake. She's been so caught up in relief and rejoicing that she's underestimated what still needs to be put right. The horrors she imagined have been banished from her mind, but that doesn't change the hard fact that they were there. That she believed Ben might have harmed Emily.

Ben doesn't know that, though, she tells herself. All he knows is that she identified him on the CCTV footage – and he must, surely he must, understand that she had to do that? Perhaps he's not angry, but in shock. Perhaps she just needs to be patient. Everything will be all right, she tells herself – but for the second time today she struggles to believe her own words.

She's stepped back to allow Ben to fill the dogs' bowls. As she watches him, his movements slow and deliberate, his eyes on the dogs' eager faces, she feels another great wave of love and remorse and fear.

'Ben,' she says, as he straightens up. 'Please talk to me.'

He turns towards her then, and in the soft light of the kitchen he looks, she thinks, like a Tintoretto Messiah. A man innocent of the complications of the twenty-first century.

'What do you want me to say?' he asks.

Rebecca frowns. That's not like Ben. 'Are you upset about the CCTV?' she asks. 'Because I had no choice, Ben. Can't you see that?'

He raises his eyebrows, but he says nothing.

'What else could I have done?' Rebecca says. 'They'd have found out who you were soon enough. They'd have identified the van.'

'Did they make you look at the footage?'

Rebecca hesitates. 'They told me there was a man with a beard and two big dogs, driving a van. If I'd said nothing, and they'd found out who you were, what would they have thought? Think how suspicious they'd have been then.'

'More suspicious than they were when they came to tell me you'd identified me as a suspect in a child's disappearance?' he demands. 'When they arrested me at a customer's property – handcuffed me in the street, right in front of her house?'

Rebecca stifles a gasp. 'I'm so sorry, Ben. I'm so very sorry about all of it. But if I'd lied, or said nothing . . .'

'That would have made you look guilty, not me. So you did it to cover yourself. And you'd only need to do that if you thought I was guilty. That I'd taken that girl.'

He turns, makes for the stairs.

'That isn't what I thought,' Rebecca protests. Although it was; of course it was. 'Ben,' she says, 'please don't walk away. We can't . . . Why don't we sit down? Let me make you something to eat.'

'I've had something to eat,' he says. 'I got something on the way home.'

'Please,' she says. 'Please, Ben. Otherwise . . .' She stops. Otherwise what? Is this the end for them? 'We have to talk,' she says desperately.

He wheels back towards her then. 'Didn't you think of talking to me this morning,' he asks, 'before you talked to them?'

Rebecca's crying now. She's never heard Ben so angry. So force-ful. 'Of course that's what I should have done,' she says. 'But it was so hard to think straight. It was all so shocking. And you'd told me – you said you were flying the kites that day. You didn't men-tion Marchboys.' She hesitates again. 'You lied to me.'

He breathes in sharply. 'I didn't lie,' he says. 'I just didn't men-tion Marchboys.'

'Why not?' she asks. '*I was near Marchboys. I went to the house.* You could have said that.' But then she stops. She doesn't need to ask why he went there, nor why he didn't tell her. She can see it in his face. She can read it in her own heart. Guilt clutches at her again, and the next time she speaks her voice is gentler. 'I could have done things differently,' she says, 'but so could you.'

'Did you really need to mention my mother?' he asks. And then, quite suddenly, his composure fractures. A great sob shakes his heavy frame. Rebecca feels something breaking inside her too.

'Oh, Ben,' she says. 'I'm so sorry. My darling, I . . .' What can she say? The truth, as she saw it at that moment: *I meant them to understand that you were damaged.* No.

'They thought I might have killed my mother,' Ben says. His voice is so tight now that there's no emotion left in it. 'Do you think that? Did you suggest it?'

'No.' Rebecca shakes her head violently. 'No.'

Pieter must have told the police his crazy theory, she thinks. Did he also tell them he'd discussed it with Rebecca? The way he talked later, back at Marchboys, he clearly assumed that she agreed with him. That she thought Ben was a killer.

This is such a terrible mess, she thinks. It's like standing beside a landslide, watching everything she cares about being swept away. And it's her own fault. She could almost laugh at the irony of it: a few hours ago she was blaming herself for having too much faith in Ben, and now she can see it was entirely the other way round.

They're still standing barely two feet apart, but it feels as though there's a vast gulf between them. And suddenly Rebecca is conscious that her legs won't hold her any longer. Heartbreak and exhaustion have felled her.

'Could we sit down?' she asks. 'I need . . .'

And then her vision blurs and she slides to the floor. The next thing she's aware of is Ben lifting her, carrying her towards the stairs. He says nothing, but he takes her up to their bedroom and lays her on the bed. And then he's gone.

23

It's dark when Rebecca wakes. She has no idea whether she's slept a whole night, or just an hour or two. Her belly is filled with an awful, sick feeling of doom, and her mind throbs with what might be the remnants of a nightmare – but which turn out, every fragment of them, to be true.

The other half of the bed is empty, the pillows undisturbed. She reaches for her phone to check the time, but it's not where she usually leaves it. Of course: she fainted; Ben carried her upstairs. He must be sleeping downstairs, she thinks. But then she hears something: a snuffle and a sigh. She sits up abruptly and reaches for the light switch. Looking up at her from the rug beside the bed are Ada and Bertha, their heads heavy with sleep.

'Dogs,' Rebecca says. 'Good dogs.'

But what are they doing here? They normally sleep in the kitchen. And if Ben's downstairs, surely they'd be with him?

Suddenly she's filled with a frantic sense of urgency. She scrambles out of bed and across the room to look out on to the road. There's her car, parked in the usual place. But Ben's van has gone.

The clock on the oven says 4:58. Five o'clock isn't impossibly early for Ben to leave, but Rebecca suspects he's been gone all night: gone to Hove, perhaps. Will he drive to work from there, then? Or – might he have been suspended, after his arrest?

Her heart contracts as she imagines the repercussions of yesterday's drama still spooling out. What if Ben's driven his van off the road? Or parked at the spot where his mother died, ready to confess to killing her, just because his heart has been broken? Because his wife suspects him of murder? She thinks of the grieving parents in 'The Moon Princess' who kill the dragon that's always protected their village because they think it's eaten their daughter. What has happened to her and to Ben is no less fantastical; the tragedies of misconception and mistaken identity are no less devastating.

If this *was* a fairy tale, she thinks, it might end here. *When she awoke, Ben had gone, and she never saw him again.* She can't let their story finish like that. But what can she do, in a world without dragons or fairy godmothers? How can she make the page turn over to the next chapter?

She finds her phone on the shelf by the front door. There's no message from Ben, no missed calls. She types: *Where are you, my love?* – but the message isn't delivered. His phone must be turned off. Despair rises through her chest, chokes in her throat. The dogs watch her, their tails hanging limp between their legs.

And then Rebecca has an idea. She knows what she needs to do. Where she needs to go.

Her father has always been an early riser.

'Rebecca!' He steps back from the door. The house is cold: much colder than None-go-bye. He looks at her for a moment. 'Have you had breakfast?' he asks. 'I'm making porridge.'

The smell in the kitchen is so evocative that it makes Rebecca want to weep, but she fights the tears away.

Her father ladles porridge into the same bowls they had when Rebecca was little: white bowls with a brown rim.

'Now,' he says, as they sit down opposite each other. 'What's the matter, my darling girl?'

Once or twice Rebecca wonders whether he might interrupt her to ask a question, but he doesn't. He listens in silence – carefully, attentively, as he always does. When she's finished, sobbing out the final paragraph about waking to find Ben gone, he takes her hand and lifts it to his lips.

'Dear Rebecca,' he says. 'How much you've blamed yourself.'

'With good reason,' Rebecca says. 'It's my fault that Ben was arrested. It's my fault he's so angry.'

'Not at all.' He's still holding her hand; he folds the other one on top now, enclosing her in his grasp. 'This is a story with several protagonists, and each of them has contributed to the muddle.'

Muddle. Rebecca almost smiles. Such a characteristic word. 'Bit more than a muddle,' she says.

Her father tilts his head. 'Even so.'

And that makes her want to smile too – the double meaning of *Even so* which she's certain he intended, both affirming and qualifying. The fact that he has space for gentle wordplay in the face of this crisis should infuriate her, but instead it reassures her. *Nothing is so bad that we should lose hope*, it means.

'Tell me what you blame yourself for,' he says. 'Let's start there.'

'For giving Ben up to the police without speaking to him first,' Rebecca says. 'For believing he might be guilty.'

'That's two things.' Her father holds up a finger to enumerate the first. 'Identifying him was your clear duty.'

'But I could have called him,' Rebecca says. 'I could have talked to him before I spoke to the police.'

'And if – God forbid – he had taken the child? That might have put her in danger.'

'Only if there was a real chance that he was guilty. I should never have believed that.'

He shakes his head. 'It wasn't for you to judge the likelihood of Ben's guilt or innocence, or to establish why he'd been at Marchboys. Why he hadn't told you about it. And given our last conversation—'

'I blame myself for that too,' Rebecca says. 'For listening to Pieter. For suspecting Ben of . . .'

'My darling,' he says, 'we are human, and therefore susceptible to doubt.'

'You said that last time.'

'Because it's true. And it's true that what you have taken on in your marriage is complicated. More complicated than most people would care to risk.' He smiles tenderly as she begins to demur. 'You are a person of great compassion, Rebecca. Yesterday morning, that little girl was at the centre of your thoughts. The same compassion that drew you to Ben was focused on her. And that was quite right.'

'I didn't marry him because I felt sorry for him,' Rebecca says.

'Of course you didn't. But compassion isn't the same as pity. It means, literally, to share someone's feelings. To stand with them. And that's what you have done. What you must continue to do.'

'How can I, if he won't speak to me?'

'He will.' Her father smiles again, as though that fact is so certain that it doesn't need qualification. Rebecca wishes she could believe him.

'You mentioned Ben's mother,' he says. 'You said he was particularly distressed that the police had referred to her murder.'

'That was my fault too,' Rebecca says. 'I told them about his mother because I wanted them to understand about Ben, to be gentle with him. Not to make them suspicious.' She hesitates. 'It was a breach of trust, mentioning something so private.'

'Hardly, when it's a matter of public record.'

'But it was years ago. The police would never have made the connection.'

'Maybe they would, and maybe they wouldn't. But I'm curious about Ben's reaction. I suspect this episode has brought the past back into his mind.'

Rebecca nods, frowns. 'Emily's disappearance,' she says. 'The police asking him questions.'

'And his guilt about his mother's death.' Her father holds up a hand again to halt her protest. 'Suppose he did stay in the car that day,' he says. 'Suppose he sat there all the time, as he'd been told, and never went to look for her. He was a big boy, you say: perhaps between them they could have chased the attacker away. Suppose that has been in the back of his mind all these years? He was her son, and he did nothing to help her. And now he's suspected of being involved in another disappearance. That little boy is still inside him. As is that guilt.'

Rebecca says nothing. What sort of compassion has she shown, she wonders, if none of this has occurred to her?

'It's too late,' she says. 'I've left it too late.'

Her father shakes his head. 'It's just the right moment,' he says.

'But what if they *do* suspect him of killing his mother now?' she asks. 'What if this whole thing makes them reopen the case? They might think it's suspicious that Ben was at Marchboys at the weekend even if he had nothing to do with Emily's disappearance.'

'That seems – far-fetched,' her father says. 'It's my understanding that old cases are only reopened when there are significant new developments. The presence of a murder victim's son at an address associated with a child who has run away from home doesn't strike me as compelling evidence.'

This time there's no smile lurking in the wings.

'But he might think that's going to happen,' Rebecca says. She remembers the idea she had, first thing this morning: that Ben had gone back to the place where his mother died. Was that so outlandish?

She glances at the clock on the wall: it's almost seven now.

'What should I do?' she asks, coming at last to the question she meant to start with. 'How should I find him?'

Her father lifts a single eyebrow. 'Have you phoned him?' he asks.

'I sent a text, but it didn't go through. His phone was off.'

'Perhaps it's worth trying again?'

As he gets to his feet and collects the porridge bowls, Rebecca takes her phone from her pocket. Ben's phone rings two, three, four times, and then he picks up.

'Ben!' Rebecca hardly recognises her own voice. 'My love, I've been so worried. Where are you?'

There's a pause. 'I went for a drive,' he says. 'I couldn't sleep.'

Where have you been? she wants to ask. *What are you thinking?*

'Where are you now?' she asks.

'On my way home.'

And that's enough of an answer. Back from wherever he's been; from wherever this terrible saga has driven him.

'Me too,' she says. 'I'm with my father, but I'll be there in an hour.' She hesitates. 'I love you, Ben. I'll see you soon.'

As the call disconnects, she feels a flare of panic. Should she have said more? Asked more? What if, after all, he's not there when she gets home? She pushes that thought firmly away. She has to trust him, she thinks. What else is there?

Her father turns from the sink. 'All well?'

'Not yet,' Rebecca says. 'But – maybe.'

She gets up from the chair and folds him in a fierce hug. He feels slighter and slighter, she thinks. There's all that – but as she draws away from him she can almost see the answer in his eyes. *Not now. Not yet.*

'Thank you, Dad,' she says. 'Thank you.'

24

Ben is sitting at the kitchen table when she comes in. The dogs are beside him, flanking him like ceremonial statues. Rebecca is so full of adrenaline and uncertainty that she can't speak. That conversation they had on the phone seems like a fantasy now. Her side of it, at least; her interpretation of it. She remembers herself saying, *I love you, Ben*, and him not answering. All the way home her anticipation has been tempered by an edge of dread, but now she's here – now they're in the same room again – the dread has come to dominate. She has no idea whether they're coming together to resolve things, or to finish their marriage.

Standing just inside the kitchen, she braces herself to speak. 'Are you all right?' she asks.

He nods. 'Tired.'

'Have you not slept at all?'

He shakes his head.

Rebecca wants to come closer, to touch him, but she doesn't dare. She remembers him flinching last night.

'Have you eaten?' she asks. 'I could make breakfast.' A second breakfast, she thinks. But she's ravenous again, despite the porridge.

'OK.'

It occurs to Rebecca that he's agreeing simply because she might stop talking if she's busy cooking, but she tells herself she must be patient. He spoke powerfully enough last night: perhaps he, too, is anxious about where this conversation might lead.

There's a packet of bacon in the fridge. They had bacon sandwiches on Christmas morning, she remembers. Perhaps they can remember what it felt like, that carefree day. Perhaps just a whiff of it will reach them, and remind them what's possible.

When she's put the bacon under the grill, she boils the kettle for coffee and slices bread and tomatoes. Now and then she glances at Ben. Her mind is doing its best to be helpful, throwing up happy memories: Ben flying his kite on the beach, carrying honeycomb across the garden.

And then he speaks.

'I'm sorry,' he says.

For a long moment Rebecca doesn't move. Did she mishear? But when she turns he's looking at her, waiting.

'You don't have to be sorry,' she says.

'I do,' he says, unblinking. 'I am. I upset you.'

'My darling,' she says. 'I upset you too.'

'And you apologised,' he says.

Rebecca bites her lip. She still doesn't know what this means: sorry and move on, or sorry and goodbye? She turns the grill off, waits a moment. Gathers her courage.

'Are we going to be all right, Ben?' she asks.

There's a pause. 'I hope so,' he says.

And then she's weeping again, weeping as she never has before. Ben pulls a chair out for her and she sits down, and at last his arms are around her, and she thinks that she didn't know, before this moment, how much she loved him. She didn't know how terrible the prospect of losing him was.

'I'm so sorry,' she says, 'about all of it. You were right to be angry.'

'I went to find him on Saturday,' Ben says, as if she hadn't spoken. 'Pieter Blake. Where I was flying the kites wasn't far from his house, and I drove back that way. I pressed the buzzer on the gate, and it opened.'

'What?' Rebecca's heart thuds. She'd imagined him leaving the van at the gate and climbing over the fence. 'Someone let you in?'

'I drove up the drive and parked at the front. I tried the door-bell, but there was no answer. So I walked round the house to see if I could see anyone. I thought there must be someone there because they'd opened the gate.'

'You rang the doorbell?'

'What else would I do?'

She shakes her head. The footage she saw didn't show the front door. Surely there must be a camera there? Did they withhold that bit of tape, then, to make Ben look guilty – like an intruder, not a visitor? But why on earth would they do that – Pieter, or the police, or Sam – when they needed to find Emily, find out who'd taken her?

'Did you tell the police all that?' she asks.

'Of course I did. They weren't interested. They probably thought I was lying.'

Rebecca wouldn't have believed that she could feel another overwhelming emotion this morning, but she does. She's furiously angry. Hopping, spitting mad. She's been deceived – and Ben has been framed. She's still trying to find the words to respond when Ben speaks again.

'I wanted to find him to tell him to leave you alone,' he says. 'To tell him you were mine, and I loved you. I know about men like him who think they can have whatever they want.' There's a tiny smile, a shake of the head. 'I felt better afterwards, even though I didn't speak to him. I felt I'd shown him I wasn't afraid of him. I'd walked round his house and looked in through the windows.'

Rebecca imagines Pieter sitting inside Marchboys House, open-ing the gate but not coming to the door. It must have been Pieter, she thinks. If one of the staff had let someone into the grounds, they'd surely have answered the bell. She remembers that feeling of cat and mouse in Pieter's kitchen yesterday, the sense of being played with. This is exactly the same, isn't it? Sitting out of sight of the windows and letting Ben walk round and round the house; watching him, perhaps, on his cameras.

Did Pieter know it was Ben, though? They didn't meet when Ben picked her up after the fall – but Pieter was there that day, she remembers; he could have looked out of a window. And if he *didn't* recognise Ben on Saturday afternoon – if he simply didn't like the look of the strange man at the door, the man who showed up on his CCTV later – surely he'd have told the police that the stranger hadn't broken in? That he'd been let in through the gate, in plain sight? It was pertinent information: it might have changed the police's approach.

And then another thought crosses her mind. A terrifying thought.

What if Pieter hadn't cared about the police finding Emily because he'd known all along that she was safe? What if her disappearance was a set-up: a trap for Ben? Could that possibly be true?

Perhaps, she thinks now, Ben's visit to Marchboys the day before Emily ran away was more than an unlucky coincidence. Perhaps it gave Pieter the idea of staging a kidnapping. That would explain why he was so calm yesterday; why he waited for her at the police station. Why all he wanted to talk about was Ben, and his idea of Ben as a psychopath.

Rebecca shivers. But it's too crazy to be true, she tells herself. Emily's return, her explanation to the police, Pieter's anger – surely that couldn't all have been staged? No, she thinks. The failure to mention the buzzer, and the missing CCTV tape – all that was just bad luck. Bad luck for Ben.

But then she remembers watching through the window when Pieter went out to meet Emily; remembers the way he put his hands on her shoulders and spoke so intently to her. What did he say to her? And then there was that edge of pride in Emily's voice when she told her story to the police: the unusual words she chose, and the way she watched her audience. She's a strange child; she's had a strange childhood. If she was offered a chance to show her father what she's made of, might she have leapt at it?

Ben's looking at her curiously. Rebecca wipes the last of the tears from her face.

She badly wants to tell him everything – so badly that it feels like a physical effort to stop herself. 'I never want to go back to Marchboys,' she says instead. 'I can't bear to.'

Ben frowns. 'But you have to finish the job,' he says. 'It's important for you.'

Rebecca shrugs. 'I'm not going today, anyway. I'm not going anywhere today.' And then she hesitates. Ben would usually have left for work ages ago. She remembers her fears first thing this morning. 'What about you?' she asks.

'I'm not going in today either,' he says. 'They said, take a couple of days.'

'So they've been nice?' she asks. 'Your boss?'

He doesn't seem to understand the import of her question, but he answers it anyway. 'They said I could pursue it,' he says. 'Wrongful arrest. But I'm not going to.'

'No,' says Rebecca. 'That's sensible.' A sigh rises through her then: a sigh of release, of emptying. 'Let's eat this bacon,' she says.

They eat almost in silence. If their thoughts could be seen, Rebecca thinks – like threads of silk, ripples of water – they would fill the whole room. Hers would, at least. She thinks about Kirsty and the diary, and about Pieter's interest in the murder. Could that really just be about the woodland, the ancient forest? It's an odd coincidence, anyway. Another coincidence. She thinks, too, about Emily and Ben and the CCTV and Pieter's sudden changes of mood. She thinks, above all, about Kirsty's death, and her father's wise words. As she stands up to clear the plates, one thought centres itself in her mind.

If she lets things run on now – if she and Ben are kind and careful with each other – their lives could go back to how they were before. But she's keenly aware now of the shadow they live under. She knows that nothing will ever be completely right between them – that they will never be entirely happy – until the mystery of Kirsty's death has been resolved. And she knows her father is right: this is the moment. She knows she can't turn away from it any longer.

'Ben,' she says. 'There's something I need to tell you about. Some things we need to talk about. I should have told you before, but . . .'

'What things?' he asks.

She takes a deep breath. 'Things to do with your mother,' she says. 'And . . .' She hesitates again; but they can't keep any more secrets from each other, she tells herself. She can't keep all that stuff shut away in her mind. 'And things to do with Pieter. With the last few weeks.'

PART FOUR

PART FOUR

25

You could say that it was the defining experience of his young life: that it transected time sharply into Before and After.

Before, you could say, there was the boy Pieter – shy and uncertain, charming in his way, eager for approval. The boy who'd been born in a place he wasn't to call home, to an English father and a mother who was half-Chinese and half-Dutch, and who named him after his merchant grandfather from Eindhoven. The boy who'd been sent six thousand miles away, to a place that was called home but didn't feel like it, when he was seven years old, and who'd made his way through a series of schools and on to university in an apparently seamless progression. Except that there had been seams, seams which were strained almost to breaking point, because the years of education had been hinged around the weeks he was allowed to spend in the place he continued, stubbornly, to call home, until he realised it wasn't any more. The boy who made friends easily but was always lonely; who knew he was good at things – exams, sport, conversation – but never really understood the point of them. The boy who had inside him a hole he was waiting to fill: who longed, always, for the time when his fierce father and his fiercer mother would welcome him back. Would declare him finished, complete, ready to take his place as their son.

Might that have happened? he wonders sometimes. He doubts it, honestly. It wasn't in their nature. But there was never time to find out, because both his parents were dead, carried off by different cancers in the same summer, within weeks of his twenty-first birthday.

That wasn't, however, the thing that defined Before and After. That was part of the story, but not all of it.

After is easy. After was the shaping, the hardening, of the public figure he's become: a businessman like his Dutch grandfather and his expat English father, but more successful – wildly more successful – than either.

After is the bit you can read about: the building of his companies and the acquisition of others; the taking apart of corporations for profit and for the pleasure of seeing what's inside them. Pieter is good at that too – very good at it – and the outcomes can be measured, just like the exam results and the sports matches, in figures on a sheet. And even if you're not sure what the point of it is, once you start there's nothing for it but to keep going, until the doing of it becomes the point. Until you've built an edifice around yourself which reminds you, sometimes, of the Tyrannosaurus rex in the Natural History Museum: something you can marvel at even though it's nothing but a collection of bones; the relics of a living creature. Until the flesh and blood, the eating and walking and breathing, is of almost no consequence, and the boy from Before is a long-lost echo inside the tycoon who makes headlines with his ill-judged affairs and boardroom battles.

But there was a time when the point of everything seemed abundantly evident. The point of the sun shining and the grass growing; of having a little money, and health, and leisure. The months he hardly allows himself to think about: that brief interval of wonder that was gone almost before he'd realised what it was.

If there's Before and After, then what would you call that time in between? Perhaps it could simply be called Life. The time when he was properly alive, and understood in infinite, blazing detail what it was to be human.

26

Rebecca Swarbrick isn't anything like Pieter expected. Perhaps he had a clichéd idea of an artist, avant-garde and exuberant – but her website gave a jaunty impression too. In person, she's shy, careful, rather plain. Perhaps that's unkind, though. Sober rather than plain. A long nose and dark brown eyes, hair bobbed above her shoulders, an unflattering heavy fringe. She's older than he expected – closer to forty than thirty – and tall. The kind of figure that ought to look good in clothes, but doesn't.

Pieter checks himself. He doesn't usually assess women in this way; not women he's employing, at least. Rebecca is sitting on the edge of the leather sofa, her face eager but anxious. She's awed by Marchboys, he thinks. Not overawed, he hopes: he wants her to accept the commission. He glances out of the window, searching for a note of easy familiarity.

'I knew this house before the fire,' he says. 'A friend of mine grew up here. They used to have wonderful parties. It was a terrible tragedy: they lost everything.'

'How awful,' she says.

He looks at her for a moment. 'They didn't have the heart to come back, after the fire. The parents were elderly by then, and it wasn't fit to live in.' He smiles. 'I'd always admired the house. The family was delighted that I bought it. That I'm restoring it.'

Rebecca gives an obedient smile. She has a scar over one eye which she tries to hide with the fringe, he notices. An old scar, faded almost to white. He files it away.

'And now we're going to tackle the ceiling in the hall,' he says. 'I'm glad you could fit the project in so soon.'

She flushes, as though he's making fun of her. That isn't what he meant, but he smiles again, tries harder.

'I'm sure you're going to do a wonderful job,' he says. 'What I have in mind for the design is fairy tales. Something more modern than Greek myths. More – unusual.'

Rebecca nods. 'Fairy tales in general,' she asks, 'or – are there specific stories you'd like me to paint?'

He thinks; forces himself to examine more closely the plan he's conceived for the ceiling. He's not sure, now, whether it's a good idea. Should he offer Rebecca the chance to make a different suggestion? No: no. She wouldn't disagree with him, anyway. And Freya will love it. She'll be charmed by it.

'I might have a book, somewhere – a book I had when I was younger.' Another smile. Rebecca Swarbrick is getting a lot of smiles. 'Are there any you'd like to suggest?'

She shakes her head. 'I was brought up on Bible stories,' she says. 'My mother didn't approve of witches and fairy godmothers.'

'Nor love's first kiss?'

She blushes again, then raises her eyebrows. 'Only if the handsome prince went to the church youth group,' she says.

He laughs, relieved to have drawn something humorous out of her. 'I'll have a look for the book,' he says, 'and perhaps you can start thinking about the general layout. Forests, castles, that sort of thing. There's a lot of ceiling to cover.'

'There certainly is.'

'Will three months be long enough?'

She screws up her face. 'I hope so. I think so.'

He nods. 'Good. Anything you need – supplies and whatnot – you can order through my assistant, Sam. We've got some scaffolding for you to approve. We could go and look at that now, if you'd like?'

As they come back into the hall, he sees her look up – sees her taking in the light, the space, the dimensions – and he sees her eyes light up too, her face opening in wonder as the possibilities of the project begin to take shape inside her. And then he feels a familiar sense of triumph; the sharp pleasure of a plan taking flight. Marchboys has worked its magic, he thinks. He's going to get his way: Rebecca Swarbrick is going to come and paint his ceiling.

27

Pieter doesn't see much of Rebecca for the first few weeks. He'd imagined her coming to him regularly with questions, but perhaps that will happen later, once the more detailed work begins. For now she stays up on the scaffolding tower all day long, painting assiduously, and Pieter waits until the evenings to go and see what she's done. He doesn't want her to feel he's watching too closely. Breathing down her neck. And he's busy too: he wants to be at Marchboys as much as possible while the painting is under way, but working remotely has its downsides. Things always take longer when he's not in the room, and there's the odd mistake, the odd oversight to sort out. One or two of them, he admits, his own fault. He's been uncharacteristically distracted, with this other business weighing on him. The project he can't discuss with anyone else. It encroaches on his dreams, like a monster from the deep. He can't seem to get a handle on it, to be sure things are moving in the right direction, and that irritates him. He hates uncertainty.

When Rebecca has been there for a month or so, Pieter's mother-in-law – ex-mother-in-law, strictly – rings to ask if he'll have Emily to stay for a couple of weeks. They've got a last-minute booking on a cruise. It might, Pieter thinks, be rather a good time to have Emily: he imagines her taking an interest in the painting, watching Rebecca work. He baulks a little, as Suzanne would expect, but not too much.

'It's not a case of not wanting her here,' he says, 'it's just short notice. There's no one to look after her.'

'She's eight,' Suzanne says. 'She doesn't need a wet nurse. And she'll be at school every day.' There's a pause. 'I assume you can arrange for her to get to school and back?'

'Of course.' No one but Suzanne speaks to him like this, Pieter thinks. Perhaps it's good for him.

They've been forced to get on, since Sally died. *The tragedy*, they call it, with that English aversion to mentioning death. It was a piece of luck, he thinks, that Robert and Suzanne had moved so close to Marchboys before he bought it. They assumed that's why he was so keen to have the house, and it suits him to let them think that. They know he'd always admired Marchboys too: not quite a Brideshead thing, but a sort of boyish awe for the place and the family, from those years when he and Michael were at school together and he used to come here as a guest. It pleases him, having Michael and his parents grateful to him now. Bringing the house back to its former glory. It's almost as though the whole thing was meant, he thinks now, as he ends the phone call. And the painted ceiling is the crowning glory, the coming-together of it all.

He sits in silence for a few moments, and then he walks down the passage to the hall. It still surprises him to see the scaffolding tower in there, occupying so much of the floor. He looks up, surveying the landscape that's spreading across the plasterwork. Rebecca is working on the sky today, applying a wash of pale blue over the central section of the dome.

'Our faces should be up there,' he says. 'Freya's and mine.'

He's not sure whether she's heard him at first, but then she peers over the edge of the platform.

'Like the Medici,' she says.

'Yes.' He hesitates, staring up at the ceiling. Three months, he thinks, might not be long enough for what he wants. He'll have to think about that. 'Come and see me in the morning,' he says, 'and we can discuss it.'

That was a good idea, he thinks, as he heads back to the study. He could have mentioned Emily's visit now, but it's better if it's an afterthought, tacked on to another conversation. Freya will love the two of them being in the picture too.

He should ring Freya tonight, he reminds himself. He doesn't do it often enough. He tells her he assumes she's busy with the filming, but she likes him to call.

The next morning, Rebecca brings a sheaf of drawings into the study. Pieter feels a prick of guilt when he sees how much time she's put into the challenge he threw out yesterday. The guilt takes him by surprise: he's used to asking things of people.

He glances at the sketches, half-hears what she's saying about cardinal virtues, murmurs vague assent.

'I like what you're doing,' he says. 'I like it very much. The style is just right.'

'Thank you.' The anxiety lifts a little from Rebecca's face; he's pleased by that. He doesn't want her anxious. She's pretty when she smiles. No, not pretty; but there's something there, if you can coax it out. Interesting, he thinks.

'I don't want you to rush it,' he says. 'I can see it's a big job. I've got more sense of that now.'

'I'm on schedule, if that's what you mean.'

He nods, makes a show of hesitation. 'How would you feel about extending the project?' he asks. 'Perhaps a frieze going up the main staircase. And the pillars in the entrance hall – what about marbling? Can you do that?'

'I could.' She looks doubtful, though. 'I'd have to ... It would mean moving things around, but I'm sure I could.'

Good, he thinks. See how we go, then. Don't push it.

'Let's start with the pillars,' he says. Then he smiles. Emily's arriving tonight. He'll keep her at home tomorrow, he thinks. She's always clamouring for a day off school. 'Have lunch with me tomorrow,' he says. 'There's someone I'd like you to meet.'

The lunch goes badly at first. Rebecca doesn't like children, Pieter thinks. Or perhaps she's just not used to them. Every time she asks Emily a question, the child bats it away with some nonsense answer.

Children have an uncanny way of knowing when an adult is ill at ease. They're halfway through before things begin to warm up.

'Where do you live?' Emily asks, her mouth full of food.

'Not far from here.' Rebecca smiles carefully at her. 'About an hour away, in a little house with a long garden.'

'Have you got pets?'

'We have bees and chickens and two dogs.'

Pieter glances at her, then looks away again. He knows where the house is. He's seen it on Google Maps. He loves Google Maps: an innocent form of stalking.

'I want a dog,' Emily is saying. 'Granny won't let me and Dad won't either.'

'Dogs are a big responsibility,' Rebecca says.

'I haven't got any brothers or sisters,' Emily says, 'so I ought to have a dog.'

'Don't lobby Rebecca,' Pieter says, in his best indulgent-father tone. 'There's nothing she can do.'

He smiles at Rebecca. He doesn't want her to be terrorised, and Emily has it in her to terrorise. He wants them to be friends.

A strange thing, he thinks then: they are all only-children. He and Rebecca and Emily. Ripe for inclusion in a fairy tale. He wonders if Rebecca has read the stories in the book he gave her. 'The Magic Mirror'; 'The Moon Princess'.

'Pudding,' he says, as Sam takes the plates away.

'What do you think of the painting?' he asks Emily that evening. 'Do you like it? Rebecca's painting?'

'It's OK,' she says, kicking at the bedclothes. She doesn't like the duvets here, she announced earlier. They're too fluffy. She prefers the kind Granny has. *Bring your own next time*, Pieter said.

'Do you like Rebecca?' he asks now.

'She's OK. I'd like to meet her dogs.'

'Maybe you could, if you were friends with her. Maybe she'd ask you to her house.'

Emily gives him a withering look. 'She's too old to be my friend,' she says. Then she wriggles down the bed and grins at him conspiratorially. 'I liked being off school,' she said. 'Can I stay at home again tomorrow?'

'Not tomorrow,' he says. 'Maybe one day next week. Is there a day you'd like to miss?'

'Wednesday,' she says instantly.

'Why Wednesday?'

'We have Miss Pinker for Maths.'

Pieter doesn't want to encourage her to fall behind in Maths. But perhaps it's just the teacher she dislikes, he thinks. Perhaps the teacher's no good. He should find a tutor.

'If you stay off on Wednesday I won't be here,' he says, 'so you'd have to make friends with Rebecca.'

'Where will you be?'

'I have to go to London,' he says. 'An important meeting.'

Emily nods. 'OK,' she says. 'Kiss me goodnight now, Dad.'

28

'Thank you for today,' he says, as Rebecca gathers her things at the end of the following Wednesday. 'I'm sorry if you were distracted. I know she can be a handful.'

'I wasn't a handful,' Emily protests. 'I was extremely good. Wasn't I?'

'An angel,' Rebecca confirms. Pieter's pleased to see her grinning at Emily.

'Rebecca painted all afternoon,' Emily says.

'Well, I'm glad to hear it.'

He shuts the front door behind Rebecca, and turns back to see Emily swinging on the scaffolding. 'Don't do that,' he says.

'Rebecca lets me,' she says. 'She lets me climb trees too.'

'Does *she* like climbing trees?' Pieter asks.

Emily turns a somersault, her feet skimming just above the tiled floor. 'She's too frightened,' she says. 'When she was a little girl she fell out of a tree and banged her head.'

'Did she?' He glances up, then, at the scaffolding tower. If she's afraid of heights that must be a challenge. 'What else did you find out about Rebecca?'

Emily pulls herself up and does another somersault. Pieter suppresses the urge to stop her. 'Her parents didn't divorce,' Emily says, 'but I *think* she didn't like them. She likes you, though. She likes that you like her.'

'What?' Pieter is thrown by this.

'I told her you liked her, or you wouldn't let me play with her,' Emily says. 'Would you?'

He laughs. 'I suppose not.'

'She's got a husband and no children,' Emily says now, 'but I don't know anything else.'

She drops to the ground again and stands before him, grinning. He grins back at her.

'That's quite a lot,' he says. 'Did you find out the dogs' names? Or the bees'?'

'Bees don't have names,' she says. 'There's too many of them.'

Sam appears just then to say that Emily's supper's ready.

'Will you sit with me while I have it?' she asks her father. 'I don't like being on my own.'

Pieter's surprised: Emily doesn't usually seem to be bothered whether he's around or not. He remembers, suddenly, lonely evenings in the flat in Hong Kong – his parents out, the maid sitting in the corner while he ate his supper. What did he eat? He can't remember. Boiled eggs, maybe. Tinned soup. Strange how the scene can feel so vivid, but the details are lost.

He goes to Hong Kong several times a year still, but never to the area where they lived. He rarely ventures further than Central. Perhaps, sometime, he should make time for it. He could take Emily, show her where he grew up. But he pushes the idea aside, files it under *later consideration*.

'All right,' he says. 'But I hope there are enough fish fingers for me.'

'I have to go away next week,' he says, while she's mashing ice cream in a bowl. 'I'll be gone for a few days. I'm sorry to leave you behind, but I couldn't change it.'

'Where are you going?' she asks.

'To Germany. Berlin.'

'Couldn't I come too?'

He hesitates. It strikes him that he doesn't have much of a relationship with Emily, but that he could. *When things are settled*, he always thinks. And they will be soon, won't they? He has an image in his head of Christmas at Marchboys: a huge tree in the hall; an open fire and piles of presents. But meanwhile, why shouldn't he take her to Berlin? If they flew out a day early, they could spend Sunday together. He could show her the city.

'Maybe,' he says. 'I'll think about it. Granny would be cross about you missing school, though.'

Emily smirks at him. Missing school is their secret currency. He must do something about a tutor, he thinks.

'Shall I read you a story tonight?' he says. 'Do you know the story of the moon princess?'

Taking Emily to Berlin is a mistake. She enjoys Sunday, especially the expensive restaurant where they have dinner, but he has back-to-back meetings from first thing on Monday, and she takes an instant dislike to the sitter Sam has organised for her.

'I wish I'd stayed at home,' she says, when he gets back to the hotel that night. 'You said it would be fun.'

'I didn't,' he says. 'It was your idea, Emily. I told you I had to work.'

'You're the grown-up,' she says. 'Grown-ups aren't supposed to say yes unless it's a good idea.'

Despite his irritation, Pieter smiles. He likes it when she shows spirit. And intelligence.

'I'll tell you what,' he says. 'You and Kristin can go to the zoo tomorrow, and maybe we can have dinner together in the evening.'

'Promise?'

'I can't promise,' he says, mindful of her stern judgement of grown-up behaviour, 'but I'll try.'

In the end he cuts the trip short, leaving others to finish up the detail. No one bats an eyelid: they know he has a lot of fish to fry, a lot of irons in the fire. Plenty of useful platitudes that enable him to please himself. He and Emily fly back on Wednesday evening and spend the night in the London flat. Robert and Suzanne are due home on Thursday, and despite Emily's protestations Pieter gets Sam to collect her at the crack of dawn and drive her to school. At least that way she'll be there for her grandparents to collect at the end of the day. There's going to be enough fallout as it is – and for no real gain, Pieter thinks, as he waves away the car, with Emily's small face looking pinched and cross in the back seat. Perhaps he should have driven her up to Warwickshire himself, but he's fixed up some meetings in town today. There's still time to squeeze a bit more value out of this week, and London has the advantage of being a safe distance away from Suzanne's wrath and Emily's reproachful gaze.

He throws himself into work that day, and by mid-afternoon the Berlin deal has been sealed and a few other loose ends tied up. Emerging from a meeting in Canary Wharf, he feels the familiar serotonin hit of power flowing through his veins, of his influence streaming out into the world. This has been his version of pleasure for too long, he thinks, to do without it.

But it's undercut today by a whiff of frustration; a kind of restlessness that has been gathering force for the last couple of weeks. Pieter stares at himself in the mirrored walls of the lift. Is it time, he wonders, to flex a muscle or two on that other front? Or has the whole thing been a mistake? It's not too late: he can back away. A rich man's prerogative. Perhaps he should be patient, give it more time – but he's not good at patience. It has never served him well.

For the few seconds the lift takes to descend to the ground floor, he lets scenarios, options, play out in his head. And then he makes a snap decision. If he takes the Elizabeth Line he can get to Paddington in twenty minutes. There's a fast train on the hour: with any luck he'll be back at Marchboys before six.

As he lets himself in through the back door, Pieter is conscious of another familiar strain of pleasure, sparked by being back at Marchboys, in this place he's remaking – but the opposing tug of irritation and impatience that caught him on the way out of Canary Wharf is stronger now. The old anger, he thinks, still simmers just below the surface.

He turns along the corridor towards the hall, noticing, as he approaches, that there's light showing under the door at the end. He stops to listen: Rebecca is still here, he thinks. Perched on the scaffolding tower, painting dragons and castles.

'Hello?' he calls, as he opens the door.

And then there's a terrible sound – a clank of metal and a muffled shout and a soft crump. Pieter sprints across the hall. There, on the chequerboard floor below the scaffolding, is Rebecca. She's lying in a strange shape, very still. Fuck: is she dead? He kneels beside her, and as he does so he hears a faint moan. Not dead. Thank God. He can't face more death.

'Rebecca?' he says. 'It's Pieter. Are you hurt?'

Stupid question, he tells himself. But perhaps not so stupid, because she answers.

'My ankle,' she says.

'How far did you fall?'

'I don't know. I was nearly down, I think.'

But she hasn't moved, and she looks bad, lying like that. He startled her, he realises; that's what made her fall. He imagines litigation, a spotlight on him: the last thing he wants.

'Shall I call an ambulance?' he asks.

'Wait.' She pushes herself up cautiously. You're not supposed to move people who are injured, he knows, but are you supposed to stop them moving themselves? Rebecca looks very pale, and he can see a bump coming up on her forehead. She bends each leg in turn, and winces.

'My ankle hurts,' she says. She touches her head. 'I'll have a bruise there too, I think.'

An idea strikes Pieter then. 'I'll call my doctor,' he says. 'He can have a look at you. He'll know whether you should go to hospital.'

James McLintock is there in fifteen minutes. He has a fast car: he can certainly afford one on the fees he charges, Pieter thinks, but he approves. He approves, too, of McLintock's view that Rebecca is just shaken up, her ankle sprained, but that – since her husband is apparently on call overnight – she should stay at Marchboys House.

'I don't want to be any trouble,' Rebecca says, when this plan is proposed.

'It's no trouble,' Pieter says. 'It's the least we can do. There are plenty of bedrooms here.'

The restless anger has gone, and he doesn't examine too closely what has replaced it. He calls Sam, and Jenny Piper, his house-keeper. She used to be a nurse, he remembers. He tells McLintock that, and the deal is sealed.

'Get her to sleep in the next room,' the doctor says. 'She might check on Mrs Swarbrick through the night, to be on the safe side.'

Rebecca protests again, but feebly.

Pieter waits until she's settled, until she's eaten the light supper Sam produces, before he knocks on the door.

'Are you feeling better?' he asks.

'Yes,' Rebecca says. 'Thank you. Thank you for everything.'

He brushes that away. 'You're better off here, if your husband's on call.' He hesitates, wondering whether he dares to sit down; whether that would alarm her. He decides against it. But a little conversation would be all right, he thinks. Host-like.

'What does he do, your husband?' he asks.

'He's a heating engineer.' Rebecca looks flustered. Does she not like talking about her husband? But her next words prove that theory wrong. 'He's a very practical person: he can turn his hand to almost anything. He grows most of our vegetables, and he keeps bees.'

'You mentioned the bees before.'

'Did I?'

He smiles. He wants to keep her talking now. There's a white glare forming behind his eyes, and his heart has started to beat faster. 'He sounds an interesting man,' he says.

Rebecca looks up at him, eagerness and gratitude rising in her face. And then he knows it's going to happen. Just like that, it's going to happen.

'He had – something awful happened to him when he was little,' she says. 'His mother was killed. He was sitting in the car. They'd broken down.'

Pieter clenches his teeth to stop his expression changing. 'An accident?' he asks. 'Someone drove into them?'

Rebecca shakes her head. 'She was murdered,' she says.

'Really?' His voice echoes in his head. 'What a terrible thing.'

And he's spiralling back, now. He can't stop himself: his mind is filling with the sights and sounds and feelings of that afternoon long, long ago.

29

He first met Kirsty on a train. Or rather, he saw her on the station platform, before they both got on the train, and somehow – even though he thought of himself as invisible – he could tell that she'd noticed him looking at her, and that she knew he'd sat opposite her on purpose. The train was almost empty, so it was conspicuous, the sitting opposite, but he meant it to be.

She wasn't beautiful, in the conventional sense. She had reddish hair and freckles, and she was small and slightly plump. She was younger than him too: he was twenty by then, and she was only just seventeen. More to the point, he was already in his final year at university, and Kirsty, as he soon found out, was still at school. But he couldn't stop looking at her: at the way she smiled and talked and laughed. She'd left the friend she'd been with behind on the platform, and he badly wanted her to look at him and say things to him in the same way she'd been doing with her friend. And wanting that made him bold.

'I'm Pieter,' he said, when she caught his eye. 'How d'you do?'

She bit her lip, then, and giggled. 'You sound like the Foxy Whiskered Gentleman,' she said, 'when he wants to eat Jemima Puddleduck.'

'I don't want to eat you, I assure you.'

'That's all right, then.' She grinned. 'I'm Kirsty. How d'you do?'

The train to Birmingham took just over an hour. Kirsty was going to do some shopping, she said. Her friend had been going to come with her, but she'd changed her mind. She hadn't got any money. She'd hoped Kirsty would lend her some, but she already owed Kirsty a fiver. Pieter was on his way back from an old school-friend's house in the countryside where there'd been a party the night before; a grand house that had made him feel small and inconsequential, however gracious Michael's family had been. He, too, was in need of company that day.

It was a Saturday afternoon in late October – a nondescript corner of the year, but the sun was out and the last leaves on the trees were lit up like magic lanterns, decorating the fields that passed outside the train windows. Pieter can't remember, now, everything they talked about. Kirsty told him about her friends, perhaps, and how her parents would kill her if they knew she'd gone to Birmingham on her own.

'Why?' he asked, and she grinned again.

'Because I might get into trouble with unsuitable men, p'raps.'

'Would they think I was unsuitable?'

'I can't tell yet.'

'Do you want to find out?' he asked. 'I promise not to get you into trouble. I'm very reliable.'

He could hear himself speak, but he could hardly believe what he was saying. He was no good with girls. He never had been.

Kirsty cocked her head. 'What do you do, then?' she asked. 'Mr Reliable?'

'I'm a student,' he said. 'I'm at Birmingham University, studying Economics.'

'Do you like it?'

'Economics?' He laughed. 'I do, actually. I did it because I thought my father would approve, but I do quite like it.' He hesitated. 'It's all about people, Economics. Why they do what they do.'

He remembers that phrase. He still uses it occasionally. It's true and not true, he thinks. Economics is about how you make people do things. How you make sure their money flows in the right direction. That's what he's done with it, anyway.

'What are you going to do after that?' Kirsty asked. He noticed the way she looked at him just then, as though this was the first question she was really interested in. She was looking for something to do with her life, he realised. She thought he might have an answer. He felt a pricking of hope – but what on earth did he know about life?

'I don't know,' he said. 'I might go back to Hong Kong and look for a job there.'

'Hong Kong?'

'I grew up there. My parents live there.' *I live there*, he might have said, but he didn't.

'What's it like?' she asked.

And so he told her. He told her about the heat and the noise; the sea all around and the mountains closer than you think; the buildings getting taller and taller every year; the food and the smells and the lights across the water at night. He told her, without meaning to, about his parents, and the lack of siblings that he'd always regretted.

'I'm an only too,' Kirsty said, and then, 'I wish I lived in Hong Kong.'

'I was supposed to wish I lived in England,' Pieter said. 'I was supposed to be pleased when they sent me to school in Dorset when I was seven.' But he didn't want to talk about that, so instead he said, 'Could I come shopping with you, since your friend isn't here? And then I could take you to a little museum I like.' He drew breath, wondering how far to press it. 'I could buy you lunch,' he said, 'if your parents wouldn't disapprove.'

'I don't ever want them to meet you,' she said, and he felt something lurch inside him. It seemed to him, in that moment, that he had chanced upon something momentous. Something too momentous, almost, to have happened by chance.

30

Rebecca looks much better the next morning. James McLintock comes back to check her over: the ankle's not too bad, he says, but she should stay off the scaffolding for a while. She could start marbling the pillars today, Rebecca says. She can do that sitting down. Pieter smiles approval, and she blushes.

He's sorely tempted to linger in the hall, but he forces himself to leave her alone. It's begun, he tells himself, as he walks back to his study. He must be patient now. He mustn't alarm her: everything must feel natural. He smiles, then, remembering his nonchalance last night when she mentioned Kirsty's death. It surprised him a bit how easily he could dissemble. But then so much of his life has involved dissembling; a concealment of his true feelings and hopes and motives. It's no wonder it's become second nature. And the sleight of hand has been there all along with Rebecca. The trail carefully laid. Although there was a prompt, of course – a prompt so felicitously timed, so apt, that it felt almost as though it had been deliberately placed in his way. As though he had no choice but to follow the path it suggested.

He shuts the study door, pours some coffee from the pot on his desk.

It was seeing her name that started it. A tiny piece online that caught his attention as he idly hopped from one website to another in the executive lounge at Heathrow. Rebecca Swarbrick. It was an unusual surname: he hadn't come across it for almost thirty years. The piece was about art in hospitals, about philanthropy, and

197

Rebecca was mentioned in passing: she'd painted a mural in the new children's ward at Banbury General.

Rebecca Swarbrick.

If the flight hadn't been delayed, he might have forgotten all about it. But he had time to kill. He found her website, a photograph of her. Ben must be in his mid-thirties by now. Could Rebecca be his wife? The piece mentioned that she lived in the Midlands, and it was easy to imagine Ben staying in the same part of the world. He'd been brought up by his grandparents after Kirsty died, Pieter knew that.

The next bit was easy. The World Wide Web is omniscient and anonymous: anything you want to know – almost anything – is at your fingertips. Rebecca had been married to Ben Swarbrick for six years. Ben Swarbrick – surely the same one? – was employed by a plumbing firm that positioned itself at the upper end of the market, offering 24-hour emergency cover to its customers. That took a little more finding out. They lived in a small village near Banbury, in a two-bedroom house that they'd bought for just under £200,000.

A small life, he thought.

But Rebecca's murals were good. She had some talent. And her website was well designed; what she had to say for herself was articulate. Her father was a retired vicar, he discovered. She'd been to university, though not to a distinguished one.

He became obsessed with their lives. He didn't, at that stage, have a particular object in mind. It was just a thread that led back to Kirsty: it was the fascination of finding that something of her had survived. That lumpen, screaming child he'd seen once in a pushchair had grown into a man. That man had a trade, a job, and a wife who made a living as a painter. They had a life together in the countryside, not far from where Kirsty herself had grown up. Every detail was a small torture, but he couldn't stop himself.

How much did Ben remember of his mother? he wondered. He'd been brought up, after her death, by the parents Kirsty had disliked, mistrusted. Perhaps he didn't have much of her in him: it had been impossible to see the slightest trace, that day in Birmingham. Perhaps his grandparents' genes had bypassed Kirsty and landed full square on him. But seven years with her must have left a trace. Seven years Pieter hadn't been allowed: that was a thorn that pricked at him. They pricked and pricked, the thorns of memory and curiosity, jealousy and disquiet. They didn't stop him pursuing his life, didn't hinder him in a way anyone could have seen, but they disturbed his nights.

The idea came to him one day, quite suddenly. Rebecca was a mural painter. The hall at Marchboys had a wonderful domed ceiling. He could commission her to paint it. He could employ her here, under his roof. He could get to know her, offer her his patronage, insinuate his way into her life. That would be a way to scratch the itch. A way, just possibly, to find out what he has never known: what he has always wanted, needed to know.

Ben was there that day. The only witness, a boy of seven. What does he remember of his mother's death? What did he see?

Those questions have plagued Pieter, he admits that now. He pretended they didn't matter, that they mattered less and less as the years passed, but that wasn't true. They mattered so much that he can see now that his whole life has been deformed by them, like a cancer that has grown and grown inside him.

He could have managed things better with Rebecca, he thinks now, but never mind. He told himself all along that it was only a matter of time before she mentioned Kirsty, and he was right. Who could be married to Ben and not think, sometimes, about Kirsty?

31

She was just an ordinary girl, he told himself, when it was all over. There was nothing special about her: nothing you could put your finger on that explained what she made him feel. At the beginning he was charmed, amused, by her ordinariness – by which he meant her unaffectedness, the fact that she had none of the same pretensions as everyone else he knew. It didn't matter a jot to Kirsty that he didn't really fit in the world he was supposed to belong to.

But there was always something more than that. She was so alive; that was one way of putting it. When she smiled, her face filled with light and hope and mischief, and her eyes had a way of fixing on his that seemed to draw something out from deep inside him. He was certain she could do anything, anything at all, because she refused to fall in with what other people expected. If her friend decided not to go to Birmingham at the last minute, she'd go on her own. If something caught her eye, she'd stop and look at it. If something confused her, intrigued her, she'd keep teasing away at it. She didn't have many answers yet, but she had lots of questions. Endless questions. What would happen if . . . ? Why does it matter that . . . ? Why don't people think about . . . ? Being with her was like stepping into a new world: it opened up possibilities he'd never have imagined for himself.

He followed her around the shopping centre that first Saturday, and every time she turned to look at him she laughed.

'You've never been to Etam before, have you?'

'No, but maybe I should have done.'

He picked up a dressing gown and held it out for her approval. 'Go on,' she said, teasing. 'Try it on.'

He'd have liked to find somewhere nice for lunch, but hunger overcame Kirsty bewilderingly fast, and they ended up at the Berni Inn. Kirsty ate every morsel of her sirloin steak and then a large slab of Black Forest gateau. Pieter thought of his mother, perpetually on a diet, and was filled with the pleasure of watching Kirsty eat.

But the highlight of that day, the thing that really sealed everything, was the Story Museum. Pieter had stumbled upon it the previous year, and had been back several times since – an unusual visitor, among the young families and school groups, but there was something about it he loved; something he'd always wanted to share with someone. The entrance was bright and colourful, but once you were inside there were dark passages and doors you weren't sure you should open. Some of them revealed rooms crammed with words and illustrations – not just covering the walls but hung from the ceiling, adorning tree-like display stands – and others led to spaces which seemed ready for stories to unfold inside them. A rocking chair beside a fire, copper pots on a blackened stove, an iron bedstead with a faded quilt. Or a forest, sprung upon you in the darkness, filled with the night-time sounds of wolves and owls and breaking twigs. It felt, to Pieter, a little like entering the temple of some alien religion. It was full of symbols he didn't entirely understand, but which affected him deeply.

Did he know that Kirsty would be able to decode them for him? Or was it chance – the alchemy of the museum and Kirsty, of his childhood yearnings and that particular, magical afternoon – that brewed up such a powerful potion of meaning and desire?

'Oh, it's the Three Bears' house!' Kirsty said – 'and look, there's Red Riding Hood, behind that tree.' She pointed out a castle turret high up in a corner, a tiny figure curled inside a flower, an indignant frog perched at the edge of a pond. She chattered on about moon princesses and sorcerers, beanstalks and spinning wheels. She laughed when Pieter looked bemused, admitting that he'd never heard any of these stories. 'I'll bring you a book next time,' she said.

And she did. And there was that next time, and another, and plenty more, through that joyful winter and the spring that followed. That first day she slipped her hand into his in the dark of the forest room, and he kissed her chastely goodbye at the end of the afternoon, then passed a tumultuous week wondering what might happen next. And the next Saturday she lifted her face to him when they met at the station and he cupped it in his hands and kissed her sweetly, deliciously, and his heart sang. After that their romance unfolded in weekly chapters. They went to the cinema, to an occasional concert, to shops of all kinds; they walked and walked around the city, and when there was a rainy Saturday he took her back to his bare room in the university hostel and they made love. Pieter was dizzy, grateful, transformed.

She never did introduce him to her parents – 'They spoil everything,' she said, 'I won't let them spoil you' – and she kept him from her friends too. But then, he kept her from his friends, such as they were. In any case his life contracted, like a vacuum pack, until more or less all it contained was his lectures and Kirsty. There was an occasional party, but Pieter felt less at home than ever in the world of drinking games and ribaldry that his peers occupied. His letters to his parents – also occasional – spoke of his dissertation, his interest in economic theory, and avoided any mention of his plans beyond graduation.

As the months passed, his certainty that his future must include Kirsty grew. But so did his doubts – not about his feelings for her, but about hers for him. Every encounter would leave him reassured and joyful, but each time they parted a seed of uncertainty would lodge in his heart, and over the days that followed it would grow and grow. What could she possibly see in him? How could she follow her dreams if she was tied to him? Did she wish their relationship would move faster, or was she happy to keep things as they were, balanced on the cusp of the light-hearted and the profoundly serious?

Because they spoke about everything, the two of them. About social policy and fashion; about classroom intrigue and pop music and the darkest secrets of their hearts. There was – there seemed to be – nothing they didn't reveal to each other. Did she see him as a mentor or as a lover, though? As a fellow traveller, or a chance encounter along the way? He bought her presents, occasionally – a bottle of perfume he hoped she wouldn't guess the price of, although of course she did, and books he thought she'd enjoy. 'I don't have anything to give you back,' she'd say, and he'd remind her about the fairy-tale book, and sometimes he'd bring it with him and ask her to read to him. The stories sounded different when she read them aloud, but he couldn't tell whether she had a particular gift, or whether she simply read them with the same inflections and cadences that every child – every child except him – learns at their mother's knee. They seemed full of meaning, those stories: he felt their echoes everywhere. Lonely children, cruel adults, inhibition and constraint; moments of magic that almost pass you by. Stories that took root in his soul, and have never left him. That still conjure Kirsty's voice, and her smile.

32

On Monday morning, Pieter catches a glimpse of Ben. He must, Pieter deduces, have driven Rebecca to Marchboys. Her car is still here: he was supposed to have it delivered to her, he remembers. But he hardly thinks any of this, in fact, because he's hypnotised by the sight of Ben getting out of his van.

It's chance, once again. Chance, or something meant. A trail of breadcrumbs. On any other day, he wouldn't have been in his bedroom at that time, but he had a headache and he'd come upstairs to find some painkillers. And so he hears the van approaching, and he glances out of the window, over the drive at the front of the house, and there is the large, bearded man who was once Kirsty's baby. Who was once the boy who sat in their car while she was being strangled in the woods, just a few yards away.

From above he doesn't look especially tall, but when he stands next to Rebecca, offers her his arm, Pieter can see that she only reaches his shoulder – and Rebecca is close to his own height. Ben is wearing a green sweatshirt with the logo of the plumbing firm he works for embroidered on it in gold. If you saw him in the street, Pieter thinks, you would notice him; notice his height. Pieter has to resist the urge to hurry out of the room, to appear casually at the top of the stairs as the front door opens to admit them. It wouldn't be a good idea, he tells himself.

He stays out of Rebecca's way that day. Let time pass, he thinks. Let there be no urgency, nothing to arouse suspicion. But that evening, after she's left, he goes into the hall to look at the newly painted pillars. He flicks on the lights and stands just inside the front door, taking it in. Rebecca has chosen a green effect for the marbling which works well with the ceiling, the swathes of forest. Pieter has paid more attention to the painting than Rebecca might imagine. Some evenings, he climbs up on to the scaffolding to see the ceiling up close, and while he's there he looks at Rebecca's paraphernalia too: the rags and brushes and palettes and the big pots of paint.

The mural is impressive. It's better than he expected: a lot better. He's pleased to find so many traces of the stories from the book he lent Rebecca. The book Kirsty gave him all that time ago. He follows the trails across the ceiling – the river curving inland from the sea, and the road winding up towards the castle. He allows himself to be reminded, sometimes, of the Story Museum. Of Kirsty's hand sliding into his in the forest room, as though they were lost among the trees. Of that first kiss, so sweet and so gentle.

He wonders, from time to time, what would have happened if he'd met someone who eclipsed Kirsty. But no – that's the wrong word. The wrong question. It wasn't like that. It was, he knows, partly about who he was then, and who he's become since. About Before and After.

All right: what if he'd met someone else who was capable of sweeping him up and carrying his life in a different direction? Sally wasn't that person, although she thought she was. Nor were any of the women he's been linked to since. And Freya isn't either: he understands that quite clearly. It's shameful how little he's thought about Freya while she's been away. How little he'd care if she never came back. But he misses having Emily around, now that her grandparents are home, and that has taken him by surprise.

There was a row about the Berlin jaunt and the missed days of school, but not as big a row as Pieter anticipated. Almost lip ser-vice. Suzanne was pleased he'd wanted to take her, he realised. Emily described the trip in glowing terms – and although Pieter felt badly that she'd had to lie, he was touched by her loyalty. She's his flesh and blood, he thinks. She knows how to spin things.

*

Towards the end of Tuesday afternoon, there's a knock on his study door.

'Come!' he calls, and Rebecca's head appears around the door.

There, he says to himself. All things come to those who wait.

Rebecca smiles nervously. 'I just wanted to say thank you again,' she says. 'For looking after me when I fell.'

'Oh! It was nothing. I'm glad you've made a full recovery.'

He tries to smile back, but sometimes his face doesn't move in the way he directs it. Could this be a pretext? he wonders. Does she, too, want to talk more about . . .

'Come in,' he says. 'Unless you're in a hurry?'

Rebecca hesitates, then shuts the door behind her. She refuses Pieter's offer of tea, but sits down on the sofa he gestures towards.

'I've been doing some reading,' he says, settling himself opposite her, 'about the story you told me.' He smiles; a better smile. A thoughtful employer, taking an interest in her. 'About the murder.'

'Oh.'

Pieter wishes she'd accepted the tea, and then they'd have to fill the time it took to drink it with conversation. But he presses on. 'It's very interesting,' he says.

Her hands are clasped in her lap. 'I only know what Ben's told me,' she says.

Pieter nods. 'Most of what's known came from Ben,' he says. 'He was the only witness.'

'Yes.'

Pieter allows a moment to pass, but not too long a moment. He can't risk her getting up, making to leave. 'There are some curious facts,' he says, in as light a tone as he can manage. 'The white car, for instance. It parked behind them, according to Ben. But if you spotted a car on the hard shoulder and decided to stop, you'd be more likely to pull up in front of it, wouldn't you, by the time you'd come to a halt?'

'Possibly,' she says.

He tilts his head. 'Unless, I suppose, it was a particularly flat, straight stretch of motorway, and you could see the car from a long way off.'

Rebecca doesn't reply. She doesn't want to have this conversation, Pieter thinks. Perhaps they have an agreement, she and Ben, that they won't discuss his mother's death with other people. Perhaps she regrets mentioning it the other night. Defeat begins to creep towards him. But then Rebecca speaks again.

'Maybe the man in the white car saw Kirsty walking along the hard shoulder,' she says.

'Walking back the way they'd come?' Pieter asks, after another feather-light pause.

'Perhaps she'd seen an emergency phone box while they were slowing down.'

He nods. 'She wouldn't have had a mobile phone, of course, in 1993.'

'No.'

'So she was walking back along the hard shoulder,' he says, 'and the man in the white car stopped. And then he lured her, or manhandled her, over the fence beside the motorway? Into the woods?'

Careful, he tells himself. Careful. There's a hair's breadth between safety and disaster.

'I suppose so,' Rebecca says.

'And Ben didn't see any of it?'

'If they were behind him, he couldn't have seen very easily.'

'But he saw the car stop. He saw the man get out. And then he stopped watching?'

Is there a glimmer of interest in her face now? Has she wondered about that day too? Surely she must have done. Perhaps she and Ben haven't talked much about it: if they had, wouldn't she say *Ben thinks*, or *Ben's always said*, rather than *maybe* or *I suppose*? Or is her choice of words deliberate?

'If the man saw Kirsty walking and then stopped,' she says, 'he'd have parked between where Ben was sitting in the car and where she was walking along. So he'd have had to walk away from Ben to catch up with Kirsty.'

'Yes.' Pieter nods. 'That makes sense. The car would have been between them.' He takes a breath. 'It's possible, of course, that the white car was following them. That the driver was someone Kirsty knew.'

Rebecca stares at him, but once again she doesn't reply. Pieter waits, letting the silence gather between them until it's almost too much to bear. And then, keeping his voice affable, curious, he changes tack.

'The other thing that seems strange to me,' he says, 'is that she left Ben in the car.'

'Why is that strange?' Rebecca asks. 'He was safer there.'

'But someone could have taken him from the car,' Pieter says. 'Or he could have got bored of waiting and wandered out on to the hard shoulder alone.' He pauses again, with a hint of a smile, a slight tilt of the head. 'I'd have kept the child with me.'

'I suppose people don't always think straight in an emergency,' she says.

'True.' People don't, he supposes.

'I should go,' Rebecca says. 'I'm still – it's a long drive.'

'Of course.' But she doesn't move, not just yet. 'He was seven?' Pieter asks, as if it's an afterthought. 'Ben was seven?'

'Yes. A big boy for seven, though.'

His heart quickens. 'Grown up, you mean?'

'Tall, too,' Rebecca says. 'He looked older. He's always . . . His mother must have thought she could trust him to stay put.'

Pieter nods. Let her leave things there. Perhaps, he thinks, she'll talk to Ben now. Ask some more questions. Will she tell him about this conversation? He has an inkling that she won't. But perhaps . . . there's a sudden flash of fascination, of terror, as he imagines Rebecca telling Ben about his interest in Kirsty's death. And what might happen then? What might that set in train?

'I've kept you,' he says. 'I'm sorry. You should get on your way.'

33

If Pieter's letters to his parents during those heady months left important things out, theirs did too. They waited until his final exams were over to tell him that they were both ill. They'd kept the news from him, they said, because they didn't want to distract him from his studies, but it would be a good thing if he came home now, without delay. They had booked him a flight.

Pieter had planned to take Kirsty camping. He'd started learning to drive, so that they didn't have to rely on the train to carry them to and from each other. He had interviews lined up for jobs in the Midlands – not the kinds of jobs his peers were applying for, but who cared about that?

But he couldn't refuse his parents' summons. He arrived in Hong Kong in the first week of June, when the heat sat heavy over the city and storms rumbled every night. It didn't take long for him to grasp the seriousness of the situation.

He had never thought of his parents' lives as being very intimately entwined, but it seemed the ends of them were destined to be closer than most couples manage, unless through catastrophic accident or careful planning. And their deaths fell into neither of those categories. They had both, in their late fifties, been diagnosed with different forms of cancer within a month of each other; had both discovered, almost at the same time, that their respective malignancies had outrun the treatment options available. They had both kept working until they couldn't, had bought in enough help to keep themselves and the household going – and were now, as Pieter arrived home, ready to move into the same hospice.

It was typical of them, he thought, in the first flush of anger and disbelief, to contrive to exit life in such a way that neither of them needed to seek consolation in Pieter, or to advance in any tiny way their connection with their only son. They presented a united front in the face of death: it reminded him of the evening they'd told him he was being despatched to boarding school.

'You'll have some money,' they said. 'You can keep the flat or sell it, as you wish.'

'I might buy a house in England,' he said. He wasn't sure whether he meant to hurt them or to please them. Nor could he tell what they thought about his plan. Whether they cared at all what he did when they were gone.

Their estates were neatly organised, and their deaths accomplished without undue delay, but even so it took some time to settle things: to get his head around what had happened and where it left him. An orphan. Not a poor orphan, though not a particularly rich one either. Someone with no one left in the world who expected anything of him. Except Kirsty, of course.

He wrote to Kirsty almost every day, and she wrote back, once or twice. Her letters took a long time to arrive and conveyed something of her, but not her whole essence. Not the bits he missed. He imagined her spending the summer with her schoolfriends, getting a holiday job, going away with her parents. 'Wales,' she'd said, before he left: 'a caravan in Wales.' She'd rolled her eyes, but Pieter had wished he could go to Wales instead of back to Hong Kong.

Now Wales felt like something out of a fairy tale – and Hong Kong, in those strange weeks after his parents' funerals, was unexpectedly vivid. The past drew him in. He saw his parents' old friends, wandered the streets he remembered so well, marvelled at the new buildings he didn't recognise. He played tennis and walked the hiking trails and considered job offers made over dinner at the Jockey Club. He remembered how homesick he'd been when he first went to school in England.

But as the weeks passed, Hong Kong's grip on him began to slacken. He hadn't been certain, when he told his parents he might buy a house in England, that that was what he intended, but as the haze of grief and nostalgia lifted, what was left behind was a vision of an English village – somewhere like the place his friend Michael lived. Somewhere his children could grow up. He would have to wait for Kirsty to finish school, to go through university, but there was no harm in buying something now. So he sold his parents' flat, and was pleased to find, when he left it for the last time, that it felt like an empty shell. And then, as September rolled into October, he booked a flight back to England.

Perhaps he'd been gone too long. Perhaps he should have written more often, or said more before he left. Perhaps he was simply naïve to imagine that nothing would change, for her, while he was living through such upheaval and watershed.

He knew Kirsty's address, but he knew better than to turn up there. She worked in Woolworths in Warwick on Saturday mornings, he remembered. He could surprise her: turn up with a bunch of roses. He imagined her blushing, beaming – and then he remembered that her friend Jackie worked at Woolworths too, and thought better of the roses.

Kirsty was on the till when he walked in. She had her back to him, and he slipped past her into the shop and wandered for a few minutes among the toys and the kitchen gadgets, his heart thumping dangerously in his chest, until he came upon the rack of pick'n'mix. He filled a large bag with a variety of sweets he'd never seen before, and made his way back to Kirsty's till.

He meant not to look up until he reached the front of the queue, but he couldn't help himself. He caught her eye when he was still two people away, and then his heart crashed and stopped. Her reaction wasn't what he'd hoped. Dismay, unmistakably. Embarrassment. He'd misjudged the occasion, the timing. But it would be all right, he told himself. He just needed to hold his nerve.

'Hello,' he said, when his turn came. 'I thought I'd come and sample your wares.'

She didn't meet his eyes as she lifted his bag of sweets on to the scales. 'When did you get back?' she asked.

Ah – so did she think he'd been home for a while and not been in touch? Was that the problem?

'Last night,' he said.

Her expression didn't change. 'That's 65p,' she said.

Pieter handed over a pound note. An apology was needed, he felt, although he wasn't quite sure what for. What she'd like to hear. 'I'm sorry I've been away so long,' he said.

She glanced up at him then. 'I'm sorry about your parents,' she said. 'I'm really sorry.'

'Thank you.' He took his change, panic beginning to stir inside him. The man behind was shifting impatiently. 'If I wait, can I see you when you finish?'

'OK.' She'd turned, now, to the next customer, but her eyes flicked back to him for a moment. 'There's a café just along the way. Tanners. I'll meet you there at one.'

He'd ordered for her: chicken and chips and a glass of Coke. A jumble of emotions he didn't want to decipher flickered across her face as she approached the table.

'I don't really have time for lunch,' she said. 'I'm expected home.'

'Don't eat it, then,' he said. But she'd slid on to the chair by then and started picking at the chips. She still didn't want to meet his eyes. She looked like a surly teenager who'd been caught smoking. He pushed that thought away.

'You don't seem very pleased to see me,' he said. 'I've been looking forward to this moment.'

Those sentences didn't seem to work together, somehow, but he let them hang in the air, even so. He couldn't think what else to say. How long had it been? Almost four months?

'I'm really sorry, Pieter,' she said.

'Sorry for what?'

She was still eating the chips, one after another, like an automaton. Outside, the autumn sun was making a poor showing over the grey bulk of the shopping centre. Suddenly she sighed, and put the chip she was holding back on the plate.

'I really liked spending time with you,' she said, 'I really did. But I'm seeing someone now, and it wouldn't—'

'Seeing someone else?' he said, before the meaning of what she'd said struck him. Semantics, he thought. Spending time; seeing. They were different things, clearly, and what they'd had, the two of them, didn't reach the threshold of seriousness that would have meant – what, though? She was seventeen: of course she wasn't dreaming about the house where they would bring up their children. But the thought of being deposed by a teenage boy, someone without the fine feeling to understand Kirsty's soul ...

She was looking at him with sympathy now, and that was enough to flip a switch inside him. An emergency circuit, designed for his own protection. He mustn't let her see how much he'd hoped for a different reception – that he'd counted on it, planned around it.

'Of course,' he said. 'I understand. It's just – we didn't really finish things off, did we? So I thought ...'

Her face cleared. 'No,' she said. 'Well, you left in a hurry, didn't you? You had to.'

He nodded. She's just an ordinary girl, he told himself then, for the first time. But every nerve ending in his body told a different story. For a long moment he couldn't take his eyes off her face, and now that the difficult bit was over she didn't seem to mind him looking at her; didn't even mind when he took her hand, until he realised that that was too painful.

It wasn't, he thought, that he cared more about Kirsty than his parents. It wasn't that simple, at least. It was that this made no sense to him. It upended the good, strong idea he'd had of his future; the way he meant to live his life.

Kirsty finished the plate of food in the end, and Pieter watched every bite, every lick of the lips, every minuscule twitch of her eyebrows, trying to extract the memory of the girl he'd loved from the reality of the girl sitting opposite him. Trying to construct for himself a sea wall that would keep the two apart: that would separate Before from After.

34

Pieter has had an idea that pleases him: he's invited a celebrity photographer to Marchboys to capture the work in progress. Everyone has a little vanity, he tells himself, and he hopes this plan will flatter Rebecca's. He needs to build bridges with her after that last conversation. Needs to reassure her that it's the painting he's really interested in.

At first she seems doubtful: she asks whether it wouldn't be better to wait until the mural is complete. But he shakes his head. 'There'll be plenty of photographs once it's finished,' he says, 'but this stage will be lost by then. The process. The scaffolding. The story unfolding.'

'I suppose so.' She smiles, then. 'Maybe I could use some of the images on my website, if you wouldn't mind.'

He spreads his hands in a gesture of generosity. He's not keen on publicity, as a rule, but he could stretch a point. He begins to imagine an article about the mural, the rehabilitation of Marchboys. Freya might like that. The chatelaine of a great house: that's what he's offering her, after all.

Sam found Clive Pettit for him. He works for the quality glossies, for *Vogue* and *Vanity Fair* and *Tatler*, but a large enough cheque has brought him skipping to Marchboys, and his charm works like magic on Rebecca. And it's probably true, Pieter supposes, that he's never seen anything like this before: a cross between Michelangelo and Walt Disney, though in truth nothing like either. Pieter gives them lunch, and afterwards the three of them climb the scaffolding tower so that Clive can photograph Rebecca close up. Pieter doesn't need to be there, of course, but he's cleared the afternoon. He wants to see the thing through with proper conviction.

He expected Rebecca to be shy of the camera, but instead she rises to the occasion. She's painting some sunflowers: they watch, he and Clive, while she mixes the colour on her palette. Clive asks questions about the paint, the technical detail, and Rebecca answers fluently, interestingly. Pieter can see that Clive's impressed by her, and that pleases him. He listens while she delivers a lengthy soliloquy on the challenges of the project. He has never heard her speak for so long.

'And with the curve, the dome, the perspective shifts all the time,' she finishes. 'While you're painting it, even. You have to keep stopping, checking. It plays tricks on you.'

Pieter watches while Clive props himself on one elbow to photograph Rebecca from below, with the mural behind her. As though Rebecca is part of the picture, he thinks.

Later, when Clive has gone, Pieter stands under the scaffolding for a few moments, thinking. He can hear Rebecca above him, the sound of the brush tinkling as she rinses it in a jar of water. Is he a monster? he wonders. Is it a monstrous thing he's doing? He tightens his fists at his side. He mustn't let himself think like that.

'Can I come back up?' he calls. 'Do you mind? Does it disturb you?'

'Not at all,' she says. He can't see her face from where he's standing, but he can hear the warmth in her voice. She's enjoyed the day, he thinks.

'To tell you the truth, I don't have much of a head for heights,' he says, as he begins to climb. 'I surprised myself, earlier.'

Why does he say that? To make himself vulnerable? Likeable? She makes a little joke of it, and he groans, playing along.

He is what he is, he tells himself. He can't help that now. It's too late.

For a while, a few minutes, he squats on the platform and watches her paint. There's something very intimate about sharing this small space, being so close to her and to the ceiling. Just the two of them now. He thinks carefully, and then he begins casually, telling her how much Clive Pettit admired her work, how pleased he is himself. Rebecca responds as he hopes: she's flattered; softened up a little.

'Has your husband seen the ceiling?' he asks next, his voice still nonchalant.

'He saw it when he came to pick me up,' she says, 'after I fell.'

'Of course.'

He was thinking of that other occasion, the Monday morning when he saw Ben from the window. He's been here more than once, Pieter thinks. He feels a frisson of excitement and fear: a rare thing these days.

'I've been talking for weeks about the stories,' Rebecca is saying, 'the ones from the book you gave me. But I don't think it made much sense to him until he saw the ceiling.'

'He's lucky to have you,' Pieter says. 'Someone so steady, so intuitive.' A tiny pause. 'After the trauma of his childhood.'

Rebecca looks disquieted. No – touched. Perhaps both. 'That's kind of you,' she says. 'Ben's a steady person himself, actually. A rock.'

She asks him a question about the mural then, but Pieter ignores it.

'You said Ben was big for his age,' he says.

'He still is,' Rebecca says. 'A gentle giant.'

'A gentle giant,' Pieter says. He remembers that oversized toddler, thrashing in his pushchair. 'Was he always gentle?' he asks. 'Was he a gentle child?'

'I think so,' Rebecca says. 'His grandparents adored him. They seem to have been fonder of him than of his mother.'

'Interesting,' Pieter says. *Kirsty never liked them*, he almost says. His heart skips, catches itself. 'The teenage pregnancy, I suppose,' he says. 'Did they disapprove of that?'

This isn't where he meant things to go, but he's fascinated, of course. And he senses something in Rebecca now: empathy. Towards Kirsty, he thinks, not Ben.

'I don't know,' Rebecca says now. 'They've always . . .' She hesitates. 'They've never had anything good to say about her,' she says. 'I've always found that strange.'

Pieter casts about for something neutral to say; something that will keep the conversation rolling.

'It would have been natural to spoil Ben,' he says. 'Given what had happened.'

But then he senses her backing away again. 'I shouldn't talk about it,' she says. 'It's not my business, really.'

'Of course,' he says. But he can't stop now. He's got to the very brink. And he has a card up his sleeve, something to draw her in with. 'There's something I haven't told you,' he says. 'I haven't been entirely straight with you about my interest in Kirsty's death.'

Rebecca stares at him. 'What do you mean?'

'There's a connection,' he says, 'with Marchboys House. A slim one, I grant you, but . . . The name is very old: it goes back to the twelfth century. It means "the house at the edge of the woods".' She looks curious now, her wariness defused. 'March means "at the edge" or "on the borders" in Anglo-Norman,' Pieter continues, 'and Boys, of course, is the French *bois*. The original manor house was on the edge of a vast forest, one of the king's prime hunting grounds. And that forest extended from here, from our remaining bit of woodland, as far as the wooded area where Kirsty was found. So in a sense – at a stretch – she was killed on my land.'

'I see,' Rebecca says.

Pieter is intensely conscious now of the lack of space up here under the dome, and of how close the two of them are. He allows a tiny pause, not enough to lose the thread of the dialogue, and then he carries on.

'This is a mad thought,' he says. 'You'll have to forgive me. But I've been turning it over in my head, and I have to say it now.'

'What?' She doesn't suspect, yet, where this is going.

'No one else saw that white car,' Pieter says. 'No one saw anything, apart from a couple of motorists who half-remembered a broken-down car.' He looks at her, holds her gaze. 'Ben was a big boy, a strong boy for seven. His mother was very slight. Perhaps he panicked when the car broke down. Perhaps he was frightened. Angry.'

'What are you saying?' She looks puzzled; not yet dismayed.

'It's not impossible,' Pieter says. 'It wouldn't even be his fault, really. A boy of seven, confused and upset.'

'What are you saying?' she asks again, her voice sharpening.

Pieter doesn't take his eyes off her. 'I'm saying perhaps he hit out. Perhaps he killed his mother. Perhaps that's the answer to the mystery.' He hesitates. He needs her to hear this, to take it in. 'Perhaps he doesn't even remember what he did.'

'He stayed in the car,' Rebecca says stubbornly. 'He didn't get out until the police stopped to see what was going on.'

'Maybe that's what he remembers,' Pieter says. 'Maybe he's suppressed what really happened.'

'No.' She's agitated now. Angry. 'No, no, no. You're mad.'

Pieter's gaze is still fixed on her face. He can see every muscle, every flicker. Does she really think he's mad? Or does she – does a little part of her – think he might be right?

'I'm sorry,' he says. He lifts his hands, as though he realises he's gone too far. 'I've upset you. Offended you. I shouldn't have said anything. I just – I'm always looking for the answer no one else has thought of. It's a bad habit – in some circumstances, at least. Forgive me.'

'It's fine,' Rebecca says, but her voice is stilted and formal. She looks at her watch. 'I should be getting home,' she says.

'I *have* offended you,' Pieter says. 'I'm sorry. Please forget what I said.' He drops his eyes at last, breaking the tension between them. 'I'm very grateful, Rebecca, for everything you've put into this project.' He attempts a smile. 'I hope it'll be worth it. I hope it'll launch your career.'

'Thank you,' Rebecca says, her voice still clipped. 'I'm grateful to you too, for the opportunity.'

She plunges her brush into a clean jar of water, and he watches the paint swilling out in thick strands that stretch and spread and fade. The same yellow she used earlier on the sunflowers. Without thinking, he reaches a hand towards them. For a moment he imagines Kirsty here with him on the platform; he imagines how much she'd love the mural. Perhaps that's the point, he thinks. Has he done it for her? Can he allow himself that comfort?

'You could almost pick them,' he says. 'I'd like to have them in a vase. Such a splash of colour.'

35

The next time Pieter saw Kirsty it was entirely by accident. Three years had passed: he was on his way up the financial tree by then, but he'd come back to Birmingham to do an MBA at Aston. He could have chosen Harvard or Chicago, but England made more sense; he had business interests there, a connection to the city. Perhaps there was more at play in his subconscious, but if there was he didn't admit it.

Certainly he hadn't expected to see Kirsty. She'd been relegated, with the fairy tales she used to tell him, to the recesses of his mind. His attention was fixed on the future, and he kept the past at a distance. He had a photograph of his parents on his desk, but that was all. He'd turned their deaths into a creation myth. More than a myth: the money from the Hong Kong flat had financed his first business venture. Give him a few more years and perhaps he could weave Kirsty into a morality tale too, but he hadn't tried that yet.

There she was, though. Pushing a pram through the city centre when he was on his way to buy a sandwich for lunch between seminars. If she'd been walking in the opposite direction he might not have recognised her, not with the pram, but she was coming towards him, and she stopped.

'Pieter,' she said.

It wasn't a pram; he corrected his terminology. It was a pushchair, and the child inside was almost too big for it. A boy with a large head, fast asleep, his feet hanging down towards the pavement.

'Hello, Kirsty.'

She didn't seem to know what to say next, and that disconcerted him.

'How are you?' he asked.

She gestured, with a smidgeon of irony, towards the child.

'I'm a mum,' she said.

'Congratulations.' Pieter's anger at the man who had supplanted him flared for a moment, like a spark from a dead fire. Kirsty looked tired, worn down. She was wearing a shapeless anorak and a pair of scuffed trainers.

'Do you live here,' she asked, 'or are you just visiting?'

'Studying again.' He allowed himself the ghost of a smile. What would she think of yet more education? 'Studying business.'

'Oh.'

Something was stirring inside him now. A voice was suggesting there could be no harm in a conversation, a shared sandwich. Not given how much time had passed; how far apart their lives had grown.

And then the child woke up. The first thing he saw, when he opened his eyes, was Pieter, and he screamed more loudly, more suddenly, than Pieter would have thought possible.

'Ben!' Kirsty was kneeling on the pavement in an instant, shushing him. 'You didn't sleep long, did you, sweetheart? You were so tired . . .'

Her son was fighting her now, struggling to get out of the pushchair, the wails getting louder and louder. People in the street turned their heads to look. Pieter stood where he was, paralysed by self-consciousness, but he couldn't just walk away. Ben was pounding his mother's arms and chest, inarticulate words emerging from the noise.

'It's not safe to get out here, Ben,' Kirsty said, her voice calmer than Pieter could credit. 'It's a busy road.' She glanced up at Pieter, apologetic. 'He wants to walk,' she said. 'He thinks he's too big for the buggy.'

Should he help? If he offered to walk with them, perhaps . . .

'Is he often like this?' he asked.

'Quite often, at the moment.' She grinned; her face crinkled around the eyes in a way it hadn't before. 'The terrible twos,' she said. 'But he'll be three in April. Maybe things will improve then.'

Pieter's mind, used to computing, laid out dates for him. If the child had been born in April 1986, he must have been conceived the previous July – so Kirsty was already pregnant when he came home from Hong Kong that October. Was that why .., ? There was a breathless instant when things swirled in his mind.

But the boy chose that moment to land a kick squarely on his mother's shin, and she leapt back with an exclamation of pain.

'Don't do that,' she said. 'You're a big strong boy now; you hurt me. You can't . . .' And then she drew breath. She turned, briefly, to Pieter. 'I shouldn't have stopped,' she said. 'I should have guessed he'd wake up. I'd better keep moving.'

Pieter could think of nothing to say. He was already an adept operator in the boardroom, but this encounter, this dismal meeting in a dismal street, had floored him. The hateful child and the girl who was now a mother, and himself a helpless onlooker, swayed by currents he'd thought long buried. She moved away almost without a goodbye. He couldn't help watching her for a few moments (was she limping? had the child really hurt her?) and then he steeled himself.

'Bacon and avocado,' he said, half-aloud. 'That was good, yesterday.' And he walked the fifty yards to the sandwich shop, feigning oblivion to the milling crowds; to the figure with the push-chair disappearing behind him.

He thought that encounter might immunise him, but it didn't. Kirsty appeared more and more often in his dreams, sometimes hostile and sometimes wheedling. The child was his, she would tell him, or her heart was. He hated the dreams. He tried to dispel them by letting her into his waking thoughts: a moment in a lift or a taxi could safely be allotted to her, he told himself.

If things had gone differently that day in Birmingham, he

wondered sometimes, what might – would could – have happened? Was it fear or pride that had stopped him from asking more questions; from walking with her? No: it was the child, screaming and pummelling. Kicking his mother so hard that she cried out. Surely it wasn't normal, that level of aggression in a two-year-old? And surely he shouldn't be so big? Could he be older than she'd said? Could he, possibly, be his own son, conceived before he left for Hong Kong? But he shrank from that idea. Surely Kirsty would have told him? Why would she have lied? He shrank, too, from any idea of involving himself with the child, although he felt a little ashamed of his revulsion. It wasn't just the boy, he admitted; it was Kirsty and the boy together. The sense of what she'd become. But that made him even more ashamed. It made him despise himself, and that made him angrier with Kirsty, and so the vicious circle tightened its grip. Sometimes he thought of giving her money – he had enough to do that, now – but that only set the circle spinning faster and more viciously. And he was certain she'd refuse, anyway.

There was only one more chapter in the story. More years had passed – four or five. No, he knows exactly how many. He knows the year, the month, the day.

He'd come back to Aston as a guest lecturer, a distinguished alumnus. Afterwards, there was to be a small dinner in a restaurant with a few members of staff. They walked across the campus together towards the city centre – walked too briskly to talk, because Pieter was irritable, his mind on a deal that was hanging in the balance.

And then, suddenly, they passed the place where he'd seen Kirsty that time. Pieter stopped abruptly. The exact place – he recognised the buildings, the flyover beyond. He could hear the child Ben screaming and see Kirsty's nervous smile; he could see himself standing hopelessly by.

He was filled, then, with such boiling rage and regret that it must have seemed to his companions that he'd had an attack of some kind. Frozen to the spot, his face flushed. He wasn't a man known for emotional lability: they couldn't have guessed at the state of his mind.

'I apologise,' he said. 'I won't join you for dinner. I'm afraid I can't spare the time, after all.'

He found a taxi and went back to his hotel. He had resources at his disposal by then, people he could call on, but he didn't need them. Her surname was unusual, and she hadn't changed it. He went down to the lobby and borrowed a telephone directory – and bingo, there was her address.

36

The day after Clive Pettit's visit is a Saturday. Emily is coming for the day, and to make up for the shortcomings of the Berlin trip, Pieter has planned an outing – or rather, Sam has planned it. They're going to a theme park, armed with VIP passes and a list, compiled by Sam, of the most desirable rides.

The trip is a success. Emily loves every moment (although her idea of desirable rides proves somewhat different from Sam's: her appetite for risk, Pieter notes, is impressive) – and for Pieter it's a welcome diversion.

That last conversation with Rebecca at the top of the scaffolding has left him in a strange, friable state. He didn't anticipate, when he began on all this, how present the past would become. How vividly it would return – not just the aftermath, the anger and loneliness, but the joy. The confusion and hope that simmered on for years, until they were brutally cut off.

He can't be sorry about reliving it all, over the past few weeks. It's been a pleasure of the most exquisitely painful kind to allow himself to go back to the beginning of the story. And since he intends to banish it for good now, to settle everything once and for all, he needs to have things clear and orderly in his mind. But the conversations with Rebecca – although they're essential to the process – don't contribute to clarity and orderliness. They're unpredictable, disturbing. They throw up things he's not expecting: things that are better not brooded on, he tells himself, as he and Emily climb aboard the most terrifying of the roller coasters.

And then he smiles to himself. It's lucky, he thinks, that it's not true that he's afraid of heights. He would be shamed, in that case, by his daughter.

Emily doesn't want to leave the theme park.

'Can't we stay a tiny bit longer?' she wheedles. 'Can't we have one more go on the Death Splash, at least?'

But Pieter shakes his head, and tousles her hair in the way that annoys her.

'I've told you, I've got a Zoom call with Freya. I've promised.'

'Couldn't you do it later?'

'No, I couldn't.' The time difference, and Freya's shooting schedule, make the timing of their calls difficult. Early evening in the UK works best, while Freya's having her breakfast. Pieter has explained all that to Emily. Emily, perhaps understandably, doesn't care for Freya – but then Freya doesn't much care for Emily, either. She's adamant that she doesn't want any children of her own.

In the car Emily tries another tack.

'Couldn't I stay the night with you?' she asks.

'That's not what's been arranged. Granny's expecting you back.'

'Granny wouldn't care,' Emily says. 'She's annoying me at the moment.'

Despite himself, Pieter laughs. 'I expect you're annoying her too,' he says, and she turns towards him, cross.

'You're supposed to be on my side,' she says.

'I'm always on your side.'

'You're not,' she says. 'No one's on my side.'

He laughs, again, at the passion in her voice, and she hunkers down into her seat to sulk. Despite his best efforts, he can't get anything more out of her until they're back in the village and pulling up in front of her grandparents' house.

'None of you would care if I wasn't here,' Emily mutters, as Pieter opens the door for her.

'Of course we would,' he says. 'Don't be silly.' But she scowls as she climbs out of the car.

He has a few minutes to spare before the Zoom call, enough time to pour himself a gin and tonic. He's just heading into the sitting room at the back of the house where he usually speaks to Freya when he hears the buzzer for the entry system at the gate. He ignores it at first: someone else usually answers it. The buzzer sounds in Sam's flat too. But it rings again, steady and insistent.

'Damn it.' Peter puts down his laptop and walks to the little office behind the kitchen where the CCTV screens are. There's a van at the bottom of the drive: a delivery of some kind, he assumes. Amazon. He presses the button to open the gate and goes back to the sitting room. Freya will be on by now. They can leave the parcel on the doorstep.

There's a brief delay as the call connects, and then there's Freya, still in her negligee, waving at him from the other side of the world.

'Hello, darling,' he says. 'Sleep well?'

He misses her reply because the front doorbell jangles.

'Sorry,' he says. 'A delivery.'

'Do you need to get it?'

'No.' He smiles, adjusts the angle of the screen. 'How are you?' But then the doorbell rings again.

'Bloody hell,' he says.

'Isn't there anyone to answer it?' she asks.

'Not on a Saturday evening.'

'You'd better go,' she says, 'or they'll just keep ringing. They must need a signature.'

Pieter nods, stands up. He has to pass the CCTV screens on his way to the hall, so he glances in. The one that should show the front door is blank – the camera must be down – but someone is walking round the side of the house now. Someone who hasn't got a parcel in his hands, but who looks oddly familiar. As Pieter stares at the screen, the man comes closer to the camera, then glances up for a moment, directly into the lens. It's Ben Swarbrick.

Pieter is transfixed. What can this mean? Surely Ben can't think Rebecca's here, on a Saturday?

Answers, theories, each more outlandish than the next, pile into his head. But above them all he can hear his own voice: *Ben was a big boy, a strong boy for seven. Perhaps he killed his mother.* And he can see Rebecca's horrified face. Did she go home and repeat every word he'd said? *Perhaps he doesn't even remember what he did. Maybe he's suppressed what really happened.*

For a few seconds Pieter thinks hard. He watches Ben make his way round the house. And then he goes back to Freya. There's only one outside window in this room, and he can't be seen from there.

'Sorry, darling,' he says. 'Here I am, now.'

37

Kirsty's death made the front pages. It happened exactly ten days after the lecture at Aston: a hot Sunday afternoon near the end of the summer, when there was no other news to report. For a week or two, everyone was talking about it. Everyone had their own theories about who had done it, and why the police had no leads.

What Pieter remembers of his feelings at the time is muddled. There was, of course, a terrible grief, but that was – of course – complicated. There was also regret, perhaps even more powerful than the grief. Regret that none of their last encounters, especially not the last of all, had gone better. But there was also a cooling stream of relief that it was over now; that he wouldn't ever see her again. That she would stop haunting his thoughts and dreams.

He was wrong about that part, though. Wrong that Kirsty's death would be the end of it; that his mind would let her go as easily as that.

PART FIVE

38

Ben doesn't say anything for a while when Rebecca has finished speaking. The remains of the bacon sandwiches sit between them on the table, the dirty plates neither of them has cleared, and the things Rebecca has just finished telling him sit between them too.

What a lot she's had on her mind these last few weeks, he thinks. It's no wonder life has felt so uncertain when they've each been plagued by their own secrets, and their own secret fears.

There are things he needs to tell her, too, but he needs a few moments to work out what he feels about it all – about Rebecca finding his mother's diary, and Pieter's interest in her death, and Emily hiding in the woods. It's funny, he thinks – it wasn't funny at the time, but looking back it almost is – that he never did find out what her name was, so when the police asked him about Emily Blake, he had no idea who they were talking about. His mind leapt to those fussy old-lady customers.

'Are you all right, Ben?' Rebecca asks. 'Are you very angry? You have every right to be.'

'No,' he says. 'No, I'm not angry with you.'

She doesn't look as though she believes him, though, so he reaches across the table and takes her hand. 'None of it's your fault,' he says.

'Not telling you was my fault. Especially about the diary.'

'But you weren't not going to tell me. You just hadn't yet.'

Rebecca smiles now, but he can see that she's struggling to hold back tears. Ben hates to see her crying, certainly on his account.

He's to blame too, he knows that. All these years he's kept his mother hidden away, not talked to Rebecca about her.

'Can I see the diary now?' he asks.

'Of course you can. Of course.'

But when Rebecca starts to move, Ben holds tight to her hand. 'It wasn't that I didn't want you to know about her,' he says. 'Or that I never think about her. It's more complicated than that. It's . . .' Rebecca puts her other hand on top of his, and that feels very nice. Very safe.

'I understand,' she says.

'I wish I remembered her better,' Ben says. 'I mean – I wish I could be sure I remember properly. She doesn't feel real, sometimes.'

'You were very young when she died.' Rebecca hesitates. 'It was a terrible thing,' she says. 'A terrible trauma.'

'Yes.'

'And you had another childhood after that, with your grandparents. It's no surprise if that's the bit you remember more clearly.'

'I suppose not.'

And then, quite suddenly, there's a powerful, painful yearning for his mother. For the real live version of her, not the dreams and shadows he's lived with all these years. What Rebecca's found – it's not her, but it's closer than anything else.

'Let's get the diary,' he says. 'Let's do that now.'

Rebecca fetches the book, and when she holds it out to Ben he takes it from her gently, in the way she imagines a pilgrim might handle a precious ikon.

'*The Peppermint Pig*,' he says, looking at the cover. 'I've never read that.'

'It's a good story,' Rebecca says. 'We could get a copy.'

A stupid thing to say, but he doesn't seem to hear her.

'Fourteen and two months,' he says. 'I remember being that age. Year 9.'

Rebecca nods. She can see Kirsty's writing in her mind's eye: Woolworths and Jackie Downey and Mr Tollitt.

'Did you read it?' Ben asks.

'Only the first few pages,' Rebecca says. 'I'm sorry. I shouldn't have done.'

'It's OK,' Ben says. 'It's just strange. I never knew her when she was this age.' He looks up at Rebecca. 'Was there just this one?'

'That's the only one I found,' she says. 'I didn't look through all the boxes.'

It seems odd, now, that she didn't, but Ben doesn't pursue it. She watches him reading; watches his face. What will he think? she wonders. Will he see anything of himself in the fourteen-year-old Kirsty? Will he recognise the person he knew? She remembers, then, all the bits about boobs and kissing and boys having chipolatas in their pants. And about wanting more than the tedious life her parents have ended up with. She knows she ought to stay quiet, but she can't. She's too anxious for Kirsty. It feels suddenly like a momentous thing, giving her diary to her son. Laying her secrets bare.

'She sounds like a nice person,' she says. 'Don't you think?'

Ben nods. He looks dazed.

'Funny,' Rebecca says, 'and interesting. And surprising.' *Stop*, she tells herself. But Ben nods again.

'Yes,' he says. 'She used to say things that were – she'd go off on a riff, sometimes. When we were in the car together.'

Rebecca smiles. She remembers Kirsty dreaming of running away while she listened to Soft Cell.

'A flight of fancy?' she says.

'Exactly. It used to make me happy when she did that. It made me feel I was seeing inside her mind.'

He looks down at the diary, and Rebecca feels a quiver of empathy and yearning. 'Take your time,' she says. 'There's no rush.'

Ben opens the book again, and Rebecca watches him reading his mother's words, her heart beating fast. She wishes they could have had this conversation before. Years before. That he could have shared even the few little things he's said in the last ten minutes. She's underestimated Ben, she thinks. No – not quite that. All this time she thought she was protecting him, but perhaps he didn't need protecting, at least not in the way she imagined. But it's not her fault they've never talked about Kirsty, she tells herself. Perhaps, all along, they needed Kirsty herself to set things in motion.

She gets up now to pour more coffee. It's only eleven o'clock, but it feels as though the day has gone on for so long already that it should almost be evening. Waking to find Ben gone, and that visit to her father at the crack of dawn – all of that was an age ago. And the great multitude of talk and feelings since she came home again and found Ben sitting here have been enough to occupy half a lifetime. She feels dizzy from it all: from the aftermath of the fear and guilt of the last few days, and the way her mind keeps ricocheting between the past and the present. From the overwhelming relief of having Ben back, and the pressure of all the things they still need to discuss.

But the diary must come first. She needs to give Ben time for that. She puts his coffee down beside him, and then she busies herself washing up the breakfast things, wiping the surfaces, rinsing out the cloths.

When she hangs up the tea towel, the dogs turn expectantly towards her. Ben looks up too.

'We should take them out,' he says. 'We could all do with some fresh air, I expect.'

There's something unfamiliar about him, Rebecca thinks, as he stands up, pushes his chair under the table. She reaches out a hand to touch his arm, and he folds her into a hug – and for a moment she imagines herself crumbling to dust in his arms. A different man would have been less quick to forgive, she knows that, and she can still feel the risk of all this destroying them. Might he be weighing her disloyalty even now, with his mother's voice to bolster him? Might he be preparing to slip out of the life they have built together? Perhaps the next twist in their story will see him turned into a tree, or a frog, or a mirror?

But the warmth of him flows into her, and she shuts her eyes. And they're both still there, standing in the middle of the kitchen, when she opens them again.

39

They take the footpath that dips down towards the stream, and the dogs scamper ahead, their tails flying. It's a beautiful morning, and there's no one else around in this quiet corner of the countryside where fields of stubble and bare earth lie in wait for the spring.

For a while they walk in silence, as though they both know enough about what's on each other's minds to make conversation unnecessary. But in a way it's the exact opposite, Rebecca thinks: there's so much to digest, to reflect on, that she has absolutely no idea where Ben's thoughts might be.

When they get down to the muddy place near the water she slips, and Ben turns.

'I'm sorry,' he says. 'I was going too fast. I forgot about your ankle.'

'No,' she says. 'It's been fine.'

But there's a twinge now, and Ben is solicitous. There's a fallen tree just along the path, and he halts beside it.

'Let's sit for a bit,' he says. 'The dogs can have a swim.'

He throws a stick into the stream, and Ada and Bertha plunge in and swim towards it, their heads bobbing like golden seals. Ben gathers more sticks so he can keep up the game, and then he sits down beside Rebecca.

'What have you been thinking about?' she asks.

He tips his head. 'My mum.' He seems very calm, as though this isn't a big deal, although it surely is.

'About the diary?'

Ben nods. 'I was wondering – you'll think this is stupid, but I wondered if there might be a clue about who my father is. Especially if there are more volumes. It was only three years later when she got pregnant.'

'Yes.' Rebecca feels a tug of compassion.

After another moment he says, 'She didn't get on very well with Grandma and Grandad.'

'I guess that's quite common for teenagers.' Rebecca hesitates, gathers her courage. 'But you know, the way they talk about her sometimes . . .' She stops again. 'It surprises me a bit,' she admits. 'They sound – I mean, your grandma does, and your grandad did – sometimes they sound a bit critical of her. As if it's only the bad bits they remember.'

'Maybe that's deliberate,' Ben says. 'So I wouldn't miss her so much.'

That possibility has never occurred to Rebecca. Can you stop a child missing his mother by maligning her? Surely that's not how most bereaved parents would behave. More likely, she thinks, they wanted to stop Ben idolising Kirsty, so that they came first in his affections.

'At least now you'll know your mother's side of things,' she says.

Ada drops a wet stick at her feet just then, and she picks it up and throws it back towards the stream. But her aim is less good than Ben's, and it lands out of reach in the bramble thicket at the side of the path.

Ben's mind is very full as they make their way back across the fields and up to the road. The diary has set off a series of firecrackers inside his head, each one illuminating some thought or idea for a moment before another one snatches his gaze away. In the midst of it, it feels like a tremendous effort to think or say anything ordinary enough for a mild March morning.

'Perhaps we could look for some more diaries this evening,' he says.

'Sure.'

He said something similar down by the stream, Ben remembers. He hopes Rebecca won't think he's being greedy. It ought to be enough, what she's found for him. A precious thing: his mother's voice. Is it wrong to want more? He'd dearly love to find a diary from the years after he was born, of course, but it's not just that. It's wanting to follow the trail of his mother's life as far as it leads. Towards that cliff-edge she had no idea was coming. And wanting, along the way, to catch hold of the things he's shied away from all this time.

He stops to hold a gate open for Rebecca, and then there's a thought, a sentence, he can share.

'She wouldn't talk about my father,' he says. 'She never told me anything about him. I couldn't stop myself asking sometimes, and she'd get cross. All she'd ever say is that he was tall and handsome, like me.'

Rebecca takes his hand. 'That's sweet,' she says – but Ben shakes his head.

'I used to worry that she didn't love me,' he says. 'She said she did, but I was afraid there was someone she loved more. My father, perhaps. I hoped it was him. I wondered—' He stops. He's never said any of this to anyone. Not even to himself, properly.

'Maybe the diaries will help us find out,' Rebecca says. 'Not whether she loved you, I don't mean—' She looks stricken, suddenly. 'I'm absolutely sure she did, Ben. She seems such a warm person. So open and straightforward.'

'She was,' he says. 'I think she was. But there were times – she'd sort of withdraw. I remember feeling she wasn't really there some of the time. But maybe that's because she *wasn't* there any more when I was remembering her.'

'Memory is difficult,' Rebecca says. 'Sometimes you get into the habit of remembering things a certain way, and when you look at the memories more closely you start to doubt yourself.'

'Yes,' he says.

'And – most people get to grow up with their parents, to develop a more rounded view of them as time goes on, but for you – it was

all suddenly cut off. And the way it happened, too, means everything is distorted. The fact that it was never resolved. It left you in
limbo. I think—'

Rebecca stops abruptly in the middle of the field. Ben can tell
she's weighing something up, wondering whether she dares to say it.

'Go on,' he says, after a moment.

'I think you need to know what happened to her.' Rebecca looks
at him. 'I think you need to know who killed her. And why.'

Ben nods, but he can't say anything for a moment. She's right,
he thinks. She's absolutely right about all those loose ends, all those
unanswered questions, and what they've made him feel. But . . .

'But there were no leads,' he says. 'The police got nowhere.'

'I know.' Rebecca's eyes are very wide. 'But perhaps – we might
find something, some new information, in the diaries.' She swallows. 'I think we need to try. Unless you . . . Perhaps it's not what
you want.'

'It is,' he says. 'Of course it is.'

So he can lay his mother to rest, he thinks. He's heard people say
that, but he's never imagined being able to do it.

The house feels very quiet when they get back. The dogs, tired from
their swimming, flop down on the rug in the sitting room.

Ben and Rebecca decide to finish the first volume of diary before
searching the boxes for more, and this time they sit side by side on
the sofa and read together. As they turn the pages, Rebecca feels a
twinge of disappointment: once the excitement of the new year is
over, the entries subside quite rapidly into a chronicle of small
events (Kirsty forgetting her homework, arguing with her parents,
falling out with Jackie). There's very little of the eager introspec-
tion which so struck Rebecca when she read those first few pages.
Through February and March the entries become more sporadic.
Oops, long gap!! Kirsty writes, several times, or *Hasn't been much
to report!*

Things pick up a bit in the summer holidays: there's a week in a
caravan in Wales and a crush on a boy called Simon, which consists

mostly of Kirsty loitering near the campsite shop in the hope of seeing him, but it comes to nothing. *Anyway,* she writes defiantly, *I like older boys better.* Then there's Kirsty's fifteenth birthday in early October, and the new clothes she buys with her birthday money (a blouse with a Lady Di collar is clearly the height of sophistication), and a Hallowe'en party reported in a self-conscious, self-deprecating tone. *Well, I should've known Hallowe'en would be a disappointment. Got soaked at the apple bobbing and everyone laughed. How did Jackie manage to make it look so sexy?* Rebecca can just imagine Kirsty trying to laugh along with everyone else as water dripped from her Lady Di fringe.

'Do you think she seems anything like me?' Ben asks, as Christmas approaches and the drama of the school disco looms large.

Rebecca risks a smile. 'I think she knew her own mind,' she says. 'That's very like you. And . . .' She hesitates, choosing her words carefully. 'I think she had a quiet side to her,' she says, 'but she had a good sense of humour too.'

'I remember her laughing,' Ben says. 'I don't know if she laughed a lot, or if I just remember the times she did.' He glances down at the book, as though it might offer up an answer. 'I remember laughing with her at something on the telly. Not something that was supposed to be funny: just someone smiling in a strange way that we both thought was hilarious.'

Rebecca makes a little noise of amusement and encouragement.

'I remember her dropping me at school,' Ben says. 'I remember her hugging me before she left, and not wanting to let her go.'

'She sounds like a good mother,' Rebecca says.

'She wasn't always,' Ben says. 'Grandma said they used to worry about me.'

'Really?' Rebecca feels a flash of anger: more propaganda, she thinks.

'Grandma said she couldn't cope,' Ben says.

'Not coping isn't the same as not being a good mother,' Rebecca says. 'She was only twenty when you were two. It must have been very tough.'

Ben nods. 'We lived in a tiny flat,' he says. 'I remember that a bit – the stairs, and the glass door at the bottom.' He takes Rebecca's hand. 'It's nice, thinking about her,' he says. 'I'm glad you found the diary.'

'Shall we have a hunt for more of them now?' Rebecca asks, but he shakes his head.

'I think we should eat something first,' he says. 'Are you hungry?'

They make fish-finger sandwiches and oven chips and eat them on their knees on the sofa. Nursery food, Rebecca thinks. And nursery teatime, too. Everything has been out of sync today, but it doesn't matter. She watches Ben spreading mayonnaise and ketchup on his bread and imagines him doing it in exactly the same way when he was a little boy. In her imagination he is very much himself: a round, solemn-faced child with curly hair and long lashes. She smiles at him, and the little-boy face vanishes into its adult self, framed by a dark beard and heavy eyebrows, as he smiles back.

Afterwards, they open up the rest of Maureen's boxes, one by one, emptying the contents on to the floor. It's not until they get to the last box – until Rebecca has almost given up hope – that Ben lets out an exclamation of triumph.

'Look!' he says. He's holding up a copy of *Charlotte's Web*.

The new volume of diary starts, just like the other one, on New Year's Day. Perhaps Kirsty bought them from Woolworths in the Boxing Day sale, Rebecca thinks. The handwriting is a bit smaller now and there are fewer exclamation marks, but it begins in the same way. *January 1st, 1984. Age: 16 and 2 months.*

She was six months old in January 1984, Rebecca thinks, living in Chattington with her parents. That's a strange feeling: baby Rebecca lying in her pram while Kirsty was thinking about her mock O levels. *Don't know why I'm doing ten subjects*, Kirsty writes, in the January 1st entry, and Rebecca detects a hint of pride. *Making life hard for myself as usual!*

But more to the point, Rebecca reminds herself, they're closing in on Ben's birth. By the end of 1984 Kirsty was seventeen, and the following summer she was pregnant. The gleam of excitement in Ben's eyes tells her that he's had the same thought. He turns the pages impatiently, searching for the first whisper of his existence.

They haven't got very far when Rebecca's phone rings.

'It's my father,' she says. 'Do you mind if I take it?'

'Rebecca,' her father says. 'I hope this is a good time. I don't want to interrupt.'

'No, no, it's fine.' Rebecca shuts the kitchen door behind her. 'I should have rung you. I'm sorry.'

'I just wanted to be sure that everything was all right.'

'Yes,' Rebecca says. 'Ben was here when I got home. We've done a lot of talking.'

She feels a little shock then, remembering that it's still the same day which began with that early-morning flit to her father's house.

'I'm so glad,' he says.

She really should have phoned him, Rebecca thinks. She hates to think of him waiting, wondering, all day. She probably shouldn't tell him about the diaries, but she wants to: she wants him to know what's going on, and to offer something in return for her thoughtlessness.

'One thing I didn't mention this morning,' she says. 'I found an old diary in some boxes Ben brought back from his grandmother's flat. One of Kirsty's diaries from when she was a teenager. We've been reading it.'

'That must be very strange for Ben.'

'Yes.'

There's a little silence then, and after it her father moves on to other things. How does he manage to understand so well, always? Rebecca wonders. How does he manage to convey so much without saying anything at all? He tells her, now, about a phone call from his cousin Jane, and an article in the *Guardian* about Italian frescoes. After five minutes he says she must be busy, and he won't keep her, but Rebecca demurs. Having a parent still alive, a connection to her past, feels more than usually precious this evening. And part of her wants to leave Ben alone with the diary for a while, too.

'Remind me about Jane's children,' she says. 'Is her son the one in Australia?'

They talk for almost half an hour in the end. Her father becomes quite animated about the antics of a neighbour's cat, and Rebecca suggests that he gets one too. They never had pets when she was growing up; not even a guinea pig.

'I'm too old,' he says. 'Cats live a long time.'

'You could get a rescue cat,' she says. 'They always have elderly ones needing homes.'

He laughs. 'An old cat for an old dog,' he says. 'Perhaps. I'll give it some thought.'

When Rebecca comes back into the sitting room, Ben is exactly where she left him, sitting on the sofa with the diary in his hands.

'There's a man in this one,' he says. 'A boy.'

'A boyfriend?'

'I'm not sure. She talks about him in a sort of code.'

'Does he have a name?' she asks.

'She just calls him Person.'

'Gosh.' Rebecca looks at him carefully. She knows what this means: what Ben thinks it might mean.

'I'm going to get a beer,' he says. 'Do you want one?'

'Sure.'

As he gets to his feet, he holds the book out to her. 'Have a look,' he says. 'You might be able to read more between the lines than me. It starts in the autumn.'

Rebecca flicks through the first half of the year, halting in August, on results day.

'Your mum did really well in her O levels,' she calls through to the kitchen.

'I saw that.'

In September, Kirsty is exclaiming over how hard her A levels are and talking excitedly about a public-speaking competition (*I thought my speech was rubbish, but Mr Tollitt said it was good, which didn't please Jackie*). For a moment Rebecca imagines a different future for her: university, a career. And then she thinks: it's Ben's existence that sent Kirsty's life off course. But she puts that thought aside. They haven't got that far yet.

In October, the boy Ben mentioned appears for the first time. From the beginning, Kirsty's account is uncharacteristically cryptic: it's not clear where or how she met him, or what his status is, but the fact that she chose to be enigmatic about him is interesting in itself, Rebecca thinks. *Met Person on Saturday*, she writes. *Don't need to write about it*.

Don't need to write about it because it was so significant – because they kissed, maybe even had sex, and Kirsty was sure she'd never forget it? Or because it wasn't important? But Person reappears almost every week over the next couple of months. It was definitely something, Rebecca thinks.

There's an upsurge in entries about day-to-day events around this time, and an increasing number of complaints about her parents. *Dad really pissing me off*, Kirsty writes, *especially when I have friends round*. And *Mum never stands up to him*. The latest tiff with Jackie is recorded, and Jackie's succession of fleeting boyfriends is documented with exclamation marks and a hint of deprecation.

Is all this designed as camouflage for the Person entries? They're brief, but Rebecca can feel a thread of tension running between them, as though these are the sentences that matter in the story of this period of Kirsty's life. *P bought me a present*, she writes, in the third week of November. And then, a few pages later, *Let Jackie try my Opium*. Rebecca puts the diary down for a moment. Did Person, whoever he was, buy Kirsty a bottle of Opium? That would have been an expensive gift for a teenager.

Ben comes back into the sitting room with two cans of beer and a bowl of crisps.

'I've got to the Person bit,' Rebecca says. 'I think he might have been a bit older than her. Either that or from a rich family.'

'Why?'

'He seems to have bought her some expensive perfume,' Rebecca says. 'Yves Saint Laurent's Opium. Even a small bottle would have cost a lot.'

'So he was her boyfriend, then?'

Rebecca shakes her head. 'It's hard to tell. She just writes *Saw Person*, most of the time. Nothing about them going on dates, or anything like that. But perhaps she chose not to write about them.'

'Why would she not, though? She writes about other stuff.'

'Exactly. But teenage girls like a bit of secrecy. Maybe she was worried someone might find the diary.' Although that didn't stop her recording her feelings about Jackie, or her parents, of course, and who else might have read Kirsty's diary? Rebecca flicks through the last few pages: there's frustratingly little detail, and then it's the end of the year and the diary stops.

'Have you looked through all the boxes?' she asks.

'Yes.' Ben picks up his beer can, takes a swig. There's a long pause before he speaks again. 'I've been thinking,' he says eventually. 'I'm probably putting two and two together and making five, but . . .'

Rebecca knows what's coming: he thinks Person might be his father. And it fits, of course. A mystery boyfriend who arrived in Kirsty's life less than a year before Ben was conceived. But what he says next takes her by surprise.

'I need to go back a bit,' he says. 'Or at least – I need to explain some things.'

Ben feels calm now, although it's the kind of calm you feel in a crisis, or when you're waiting for bad news. For something dramatic to happen. And perhaps it is.

He hasn't worked out which order things should go in yet, but he knows where he needs to start.

'That book,' he says. 'The fairy-tale book Pieter Blake gave you. I had that book when I was little.'

'Really?' Rebecca looks surprised: that isn't what she was expecting. 'I always thought you weren't interested in the fairy tales.'

'It was my special book,' Ben says. 'Our special book. My mum used to read it to me.'

'I had no idea,' Rebecca says.

Ben shakes his head. 'How could you? I don't know why I didn't tell you, except – there are other things too. Other things connected to the book, which . . .'

Rebecca waits, looking at him. He wants to tell her everything now. About the dreams, and his mother appearing in his flat. But he needs to stick with the story he's telling.

'My mum had the same book when she was a little girl,' he says. 'That's why she got it for me. But she didn't have her old copy any more. She told me she'd given it to someone. She wouldn't say who, but I could tell it was someone important. Someone who made the book special for her. And when you came home with it, I had this crazy idea that—'

'That it was Pieter she gave it to,' Rebecca says.

Ben nods. 'I didn't think that at first,' he says. 'At first I felt – it just felt significant, somehow, him giving it to you. But because I was anxious – because I was curious – I googled him.' He looks at Rebecca: she's frowning slightly, the way she does when she's thinking. 'He went to university in Birmingham, from 1982 to 1985. So he was there when Mum was a teenager. I know it's not that close to where she lived, but—'

'He could have met her,' Rebecca says. 'He might be Person. P for Person; P for Pieter. Oh my goodness, Ben . . .'

'There's no evidence,' Ben says. 'It's just a guess. I—'

'But there's more,' Rebecca says. 'Pieter knew the family who owned Marchboys House before him. He told me he used to visit them. That's a lot closer to where your mother lived.'

In his mind's eye Ben imagines pins stuck into a map: Birmingham; Marchboys House; the village near Warwick where his mother grew up. A triangle planted in the middle of the country. And he thinks about triangles connecting people together too: his mother, Pieter, himself.

'There's something else,' Rebecca says. 'Something Pieter told me. The woods around Marchboys – they used to be part of a huge forest. And that forest included the woodland where your mother was killed.'

'What?' Ben says. 'How does he know where she was killed?'

'He said he'd been reading up about the case.' Rebecca looks at him, and Ben knows they're both thinking the same thing.

'Perhaps he knew about it all along,' he says. 'Because he was Person: because he knew my mother. Do you think that's why he bought the house?'

'Maybe,' she says. 'Maybe it is. But listen. You know how you rang the bell at Marchboys that day, and no one answered? And how the CCTV from above the front door was missing, and how Emily reappeared immediately after Pieter heard your alibi had been confirmed?'

Ben nods.

'I just wondered whether all that added up to something,' Rebecca says. 'Perhaps Emily's disappearance was a set-up. Perhaps Pieter meant to frame you.'

'You mean he kidnapped his own daughter?'

'That's ridiculous, isn't it?' Rebecca's face is flushed now. 'No one would do that, except a psychopath.'

Ben stares at her. There's too much happening, he thinks: too much to process all at once. But he can't stop now. He can't resist the momentum that's carrying them along.

'Perhaps he is a psychopath,' he says. 'There's a lot of very interesting stuff about him on the internet.'

'What sort of stuff?'

'Affairs, business scandals. Accusations of bullying. And—' He swallows. 'It turns out his first wife wasn't ill, like Emily told you. There was an accident – except that it might not have been an accident. I know the tabloids will write anything, but Pieter was on holiday with her, even though they were divorced, and while they were there she fell off a hotel balcony and died.'

There's a pause, then, that probably only lasts a few seconds but feels like an age. Long enough for time to reverse back through three decades, then catapult them back to the present, to their little sitting room at None-go-bye.

'You think Pieter might have murdered his wife,' Rebecca says. 'And your mother.'

Ben can't speak for a moment, but he nods again.

'You might be right,' Rebecca says. 'It feels like too many coincidences, doesn't it? Too many things pointing in the same direction.'

Ben waits, but she doesn't speak again.

'What are you thinking?' he asks eventually.

She looks at him then. 'I thought, when you started telling me about the book, that you might be wondering if Pieter was your father.'

Ben's stomach turns inside out. 'He could be both,' he says. 'My father, and my mother's murderer.'

Rebecca hasn't touched her beer; she picks it up now, and takes a careful sip.

'Well,' she says. He can hear the effort it takes to keep her voice steady, and he feels a rush of love. 'Person could certainly be your father,' she continues. 'Let's start there. You were born in April 1986, so you'd have been conceived in July 1985. That's nine months after your mother met Person, so the timing definitely works, although we don't know what happened after December 1984 because the diary stops. And we're not sure Person was her boyfriend.'

'What was he if he wasn't her boyfriend?' Ben asks.

'A mentor?' Rebecca suggests. 'She was ambitious. She wanted more from life. But he could still have been your father. Isn't there something in the diary about liking older men?'

'Pieter was only a few years older than her,' Ben says. 'But at seventeen the gap would have felt bigger.'

'Exactly.' She frowns. 'But at the moment it's still guesswork. Person wasn't necessarily your father. And Pieter wasn't necessarily Person.'

He'd like the first to be true but not the second, Ben thinks. He'd dearly like there not to be such a mystery about his birth. He's the wrong kind of person to be at the centre of an enigma.

And then he sees Rebecca stifle a yawn.

'It's late,' he says.

'It's not really,' Rebecca says, 'but I am tired. It's been a long day.'

'Let's go to bed,' Ben says. 'I'm tired too. I can't think straight any more.' He smiles at her; at his wise, kind Rebecca. 'We're not going to solve this tonight.'

She kisses him then: a tentative kiss at first, until he puts his arms around her and draws her in close. And for a moment, a long moment, his mother and his father and all the rest of it fades from his mind.

40

Perhaps it's habit, or perhaps it's because they were asleep by ten o'clock, but they're both wide awake again before six. Ben stays quiet, lies still, until he hears Rebecca sigh.

'It doesn't seem real, does it?' he says.

Rebecca rolls towards him. 'I didn't know you were awake.'

'Me neither.'

She reaches for his hand under the covers. 'I don't know what to do about today,' she says. 'About Marchboys.'

'Can't you take another day off?' he asks. 'I'm not going back until tomorrow.'

'But it'll only get harder.' She looks miserable: his heart contracts in sympathy.

'If you go today, I could drive you,' he says. But even as he says it he knows he doesn't want to do that, and that Rebecca won't ask him to.

She shuts her eyes again, and rests her head back on the pillow. 'I can't leave the mural unfinished,' she says. 'We need the money, for one thing.'

Ben doesn't like the idea of taking money from Pieter Blake, but he doesn't say anything. They do need the money. But he needs Rebecca to be safe too.

'Let me make some tea,' he says. 'We can think about it.'

He's just filled the teapot when Rebecca appears in the kitchen.

'Look,' she says. She holds out her phone: there's a text message from Pieter Blake.

I have to go to Hong Kong for a couple of weeks. Sam will be at Marchboys and can give you any help you need. Best regards, Pieter.

'Running away,' Ben says. 'What does that tell you?'

'His business started in Hong Kong,' Rebecca says. 'He goes there a lot.'

'It seems like convenient timing to me.' Ben hands her a mug of tea. 'We're allowed to be suspicious of him, don't you think?'

Rebecca smiles suddenly. 'This is a new Ben,' she says.

She slides a hand around his waist, and he shuts his eyes for a second, giving thanks again for the fact that his worries about her have gone.

'Do you like the new Ben?' he asks.

'I liked the old one too,' she says, 'but – yes.' She reaches up to kiss him. 'What should I do, then? Should I go today?'

'Stay here today,' Ben says. 'Go back tomorrow.'

Rebecca hesitates. 'I'm no good at skiving,' she says. 'I've never been any good at it.'

'The new Rebecca,' Ben says, and she laughs.

'OK.' She slips out of his arms then. 'OK.'

'There's more to talk about, anyway,' he says.

'Yes,' she says. 'That's certainly true.'

But they don't pick up last night's conversation straight away. Ben's not sure which of them is responsible for that, or whether they both are. Probably they both feel the need to let things settle; to think about something else for a bit. There's a fence post that needs mending, and after breakfast he gets out his tool box to fix it. While he's doing that, Rebecca starts on some sketches for her next commission, and that pleases him too, the sense that she's already thinking beyond Marchboys.

And then, as the sun comes out, they take the dogs for a walk – in the opposite direction today, through the woodland behind the church and along the footpath that leads to the next village. There's no one about, so they let the dogs off the lead and watch them romp like puppies among the undergrowth. Now and then Ben hears a twig crack, or glances up at a network of bare branches over his head, and he feels a quiver of recognition, stronger for that glimpse of his mother through her diaries. His mind is conditioned to recoil – but he won't shy away from it any more, he tells himself. He'll face it head on. He owes that to himself, and to Rebecca.

After half an hour they reach the top of a little rise where there's a gap in the trees and a view down across the sloping fields. Ben stops, and Rebecca stops beside him.

'Lovely,' she says. 'What a pretty place this is.'

Ben glances at her, then back at the view. This is the moment, he thinks. He can't let it pass or his courage will fail.

'I don't know if you noticed the cover of that book,' he says. 'The fairy-tale book. Two people walking through a forest.'

Rebecca turns towards him. 'Yes.'

'I think it's where my nightmare comes from.' Ben holds his breath for a second. 'My mother's always with me,' he says. 'It's always the two of us, running through the trees. And at the end she's dead. I find her, underneath a tree. Her head's been chopped off, and I'm holding an axe covered in blood.'

Rebecca stares at him. Ben makes a sound which is part nervous laugh and part whimper.

'What are you thinking?' he asks. 'That Pieter was right? That I killed her?'

'No.' Rebecca shakes her head. 'Of course not.'

She wants to hold him, to reassure him, but she can't move just yet. She can still feel the shock of his words percolating through her.

'What an awful thing,' she says. 'I'm so sorry. It's no wonder . . .'

No wonder he was so upset by Pieter's accusation, she's thinking. No wonder he didn't tell her the whole truth about the nightmares, either. No wonder they keep coming back. She remembers her father's words: *an experience like that leaves terrible scars*.

'Sometimes I think maybe I did,' Ben says, and she can tell by his voice, by the tiny space it comes from, how painful it is to speak these words. 'There's so much I don't remember. Maybe . . .'

'But you were in the car when the police came,' Rebecca says. 'There was no axe, was there? And no blood. Nothing to suggest—'

'No,' he admits.

'Of course you felt guilty,' she says, remembering more of her father's wisdom. 'You sat in the car all the time she was being killed. You weren't there to help her.'

To her horror, Ben's crying now.

'Oh Ben,' she says, 'I didn't mean to upset you. That's the last thing I wanted . . .'

'You haven't,' he says. 'It's not—'

He takes her in his arms now, and for a while they stand in silence under the trees, and Rebecca feels so full of love and pain and regret, so much in need of giving comfort and of being comforted, that she can't imagine ever breaking this embrace. She can't imagine them going back to being two separate people, going about their lives. She wishes they could be Elvira and Arkady, turned into two trees whose branches are intertwined forever.

'If Pieter killed her,' Ben says at last, 'then we need to prove it. You're right: I need to know. And my mother deserves justice.'

41

When they turn towards home, things feel different. Lighter, Rebecca thinks, but also more purposeful. There's something of that momentous, fizzing feeling of being in love for the first time.

After a few moments, Ben says, 'So where are we?'

'On Pieter?' Rebecca asks. Ben nods. 'He could be your mother's Person,' she says. 'And there's his interest in her murder, and the thing about the woods, and his wife's death . . .'

'And trying to put me in the frame,' Ben says. 'There's no reason to do that unless he wanted to divert attention from himself.'

Rebecca feels a twinge of anxiety. She's more conscious, this morning, of the perils of this quest they've embarked on: looking for Ben's father and his mother's killer at the same time, possibly in the same person. She's more concerned about what it might do to Ben if that turns out to be true. She can't detect the tiniest trace of Pieter in Ben, but genes are strange things. She is her mother's daughter, after all.

'It does all feel quite suspicious, doesn't it?' she says carefully.

'Do you think he hired you on purpose, then?' Ben asks.

Rebecca stops dead and stares at him. That question hadn't occurred to her, but of course it's the obvious one. It's the key to the whole thing. Swarbrick's not a common surname, and if Pieter was looking for Ben, for anyone in Kirsty's family, he could easily have found her website.

'He must have done,' she says. 'If he knew your mother, it can't be chance that I've ended up working at Marchboys.'

'So either he's not Person at all, or he planned all of this?'

'Yes.' Rebecca nods slowly. 'Because if he knew your mother back in 1984, and they lost touch, and there was no more to it – and then by total coincidence he happened to employ me – he'd have reacted differently when your mother's name came up. When he realised who I was.'

'Did he mention her name first, or did you?' Ben asks.

'I did,' Rebecca admits. But if Pieter knew what there was for her to reveal, perhaps he'd have persisted until she mentioned Kirsty, guessing that she'd be flattered by his questions about her husband, his interest in her. Was that why he introduced her to Emily, invited her for lunch – so he could put her, gradually, at her ease?

'But I think he might have been steering me towards it,' she says. 'And if he knew your mother, wouldn't it have been natural to say so when her name came up, rather than pretend to read up about her murder? Doesn't it suggest he had something to hide?'

'So if he *is* Person, it seems likely that he killed her,' Ben says.

'Exactly. And he's got away with it, hasn't he? No one's come close to identifying him for almost thirty years. But suppose he's been afraid, all this time, that you might recognise him? You saw the man who got out of the white car that day. Pieter's photograph is in the papers sometimes. What if the only way to be sure he was safe was to find out what you knew? What you remembered? And then he stumbled on a way to do that.'

This is the crux of it, she thinks. She can see, now, how it all hangs together.

'Did he ask you if I recognised the man in the car?' Ben asks.

'Not directly, but he talked about how much you saw. How much you could have seen.'

'Maybe he still wasn't satisfied,' Ben says. 'Maybe he thought it would be safer to make you suspicious of me. To suggest I'd killed my mother, and then frame me for his daughter's kidnap.'

'Yes,' Rebecca says. 'He was never going to get you convicted for a crime that didn't happen, and he couldn't have kept Emily missing forever – but maybe he thought once the police had you locked up he could feed them his line about you killing your mother, and they might believe it. Might pursue it. And certainly, if you ever tried to identify Pieter as the man in the white car after that, they'd dismiss it out of hand.'

'But he couldn't have done all that,' Ben says, 'if I hadn't gone to Marchboys that Saturday evening.'

'No,' Rebecca admits. 'That was a bit of luck for him.'

She thinks back to Monday now, remembering the strangeness of Pieter's behaviour with a shudder. How he waited for her outside the police station and insisted she came home with him, then asked all those questions about living with a psychopath. He enjoyed tormenting her, she thinks. Why didn't it strike her then how strange it was that Emily appeared out of the woods almost immediately after Ben's alibi was confirmed? Did Pieter text Emily from his study to let her know the game was over? Was he watching her walk towards the house when Rebecca burst in to tell him the good news? And when he went out to greet her, grabbed her by the shoulders, was he reminding her what to say to the police? Warning her that he needed to seem angry with her?

Perhaps Ben has followed some of this train of thought, because he says, 'He might have harmed you. He's had you in his house all this time.'

'But if he'd harmed me, it would have blown his cover,' Rebecca says. She hesitates. '*Do* you remember anything about the man who got out of the car that day?' she asks. 'Is there any chance you'd recognise him?'

There's a long pause before Ben replies. 'I really don't know what I remember,' he says. 'I can call up a picture – but it was so long ago, and . . .' Rebecca waits. 'He was wearing things that made it hard to see what he looked like.'

Rebecca's heart quickens. 'What sort of things?'

'A hat, I think. A white hat. The kind you might wear on the beach.'

'It was August, wasn't it?'

Ben shakes his head. 'But he wasn't wearing summer clothes. He was wearing some kind of long coat. All of him was pale, like the car. At least, that's what the picture in my mind looks like.'

'A raincoat?' Rebecca asks. 'A mac?'

Ben nods. Nothing like that was found, Rebecca thinks. No trace of the man at all. Could a sun hat and a raincoat be an attempt to disguise himself? She remembers something Pieter said: *It's possible that the white car was following them.* Was he doing that thing killers sometimes do in TV dramas – raising the stakes by planting a clue? Or offering a lead she could feed Ben, to jog his memory?

They've almost reached the road again, and they stop to put the dogs back on their leads. Rebecca has the same feeling, just then, that she used to get sometimes when she climbed down from the scaffolding at Marchboys: the feeling of emerging from a land of fairy tales and rejoining the real world. Except that the fairy tale has insinuated itself into the real world this time, she thinks. And the truth is that it's been there all the time, in the background of their lives.

When they get back to None-go-bye, Ben heats up tomato soup while Rebecca makes toast. They need to be practical, he thinks, as he pours the soup into bowls. It's not enough to work out for themselves what has happened.

'What should we do, then?' he asks, when they're sitting down. 'Should we take the diaries to the police?'

'I think we need more information,' Rebecca says. 'It would just sound like a conspiracy theory, and . . .'

And after the Emily saga – after his arrest – the police would be highly sceptical, Ben thinks.

'But if we're right,' he says, 'then we can't let him get away with it. We have to make the police listen. However rich and powerful he is, we have to stand up to him.'

Rebecca looks uncertain: is she worried they've hit a dead end? He's not going to let that happen, Ben tells himself. This matters too much.

'There are things the police could look into,' he says. 'They could find out where Pieter was living when my mother died. They could investigate the CCTV system at Marchboys House. They could check his phone records for the day Emily was missing, to see who he called that afternoon.'

'But they'd need a warrant for most of those things,' Rebecca says. 'And I'm afraid they'd need a better reason than we can give them.'

'Then perhaps we could ask to see the case files for my mother's murder,' Ben says. 'There might be things – details that meant nothing at the time, or weren't followed up – which point to Pieter.'

He can see that Rebecca is impressed by his determination. The new Ben, he thinks.

'It's worth trying,' she says. 'Under the Freedom of Information Act, perhaps. I don't know if that covers police records, but we can find out.' She looks at him. 'But the most useful thing would be to find some more of your mother's diaries. If we're right that Pieter is Person, she must have written more about him. And that's information no one else can find. That's something we might be able to take to the police.'

'So if we could prove that he knew her . . .'

'It would be something concrete to tie everything together.'

Ben nods. 'There might be more diaries at Hove.' He thinks about that: about how small the flat is; how they couldn't look anywhere without his grandmother knowing. 'Do you think Grandma knew about them?'

The way Rebecca looks at him tells him she's been wondering the same thing. 'Would she have left them in the box if she did?' she asks. 'If she knew about them, wouldn't she either have given them to you, or . . .'

Or got rid of them, Ben thinks. He can see that that possibility seems monstrous to Rebecca – but she's right. Grandma would probably have chosen to throw the diaries away rather than talk to him about them. He knows all too well how much has never been said.

'She must have gone through Mum's things after she died,' he says. 'They must have cleared our flat. Maybe she threw the rest of the diaries away, but missed the two we've found.'

Rebecca reaches a hand across the table. 'There are other things we can do too,' she says. 'Finding out more about Pieter, for example. Maybe when I'm back at Marchboys . . .'

She doesn't finish her sentence. Ben twists his hand round beneath hers and takes hold of it.

'Be careful,' he says. 'You will be careful, won't you?'

'Of course,' she says. 'But Pieter's away, isn't he? I'll see if I can draw Sam into conversation. There aren't many people he can talk to, and I'm a very safe person. A very dull, unimportant person.'

42

It feels very odd going back to Marchboys the next morning. Rebecca has to steel herself to press the buzzer on the gate, imagining herself captured on the CCTV cameras. She parks in the usual place and rings the front doorbell, and as she waits for someone to answer it she thinks of Ben standing outside the house on Saturday afternoon – less than a week ago – and she feels a burning rage which is briefly eclipsed by a flash of terror. What if Pieter hasn't gone to Hong Kong? What if he suspects she and Ben are on to him, and he's planning to silence them? Another fall from the scaffolding – Ben's van sabotaged in some way . . .

'Have you lost your key?'

Sam smiles, conveying – what? Some kind of fellow feeling, Rebecca decides. His next words confirm this impression. 'I wasn't sure you'd come back.'

He makes a grand gesture of ushering her inside. What she said to Ben last night about gossiping with Sam – she didn't entirely believe in it then, but perhaps, Rebecca thinks, it might be possible.

'Everything is as you left it,' Sam says, 'but if you need anything, just shout.'

The painting is indeed exactly as she left it, although it surprises her as she approaches. Some parts have the completed look that always makes things recede a little from her, as though they've settled into a final form that no longer requires their creator. And other parts are less advanced than she remembers, in need of more work than she thought.

But what has changed most is her enthusiasm for this project, her eagerness to be rid of it. She resolves to do her best to get it finished before Pieter comes back from Hong Kong. She'll start with the sky, she decides. The sky is blameless, and it requires less concentration. It's a matter of floating, catching the wisps of cloud as they pass: a light wash of blue, and a multitude of pale greys.

Despite her reluctance, she's soon engrossed. The brush, the colour, fill her mind. She climbs down the ladder a couple of times and moves the scaffolding tower across the floor, locking the wheels carefully in place before she ascends once more – and listening, half-scornful of herself, for noises. But the house is silent. Even Sam must have retreated into its depths – although he appears, unexpectedly, at eleven o'clock, carrying a cup of coffee on a small tray. Rebecca happens to be on the ground just then.

'That's very kind,' she says. 'Thank you.'

She doesn't say any more – doesn't express surprise – because she knows what that would do. That Sam has opened a door, and she must take care not to shut it.

'How is Emily?' she asks.

'No one's favourite person.' Sam pulls a face.

Ah, so she was right: right about Sam, that is, and the coffee. The willingness to gossip.

'Were they all very cross with her?'

'I think Pieter was secretly rather proud of her, once he'd got over the shock. He likes risk-takers. Chutzpah.'

'What about her grandmother?'

'Furious. But partly because she was afraid Pieter would blame her. That's my theory, at least.'

'And the police?'

'I've no idea.'

Ah, that was a misstep, Rebecca thinks. Reminding Sam that this wasn't just a domestic intrigue. But then he ventures his own little piece of daring.

'How's your husband?' he asks.

Rebecca hesitates. Sam's keen to know what Ben was doing at Marchboys, she thinks. To hear her side of it. She hates the idea of using Ben as currency – but it's a way in.

'Shaken,' she says. She weighs up other words – angry words – and decides against them. 'You know he was buzzed in through the gate on Saturday afternoon,' she says. 'He rang the front doorbell, but no one answered.'

Sam's eyes widen. 'I wasn't here,' he says. 'I'd gone to visit my mum.'

'Oh.' Rebecca musters her most casual tone. 'So I suppose Pieter buzzed him in, then?'

Sam doesn't answer. Rebecca tries another tack. 'I thought it was odd that the CCTV didn't show Ben standing on the doorstep.'

'The camera over the door is broken,' Sam says.

That removes a small cog from their theory, Rebecca thinks – but Sam has been more forthcoming than she expected. She remembers Pieter's tactics when he talked to her about Kirsty's death, though – a little and often, building up to his *coup de grâce* over several conversations – and she swallows down the questions she still wants to ask. But it seems Sam's appetite for loose talk hasn't been satisfied yet.

'Pieter does have an unlucky streak,' he says. 'His wife died, you know. Emily's mother. And both his parents, when he was twenty-one.'

'Really?' Rebecca widens her eyes, all eagerness. 'An accident?'

'The wife was. She fell off a hotel balcony. She'd been drinking, apparently. The parents both had cancer.'

'Gosh.'

'And the story goes,' Sam continues, 'that he lost the love of his life not long after his parents. His first girlfriend.'

'She threw him over, you mean?' Is that the right term? Rebecca doesn't care. Sam is opening his mouth to reply.

'Threw him over then died, from what I heard.'

'Who did you hear that from?' Rebecca's heart is capering in her chest now, but she keeps her voice as casual as she can manage.

'My predecessor, Mark. Pieter's previous assistant.' Sam raises an eyebrow. 'Inside information, passed down the line. He reckoned it was the key to understanding Pieter. He never trusted anyone again, Mark said. Never trusted life.'

'Do you think that's true?'

'The story, or the interpretation?' Sam shrugs. 'People like to tell stories about men like Pieter. And passing the stories down through his assistants, something never to be breathed to anyone –' he grins at Rebecca '– it's part of the mystique, isn't it? But yes, I can believe it. That his heart was broken. He certainly doesn't have . . .'

He stops. Rebecca pretends she hasn't caught the last few words. She's still reeling from what Sam has revealed: a hint of Kirsty's presence in Pieter's past. *The love of his life*. Could that be true?

'Poor Pieter,' she says. 'And his wife – it was in the papers, wasn't it? They were divorced, but he was there when she died?'

Sam gives her a lofty look. 'They were having a weekend together with Emily,' he says. 'It was part of the arrangement. Pieter had taken Emily out when Sally fell. She was . . .' He hesitates. 'She was in a mess,' he says. 'On medication. Not all of it prescribed. And drinking too much.'

Rebecca nods, as though none of this is of any great importance to her. But that might account for the story Emily was given about her mother being ill, she thinks. You wouldn't tell the whole truth to a little girl, would you? Not until she was old enough to understand. She takes a sip of her coffee – too milky, too sweet for her taste – and glances up at the ceiling, as though she's keen to get back to work, just making conversation to be polite.

'Well,' she says, 'thanks again for the coffee. I'd better get on.'

'Me too.'

There's a hint of that loftiness in his voice still, but something else as well: he's worried that he's said too much, Rebecca thinks. That's no bad thing, though. She's got something over him now. She's better at this than she thought.

*

Ben's only just got in when the phone rings. They hardly ever use the landline, and the sound of it puts him instantly on the alert: the police, he thinks, following up on something. Suspicious, still.

It takes him a few moments to locate the handset, in a corner of the sitting room, and he's worried whoever it is will have rung off by then. But they haven't.

'Is that Ben Swarbrick?' a voice says.

'Yes.'

There's a tiny pause. 'I'm calling from Hove General Hospital,' the voice says. 'It's about your mother. I'm afraid she's had a fall.'

Ben breathes out. They don't mean his mother, of course. They mean his grandmother.

'Maureen Swarbrick,' the voice says, as if he's spoken that thought aloud.

'Is she OK?' he asks.

'She needs an operation,' the voice says. A nurse, Ben thinks. Or a doctor.

'Is it serious?' he asks. 'Should I come down?'

'There's no rush,' the voice says. 'They're taking her to theatre now, and she'll be there a couple of hours. But I think you should come as soon as you can.'

Ben listens to the other things they say without hearing them clearly. The nature of his grandma's injury (*neck of femur*), the risks of the operation in someone of her age and state of health. All the time he can't help imagining that it *is* his mother they're talking about; that he's about to lose her again. The dogs have followed him into the sitting room and positioned themselves on either side of him, but it's Rebecca he wants. After he puts the phone down, he stands in the sitting room, in the dark, willing her to appear. And as if by magic, there are her headlights coming up the lane, stopping outside the house. There is her key in the lock, and her voice calling to him.

His colleague Jamie agrees to have the dogs for the night, and they drop them off at his house on the way to the motorway. They ought to be thinking only about Grandma, Ben knows that, but they both have things to tell each other, and once they've passed the first half hour of the journey in picking over the sparse information Ben got from the hospital, Rebecca mentions her conversation with Sam that morning.

'Tell me,' Ben says. 'It's OK. It won't hurt Grandma.'

So Rebecca recounts Sam's version of Pieter's wife's death – and then, more surprisingly, the story about Pieter's first girlfriend.

'You think that might have been my mother?' Ben asks, when she's finished. 'The love of his life?'

'It could have been her,' Rebecca says. 'She threw him over then died, Sam said. That fits, doesn't it?'

But the idea of Pieter Blake being in love with his mother is hard to get his head around. 'If Pieter was Person,' he says, 'and she broke his heart, why would he kill her so many years later?'

'He could have come back into her life,' Rebecca says. 'Perhaps he found out about you. Perhaps he was angry that she'd never told him, and they argued. That could be a motive for a crime of passion.' Rebecca looks sideways at him. 'Especially if she told him you weren't his son, and he suspected that she'd been seeing someone else at the same time as him.'

'Yes.' Ben doesn't take his eyes off the road, but he reaches across and puts a hand on her knee, and Rebecca lays her hand on top of his. For a moment or two neither of them says anything more, and then Rebecca speaks again.

'The thing I can't work out, though, is how he could have arranged things. Even if he'd followed you both that day, how could he have guessed the car would break down?'

'It could have been chance,' Ben says. 'He could have been stalking her, waiting for an opportunity.' That fits with what they know about Pieter, he thinks. With him sitting in his house, ignoring the doorbell. 'I've found some things out today too,' he says. 'You *can* make Freedom of Information requests to the police. They're allowed to redact things from what they give you, but you can ask for whatever you want, if it involves you. It says so on the police website.'

'That's good,' Rebecca says. 'We can ask for the files about your mother's death, then.'

But after that they fall into silence, and somehow the silence extends and extends. Because the hard reality of police records is a different thing from speculation and guesswork, Ben thinks. And because what's happening to Grandma is more urgent. Because that's the thing they need to turn their minds to now.

43

The news at the hospital is mixed. Maureen is out of theatre by the time they arrive, and the nurse who comes to talk to them tells them the operation was a success. Maureen's had a total hip replacement, and at her age (Rebecca has never been quite sure how old Maureen is, but is surprised to learn that she's only seventy-three) the outlook is good. But it took a while for Maureen to get to hospital, the nurse says. She glances at Ben, perhaps worried that he'll take this badly.

'I see.' Ben looks pale. Rebecca takes his hand, squeezes it.

'We'll have to wait and see how she is when she wakes up,' the nurse says. Rebecca catches a hesitation over that *when*. She knows, too, that ambulance response times have been scandalously long recently. She catches the nurse's eye, but says nothing. Perhaps sensing this restraint, the nurse gives her a quick smile. 'The sooner you get to theatre the better, in these situations,' she admits, 'but we've done everything we can.'

'Can we see her?' Rebecca asks.

'Once she's out of recovery,' the nurse says. 'But I don't expect she'll wake up tonight.'

'So we need to stay,' Ben says. 'Stay in Hove, I mean.'

The nurse nods. 'That might be a good idea,' she says. 'At least for tonight.'

It's not good timing, Rebecca thinks. They only went back to work today. But it doesn't matter about Marchboys, and Fortescue's will understand, surely.

*

It makes sense, they agree, to stay at Maureen's flat. But her spare room is tiny, the bed hardly big enough for Ben, let alone both of them. One of them could have Maureen's room, Rebecca thinks, but she knows that's out of the question. While Ben potters in the kitchen, she finds some sheets and makes up the spare bed.

Ben's sitting at the dining table when she comes through. He pushes a mug of tea towards her. 'I was thinking,' he says, 'that maybe we should . . .'

He doesn't finish the sentence, but Rebecca knows what he means. He wants to search the flat for more diaries, and he's wondering if she's shocked.

'Yes,' she says. 'Why not? Seize the moment.' After all, Maureen herself is a past master of pragmatism, she thinks.

They start with the sitting room. The shelves below the TV hold a selection of DVDs and a few books, and there's a small desk containing bills and papers, but there's no sign of another diary in either place. They rifle through the drawers under the spare-room bed, check the chest of drawers in the corner, and then they move on to the box room. Inside the door is a stack of boxes similar to the ones Ben brought back from Hove.

'This looks more promising,' Rebecca says.

But although they find plenty of clues to Maureen and Terry's lives (old magazines, laddered tights rolled together in a ball, rusty tools) there's nothing of any relevance to Kirsty. Behind the boxes there are various household appliances, most of them broken. Apart from the bathroom and kitchen, that only leaves Maureen's bedroom.

As they shut the last cupboard in the kitchen, Rebecca looks at Ben. For such a small place, it has taken a long time to search. Ben must be tired; she certainly is. They've been up since six, and he's done a lot of driving. And it's exhausting, going through all this stuff: the weight of other people's possessions, other people's lives, with the smell of the past coming off them.

'It's almost midnight,' she says.

'Do you want to stop?'

Rebecca hesitates. They're down to their last chance of finding another diary, and it would be better, she thinks, to go to bed with some hope still alive. And there's another twist too: if there's anything to be found in Maureen's bedroom, then surely Maureen must know about it. She must have kept it from Ben deliberately.

Can Ben read any of this in her face? She can't bear the idea of Maureen keeping the last vestige of his mother from him – and nor can she bear the idea that Maureen might never have troubled to look through Kirsty's possessions carefully enough to find the diaries. That she might have thrown some of them away long ago, without even realising.

But she's suddenly conscious of something that lifts her heart, despite herself. She has a sense, in that moment, standing on the threshold of his grandmother's bedroom, that something has changed: for the first time she and Ben are on one side and Maureen is on the other. It's wrong to rejoice about that, especially when Maureen is lying unconscious in a hospital bed – except that Ben is her husband, she tells herself. They should be on the same side. Them and Kirsty.

'OK,' she says. 'Let's go on.'

It happens this way sometimes, Rebecca thinks: you almost stop hoping to find what you're looking for, and suddenly there it is. There's a small bookshelf in the corner of Maureen's bedroom. It contains a strange selection: *A Christmas Carol*, a couple of Jilly Coopers, a book of word games, a volume of nursery rhymes that looks old enough to have been Maureen's when she was a child. And then there's a row of books that must, Rebecca thinks, have been Kirsty's. Classic children's books like the ones that came to None-go-bye. And there, inside *The Secret Garden*, is another diary.

'Look,' Ben says, pointing at the date on the first page, but Rebecca is already looking.

This volume is later than the others they've read. It picks up Kirsty's story in January 1986, a year after the last one finishes. The year before would have been even better, Rebecca thinks – the year that began with Kirsty seeing Person and ended with her pregnant – but this one has its own thrill in store. This one ought to see Ben born.

They read the whole of the first entry together, sitting on Maureen's bedroom floor. After the first couple of lines it's impossible to stop.

January 1st, 1986. Age: 18 and 2 months. Height: 5'1". Weight: 9 stone 2. I've put on more than I should, the midwife says. You'll have to watch it a bit, Kirsty, or you'll have too much to lose after Baby arrives. But then she feels my stomach and says, my goodness, he's going to be a big chap. She looks at me with a mixture of admiration and pity. Better than disapproving, though. We've got past the point for disapproval, I suppose. Anyway: eyes still green, hair still brown with a bit of ginger, bra size 34D. My boobs have certainly come on this year, ha ha.

Best friend: still Jackie Downey, I think. Jackie's been a bit funny lately. No one actually ends up pregnant in Jackie magazine, so it's like I've shown them all what the game is really about – me, Kirsty Titch Swarbrick, the last person you'd expect, zooming up a ladder to the winning square. Not that anyone could possibly fancy me any more, but they all know someone did. Someone really did. And I'm not saying who, which makes Jackie really furious. At first she tried to tease it out of me. Bet it's Mr Tollitt, she said. That made me laugh. Then she tried sulking, but I didn't budge. I've always been a stubborn little cow, my mum says. But I've got my reasons.

The midwife tried to get me to tell too. It's important for Baby, she said. She said it was in case there's any diseases in the family, but I know there's other reasons, like child support. I said I didn't know. I gave her a little smirk, like I was the kind of girl who'd slept with loads of boys and never knew their names, but she didn't look convinced.

Anyway. Favourite subject: nothing, really. I kept going into school for a while, but it got a bit awkward, to be honest. I'm doing antenatal classes instead now. But since they've decided I need a Caesarian I don't need to know all that stuff about breathing and the cervix, which is a relief. Baby's too big and you're too little, Kirsty. One advantage of being a Titch. The other way doesn't sound like much fun.

You sound a bit doubtful about it all, the midwife said the other day, when I made a joke. You're supposed to be dead serious, as a teen mum. But I am serious really. It was my choice to have the baby. I was a bit surprised they were pleased. Not Mum and Dad, I don't mean – they're not pleased about any of it – but the doctors and midwives and all that. And I was pleased they were pleased. I felt like I'd done the right thing for once. Keeping it too – although they keep reminding me I can change my mind about that. I could let some nice childless couple adopt my baby.

I know I won't change my mind, though. It's funny – I'm never usually all that sure about things, but I am about this. I know I won't ever give away my baby. Sometimes I lie there at night with my huge great stomach and I can't believe it's really happening to me, but I'm not sorry about it. About him – they told me that at the scan. A little boy. I lie there with him inside me, kicking away, and it's like my body's made a choice – it's chosen this for me, and that's what I'm meant to do now. It's my baby, and I'm its – his – mother.

I can't imagine what it's going to be like, though. If you can stand having a huge stomach, this bit's easy – lots of people looking after you, asking how you are, and all the time you're magically growing another person inside you without even thinking about it. But when it's born, when you have to look after it – they try and teach you about that, but it feels like a game, playing with dolls and bags of flour. You just wait, my mum says. No lying around all day then. You're in for a shock. Other girls in the antenatal group, their mothers come to the classes and make things for the baby, and they seem really excited about it. Sometimes I feel a bit jealous, but then I think – I won't have to share my baby with my mum. She won't always be trying to take it off me and showing me how to hold it. She's never liked babies. That's why there was only *one of me. One look at you, she used to say. She doesn't really mean it, I know, but I hope I'm going to like babies. I hope I'm going to like mine.*

Whoa, Kirsty – don't get ahead of yourself, eh?

So, best Christmas present: rainbow leg warmers. Wow, a fashion item you can wear when you're as pregnant as a whale! I really like the rainbow ones, and Jackie hasn't got a pair like them. Yet. Worst Christmas present: a bottle steriliser. It was on offer in Boots, I know, because I saw it there, but I'm not giving my baby bottles, I've told Mum that.

Favourite film of the year: Terms of Endearment. I saw it on the telly and I couldn't stop thinking about it afterwards. It's a real weepy, but I felt like I was crying for different reasons from everyone else. Most people cry because Debra Winger was really young and beautiful and she only found out the truth about love and about her mum when she was dying. I cried because I wished I loved my mum more, and I wished she loved me more. I cried because I hated the idea of dying and leaving my baby. And because being pregnant makes you feel everything more, but at the same time it makes you feel fuzzy and muffled, as though you've got leg warmers over the whole of you.

Favourite single: 'Every Breath You Take' by the Police. Yeah, that's not new either. Maybe I like old things, now I'm so old. But I love that song, I love those words. I love the idea that someone is watching every breath I take, and I know who it is. It's my baby. The baby's taking them with me, every breath, every step. He's listening to every word too, and I talk to him now, I tell him everything. I don't even feel like an idiot doing it, because he's part of me, and he understands.

When they get to the last paragraph, Ben takes Rebecca's hand, and she thinks that she's never been so touched by anything in her life. By Kirsty's words, and what they must mean to Ben, but also by the fact that he reached for her hand while he was reading them. There are tears streaming down her face, and she knows without looking at him that Ben is weeping too. *He's listening to every word too, and I talk to him now, I tell him everything.* Did Kirsty ever imagine her son reading her diary? Would she have shown it to him, if she'd lived?

Rebecca wants to say something, but there's nothing she can say that won't sound trite. Instead she sits there, with Ben holding her hand, letting Kirsty's voice echo in her head. She sounds just the same as she did four years earlier, Rebecca thinks – the same wit and honesty – but older, wiser, too. Someone you'd be proud to have as your mum.

And then, at last, Ben says, 'I'm glad we found this one.'

'Yes.'

'I'm glad she wanted me.'

'Yes.' Rebecca's tears are choking her voice, filling her mouth with salt. 'She was a lovely person, Ben. I wish I could have met her.'

'I wish that too. And I wish I'd known her for longer.'

Rebecca rests her head on his shoulder.

'Shall we stop?' Ben asks.

'Do you want to?'

He strokes her hair. 'You're tired.'

'Don't stop for me,' she says. 'Let's carry on reading, if you want to.'

But he shakes his head. He wants to save the rest up, she thinks. There can't be much more: you can tell the second half of the book hasn't been written in. Perhaps he's hoping there'll be something about him being born, what he was like as a baby, but he doesn't want to turn the pages and find out.

'We've found it now,' he says. 'It's not going anywhere.'

Rebecca sleeps better than she expected in the narrow spare bed, but when she wakes up and finds herself alone she wonders whether she's slept because Ben hasn't. She climbs out of bed and goes through to the kitchen – and just as she gets there, the front door opens.

'I went to buy milk,' Ben says. He's bought other things too:

croissants and bananas and yogurt. It feels, just for a moment, like the first morning of a holiday.

'Have you been up long?' Rebecca asks.

'About half an hour,' he says. 'I rang the hospital.'

'Oh?'

'They said we should come in at eleven to see the doctors.'

'OK.' Rebecca hesitates. 'Did they say how she was?'

He shakes his head. Behind him, Rebecca can just see the sea, grey and choppy. It's not a beach day, she thinks. But they've got something else to fill the morning. They've got the rest of the diary to read.

Like the other volumes, this one falters after the first few entries, sometimes leaving gaps of a week or two. The subject matter is different from the previous years: Kirsty records antenatal appointments, negotiations with the housing department, discussions about benefits – but the perennial complaints about her parents continue. At the end of February there's a triumphant announcement that she's been promised a flat, but that she hasn't told her parents yet. *Don't want to get their hopes up*, she writes, with an attempt at bravado.

Ben and Rebecca read on, alert for any hints about the baby's father, any mention of P for Person, but find neither. Perhaps, Rebecca thinks, the thrill of that first entry, revealing Kirsty's thoughts about the baby so movingly, will be their reward for finding this volume. Certainly those few pages are enough to justify the anticipation: enough to make a difference to Ben's life. But they keep going, hoping for more.

And then, in early March, only a few weeks before Ben is due to be born, there's a bombshell.

I'm shaking so much I don't know if I can write this down, but I have to. I need to tell someone, but I can't bear it to be anyone else, so it has to be me. Not that I'm going to forget this. Never.

It happened by accident. I'm sure it did, because neither of them wanted to tell me. Not to protect my feelings, nothing like that, but because it was their secret and they wanted to keep it that way.

Slow down, Kirsty. Start from the beginning. Another row, at teatime. Fish fingers and chips, just like every Friday, and they grumbled at me because I took too much ketchup. Just like every Friday. Then Mum called me ungrateful, and I said well, you won't have to put up with it much longer, because I won't be here to eat your ketchup when I've got my new flat. I didn't mean to say it like that, but they had to know sometime, and I didn't feel like breaking it to them nicely. And then they started in on me, both of them, asking what made me think I could look after myself and the baby on my own, all that kind of stuff, and suddenly it slipped out. Mum said, 'Well, you'll have to hope someone comes along like Terry' – and I wouldn't have thought anything of it, except they both went silent all of a sudden, and I could tell she hadn't meant to say it. And that she didn't just mean someone to marry me, but someone to marry me and take on the baby. Or rather – I'm not explaining this very well – she meant that Terry – Dad – had taken her on the same way someone would have to take me on.

I sat there staring at them, looking at their faces, and before they could find a way out of it I asked straight out whether Terry was my real dad, and Mum said no. Said it through gritted teeth, but said it.

So. All this time they've gone on at me for getting pregnant when Mum did exactly the same. It's a lot to take in. They've lied to me for eighteen years.

But it makes sense of things, that's what I'm thinking now. Makes sense of them resenting me – Dad because I'm not his, and Mum because she never meant to have me, and maybe because it landed her in a marriage she didn't really want. Makes sense of me never being able to believe, ever, that they loved each other. Makes sense of the age difference too, which I'd never thought much about before. Stupid me, not thinking it was a bit weird that Mum was only just twenty when I was born and Dad was thirty-two. Not thinking how young Mum would have been when they met, if they'd had a proper courtship. It gives me the creeps. Makes sense of Mum being so upset about me being pregnant too – not

276

*wanting me to follow in her footsteps – although you'd never
guess she cared all that much what happened to me. Makes sense
of other things, too, which I need to think about. All those times I
felt uncomfortable having my friends over. All those remarks
about Top of the Pops.*

*It makes me shiver, all of it. I AM shivering, curled up under my
duvet. It feels like I'm not who I thought I was. And although I
don't mind not being Dad's daughter (I'll have to stop calling him
that, at least to myself), it makes me wonder whose I am. Who I
am. I would've asked Mum, but I knew she'd just throw the question back at me – who's YOUR baby's father, eh? – and I'm not
telling them that, so maybe I can't expect Mum to tell me.*

They get to the end of the entry at more or less the same time.
Rebecca swallows. This isn't what they were expecting – a different
kind of secret altogether. She looks at Ben.

'Did you know?' she asks, just to be sure.

Ben shakes his head.

'He worked for Grandma's dad,' he says. 'He took over the
business in the end. Maybe that was Grandma's dowry. Maybe he
was promised it.' He does a little ironic sniff, a *who'd-have-
thought-it* gesture. 'I thought she fell for him,' he says. 'I thought
they must have loved each other at the beginning.'

Rebecca waits a moment, weighing things up. 'Does it upset you?'

'I suppose it does. I've never known who my dad is, and now I
don't know who my grandad is either.'

He's missing three-quarters of his ancestors, Rebecca thinks.
That's a lot to get your head round. He hoped to find out new
things from this diary, not to lose things he already had.

'He wasn't always nice to her,' Ben says. 'Grandad, I mean,
wasn't always nice to Grandma. I saw that, even when I was little.
And Mum saw it too, didn't she? Saw that things weren't right.'

Ben's still staring at the pages they've just read, and Rebecca sits
quietly beside him, but her thoughts are racing on now. Might this
revelation be important, she wonders, even though it wasn't what

they were looking for? A piece of the jigsaw they can't place at the moment? Perhaps Kirsty tried to find her real father. Could that have led her, somehow, into danger?

She glances at Ben, wondering whether to say that – and wondering, too, whether finding out how his mother got pregnant, and why it was such a secret, feels more important just now than finding out who killed her. There have always been two threads running alongside each other, she thinks, and there has always been the difficult possibility that both of them lead to the same person. Has the frame shifted now? Because Kirsty found herself on the same quest as Ben?

She looks at him, at his large hands resting on the table.

'Are you OK?' she asks.

'Yeah.' Ben sits still for a moment longer, then he closes the diary with a sigh. 'Let's go,' he says. 'Better to be early for the doctors.'

44

Grandma is on a normal ward now, a surgical ward with patients of all ages. The nurse who points out her bed follows them over, then shakes her shoulder gently.

'Your son's here, Mrs Swarbrick,' she says.

'Grandson,' Ben says. The nurse smiles. She looks nice, Ben thinks. About their age; someone you could trust.

'She's sleepy still,' the nurse says. 'You might not get much out of her.'

'But she's awake?' Ben asks. 'She's been awake?'

'On and off.' She nods at the drip stand beside the bed. 'She's not really eating or drinking yet. But it's early days.'

Ben raises his voice a little. 'Hello, Grandma,' he says. He reaches out his hand tentatively to touch her arm. 'It's Ben. We've come to see you.'

Nothing happens for a moment, and then her eyes snap open.

'Where've you been?' she mumbles. 'I've been waiting.'

Ben leans in a bit closer. 'We were here last night, but you probably don't remember.'

'You've been gone a long time,' Grandma says. The words are a bit slurred, but it's her voice. 'You've missed Kirsty and the boy.'

Ben's heart leaps and falls. He looks around at the nurse, and she smiles reassuringly.

'I'm here, Grandma,' he says. 'I'm the boy. I'm Ben.'

'A bit of confusion is very common after an operation,' the

nurse says. Ben can't be sure whether Grandma heard her, or whether her scowl is directed at him.

'Where've you been?' she asks again – and then her eyes drift shut once more and her face slackens.

'OK,' he says, in the way he might when faced with a broken boiler. Keeping calm, assessing the situation.

'They explained,' Rebecca says, 'about how long it took for her to get here, and . . .'

The nurse nods. 'One of the doctors will come and talk to you,' she says.

It's a long day. Time feels different in a hospital, though – sometimes two hours pass without you noticing, but then half an hour can stretch out and out so you wonder how you'll ever get through a whole day. When they're not sitting with Grandma, they wander the corridors, buy cups of coffee from the café, talk about anything except his mother and the diaries.

The doctor does come and speak to them, but no one can really tell them anything definite about Grandma's condition. It's a matter of time, they say. It's a waiting game. Now and then she opens her eyes and they lean forward eagerly – *Hello, Grandma, how are you feeling? Do you remember what's happened?* Once or twice she mumbles something in reply which they try to decode, and then she slides back into sleep. Sometimes the bustle on the ward, the other patients coming and going to physiotherapy and X-ray, makes Ben feel hopeful, and at other times the contrast with Grandma, lying so still in her bed, makes things feel worse.

And beyond that, beyond the hope and the discouragement, is the question of what he's hoping *for*, exactly. Not just for Grandma to get better, he admits. He's hoping for answers. For information she's kept from him, all this time. He doesn't want to believe she's slipped into this state of delirium for good.

He thinks a lot, during these shapeless hours. He thinks about all those words his mother wrote. *I cried because I hated the idea of dying and leaving my baby.* Words almost too painful to bear, but more precious than he can begin to explain. He thinks about his childhood, and about his mother's childhood too – about what her life was like, in the years before he was born, in that cramped little house he came to know so well. He thinks about all the unanswered questions that have kept tugging him back into doubt and guilt and nightmares, and there's a moment when a furious rage bubbles up inside him – rage that settles on Grandma, because she's the only one left, and because now her mind has retreated into confusion it might be too late for answers. And then the rage is gone, and it leaves behind pity, and bewilderment, and sorrow. Poor Grandma, he thinks. Poor old lady. Why didn't she ever tell me about Grandad – about why they got married? Why did she keep so much from me?

When the catering trolley arrives to deliver the patients' evening meals, Ben realises the day is almost over. There's been no change in Grandma's condition. *It's a matter of time*, the nurses say again, whenever they come to check on her. But how much time?

Rebecca is reading a magazine she bought in the hospital shop. Ben watches her for a few moments, noticing the tightness in her face. The tiredness.

'It's lucky it's Friday,' he says. 'We don't – I mean, we don't have to stay here all weekend, but we don't have to worry about work either way.'

Rebecca looks up. Ben can see her thinking now – about that bed, maybe. About how long things might stay in this limbo. But suddenly she smiles.

'Let's go and get something to eat,' she says. 'Something – proper. Let's find somewhere nice.'

It's such a relief to get out of the hospital. It's almost six o'clock, but there's still some light left in the sky, a hint of the shimmering expanse of sea a few hundred yards away. The pavements are full of people heading home – people who haven't spent the day beside a hospital bed, Rebecca thinks. It would be easy to be jealous of them, but her feelings are more benevolent. You need the world to keep going, she thinks. That's all part of the relief.

They find a little Italian restaurant ten minutes' walk from the hospital which reminds Rebecca of the place her parents took her occasionally as a child. A birthday treat, instead of a party. Piccolo Mondo, that was called – the waiters all had moustaches and wielded giant pepper grinders. There are no moustaches here, but the smiling welcome and the packets of breadsticks on the table are the same. The prices are higher than Rebecca imagined, but that leads her to hope that the food will be good. She wonders if it would be unseemly to order a bottle of wine.

Ben chooses seafood linguine followed by *bistecca alla fiorentina*, and Rebecca, encouraged by his ambition, settles on bean soup and *pollo alla cacciatora*. If she manages to eat all that, she thinks, there will be no room for a single troubling thought inside her. That would be a relief, after a day of rumination and queasy anxiety.

And indeed, as the time passes, Rebecca feels something more than a pleasant repletion filling her belly. Safety, she thinks. Being here with Ben, eating this nice food, she feels safe. That thought surprises her: it's not her life that's been upended by a fractured hip. It's not even her childhood she's been thinking about today, at least not until she remembered the Piccolo Mondo. But she remembers, suddenly, the first time they met, when Ben looked at her scar and she felt that he knew what it meant. She remembers the gush of release and joy she felt then – and she feels it again now.

She takes his hand as the waiter brings their main courses.

'This was a good idea,' she says. 'It's lovely here. We should do this sort of thing more often.'

But even as she says it, even as she feels Ben's fingers squeezing hers, there's an answering voice in her head reminding her that safety and joy and pleasure are never certain. Never forever. That although the candlelight and the soft music and the red wine are powerful totems, they can't conceal the sharp edges of life. She and Ben have brushed up close to darkness over the last few weeks, and the pleasure of finding Kirsty's diaries is made more poignant by the ineluctable fact that she was murdered, and that her killer has never been found. That that person is still, in all likelihood, alive and at large – and that however hard they try to pursue the truth, they may have to live with that knowledge for the rest of their lives.

She forces herself to smile again. All the more reason, she tells herself, to savour pleasure and comfort when they can. To enjoy the sight of Ben tackling a large steak. But when he meets her eyes, she can tell his thoughts haven't been running far from hers.

'I've been thinking about my mum,' he says. 'I've remembered something. There was an evening – I don't know exactly when, but I think it wasn't long before she died. One of her friends came round, and she brought me a present – a plastic troll with fuzzy hair. Do you remember those?' Rebecca nods. 'I called it Jackie. And I think – I'm wondering if it might have been Jackie from the diary who gave it to me. If I called it after her.'

'Did they keep in touch, then, your mum and Jackie?'

Ben shakes his head. 'I don't know,' he says. 'I don't remember her coming round any other time. I don't think I'd met her before. But what I remember about that evening, apart from Jackie the troll, is that they had an argument. I could hear them shouting, and I didn't like it.' He screws up his face. 'I think I'd taken quite a shine to her, to Jackie, and I was worried that she might not come back again. And it frightened me, hearing Mum so upset.'

'She was upset, then?' Rebecca asks. 'Not angry?'

'I think so. I remember Jackie, if it was Jackie, saying, *It's too late now*, and Mum saying it wasn't. And something about *your dad*. But you know what you said the other day about remembering things you haven't thought about for a long time? How once you've – you know – viewed a memory, what settles in your mind is the remembering, not the thing itself? And then you can't tell whether it ever actually happened.'

'Yes,' Rebecca says. 'I know exactly what you mean. But I don't think you'd have made all that up. Not if the troll was real.'

'That's true.' He hesitates. 'I kept the troll for ages. I remember having it under my pillow when I first went to live with Grandma and Grandad. I remember it was still quite new then. And why would I have called it Jackie if it wasn't Jackie who gave it to me?'

'It could have been a different Jackie,' Rebecca says, 'but let's assume for now it was Jackie from the diaries.' She stops, then, as a thought occurs to her. Could Jackie's father have been Kirsty's real father? Could that have been what the argument was about? Or – even more fantastically – could he have been Ben's father?

'And you think Jackie and your mum had an argument that evening about her father?' she asks.

'Not Jackie's father. Mum's father. My grandad.'

'Are you sure?'

Ben nods. 'It was Jackie who kept saying "your dad".'

The pieces in Rebecca's mind hover for a moment, then start spinning in a different direction. A few lines from the diary – from the entry they read this morning – come back to her now. *Makes sense of other things, too, which I need to think about. All those times I felt uncomfortable having my friends over. All those remarks about Top of the Pops.* She remembers all the references, over the years, to Terry being creepy and overbearing: *He's such a weirdo,* Kirsty wrote, more than once; and *He's a tyrant. He frightens people so he can get his own way.*

What price did Maureen pay, Rebecca wonders now, for the respectability and security of that marriage? What was it, exactly, that Kirsty saw, or suspected – that she wanted to think about when she learned that Terry wasn't her real father?

She's about to speak again when the waiter appears to collect their plates and deliver the dessert menu. Rebecca casts her eyes down the list: lemon sorbet, tiramisu, chocolate tart. The memory of being hungry seems distant now. She shakes her head, smiles.

'Maybe we could contact Jackie Downey,' she says.

'I've tried,' Ben admits. 'I googled her this morning, before you were awake. Looked on Facebook and all that. I couldn't find her. She must have got married, changed her name. I think that's what brought back the memory of that evening, though.' He hesitates. 'I remember clutching the troll in my hand while I listened to them, hoping the row wasn't about me. I was relieved when I realised it was about Grandad.' He stops. 'But maybe it wasn't. Maybe Jackie knew who my real grandad was.'

'Maybe.' Rebecca takes Ben's hand again. Maybe it's better if she doesn't mention those other thoughts just yet. There might be more in the diary – the results of Kirsty thinking about it all, perhaps.

The waiter returns just then and sets a slab of chocolate tart in front of Ben, and Rebecca watches him eat it: watches the way he takes a piece from each side in turn so the tart keeps its shape. It's funny, she thinks, how much you can know about another person, and how much more there always is to know. And how even the most familiar things can seem surprising, sometimes.

It seems to be agreed between them that when they get back to the flat they're going to finish reading the diary. And that they'll make tea first, and sit together at the table just like they did this morning. None of that is discussed, but there they are, ten minutes later, with *The Secret Garden* in front of them.

They start again at the revelation about Maureen and Terry. Kirsty doesn't write anything for a couple of weeks after that entry: there must, Rebecca thinks, have been some fallout, some shockwaves from that evening, but Kirsty must have decided not to commit them to paper. When she does pick up the diary again, the tone is different, and there's some evidence of a thaw between her and Maureen.

Mum and I got some baby stuff out of the loft, Kirsty writes, in the middle of March. *It's all pretty crappy, but it's the thought that counts, eh?* And then, a few days later, *Looks like Mum's coming with me when I have the baby. Not that I really need anyone to hold my hand, but I suppose it would be weird to be alone. I'd have liked Jack to be there, of course, but obviously that's not happening.*

'Jack,' Rebecca says. 'That must be Jackie. I wonder why she didn't want to be your mum's birthing partner?'

'I guess she was only eighteen too,' Ben says. 'Squeamish, perhaps. All that blood.'

There's more, then, about cots and pushchairs and the latest news about her council flat (*it looked like I was going to get one of those horrible ones out by the railway, but now they're saying there might be one near the shopping centre*). Rebecca's on the lookout for any mention of Terry, but for a long time there's nothing. It's almost as if Kirsty deliberately stopped mentioning him, Rebecca thinks. As if it felt too important for the diary, maybe – or had her suspicions faded away by then?

And then at last, at the beginning of April, there are a couple of paragraphs that catch her attention.

> *I'm really happy I'll be moving into my flat before the baby's born. I really can't stand to be in the house with Terry any more. It's been so awkward since I found out he wasn't my dad. I've been trying to avoid speaking to him, but to be honest I think he's been trying just as hard to avoid speaking to me, and when he does he's all stilted and polite, which is almost worse than how things were before. I thought it would settle down after a bit, that he'd go back to criticising and shouting at me, but he hasn't.*
>
> *Sometimes I wonder if he realises I've put two and two together about how old Mum was when they got married, and the way he's always looked at my friends. And him being so weird now makes me more sure there's something to it. Maybe I ought to confront him about it, but I don't have the energy for that at the moment. And I don't have any evidence either. Nothing except a feeling, really. I suppose I could talk to Mum about it, but I'm not going to do that. We might be getting on a bit better, me and Mum, but there's no way she'd ever be on my side against Terry.*

When they get to the end of the page, Ben doesn't turn over. For a few moments neither of them speaks, and then he says, 'Is this what she meant about making sense of other things?'

Rebecca nods. 'I think it must be.'

There's another silence then. 'I never suspected anything like that when I lived with them,' Ben says. 'I mean – he'd speak about women in a way even I knew wasn't right, but ...'

'Your mum may have put two and two together and made five,'

Rebecca says. 'And your grandad being awkwardly polite with her – that could just be because she'd found out the big secret. Because she knew he wasn't her father.'

'Yes.'

Maybe that is right, Rebecca thinks. Kirsty wouldn't be the first teenager to come up with a scandalous theory about her stepfather. But what about that evening with Jackie, and the row about *your dad*? She waits another moment, and then she turns the page of the diary.

The next entry is from the day before Kirsty went into hospital for her Caesarian, and there's only one thing on her mind by then. *Well, this is it*, she writes. *My big moment, God help me. I hope me and the baby get out of it alive. You're not meant to think like that, I know, but somehow I feel like I'm just not a lucky person.*

Rebecca feels a jolt, reading those words. For the first time she feels like a voyeur, eavesdropping on Kirsty's fears and her vulnerability: a frightened teenager, facing the unknown. But she and Ben read on – and there's a reward, in the very last paragraph. Another precious passage for Ben.

I've decided on a name, at least, Kirsty writes. *I haven't told anyone else yet, but I'm going to call him Ben. It means 'son', apparently, and that seems like the right name for him. For my son. I hope I'll be able to do OK by him. I want to. I want him to grow up in a better family than I did, to have more chances than I've had.*

Rebecca can almost hear those words echoing in Ben's head. The same voice, she thinks, that read the story of the magic mirror to him, coming back from beyond the grave to speak to him now. She sits very still, not wanting to intrude on his thoughts, while he turns the final pages, with their account of the arrangements for the next few days.

And then, quite suddenly, there's nothing more in the diary. Nothing at all after Ben came into the world. Half a volume: the last months of Kirsty's life before she became a mother.

'It feels funny getting to the end,' Ben says. 'It's almost like saying goodbye to her all over again.'

Rebecca slides an arm around him. 'It's a funny place to have to stop,' she says. 'When you're about to be born. But at least you've got the diaries now. You can read them again whenever you want.'

'Yes. But I know it all now. I know where the trail ends.'

Rebecca leans her head against his shoulder. It's the end of the trail in lots of ways, she thinks. And it occurs to her, then, that there is no mention of Person anywhere in this last volume. That trail in particular has gone completely cold.

45

On Saturday morning, they decide they'll stay in Hove for the rest of the weekend. Jamie and his girlfriend are happy to keep the dogs, and there's no point going home now, Rebecca says. If Grandma wakes up properly, they ought to be on hand.

But the time drags, now there are no more diaries to find, no more leads to follow. Now they've said everything they can to each other about it all. *So do you think Pieter might* ... one of them begins, every so often – but Pieter's place in the story feels less certain, Ben thinks, since they've established that there's no definite mention of him in the diaries. Since even Person had vanished by January 1986.

'We should do the application to the police,' he says to Rebecca on Saturday afternoon, when they've escaped for a walk on the beach.

'Yes.' It's not raining today, but it's cold and windy. Rebecca has the hood of her jacket pulled up over her head. 'And we can keep trying to track down Jackie Downey,' she says. 'We could search for her marriage records online.' She bends down to pick up a pebble and holds it in her hand for a moment before slipping it into her pocket.

'We'll find out everything we can,' she says. 'We might not—'

She stops. Neither of them has said this yet, but Ben knows it's true. They might not find out who killed his mother. They might not find out who his father is, either.

'But we won't give up,' Rebecca says. 'There are still plenty of things we can try.'

'Yes,' he says. There's a strong gust of wind just then, and Rebecca pulls her hood closer over her face. 'We should have brought the kites,' Ben says. 'They'd have flown well today.'

They stay out for longer than they meant to. The sea air feels good, and the sound of the shingle under their feet lulls their steps into a steady rhythm. Rebecca fills her pockets with pebbles, the way she remembers doing as a child. Pebbles that were never allowed into the house once they got home.

When they get back to the hospital, the catering trolley has already been round. Maureen has been propped up in bed with a plate of food on the tray table in front of her.

'We thought you might help her with her tea,' the nurse in charge says, when she sees them.

'Can she eat?' Ben asks.

'No reason why not.'

It's the first time they've tried giving Maureen a proper meal. Perhaps it's the smell of the food – something uncannily like Maureen's stew, Rebecca thinks, reduced to a thick mush – but Maureen seems more alert. She's eager to eat too. She manages half the plateful, and then she shakes her head.

'Enough,' she says.

It's the first thing she's said that has made sense.

'Are you feeling a bit better, Grandma?' Ben asks.

She looks uncertain now, and Ben picks up her hand.

'Do you know what's happened?' he asks. 'You had a fall. You've broken your hip, and they've put a new one in.'

'Bloody waste of money,' she says.

'Of course it's not,' Ben says. 'You'll be good as new.'

She makes a *hmph* sound, and her eyes shut, and Rebecca wonders if that's it for now. If she's slipping back into sleep. But then her eyes open again and she fixes them on Ben.

'You're a good boy,' she says. 'You always were a good boy.'

They go to bed early that night, and the sea air sends them to sleep quickly. But when Rebecca stirs, sometime in the middle of the night, Ben shifts in the bed beside her.

'Are you awake?' he whispers.

'Yes.'

'I've been thinking,' he says. 'I've remembered something else.'

Rebecca wriggles herself against his warm bulk. 'What?'

'The day my mum died,' Ben says, 'there was something wrong with our car, and Grandad tried to mend it. I've never thought of it, all the times people asked me about that day, because it was before we set off.'

Rebecca says nothing for a moment. She's woozy, still, with sleep.

'Did your grandad often mend her car?' she asks eventually.

'He was good with cars,' Ben says. 'He was always fiddling around with them at the yard, cars that had been written off and things. But he and Mum argued about it that day. I remember that too. He said our car was making a funny noise, and Mum said he was fussing, or something like that.' He stops. 'Isn't it funny that I can remember that now? It's as if the diaries have opened things up in my mind. Brought my mum's voice back again.'

This time when Rebecca doesn't speak it's because her mind is racing ahead again. She hauls it back: it's important not to get out of step with Ben, she thinks.

'Are you thinking he might have deliberately sabotaged the car?' she asks.

'Why would he do that?'

'I don't know. I thought that's what you meant.'

'No,' Ben says. 'I just thought that if there was a problem with the car it might explain why we broke down. If Grandad tried to fix it but it didn't work.'

'OK.' Rebecca squeezes his hand. 'I see.'

But perhaps, she thinks, there was more to it than that. Perhaps

Terry did something that would make the car break down but wouldn't cause them to crash. Something to do with the battery, for example? She doesn't know enough about cars to know what's possible, but maybe he wanted to make Kirsty look incompetent. Maybe Kirsty had tried to keep Ben away from them, and he and Maureen wanted to get custody of him. Could that have been their plan? But if Terry had tried to mend the car, she thinks, it would hardly look like Kirsty's fault.

She turns on to her side, then sits up. This bed is too uncomfortable to lie awake in. 'Do you want some tea?' she asks.

Five minutes later they're settled at the little table by the window. It's three o'clock, and it's eerily quiet outside.

'I was thinking,' Ben says, 'that Grandad might have felt guilty afterwards, about the car. Grandma might have blamed him. Because if we hadn't broken down, my mum wouldn't have been killed.'

'Yes,' Rebecca says. 'That makes sense.' And guilt might explain the way they talked about Kirsty afterwards, she thinks. Guilt and the continuing ramifications of the secret of her parentage.

'Did you visit your grandparents often, before your mother died?' she asks.

'Not that often. I remember Mum grumbling about it.'

'So they still didn't get along?'

Ben hesitates. 'She got on better with Grandma than Grandad, I think.'

'But they were on speaking terms, she and your grandad?' Rebecca is thinking of that line in the diary: *Maybe I ought to confront him about it*. If Kirsty had done that, there'd have been more of a rift, surely.

'It was—' Ben stops, looks at her. 'It was quite like when you and I used to go and see them both,' he says. 'Grandad would get at her. There was a bit of an atmosphere.'

'You've never said that before,' Rebecca says, 'about me and your grandad. I didn't realise . . .' She smiles. It sounds as though Terry went back to criticising and shouting after all, she thinks. 'So it wasn't much fun, visiting them with your mum?'

'I still liked going there,' Ben says. 'I guess most kids like seeing their grandparents, don't they?'

'I never met mine,' Rebecca says. 'They all died before I was born.'

'I didn't know that.' Ben frowns. 'All four of them died young?'

'Not that young. My mother was thirty-nine when she had me, and my father was forty-three: their parents were all born before 1920. But actually my father's father died at Dunkirk. He was a posthumous baby.'

'A bit like me,' Ben says. 'But your dad knew who his dad was, at least.'

'He had photographs,' Rebecca agrees. 'We had photographs of all of them. I was fascinated by them when I was little. They felt like ghosts.'

'What were their names?' Ben asks.

Rebecca is touched by his interest. It strikes her, suddenly, that all this time when she's wished Ben would talk more about his family, she's said just as little about hers. 'My mother's parents were Hilda and Stuart,' she says, 'and my father's were Robert and Audrey.' It's curious: she hasn't thought about them for years, but they're there, in the back of her mind. Her ancestors. She has a glimpse, now, of what it might feel like to see the threads of your family history unravel. 'Audrey lived the longest,' she says. 'She died the week before I was born. I was nearly an Audrey too.'

'It's a nice name,' Ben says.

'I called my dolls Hilda and Audrey,' Rebecca says. 'I used to think I'd call my daughters after them too.'

She stops. She didn't mean to say that. But the tenderness in Ben's eyes now opens something raw inside her.

'I'd like that,' he says. 'If we . . .'

He breaks off, his expression moving towards dismay. It's struck him, she thinks, that this is a conversation they should have had earlier. That they might have expected to be naming children by now.

'Rebecca,' he says. 'Do you . . . ? Is there . . . ?'

She shrugs. Tears rise in her eyes, but she brushes them away. 'It just hasn't happened,' she says. 'Maybe I can't.'

He stares at her. 'I didn't . . . I'm so sorry. You always seemed so involved in your work, and I thought . . .'

'It's not your fault,' she says. 'I didn't say anything either.' She swallows. 'Would you like to have children?'

'Of course.' He lifts her hand to his lips. 'Did you think I wouldn't? Did you think I'd prefer bees and chickens to babies?'

She can't hold the tears in now. 'We're ridiculous, both of us,' she says. 'Like some Victorian couple.' She chokes a little as a laugh and a sob collide. 'I wanted to put you first,' she says. 'But I hoped . . .'

He comes round the table now and puts his arms around her, enclosing her in the warm certainty of his embrace. 'I hoped too,' he said. 'But it's not too late. We'll go and see someone. We'll go to a doctor.'

She nods, her forehead brushing against his shoulder.

'I'm sorry,' she says. 'We weren't meant to be talking about that.'

Ben lifts her away from him for a moment. 'This matters far more,' he says. 'Of course it does. The rest is just the past.'

And then he kisses her, gently, on her eyes and across her forehead and down her damp, salty cheeks. When he reaches her mouth, that rawness inside Rebecca aches and trembles. She shuts her eyes and leans into him, letting all the hurt and want and need flow between them.

46

Grandma is sitting up in bed when they arrive at the hospital on Sunday morning. She spots them coming towards her, her eyes settling on Ben first, then flicking to Rebecca.

'Morning, Grandma,' Ben says. 'You look better today.'

'I broke my bloody hip,' she says.

'I know. But they've given you a new one.'

The look in her eyes is unfamiliar. Uncertain. 'It's nice of you to come,' she says.

Ben is taken aback. 'Of course we came, Grandma,' he says. 'We've been here all weekend. You had us a bit worried.'

She makes a harrumphing sound. Ben sits down beside her while Rebecca finds a chair on the other side of the bed, at a discreet distance.

'How are you feeling?' he asks. 'Does your hip hurt?'

'What d'you think?'

Ben's relieved – mostly – to see her fighting spirit returning. 'Are they giving you enough painkillers?' he asks. 'Shall I call someone?'

She shakes her head. There's a tremor in her face, perhaps a smile doing battle with something darker.

'Are you sure?' Ben asks. 'You don't need to be in pain.'

'You're a good boy, Ben,' she says. 'You've always been a good boy.'

Ben takes her hand. 'Thank you, Grandma.'

'I was there when you were born, you know. Your mother's friend wanted to be there but she chose me.'

For a moment Ben freezes. Has she guessed they've found the diary? That they've been staying in her flat, searching it? No, surely not. And anyway, that's not quite what the diary says. *I'd have liked Jack to be there, but obviously that's not happening.* Maybe Grandma remembers it differently.

'Which friend was that, Grandma?' he asks.

'Jackie,' she says. 'Jackie Downey. They were thick as thieves, your mum and Jackie.'

Ben smiles, trying to conceal his excitement. 'What happened to her?'

'Got married, I think. Or maybe she went abroad. There was a teacher at their school moved to Canada, and they all wanted to emigrate after that. Canada or Australia or wherever.' She looks at Ben. 'Your mum might've gone, you know.'

'I didn't know that.'

Might've gone if she hadn't got pregnant, does Grandma mean? Was that – perhaps it wasn't a person she used to daydream about when he was little, Ben thinks, but a plan she'd had to give up. He feels shaky, suddenly. About all these things he never knew, and about Grandma being better, talking properly. And: *Your mother's friend wanted to be there but she chose me.* He can hardly bear the whisper of pride in that sentence. He's wondering what to ask next, whether he dares ask about Grandad – and then Grandma's face changes and he understands that the door has shut again.

'The food's terrible in here,' she says. 'Mush, every meal.'

Ben's reluctant to leave on Sunday evening, but they can't stay in Hove indefinitely, Rebecca says, and Maureen is out of danger now. She's being well looked after. And they both need to get back to work: Pieter's only away for one more week, and Rebecca's still hoping she can get the ceiling finished before he comes home.

It's a relief to get on the road to None-go-bye that evening, anyway. To be heading home to the dogs, and their own life. And if Rebecca feels a twinge of disappointment that they haven't got any closer to incriminating Pieter, she tells herself that the things they've found this weekend are important. Things that have less to do with Kirsty's death than with the landscape of Ben's childhood, but that matters too.

When they set out on this quest, she thinks, what she wanted for Ben was a better understanding of where he came from; of who he is. She's very happy that he's started to remember things about his early life, and that Maureen has started talking to him about Kirsty. It's a breakthrough, a little miracle, and she can sense the change it makes to Ben. He's particularly excited about Maureen mentioning Jackie Downey: about the idea that she emigrated to Canada or Australia – *that would explain why she didn't come and visit us more often*, he says – and the possibility of getting in touch with her.

But Rebecca doesn't want to lose sight of Kirsty's murder. It was crazy to think they could catch her killer, of course, but that's what Rebecca's hoped for. What she promised Kirsty they'd do. She wanted a fairy-tale ending, with wrongs righted and mysteries solved, and she's not ready to give it up just yet.

And then, she thinks, as they follow the trail of weekend traffic up the M23, there's that other fairy-tale ending – the one she's hardly allowed herself to think about. *Did you think I'd prefer bees and chickens to babies?* Perhaps she did, Rebecca admits. Perhaps she thought it wasn't meant to happen. That they had enough on their plates, between them, with each other. But now that the seed has been sown, she can feel the ache growing inside her. And the knowledge that it might not happen, now. All that time when she was painting the moon princess, and the old couple who were so overjoyed to find a tiny child in their garden because they couldn't have children of their own: did it never occur to her that she was painting her own fears and desires?

Everything feels very quiet at Marchboys on Monday morning. Rebecca is looking forward to getting on with the painting, after the stopping and starting of recent weeks: a straight run to the finishing line, she thinks, as she mixes a pale green to catch the sunlight on the distant hills.

Sam, perhaps fearful of having said too much last week, of having trusted someone he shouldn't with the secrets of the house, keeps his distance. For a couple of days Rebecca suspects he's not there, but then she catches a glimpse of him and realises he's been avoiding her. Or perhaps he's just busy. She mustn't see conspiracies wherever she looks. And she's not sure what more he could tell her about Pieter, anyway. She can't, for the moment, see a way forward, but perhaps it will come to her. Perhaps this is the calm before the storm, she thinks. The lull before the grand denouement.

Wednesday of that week is her father's birthday, and she leaves Marchboys early and drives straight to Chesham to have supper with him. Ben's supposed to meet her there, but he's held up at work. A troublesome boiler, he tells her, on the phone.

'I'll come on when it's sorted,' he says, and Rebecca pushes away the pleasurable anticipation of seeing her father on his own.

Her father has roasted a chicken.

'It's awfully easy,' he says, as he always does when Rebecca admires his cooking.

'A treat, though,' she says.

The chicken is ready at six, but they decide to wait a little longer for Ben. Rebecca carries crisps and a bottle of wine into the sitting room.

'A small glass,' Rebecca says. But the glasses in her father's house are all small, left over from the days when a single bottle of wine would do for twelve at a PCC meeting. Rebecca smiles, thinking of that. Feeding the five thousand, her father used to say, after every parish event.

'How is Maureen?' her father asks.

'All right, I think. I haven't heard anything today. They've been talking about rehab. Physio and so on.' She takes a deep breath. 'There's lots to report about Kirsty,' she says. 'We found another diary in Hove.'

She tells him about Kirsty's account of her pregnancy, and about the bombshell news that Terry was not Kirsty's real father.

'That paints him in a rather positive light,' her father says. 'Taking on another man's child has always seemed a noble act to me.'

'I hadn't thought of it like that,' Rebecca says. 'But I suppose you're right.' She raises an eyebrow. 'Kirsty saw it rather differently,' she says. 'She disapproved of the age gap: her mother was only twenty when she was born, and Terry was twelve years older.'

'That was more common back then,' her father says.

'True.' Rebecca hesitates. The temptation to lay everything before her father is so powerful, she thinks. Perhaps she shouldn't – but she can't stop herself.

'Kirsty complained about how Terry behaved with her friends,' she says. 'How he looked at them. I think she suspected him of having a penchant for younger women.'

'For girls?' her father asks.

Rebecca nods. 'He wasn't a nice man,' she says, 'but . . .'

'He certainly had an unattractive manner at times,' her father admits.

Rebecca smiles. For him, that's a strong statement. 'He liked to get his own way,' she says. 'He liked controlling people. I've been wondering . . .' She hesitates again. 'Ben remembered that Terry tried to mend Kirsty's car the day she died. I've been wondering if there's anything to that. Whether he wasn't actually trying to mend it. Whether – oh, I don't know. Whether he wanted the car to break down. Whether they were trying to make Kirsty look incompetent, perhaps as part of a plan to get custody of Ben.'

Her father looks at her.

'Or perhaps,' he says, 'he wanted to make sure they broke down because he was following them.'

'What?' Rebecca is astonished. 'You mean . . . ?'

'It's possible, isn't it?'

He sounds perfectly calm. She forgets sometimes, Rebecca thinks, that her father comprehends the full possibility of human evil. That it's as much his food and drink as the unconditional love of God.

'Did they have a white car?' her father asks.

He was always fiddling around with them at the yard, Rebecca thinks. *Cars that had been written off and things*. 'Terry certainly had access to cars,' she says. 'But . . .'

'I'm probably wrong,' her father says. 'Forgive me: I'm not very experienced at solving crimes.'

But Rebecca remembers, then, the other memory that came back to Ben: the argument with Jackie Downey. The words *your dad* and *too late*, and Kirsty protesting that it wasn't too late. And only a few weeks later, if Ben's memory is accurate, Kirsty was killed.

Was Jackie's visit – her return from Canada or Australia, if Maureen was right about that – the key to it all? Did she finally give Kirsty the evidence she needed to confront Terry? And is that what happened, on that last day? Did Kirsty make him angry enough – frightened enough – to kill her?

The doorbell rings just then, and Rebecca jumps.

Her father gets up and goes to answer it.

'My dear Ben,' he says. 'How nice to see you.'

They have to drive home separately, Rebecca in her car and Ben in his van. They leave early – before nine o'clock – but the hour the journey takes feels endless.

They didn't talk any more about Kirsty or Terry after Ben arrived, but Rebecca couldn't stop thinking about it. All evening she veered between conviction and doubt, and she's desperate, now, to talk to Ben. All this time, she thinks, they wondered whether Ben's father might have killed Kirsty, and perhaps after all it was Kirsty's father. Stepfather, rather. No one in this story is quite who they first seemed.

But she has thought of Terry as a bullying thug from the first time she met him. That much is true. Is that why she's so thrown by this idea – because she wonders why it had never occurred to her before that he could have killed Kirsty? Because it's alarming when your instinctive judgements about people turn out to be so accurate?

*

Ben can tell Rebecca has something on her mind. He's been aware of it all evening, so he's not surprised when she sits him down at the kitchen table. But what she has to say comes out of the blue. So much so that he doesn't say anything for a while after she's finished speaking.

It's totally plausible, he thinks, the theory she's set out. But the Pieter story made sense, too, and he'd so much rather Pieter Blake turned out to be the culprit, not Grandad. Because he wants to hold on to the idea that he had a happy childhood with Grandma and Grandad? Because he doesn't want there to be any more scandal in his family? Maybe. But the main reason is that he can't bear to talk to Grandma about it, and he knows that he'll have to. Somehow, he'll have to find a way to ask her unthinkable, unsayable things.

Rebecca is flicking through the diaries now, looking for more mentions of Grandad's behaviour.

'Look,' she says. '*I hate what he's like when I bring friends home. He thinks it's OK to say things about them but it gives me the creeps.*'

'I've been thinking about that since you mentioned it before,' Ben says, 'and you're right, he was like that when I was little too. Making comments about women. Girls he saw on the street, or on the telly. I thought he meant it as encouragement to me, to – you know – let me know it was OK to think about girls that way. But it put me off.'

'I'm sorry,' Rebecca says.

Ben shrugs. 'It didn't really affect me,' he says. But he knows that's not quite true.

'We don't know that he did anything,' Rebecca says. 'Plenty of men are creepy. Not many of them . . .'

She doesn't finish the sentence, but she doesn't need to.

'I'm sure that's what Mum and Jackie were arguing about that evening,' Ben says. 'I think I had an idea at the time, but I couldn't really make sense of it.'

He has a terrible feeling, suddenly, that he's going to cry.

'Look,' Rebecca says, 'we don't have to do anything. Terry's dead. We can let all this settle down, come to terms with the idea that it might be true. We can—'

'No,' says Ben. 'That's not enough.'

There's silence for a moment. The dogs, who were ecstatic to see them when they got in half an hour ago, are lying flat on the floor at their feet. Poor dogs, Ben thinks. He called in on his way to Rebecca's father to feed them, but they haven't had a walk since first thing this morning. They seem happy enough, though. Their needs are simple. There was a time when he thought his needs were almost that simple too – and perhaps they still are. Perhaps when all this is over, he thinks, things will go back to being simple: a better kind of simple from before.

'It could still be Pieter,' he says. 'If he was Person, he has a motive too.'

Rebecca has that burning look in her eyes again, that ferocious pity.

'I don't think it was Pieter,' she says.

'Maybe not.' Ben shuts his eyes for a moment. 'We have to talk to Grandma,' he says. 'If Grandad went out that day, after we left, she'll know.'

Perhaps she knows everything, he thinks. Perhaps she always has.

'It'll keep until she's a bit better,' Rebecca says.

'Yes.' He hesitates. 'But I was thinking we'd go down to Hove again at the weekend, anyway. If you don't mind.'

Rebecca paints furiously for the next couple of days. She's very much on the final phase now – making sure there's a consistent texture across the ceiling, the same density of paint and the same level of detail. It involves a lot of climbing down the ladder, squinting up at the great dome above her, then scrambling back up to add something in a particular place. She doesn't think about falling, though. That episode is well behind her now. She doesn't think, either, about the stories: the mural has become a painted surface, no more. And she does her best not to think about Pieter. All his questions, putting her in such an uncomfortable position, were born simply out of arrogant curiosity, if they're right about Terry – about Pieter having nothing to do with Kirsty – and that makes her angry. But there's also the matter of what she and Ben have suspected Pieter of. She cringes when she remembers asking Sam about his first wife's death. She remembers the expression on Sam's face, as if she'd lowered herself in his opinion.

But if Pieter *did* kill Kirsty, after all, and might guess that she suspects him, and she's here in his house, at the top of a ladder above that hard tiled floor – that doesn't bear thinking about, either. The only thing to do is work as fast as she can, and not think about anything except the application of the paint.

Ben is happy to be back at work again. He hadn't thought about what it would be like returning to Fortescue's after the fiasco of his arrest, but if he *had* thought about it he'd have assumed no one would know, and certainly no one would say anything. But he'd have been wrong. Each time he goes into the yard now he's greeted as a kind of celebrity, and he's surprised to find that he likes it. The only people he told were the boss and young Jamie, but one of them – Jamie, he guesses – must have felt the story needed sharing. It's like being a schoolboy who scored a dramatic winning goal, or a bystander who dived into a lake to rescue someone from drowning. He ought to feel embarrassed, Ben thinks – all he did was be wrongly accused of something – but instead he enjoys the fuss, the pats on the back from colleagues who'd barely spoken to him before, the new nicknames. The best thing is that he doesn't have to say anything himself – the others are happy to answer their own questions, to fill in the gaps in the story. *Bet it was . . .* they say. *Bet you felt . . .* Ben smiles modestly, adding to the legend that is growing up around him.

The customers don't know anything about it, of course, and that's a relief, because they might take a different view. Bill Fortescue dealt with the couple whose house Ben was arrested at – he went in person to explain it was a case of mistaken identity, and finished the job himself. Ben was very touched by that, even though he knew it was for the sake of the company's good name, not his. And Mr Fortescue was just as nice about Ben having to miss another day's work because of Grandma's fall. He's determined to repay the boss by being more than ever the model Fortescue's employee. He's picked up some of Jamie's charm, his smiles and his patter, and he likes the way it smooths his path through the encounters of the day. He's plumbing in a couple of bathrooms in a new-build this week, for a local builder who's already offered him a ready supply of freelance work if he ever wants to make a go of it on his own. Ben was flattered by that, too, even though he knows it would cost the builder less to do it that way – *everyone'd be quids in* – but he shook his head politely and said he was happy where he was.

But there comes a moment each day, when he's on to the mechanical part of the job, the bit that doesn't take much thought, when the events of the last couple of weeks filter back into his mind. When he remembers that his arrest is part of a bigger picture that's about more than a bit of fame among his colleagues, and that Grandma's fall has turned everything he thought he knew about his family upside down. He tells himself he doesn't need to think about it, not while he's at work, but he can't help it. Just a few minutes, he thinks, while he's on his way to pick up some materials, and then it draws him in again and won't let him go.

Could Grandad really have killed his mother? Could what she suspected him of be a motive for murder? Maybe they're wrong to let Pieter Blake slip out of their sights, he thinks: maybe the wheel hasn't finished spinning yet. He shakes his head, as if to make the pieces of jigsaw settle in a different pattern.

Grandad. Pieter Blake. Person. The man in the white car. His father. His mother's real father. Any one of them could have killed his mother. Will they ever be sure who did?

PART SIX

47

Pieter doesn't do regret. It's one of the things he left behind, years ago. You don't build a business like his if you allow yourself to worry about the things you've got wrong, or about the people who've lost out while you've gained. It's much better if you don't feel anything very much about any of it – about the triumphs, the ascent, as well as the failures. If you care too much, things get distorted. If one deal means more than another. He's seen it many times: seasoned financiers, people he's admired, allowing their emotions to get the better of them. Opening a chink in their armour. It never ends well. He's taken the same view about his personal life – the affairs, the dalliances. Freya is perfect because she doesn't care any more for him than he does for her. Whether that's a good basis for a marriage time will tell, but it could hardly be a worse basis than the last one.

It's not his engagement he's at risk of regretting, though. It's this other matter. And it's brought him close to the edge. Did he know it would? That worries him: that he knew exactly what he was doing. What it would mean. Where it would lead. He's in a quandary, and he's not used to that, still less to it being a quandary of his own making. And even if he can extract himself without further damage, he'll have that damn ceiling to remind him, every day. There's an irony in that which he ought to enjoy, but he doesn't.

What to do, then?

If this was a business venture, he'd be thinking about risk

management, damage limitation. Perhaps about hedging his bets. Does that help? He shakes his head. He's not sure that it does.

It disconcerts him, too, that Hong Kong feels so different these days. His parents would be shocked, he thinks, emerging from the Jockey Club after a lunch meeting where the political situation simmered beneath the surface of everything that was said. Might his parents have lived this long? They'd be nearly ninety by now. For a moment he pictures them white-haired, frail, venerable – and then he catches himself. Sentiment. Affect. He needs to be careful. Or . . .

He feels very tired suddenly. What's it all been for? The bravado; the success. The iron self-control. Has he been fighting a losing battle all this time? A battle against himself? He thinks, then, about Before. About the way the world looked that summer.

Did he mean to lose so much? Did he ever stop to count the cost?

Perhaps, after all these years, it's time for a different sort of reckoning.

48

Ben has been ringing the hospital every morning. The news has been encouraging: talk of home assessments and rehab centres. Ben has been pleased to hear it, but at the same time it's felt like lead dripping into his stomach. *It'll keep until she's a bit better*, Rebecca said. But how much better is better enough to ask her the questions they have to ask? How will he psych himself up when that moment comes?

And then, on Thursday evening, the hospital rings him. A nurse he hasn't spoken to before. Not to worry you, she says, but she's not so well this evening. An infection, the doctors think. They're starting her on antibiotics. She's a bit confused, a bit short of breath. We thought we should let you know.

'Should we go down tonight?' Rebecca asks.

'I don't know.'

'She might be a bit better by tomorrow if the antibiotics kick in,' Rebecca says. 'But they wouldn't have rung unless . . .'

Ben nods. He knows they're both thinking the same thing: if this is something serious, they need to get there before it's too late. He thinks of Grandma saying, *You're a good boy*. Of the custard-cream afternoons, the stews. His stomach squirms at the thought that his eagerness to be at her bedside isn't quite what it might seem. What it ought to be.

He catches the same nurse on Friday morning, at the end of her night shift. If it was my grandmother, she says, I think I'd come down as soon as possible.

*

It's pneumonia, the doctor says, when they arrive at the hospital. It's not uncommon at this age, after such a big operation. An emergency.

Grandma's got an oxygen mask over her face and a new drip in her arm. She looks even more frail than she did the previous weekend: a little old lady in a hospital bed.

'Is she conscious?' Rebecca asks.

'Intermittently,' the doctor says. She only looks about twenty, but she sounds as though she knows exactly what's what. 'Talk to her,' she says. 'It's always a good thing.'

She draws the curtains around Grandma's bed and they sit down.

'Hello, Grandma,' Ben says. 'We're back now. I'm sorry you're not feeling too good.'

Despite his cheery tone, he can see how ill she is. She can't really speak with the mask on, but in any case it's clear her mind is wandering again. Part of him is relieved, the part that couldn't bear the idea of asking her those painful questions, but another part is dismayed, because he can't bear not to know now. He can't bear having got so close, then having to turn away and leave behind the impossible theory that might just be true.

They spend another day toing and froing from Grandma's bedside. They've brought the dogs with them this time, and they take them for a run on the beach at lunchtime, before returning to the hospital for a few more hours. When they leave in the evening they go back to the beach and walk as far as they can go, with the dogs just ahead of them, padding along the shingle. The moon is almost full, and there's plenty of light to see by. It's so beautiful, so ordinary and beautiful, that all Ben's pent-up emotion spills over and he feels tears trailing down his cheeks. Not just tears for Grandma: tears for his mother, who died when she was the same age as that young doctor. Who might have emigrated to the other side of the world if she hadn't been landed with a baby whose father didn't even know he existed. Who was killed, on that long-ago August day, by someone who has never been caught.

They're almost back at the van when his phone rings.

'Your grandmother's asking for you,' says the night-shift nurse.

That might be a euphemism, Ben thinks. It might mean she's about to die: maybe they don't say that sort of thing over the phone. His heart races as they drive the short distance back to the hospital, hunt for a place in the car park.

But it's not a euphemism. Grandma's awake. They can see as soon as they come into her bay that she's alert, agitated. As they approach the bed, she tugs the oxygen mask away from her face.

'Where've you been?' she asks. 'I've been waiting.'

Ben takes her hand. 'We just went out for a bit, Grandma.'

She stares at him. Her breath heaves, as though it has to be forced through a layer of sponge. 'Ben,' she says.

'Yes.' Ben smiles. 'Who did you think it was?'

It's strange, Rebecca thinks, how sometimes, at the most unexpected moments, you can suddenly see the resemblance between people. Ben could almost be a different species from this sick old woman, but just now, just for a moment, you can see beyond doubt that they're related. Ben's only living relative, she thinks. The only one he knows, at least.

Maureen moves her head fretfully on the pillows. 'I was waiting all afternoon,' she says.

'For us?' Ben asks. 'Were you waiting for us?'

There's no reply. Maureen is staring at the ceiling now, her breathing noisy and effortful. Ben slips the oxygen mask back over her nose and mouth and for a minute or two, maybe longer, they sit quietly, watching her. When she tries to speak again, they can't understand her through the mask. She scrabbles at it with her fingers, and Ben reaches across to help her. Her voice is so hushed this time that they both have to lean forward to hear what she's saying.

'She was my baby,' Maureen says. 'She was my baby, not his.'

Rebecca glances at Ben. If Maureen's talking about Terry and Kirsty, then that's a huge thing for her to confess. It feels surreal, sitting on a hospital ward at night, wondering whether deadly secrets are being disclosed in these breathless, feverish words.

Ben takes Maureen's hand.

'Grandma,' he says, 'did my mum know anyone called Pieter?'

Oh Ben, Rebecca thinks. Is he still hoping to head things off that way? Maureen looks at him, and Ben smiles at her encouragingly.

'We wondered if Mum ever met Pieter Blake, who Rebecca's been working for,' he says. 'He wouldn't have been famous then, of course. He'd have been just a bit older than her.'

Maureen frowns. Her expression sharpens, as though she needs to try harder to make them understand, and her head lifts slightly forwards from the pillows. 'He was gone all afternoon,' she says. 'I should've told.'

'Do you mean Grandad?' Ben asks.

Maureen nods. There's no mistaking, now, what she wants to talk about.

'When was this, Grandma?' Ben asks. 'Do you mean the day Mum died?'

'She made him angry,' Maureen says. 'She was angry and she made him angry too.'

Her breath is sharp, tight. She clasps the mask back on to her face.

'Was she angry about what he did to Jackie?' Ben asks, and Maureen's eyes widen. 'He fixed the car that day,' Ben continues. 'I remember that. Maybe there wasn't anything wrong with it until he got to it.'

Maureen reaches for Ben's hand, but he pulls it away. At first Rebecca thinks the shock of that rejection might drive Maureen back inside herself, but instead tears start to fill the pouches below her eyes. She tugs the mask down again.

'She was my baby,' she says, 'I should've told.'

'Why didn't you, Grandma?' Ben asks. He's breathing almost as fast as Maureen, and his face is flushed, little circles of colour staining his cheekbones. 'Why did you let him get away with it?'

But Rebecca knows why. She can see it in Maureen's face.

'She didn't want to lose you, Ben,' Rebecca says. 'She was afraid they'd take you away.'

'But if the police had ever caught Grandad,' Ben says to Maureen, 'then they'd have known that you'd lied. Covered for him. They'd definitely have taken me away then, wouldn't they? They'd have taken you to prison too.'

Maureen looks terrified, panic-stricken. 'I thought you'd seen him,' she says. 'Thought you'd say something, one day.'

'No,' Ben says. 'I was too far away. He was wearing – the man was wearing . . .' He stops. It's too much for him, Rebecca thinks. For the little boy who is still there inside him, still plagued by those nightmares.

'We never spoke about it,' Maureen says. She swipes at her tears, blurring them across her face. 'All those years. But he knew I knew. He knew what I felt.'

Ben reaches for his grandmother's hand then, and tears well in Rebecca's eyes this time. In Ben's too. He takes a deep breath.

'I'm glad you've told me,' he says. 'I've carried it with me, all this time. Wondering who did it. Blaming myself for not saving her.'

'I'm sorry.' Maureen's lip trembles. 'My little Ben. I couldn't stand to lose you. So I just went on as if I didn't know.'

That last speech is almost too much for her: she clutches at the oxygen mask.

'Don't talk any more,' Ben says. 'You need to rest.' He puts a hand on her forehead – like a blessing, Rebecca thinks. An absolution.

Somewhere on the ward someone cries out, but inside their curtained bay the three of them sit in silence, the echoes of what's been said in the last few minutes filling their heads. When Rebecca shuts her eyes, she can almost believe she's imagined it all, but then she opens them again and there's Ben grasping Maureen's hand, an expression on his face she's never seen before. There are impossible things to think about – what they ought to do, what they need to say – but just for now, she thinks, it's very simple. Just for now what matters is that there's love at the centre of it. Maureen's love for Ben, which has been twisted out of shape all these years by guilt and grief and fear and regret. And her love for Kirsty too. The thread of mother-love that links Maureen to Ben through her poor murdered daughter.

49

Leaving the hospital that night, Rebecca has a strange feeling of dislocation: the kind of feeling you might have, she thinks, if you'd been caught in a siege. Neither of them wants to discuss what they've learned this evening or to speculate about what comes next. To start a sentence with *So* . . . or *Well* . . .

They walk back to the van in silence, then drive to the beach to give the dogs a last run.

'Will she be all right?' Ben asks at last, as they stand on the damp shingle, feeling the chill coming in off the sea.

'The pneumonia, you mean? I should think so.' Rebecca slips her hand inside Ben's. 'She was very brave,' she says. 'And so were you.'

'I don't feel brave,' Ben says. 'I feel – hollowed out.'

'I'm not surprised.' Rebecca looks out towards the dark horizon. 'It's a lot to take in. The truth.'

Ben breathes deeply in and then slowly out again. 'The truth,' he says. 'Yes.' There's that little sniff of a laugh again. 'I wanted it to be Pieter Blake.'

'I know. He'd have made a good villain.' But she shouldn't joke, Rebecca tells herself. 'I'm so sorry it turned out this way.'

'It's hardly your fault,' Ben says. 'It makes sense of things. It makes sense of Grandma.'

'That's a good thing,' Rebecca says. 'I'm glad that's happened, at least.'

'And it's an answer,' Ben says. 'I just wish I could have had it earlier.'

'But when?' Rebecca asks. 'When would have been the right moment? She couldn't have told you when you were little. And if she'd told you when your grandad died – well, maybe you'd have cut her off. And she needed you then.'

Ben nods. 'I suppose you're right. But even so . . .'

'Even so,' Rebecca says, 'it's been a terrible thing for you to bear. And it must feel very odd to have it lifted. All that uncertainty.' She hesitates. 'Are you going to tell anyone?'

'What do you mean? Tell the police?'

Rebecca shrugs. 'I don't know. For your mum's sake, I wondered . . .'

'No,' Ben says. 'Grandma doesn't deserve that. She deserves a bit of peace now.'

'Yes,' says Rebecca.

Is she surprised by his response? No, she thinks. It's the right thing to do, isn't it? The compassionate thing to do. Her father, she feels sure, would approve.

'I don't like leaving her tonight,' Ben says.

Rebecca squeezes his hand. 'She was asleep,' she says. 'She was exhausted. We'll go and see her in the morning.'

When the phone rings in the night, Ben knows almost before he's fully awake what it is.

'Is that Ben?' The same nurse; the nice one he's spoken to so many times this week. 'I'm so sorry, but I'm ringing with bad news.'

She knew she was dying, Ben thinks. She wouldn't have said anything otherwise. It was her last gift to him: the clearing of her conscience, and of the cloud that has hung over Ben for most of his life.

Rebecca holds him in her arms in that terrible bed in Grandma's little flat, and he weeps. Weeps for more reasons than he can list, or perhaps even understand. For the loss of his grandmother and the time they might still have had together. For the severing of his final link to his mother. And for the end, at last, of his complicated, confusing childhood.

50

Rebecca could almost get away with not going back to Marchboys, but she knows she has to. There's all her equipment to collect, for one thing, and her professional pride won't quite allow her to leave the final touches undone: the handful of little jobs she'd left for that Friday when they were summoned back down to Hove. There's a clear day before Maureen's funeral, and she texts Sam to let him know she's coming. She's messed them around a bit, she thinks, but she's had a good excuse. And there's still a couple more weeks until Freya is due back from her filming. They'll be able to get rid of the scaffolding in plenty of time.

She dreads the prospect of meeting Pieter, but she's hoping he'll still be in Hong Kong – or, failing that, in London, or America, or wherever else he carries on his business. And if he's back in England, she's hoping that Sam will finesse things somehow. That having let her in on his secrets about his boss, he'll want to keep them apart.

For most of the day she's left entirely to herself, just as she hoped. It feels nostalgic, almost, to be back up on the platform one last time. It's so familiar now: that view of the chequerboard floor; the arch of the ceiling above her, and the great chandelier at its apex. She takes things slowly, examining every bit of the mural. Following through the stories that almost overwhelmed her a couple of weeks ago: 'The Magic Mirror'; 'The Toad Prince'; 'The Moon Princess'. If they ever do have a child, she and Ben, perhaps she won't read them those particular fairy tales, she thinks. But she's not counting her chickens, even though Ben is so sweetly eager, now, to make sure they get some help.

She thinks about Kirsty too, that day. About her courage in standing up to her stepfather, calling him out on his behaviour, when she could easily have let things lie. About the price she paid for it: about how terrifying it must have been to encounter him beside the motorway that fateful afternoon. When, Rebecca wonders, did she realise what he meant to do? Did she fear that he'd go back afterwards and harm Ben? That's almost the worst of it: the suspicion that that might have been her last thought. Her little boy, left all alone in the car. He's safe, Rebecca wants to tell her, that smiling girl whose photograph sits on their own mantelpiece at None-go-bye now. He's grown up safe and sound, and I'll always look after him. I'll always love him. On an impulse, she takes her smallest brush and sketches in two tiny figures on the track that winds across her painted landscape. Ben and Kirsty reunited at last, walking together along a different road, towards a different ending to their story.

It's three o'clock by the time she sticks the final brush into her jar of water and wipes off her palette with a rag. Sam has promised to deal with the big pots of paint, but Rebecca makes three or four journeys with her own things, packing them carefully into bags so she can carry them down the ladder.

She's almost finished when she hears footsteps coming into the hall. Sam, she hopes, but somehow she knows it's not.

Pieter is waiting for her when she reaches the floor.

'I hope I didn't startle you this time,' he says.

Rebecca manages a smile. 'No,' she says. She twists her head towards the ceiling. 'It's finished at last. I'm sorry for the delay.'

Pieter shakes his head. 'It's perfectly all right,' he says. 'I was sorry to hear about your mother-in-law.'

'Thank you.'

'And the ceiling has been worth the wait. It's magnificent. Better than I could have hoped.'

Rebecca smiles again, murmurs something self-deprecating. Pieter doesn't move.

'I won't—' He hesitates. 'I don't suppose I can persuade you to have a cup of tea, but I feel I owe you an apology.'

Rebecca feels the ground shift beneath her feet, the chequer-board floor tipping itself back towards the ceiling. She reaches a hand to the ladder.

'I haven't been entirely candid with you,' Pieter says, 'and I fear I might have alarmed you at times.'

Rebecca grips the metal railing more tightly. If they're going to do this, she wants to be on the front foot. 'You knew Kirsty,' she says.

'Yes.' He still doesn't move, but there's a flicker of pain in his face now that makes up Rebecca's mind for her.

'I will have a cup of tea,' she says. 'Thank you.'

'Kirsty wrote about someone in her diary,' Rebecca says, when she's settled on the leather sofa in Pieter's study. 'She didn't use a name. She called them Person. She met them on Saturdays, when she was about seventeen. They bought her some perfume once.'

'Opium,' he says.

Rebecca nods. 'We don't have the next diary, so we don't know what happened. We don't know . . .'

'I'm not Ben's father,' he says. 'If that's what you mean.' And then his face changes, as if he's caught sight of something in the distance. 'She wrote a diary?'

'I'm afraid it doesn't say much about – about you,' Rebecca says. 'She was very secretive about it.'

'She didn't want her parents to know,' he says. 'She never let me meet them. She wanted to do better than them. To get away. I thought—'

The door opens just then, and Sam brings in a tray. Rebecca smiles at him.

'I've finished the painting,' she says. 'I'll be leaving soon.'

'Congratulations,' he says, his manner exactly as it was the first time Rebecca met him. Bland, professional.

And then he's gone, and it's just her and Pieter again. Pieter as she's never seen him before, his hands twisted together in his lap.

'I had to go home to Hong Kong at the beginning of the summer,' he says. 'My parents were both ill; they both died, in fact. I hoped Kirsty and I could pick up where we'd left off when I returned to England, but I was gone for several months. I wrote, but . . . Kirsty had found someone else by the time I got back.'

He hesitates, as if he's doing battle with himself.

'I loved her,' he says, and Rebecca's eyes jerk upwards. 'I wanted to marry her. We were both very young, but I thought that was what she wanted too.'

Rebecca says nothing.

'I saw her again, quite by chance, a few years later. With Ben. I thought – but when she told me how old he was, when he'd been born, I knew he wasn't mine. We didn't have much time; I didn't even find out whether she was married. I tried to put her out of my mind after that. I was busy with work by that stage, building my company. But then – I was back in the area some years later, and I thought of her again. I found her address, and I went to see her. When I realised she was on her own still, I offered to marry her. But that wasn't what she wanted. She told me she was hoping to trace Ben's father. She thought he'd gone abroad. He'd never known about Ben, and she wanted to tell him he had a son. I offered to help her. I thought my contacts—' He stops. 'Ten days later she was dead.'

For a few moments Rebecca stares at him.

'I'm sorry,' she says.

He shakes his head. 'You don't need to be,' he says. 'Thank you for listening. I've never told anyone else.'

'So—' Rebecca starts speaking, then stops again. She's imagining how different Ben's life would have been if Kirsty had accepted Pieter's proposal. And if Pieter had been with them that day, she thinks . . . But he might not have been. He might have been away on business. Who's to say.

'You hired me on purpose,' she says. She meant to be more delicate, but Pieter doesn't seem surprised.

'That's one of the things I need to apologise for,' he says. 'Although – please believe me when I say that I couldn't be more delighted with your work. That's an outcome I didn't deserve.'

'Why?' Rebecca asks. 'What did you want from me?'

He looks pained now. Embarrassed. Curiouser and curiouser, Rebecca thinks.

'I didn't have a very clear idea,' he says. 'I wanted to find out – what Ben was like. Whether you – he – knew anything about Kirsty's death.'

'Whether he might have killed her,' Rebecca says.

'I'm sorry,' Pieter says. 'I couldn't get that idea out of my head. It's tormented me all these years, and I couldn't stop myself asking you about it.' He looks straight at Rebecca now, and she doesn't look away. 'When I met Kirsty with Ben that first time,' he says, 'he was two, nearly three. He had a tantrum in the street. He kicked his mother. He hurt her. He was such a big child: I was shocked. And when she died, I imagined how big he'd be at seven. I remembered that rage and that strength.'

In the distance, a clock strikes four. It reminds Rebecca of the day of Emily's disappearance, but she pushes that thought out of sight.

'It was a kind of madness,' Pieter says, 'but the idea of a random stranger murdering Kirsty seemed – unthinkable. I was sure there was a different answer.'

'We thought you'd killed her,' Rebecca says. 'We thought you were trying to throw suspicion on Ben to cover your own tracks. That you were afraid he'd seen you that day and might still identify you.'

'What?' Pieter looks so shocked that Rebecca almost laughs. 'And what made you stop suspecting me?' he asks. 'Or haven't you?'

'We found out who really killed her,' Rebecca says – and then she shuts her mouth so fast that she almost bites her tongue. No one except her father, they agreed. But she can tell that she's not going to be able to keep it from Pieter now. And perhaps he deserves to know, she thinks. She takes a deep breath, and then she tells him the story they've gleaned from the diaries, from Ben's memory of Jackie's visit, from Maureen's confession.

There's a long silence when she's finished.

'Her father,' Pieter says at last.

'Stepfather.'

'And Ben didn't recognise him?'

'He was wearing a raincoat and a hat,' Rebecca says. 'And I'm sure he'd have been careful to keep his back towards Ben.'

Pieter nods. 'He'd have known Ben was sitting in the car because he'd have seen Kirsty walking along the hard shoulder alone.'

Rebecca feels a quiver of unease. This exchange reminds her, now, of those other conversations. 'Yes.'

'What did he say to her?' Pieter asks. 'How did he get her over the fence? If she knew he was angry with her – if she realised he'd followed her, sabotaged the car on purpose . . .'

'We'll never know,' Rebecca says, 'but she must have been terrified. I hope he pretended he'd come to apologise. To make peace with her. Perhaps he had, but . . .' She shakes her head. 'He wasn't a nice man,' she says. 'I mean . . .' But she doesn't know what she means.

'Thank you for telling me,' Pieter says. 'It makes a difference.'

'I'm glad,' Rebecca says. And she is: she can tell how much it matters to him. It was the right thing to do. But she's worried, now, about what he might do with the information. His agenda might be different from theirs. His perspective. 'We're not—' she begins. 'Terry's dead, and Maureen too. Ben doesn't want to stir things up.'

'I won't say anything. It wouldn't do anyone any good. And it would be no more than hearsay, anyway.'

'Thank you.'

Rebecca's finished her tea: it's time to go. But there's one more question she wants to ask. 'You told me once before that you hadn't been candid with me,' she says. 'You told me you were interested in

Kirsty because of the woods. Because, once upon a time, your woodland ran all the way to where she was killed.'

'That was the truth,' Pieter says. He smiles, rueful now. 'It's part of the reason I bought the house. The main reason, perhaps. It made me feel closer to her. Made me feel, somehow, that the truth about her death was within reach.' And then he stands up, ready to release her.

'I can't excuse my behaviour,' he says, 'but I hope you can forgive me.'

What exactly, Rebecca wonders, is he apologising for? For a moment she hovers on the brink of asking whether he staged his daughter's kidnapping, but she holds herself back. It can't possibly be true. He's not a monster. Maybe, she thinks suddenly, Pieter reads fairy tales to Emily. Maybe she's grown up with stories of intrepid little girls who venture out into the forest. And maybe it's appropriate, in this particular story, that the child has the last laugh.

'I hope Emily's OK,' she says instead.

'Very well,' he says. 'Unchastened, I'm happy to report.'

And he seems, in that moment, more normal – more human – than Rebecca has ever seen him. She smiles.

'Send her my love,' she says. 'Tell her to keep climbing trees.'

On her way out of the house, she glances across towards the woodland, the last remains of that ancient forest where kings and princes hunted, centuries ago. If she'd never come here, she thinks, to the house at the edge of the woods, they might never have solved the mystery of Kirsty's death. She should be grateful to Pieter for that: for asking the questions that set her on the trail. For goading her into seeking out the truth.

51

MAY

When Pieter's eyes have adjusted to the darkness, he looks around him. There are no more than a dozen people in the church: Rebecca and Ben, a small group who must be old family friends, and a couple of women in their fifties Pieter takes for schoolfriends of Kirsty's. He was touched to be invited – surprised and touched – but he nearly didn't come. Mortification is a difficult emotion to put behind you, even for someone as expert at dismissing emotion as Pieter.

But he's very glad to be here. It's a beautiful afternoon, the sky clear and the horse chestnut trees around the churchyard in radiant bloom. The world looks like a good place today. Rebecca's father, an archaic figure in his cassock and surplice, presides with the kind of benign authority that Pieter remembers from the school chaplains of his childhood. There are readings by Ben and one of the schoolfriends, and when the little congregation sings 'All Things Bright and Beautiful' the lump in Pieter's throat makes his voice crack.

He'd planned to slip away quietly at the end, but Rebecca's father is waiting outside the porch, and grasps his hand with a firmness that takes Pieter by surprise.

'I think you must be Pieter,' he says.

'Yes.'

'I'm glad you could come. I hope you felt we did Kirsty justice.'

'It was a lovely service,' Pieter says. 'A lovely idea.'

'She was baptised in this church,' he says.

And might have been married here, Pieter thinks. But he dismisses that thought. Rebecca's father releases his hand and he smiles, turns towards the lychgate and his waiting car.

'Pieter!' Rebecca's voice. He halts. 'The church hall is down the road to the right,' she says. 'There are sandwiches and things.'

'I wasn't—' He turns back to face her. 'Thank you,' he says.

Ben looks different at close quarters. He's unmistakably Kirsty's son, Pieter thinks: he has her eyes, her mouth. Ben holds out a hand, and Pieter takes it. He'd been dreading this moment, but now it's here what he feels is a flow of relief. The reckoning is over, and what they share matters more than what they have thought about each other.

'You were only two when I last met you,' Pieter says.

'Screaming in my pushchair,' Ben says.

'Yes.' Pieter smiles. He wants to say something profound, something memorable – *I loved her*; *she would be proud of you* – but he can't. Understatement is the measure of today. His parents would understand that, he thinks. They would approve. It occurs to him that he should have thought of them during the service – should, perhaps, have thought of arranging a service like that for them, all those years ago. They would have liked a memorial service in an English country church. Perhaps he could put up a plaque somewhere. *In loving memory.*

'Thank you for coming,' Ben says. 'It's nice to have people who knew her here. You should meet her friend Jackie.'

At the sound of her name, one of the women turns.

'You're the mysterious boyfriend, I hear,' she says, her Midlands inflection overlaid now by broad Australian. 'The giver of expensive presents.'

'That's me.'

Jackie narrows her eyes. 'She should've kept you,' she says. 'Kirsty never did know which side her bread was buttered.'

*

He doesn't stay long, even though there's something strangely compelling about this motley collection of people, standing around in a chilly church hall drinking tea from cheap white cups. Perhaps that's why he doesn't want to linger: because what it evokes, deep inside him, is too confusing. But before he leaves, he finds Rebecca.

'I wanted to let you know that the article is coming out soon,' he says.

'Article?'

'About the ceiling. It's going to be in *Country Life*.'

'Oh!' He's pleased by her reaction. He smiles.

'Would you talk to the journalist?' he asks. 'They'd like your input.'

'Of course.'

'Clive's photographs are wonderful. I'll send them to you. And there are more, of course, of the finished piece.'

'*Country Life*?' Rebecca says, as though she's only just taken in that detail. 'And you're pleased with it? Your fiancée likes it?'

'I'm very pleased with it.' He hesitates. 'My fiancée isn't my fiancée any more, I'm afraid, so it's turned out to be a present to myself, but I couldn't be a more grateful recipient.'

'I'm sorry,' Rebecca says. 'That's a shame.'

He shakes his head. 'Don't be sorry. It's for the best.'

Someone calls her name just then, and Rebecca glances over her shoulder.

'I'm sorry,' she says again. 'I ought to . . .'

'Of course,' he says. 'I have to go, anyway.' He grins. 'A meeting. And then a plane to catch.'

52

SEPTEMBER

It's too hot for Rebecca. She's not even that big yet, but it's as if she's got a small furnace inside her, compounding the effect of the late-summer heatwave. Ben has rigged up an awning over the terrace so she can sit in the shade this Sunday morning, her drawing things spread across the garden table. The familiar view of the apple trees and the beehives is always a pleasure, and at this time of year the garden is alive with the buzzing of Ben's bees, bright with the garish heads of dahlias and gladioli. The fruitfulness of late summer feels like a joyful metaphor – she's not quite old enough for this child to be an autumn leaf, she thinks, but it could certainly be called a late-summer bloom.

By midday, though, the heat is too much for her. The thick walls of None-go-bye are a blessing just now: the temperature inside is several degrees cooler. And she needs to deal with her email, anyway. Since the *Country Life* article came out, enquiries have been flooding in through her website. It's a nice feeling to have so much interest, so many enticing projects to choose from, but if she allows the emails to build up for too long her inbox starts to feel overwhelming. You need a secretary, Ben said last night. Or an agent. But the excitement won't last, Rebecca thinks. It's best not to get carried away.

Her laptop is plugged in on the kitchen table. She pours herself a glass of cold water, opens the biscuit tin, then shuts it again and cuts up an apple for herself. Midwives haven't changed their tune since Kirsty's day: *You'll have to watch it a bit or you'll have too much to lose after Baby arrives.* Rebecca reread that entry last night. She knows it almost by heart, but she likes to see Kirsty's handwriting. She loves the loop of her Y at the end of *Baby*, the way it curves round below the B almost as though it's making a little hammock for the baby to lie in. A hammock big enough for a moon princess, she thinks.

She wouldn't admit this to Ben, but she's had a strong feeling that Kirsty has been close to her these past few months. It's helped: she was so anxious at the beginning, and so sick. Ben's been wonderful, of course, but Kirsty's voice, as clear as it was that day when Rebecca found the first diary, has been a secret comfort to her too. *Can't believe I'm going to be a grandmother*, she says. *It'll all be worth it, I promise.* Rebecca wouldn't admit this to Ben, either, but part of her pleasure – part of her excitement about the baby – is for Kirsty. That late-spring morning when she woke up feeling awful and wondered why; when she counted the days and wondered whether it might possibly be; when she went to the chemist to buy a test before she said anything to Ben: it was Kirsty she spoke to in her head. It was Kirsty she shared the suspense with. And it was almost her first thought when she looked down at the positive result – not that Kirsty hadn't died in vain, of course not that, but that something of her would continue. That this was something – the only remaining thing – that Rebecca could do for her.

There've been ten new emails through her website over the weekend. Four of them are sales pitches for marketing companies and art suppliers, three are enquiries from potential clients. Two others she saves to reply to later – one from a young woman who wants to become a mural painter, another from a couple who've sent photos of ceiling frescoes from their holiday in Italy.

The last email, though, is rather different.

Dear Ms Swarbrick, it begins, *I hope you won't mind me getting in touch. My sister sent me a copy of the article in* Country Life

*about your painting at Marchboys House. I used to live in the area
and she thought I might be interested, and indeed I was. Your work
is extraordinary, and I wish I could see it in person.*

*But what interested me even more is your name. I'm sure it's too
much of a stretch, but are you by any chance related to Kirsty
Swarbrick? She was a pupil of mine years ago. I know she died in
tragic circumstances, and I've always felt badly that I didn't write
to her family at the time. I had moved to Canada by then, but that's
really no excuse.*

The email is signed Jack Tollitt. Mr Tollitt, Rebecca thinks, of
the Five Pillars of Islam. He must have been the teacher whose
emigration to Canada inspired Kirsty and Jackie to dream of new
lives on far-flung continents – and Jackie to follow through on the
plan. How funny.

She ought to show Ben the email before she replies, but it feels
like too much of an effort to get up just now.

Dear Mr Tollitt, she writes. Somehow she can't bring herself to
call him Jack. *Thank you for your email and your kind words
about my painting. I am in fact married to Kirsty Swarbrick's son,
Ben. I'm afraid her parents are both dead now, but Ben will be
pleased to hear from you. You may be amused to learn that we
found some of Kirsty's old diaries recently, and your name appears
in them. You taught her RE, I think?* She hesitates. She doesn't
want to over-egg the pudding, but on the other hand he took the
trouble to look her up, to write that nice email. *Her mother
remembered you moving to Canada,* she adds, *and she said Kirsty
and her friends talked about doing the same thing. In fact Jackie
Downey ended up emigrating to Australia – perhaps you remember Jackie too?*

She's not sure which part of Canada he lives in, nor what the
time difference would be, but she doesn't expect a quick reply. She
moves on to the enquiries from potential clients next – two of them
promising, and one more exciting than usual. A church which is
undergoing a major refurbishment is looking for a fresco painter.
The project is well funded thanks to a generous donor, the email

assures her. It would please her father if she could take on that one, Rebecca thinks, but there won't be time for it now before the baby is born. She hopes they'll be prepared to wait.

She's halfway through her reply when Ben comes in from the garden.

'Hungry?' he asks.

'Always.'

Rebecca smiles, and Ben does too. He doesn't believe in the midwives' advice to watch what she eats. We don't want a shrimp for a baby, he keeps saying.

Another feature of pregnancy is the ease with which things slip from her mind these days. It's not until the end of the day that she remembers Mr Tollitt's email.

'Let me show you this, Ben,' she says. 'You'll never guess who wrote to me about the article.'

She can see as soon as she opens her inbox that Jack Tollitt has replied to her message. She lets Ben read the first email, and then she opens the new one.

I was surprised and happy to get your reply, he writes. *I remember Kirsty very well – she was a lovely girl, bright and enthusiastic and full of life. Her death must have been devastating for her family. I didn't realise that she had married: her son must have been very young when she died.*

'He obviously didn't read the newspapers,' Ben says. 'It was hard to miss my part in the story.'

'Perhaps it didn't feature so prominently in Canada,' Rebecca says. 'It was before everyone got their news from the internet, remember.' She looks at him. 'Shall we write back?'

'To say what?' Ben asks.

'I wondered if we should send him photos of the diary pages,' she says. 'But not if you don't want to.'

He shakes his head. 'Whatever you think.'

Rebecca shuts the lid of the laptop. Perhaps she will write back, she thinks, but later, when Ben's not around. Or perhaps she won't:

she feels a bit odd about it now. As though she's making more of it than she ought to.

The churchwarden responds effusively to Rebecca's email. They hadn't realised her father was a vicar, but that makes her interest all the more welcome. They are happy to wait until the new year, but perhaps she would like to come and visit them to discuss the project?

It takes several more emails to nail down the arrangements. In between, Rebecca allows herself to write to Mr Tollitt again. She's not quite sure why; it's unlike her to pursue something Ben isn't keen on. Especially since her reply includes information that he might prefer her not to share. But he knew Kirsty, she tells herself. He might remember a boyfriend. She might even have confided in him.

You probably won't be able to shed any light on this, she writes, one evening when Ben is out on call, *but I feel it's worth asking. Kirsty was never married, and she never told anyone who Ben's father was. I know you were her teacher, not a friend, but I wonder whether by any chance you remember her having a boyfriend? I think you must have left for Canada soon after she got pregnant, in July 1985. Do you remember anything about that last summer term which might be helpful?*

The next time Rebecca sits down at her laptop, Mr Tollitt has replied again. And when she opens his email, she knows at once that she was right to tug at this thread. She stares at the screen for a long time, and then she checks the app Ben installed on her phone that allows her to see where he is. Two miles away: on his way home. She gets up to put the kettle on. But for the first time in months she feels more in need of whisky than herb tea.

Dear Rebecca

I can't fully describe the impact of your last email. I'm afraid I have been disingenuous with you, but the truth is that I have been even more disingenuous with myself.

I know that you will be dismayed by what I have to say, and the fact that Kirsty was no longer, strictly speaking, a pupil of mine in late July 1985 is no defence.

We had always got on well: she was the kind of pupil who could have been a friend, in different circumstances. I was only six years older, in fact, and Kirsty was very grown up for her age. She had thought a lot about life for someone so young. That summer term she was unhappy: she'd had a boyfriend, a university student I think, who had gone away suddenly, and for some reason she didn't want to talk to her friends or her parents about it. She took to coming to my classroom at lunchtime, and sometimes after school, and gradually the conversation moved on from the boyfriend to other things. When term ended, I suggested that we met for coffee in town one day, and things – to coin a phrase – carried on from there.

For a long time it was entirely innocent. I told myself I was well aware of the perils of the situation and of where the boundary of acceptable behaviour lay. Apart from anything else, I was about to fly out to Canada, and the last thing I wanted was to replicate the situation that had made her so miserable. But we did cross the boundary. Just once, just before I left. I felt very bad about it, but Kirsty assured me she was happy that it had happened. That it was a good way for things to end.

I thought about her a great deal in my first year or two in Canada. I wrote to her more than once, but she never wrote back, and I guessed that she had moved on – or perhaps the boyfriend had come home. I assumed her feelings were less hurt than mine, in fact. It never occurred to me that she was pregnant, but I think there is every chance that her baby, your husband, is my son. I wonder, now, whether she ever got my letters.

'Jack,' Ben says. 'Do you remember? *I'd have liked Jack to be there, but obviously that's not happening.* We thought she meant Jackie, but she didn't.'

Rebecca doesn't reply at once. There were other clues in the diaries, she's thinking, but they didn't spot them. *Everyone fancies Mr Tollitt.* And something later, when she wouldn't tell Jackie who the father of her baby was: *Bet it's Mr Tollitt, she said. That made me laugh.* Why did they never think of it? Didn't Pieter say that Kirsty thought Ben's father had gone abroad, even?

She can see the joy of the revelation seeping slowly into Ben's face. And she feels joyful too, but she feels something else even more strongly. A sense of relief so powerful, so overwhelming, that it hollows out the inside of her mind. Because the terrible truth is that she's wondered, ever since the shocking revelations about Terry, whether he might have been Ben's father. She has barely admitted it to herself, still less to Ben. She has told herself that Terry was too short; that Maureen would not, could not have stood by and said nothing. That Kirsty would surely have written different things in her diary. But even so, it's been gnawing away at her. She's wondered whether Kirsty could have suppressed the memory of being abused by Terry; whether it only came back to her when Jackie finally admitted what he'd done to her. That would have been a motive for murder, all right. And she has lain awake at night wondering whether Ben has had the same thought. Whether there might be a final twist of the tale that had the power to corrupt their lives with a cloud they could never hope to banish.

But it's not true. It's not true, and Terry is not the grandfather of her baby. Instead it's this nice man from Canada: a man who cared about Kirsty. Who would have cared for Ben. Whom Kirsty was making plans to search for, just before she died.

It's much too late now to make amends, the email continues. *I won't pretend, either, that my life has stood still. I have a wife and two children, both of them grown up now. I am the headmaster of a school in Winnipeg, where I've lived for twenty years. But I'm coming to England this Christmas to visit my parents, and I wonder – of course it may be the last thing Ben wants, and I would quite understand that – but if he would like it, I would very much like to meet him. To meet you both. But I won't expect an immediate response. Please take as much time as you need to think about it.*

'I don't need to think about it,' Ben says. 'Of course I want to meet him.' But he frowns as he reads through the email again. 'I wonder why she didn't answer his letters,' he says. 'Do you think he's right that she never got them? Do you think – could Terry have kept them from her?'

'Possibly,' Rebecca says. 'Or perhaps – he was a teacher. She knew what it would mean for him if people found out he'd had an affair with a pupil. Perhaps she kept it a secret to protect him.'

'Because she loved him?' Ben asks.

Rebecca nods. 'Because she was a good person. A kind person.'

'And that's why she faced up to Terry too.' Ben has stopped calling Terry Grandad, Rebecca has noticed. She's glad about that. She's glad that Terry and Maureen have been separated in Ben's mind; that Kirsty isn't the only person Ben has been granted a new relationship with.

'Yes,' she says. 'Because she was strong too. Brave. Unafraid.'

Ben doesn't say anything for a few moments. The baby's kicking: Rebecca rests her hand on her swollen belly so that it knows she's aware of its presence. Her presence: it's a girl, they know that.

'I'm curious to meet him,' Ben says at last, 'Mr Tollitt. But I'm not sure I can think of him as my father.'

'I understand that,' Rebecca says. 'We've got used to him being your mother's teacher.'

'It's not just that,' Ben says. 'It's funny: all this time I longed to find my dad, but now that we've found him . . .' He screws up his face. 'I think what I really wanted – all I really needed – was my mum. A chance to make my peace with her.'

Rebecca smiles. 'I'm glad,' she says. 'I'm glad you have.' And then she raises her eyebrows. 'All you wanted?' she asks, an edge of playfulness in her voice now.

'No.' He smiles too. 'Not quite.' He puts his hand on her belly, and their daughter chooses that moment to land a kick squarely in the middle of his palm.

'Do you think she'll keep a diary?' Rebecca asks. 'Little Hilda?'

'Of course she will,' Ben says. 'Where else will she complain about her dull old parents? Or record all the things she can't possibly tell us?'

'Her first kiss,' Rebecca says. 'Her worst Christmas presents.'

And in that moment she sees the future spooling away from them: their child growing up, and them growing old. The sorrows that inevitably lie ahead, but the happiness too. The happiness that will make it all worthwhile.

THE FAIRY TALES

The Moon Princess

Once upon a time there was an old man and an old woman who lived in a cottage on the edge of a forest. They were very poor, but they had everything they needed: their snug little house, plenty of wood to keep them warm, and all the berries and fruit they could eat from the forest and the orchard behind them. The old man caught rabbits and the old woman grew potatoes and swedes, and at night, by the light of the fire, she sewed rabbit skins into coats and stockings and hats.

They had everything they *needed*, but there was one thing they wanted more than anything: a child. When they'd first been married, they'd planned to have dozens of children. One for every letter of the alphabet, the man had said. Thirteen boys and thirteen girls, the woman had said. Lying in bed at night, they named them all: Anna, Bobby, Clara, David. Then Elsa, Frederick, Gretel, Henry, Ingrid, Jack, Kirsten ... Sometimes the man fell asleep before his wife, and she lay awake wondering about the names of the children who came later in the alphabet. What could you call a child beginning with Q, she asked herself? She could never think of the right name. 'Quarrel', she thought one night, might be appropriate for a child near the end of such a large family. 'Question', perhaps, for all the things she would have to ask the others about. Or

'Quietness'. Quietness would come between Pieter and Rudolf, two noisy little boys. Perhaps she would love Quietness best of all.

But the woman waited in vain for these children to arrive. The years passed, and there were no children to name, not even Anna. Every Christmas the husband hung up a stocking by the hearth for the baby they hoped would be there by the next year, and every January the wife made a beautiful pudding from dried fruits and berries to bless their home, but every summer came and went without a child in her womb.

Gradually the woman began to give up hope. Now, she lay awake at night wondering what she'd done wrong. Perhaps she had mistaken the ingredients for the pudding, she thought. Perhaps she hadn't stitched that little stocking carefully and lovingly enough. She never spoke these thoughts to her husband, but he knew what was in her mind as she lay awake beside him, and it grieved him. He loved his wife more than anything in the world, but he knew he could never make her truly happy until she had a child.

One January, when the frost was sharp and beautiful on the ground, the old man went out early one morning to bring in firewood. The winter sun was pale gold, its rays lighting up the fringes of the sky and glinting on the bare branches of the apple trees and the currant bushes. How beautiful the world is, the old man thought. Perhaps this is the year that our luck will change.

As he stood gazing at the garden, he noticed a single apple hanging from a branch of the smallest apple tree. That's strange, he thought. They had picked all the apples months before, but this one must have been too small for them to notice then. It must have grown through the cold days of autumn and winter into a new-year gift. How his wife would love a fresh, ripe apple for her breakfast! But as the old man came closer, he found that he couldn't pick it. It was such a perfect apple, so plump and red and shiny. It belonged to the tree, he thought. For a few moments he gazed at it, taking in every detail so that he could describe it to his wife. And as he stood, he noticed something else. Close by, in a currant bush, a tiny basket was resting among the sharp tangle of branches.

The old man had never seen anything like it before. It looked a little like a bird's nest, and a little like a seashell, and a little like an egg without a top. It was made of the finest filigree of twigs and hair and feathers, silvery-white, and lined with rose petals. And in the middle of it, curled up fast asleep, was the tiniest child he had ever seen.

Gently, very gently, the old man reached down to touch the little nest, and before he knew what he was doing he had it cupped in the palm of his hand. The child was still asleep. She was no bigger than a robin's egg, but perfect in every way, her dark hair curling around a face with plump cheeks and the tiniest, sweetest little cowrie-shell of a nose. He was very much afraid of hurting her, but he couldn't stop himself now: he carried her inside, and up the stairs to the bedroom where his wife still lay sleeping.

'Look!' he called as he came into the room. 'Look what I have found in the currant bush!'

His words woke the child as well as his wife, and as he laid the glowing silver nest into her trembling hands the little girl stretched and sat up. Her face was very solemn, but not afraid.

'Oh!' his wife exclaimed. 'Oh, my dear, where do you come from? Who are your parents, sweet child?'

The little girl put out her tiny hand to touch the old woman's finger. Her voice was as soft and pure as birdsong.

'I am the moon princess,' she said, 'but you are my parents now.'

The old woman gazed down, her face alight with pleasure. 'I am so happy,' she said. 'We will be the best parents you could wish for. But what should we call you, my daughter? Do you have a name?'

The girl smiled, and as she looked from the old woman to the old man, sunlight flooded into the room. 'My name is Quietness,' she said. 'You may call me Quietness.'

And then she shut her tiny rosebud mouth, and from that moment onwards she never spoke again.

The old woman's joy at the arrival of the little girl never faded. As the weeks turned into months and the months turned into years, she fed and clothed her tiny daughter, tucking her into her little bed at night and watching her blossom, day by day, into a beautiful young woman. Her only sadness was that the child never spoke, although she smiled and laughed enough to satisfy her parents that she was happy with the home they had given her. She played with the harvest mice and the spiders, who gave her rides around the garden and spun webs for her to climb, and she danced in the sunlight and turned somersaults through the dewy grass, and every January the old woman laid gifts of fine needlework and candied fruits in the currant bush as a thanksgiving for the blessings it had brought them.

As she got older, Quietness became more adventurous. One spring day she slipped through the garden gate and out into the edge of the forest.

'Be careful,' the old woman warned. 'There are dangers in the forest. Don't go too far, my dear.'

The girl smiled and shook her head, and came back safely. But every day she went further, and was away for longer.

'Please be careful,' the old woman said. 'It's not just the owls and the hawks who might snatch you away. There are wolves and bears in the forest too.'

She didn't tell her that there was also a dragon, living in a cave on the far side of the forest. She didn't imagine the child would ever stray so far, and the dragon was peaceful. As long as no one bothered her, she stayed in her cave and slept. Some of the village elders had tales to tell about how the dragon had protected the village when danger came. Besides, she was a very old dragon.

But one day, the little girl didn't return by nightfall.

The old man and the old woman took lamps and searched far and wide, calling and calling to their tiny daughter.

'Quietness!' they shouted. 'Quietness, where are you?'

When daybreak came, they were both exhausted.

'Go home,' said the old man. 'Go home and rest, and prepare a warming stew for the child. I will go to the village and gather the men to help me find her.'

But the old woman wouldn't leave him.

'I can search as well as you,' she said. 'She's my daughter too.'

So together they went to the village to ask for help. The little girl was popular with the villagers for her sweet smile and her quaint ways, and everyone was keen to join the search. All day they tramped through the forest, calling and calling. The forest echoed with their voices: *Quietness! Quietness!*

At last, as that day drew towards its close, they came to the dragon's cave. The dragon usually stayed deep inside, but even so they approached cautiously, step by step. And then, with a tremble of her heart, the old woman spotted the little girl's coat, torn and bloodstained, lying right in the mouth of the cave.

'Murderer!' she cried. 'Oh, evil dragon! She has eaten our daughter! This is all that is left of her!'

And so the villagers brought their pikes and pitchforks, their swords and ploughshares, and together they stormed into the cave and attacked the dragon. The dragon was old and sleepy, but even so they were surprised that she didn't even raise her head to resist them. Some of the villagers hung back, wondering.

'Don't hesitate!' shouted the old woman. 'The evil dragon has eaten my daughter! Kill her now, before she eats anyone else!'

And so the villagers pressed forwards again and thrust their pikes and pitchforks and swords and ploughshares into the dragon's side, until rivers of blood flowed out of the mouth of the cave and the dragon lay dead.

It was only then that one of the women saw something else. Deeper in the cave, singed and scorched by the dragon's breath, a great wolf lay dead, and in his claws was caught the dress of the little moon princess.

'We have killed the wrong creature,' said the villager. 'The dragon wasn't evil. She tried to save your daughter's life. She didn't resist us when we attacked her because she had no fight left in her.'

Another woman joined in. 'We have killed the dragon for nothing and now she won't protect the village any more. This is a bad day for us all.'

'The moon princess has brought bad luck,' said a third. 'It would have been better if she had never come to the village.'

All the villagers were murmuring now. 'These people should never have taken her in,' they said to one another. 'They were greedy and foolish, and they took a child who wasn't theirs.'

'There will be a curse on the whole village now,' said others. 'Together we have killed the dragon and brought evil on ourselves.'

Shunned by the villagers, the old man and the old woman went home with heavy steps and heavy hearts.

'It's true,' the old man said. 'That child brought bad luck.'

'She was my daughter,' wept the old woman. 'I loved her.'

'No,' said the old man. 'She was never our daughter.'

The next morning he took the moon princess's silvery nest deep, deep into the forest and threw it away where no one would ever find it. But both their hearts were broken. And from that day onwards, neither he nor his wife ever spoke again.

The Toad Prince

There was once, in a far-off land, a princess called Elvira, who was beautiful and kind and clever. She lived in a castle beside a lake with her mother and father, and her friends the skylarks sang outside her bedroom window every morning while she plaited her long auburn hair.

Everyone loved Elvira, and each year on her birthday the whole kingdom had a party: bunting was stretched from house to house, from tree to tree, from village to village. Every kitchen in the land baked cakes and sweetmeats, and the streets were filled with music and dancing to celebrate the birthday of the young princess.

But when Elvira was still a child, a terrible plague came to the land. The kingdom had many fine doctors, but they were mystified by this new illness. It passed over the men and the boys, even if the plague was rife in their houses. It passed over the old women too, but throughout the land, young women fell ill and died, and nothing could be done to help them. It must be a curse, the people said, and although the doctors didn't believe in curses, they shrugged their shoulders and agreed. They had never seen anything like this, and they had no explanation to offer, no cures to suggest. The kingdom that had been so happy fell into sadness and fear.

Elvira's father, the king, ordered the castle gates to be locked and the servants and courtiers to be sent away, and Elvira and her mother were shut away in the tallest tower in the castle. The king himself carried their food up the long stone staircase and left it outside their door, lingering for a few minutes to listen to the queen and the little princess laughing and singing inside.

For a time all was well in the royal castle. Although the king's heart was heavy with sorrow for the plight of his kingdom, he rejoiced that his family was safe. But one dreadful morning Elvira woke to find her mother lying pale and feverish beside her.

'Do not lose heart, dear Mother,' she said, stroking her face. 'You have caught a chill, that's all. Listen to the skylarks: they will cheer you up, and you will soon be well.'

But although the king had the best medicines in the land brought to the castle, the queen grew sicker and sicker. Elvira begged to stay by her mother's side, but the king was terrified that she, too, would catch this dreadful illness. And so the queen died alone, with only the skylarks for company, singing their sweetest songs to carry her soul away to Heaven.

Soon after that, as swiftly as it had arrived, the plague left the kingdom. Every family in the land had lost a mother or a daughter, a sister or a sweetheart, and no one was ever as happy or as care-free again. But slowly, slowly, life returned to normal. Lovers were married, babies were born, and the sickness didn't return.

The king's heart was broken by the loss of his beloved wife. Elvira's heart was broken too, but she was determined to look after her father and to take her mother's place in the kingdom.

'I am nearly a woman now,' she said to him. 'Let me sit beside you on my mother's throne. Let the people see that they still have their princess.'

But the king was frightened for Elvira. Although the doctors assured him that the plague had gone, he didn't dare to risk allowing her to appear in public.

'It's best if you stay in your rooms in the tower for a little longer,' he said. 'You're safe there.'

Elvira pleaded with him, but to no avail. She knew her father was acting out of love, and she had no choice but to accept his wishes. The king had the tower decorated with the finest silks and tapestries, and he made a garden for Elvira on the roof outside, so that she could feel the sun and the wind on her face and could spend her days with the skylarks she loved so much. He even gave her a dog to keep her company, a strange-looking mongrel who turned up at the castle gates, and whom Elvira loved from the first moment she saw him. She called him Arkady, which the queen had once told her was the word for friend in her mother tongue.

Although Elvira was often lonely, Arkady was the most faithful companion she could wish for.

'We won't be shut up here for ever,' she told him every night. 'When my father understands that the plague is over for good, he will change his mind. One day I will travel the world, and you will come too. You will always be with me, Arkady, my dearest friend.'

Arkady would wag his tail and rest his soft muzzle on her knee and look up at her with his beautiful brown eyes, and Elvira would smile, because she was sure he understood her.

The king had vowed never to marry again, but when a few months had passed, he invited his sister to come to the castle and take the place of the queen. Elvira tried to love her aunt, but she was a cold woman, nothing like the loving mother Elvira had lost, and however hard Elvira tried to win her heart, it was clear that she did not like Elvira.

'Your father is right to shut you away,' she said. 'You can do this kingdom no good.'

She began to whisper to the king that there had been a reason for the plague to come to the country, and that that reason was Elvira.

'She is too pretty,' she said. 'She is too spoilt. She has caused envy and anger.'

'But the people love her,' the king protested. 'She has always been kind and good.'

'The people know nothing,' said the new queen scornfully. 'She has offended the spirits of the land. You must make sure no one ever sees her again, or the plague will return.'

And so, reluctantly, the king put new locks on the door to the tower, and built a high wall around Elvira's little garden so that no one could see in or out. Only the skylarks, soaring over the castle, brought her news from the outside world.

The years passed, each one more slowly than the last. Elvira spent her days painting the flowers in her garden, playing her lute and brushing Arkady's soft coat.

'Poor Arkady!' she said. 'It is one thing for a human to be shut away from the world, but quite another for a dog. If it were not for me, you could run through the fields and splash in the rivers. You could see the mountains and the forests in the far corners of the kingdom.'

But Arkady looked at her with his soft eyes and wagged his tail to reassure her that he could never wish to be anywhere but by her side.

One spring day, when she was watching the little fish darting among the water lilies in the pond she had built in her garden, Elvira noticed a little creature climbing out of the water on to a large stone. For a few moments she stared. It was such a long time since she had seen another living being, apart from Arkady and the skylarks and the fish, that she suspected her eyes were deceiving her. But the creature squatted, blinked, then turned its bulging eyes towards her.

'You're a frog!' she exclaimed. 'Welcome, little frog! How did you come to my secret garden?'

'I am not a frog,' said the creature. 'I am a toad.'

Arkady barked, his hackles rising.

'Excuse me?' Elvira said. She must have imagined him speaking, she told herself. She had been alone for too long: her imagination had grown wild.

'I am not a frog,' the creature said again. 'I am a toad.' His voice was deep and refined and just a little haughty.

'I beg your pardon, Mr Toad,' said Elvira. 'Be quiet, Arkady. Mr Toad is a friend.'

But Arkady would not stop barking. The toad looked at him sideways.

'Your dog is a fool,' he said, 'and I am not Mr Toad. I am Prince Malvado.'

'Oh!' Elvira's sorrowful heart began to skip. A princely toad in her garden! Nothing as exciting had happened to her for a long, long time. 'How did you come to be a toad?' she asked.

The toad blinked at her. 'You are clearly very poorly educated,' he said. 'That does not matter. I will teach you.'

'I didn't mean to offend you, your highness,' Elvira said. 'Have you always been a toad?'

'Of course I haven't,' said Malvado. 'I was turned into a toad by a witch. The same witch who sent a plague to your kingdom.'

'Oh!'

'If you had had a proper education, you would know that the witch's curse can only be lifted by a kiss from a princess. No –' Elvira had already begun to move towards him, but he held up a webbed hand to stop her '– it must be true love's kiss, or it will not work, and the spell will last forever. First we must get to know each other, and you must fall in love with me.'

'Of course.' Elvira nodded earnestly. If she could break the spell the witch had put on Malvado, she thought, then the truth about the plague would be known at last. The witch could be discovered and punished, and her father would let her leave the tower.

Arkady was still growling.

'Dear Arkady,' she said, 'you don't need to worry. Prince Malvado is a friend. You are very good to protect me, but although I like to think you can understand what I say to you, you are just a dog.' She smiled at him and stroked his neck, and he whined softly and leaned his head against her.

'I do not like dogs,' said Malvado, 'and this one is a mad dog. You must keep him away from me.'

For the rest of that day, Malvado and Elvira talked. Malvado told her about the long, arduous journey he had endured in order to reach the castle and climb up the high wall to reach her garden. He told her about the palace where he had grown up, and the land where he would one day be king. He related the history of that kingdom, and he began to teach her his language.

'Will I visit your kingdom one day?' she asked, and he turned his large eyes towards her.

'Of course you will,' he said. 'You will be my queen.'

Elvira smiled, and her little heart beat faster. Perhaps there would be a happy ending for her after all, she thought.

'Shall I kiss you now?' she asked.

'No,' said Malvado. 'You do not love me yet. We must be patient.'

The days passed, and everyone was happy except for poor Arkady. All day long he whined and growled and scratched at El-vira's ankle, begging her to attend to him.

'Your dog is jealous,' Malvado said. 'He wants to keep you to himself. He does not want you to leave your tower. I am afraid that he will hurt me. It would be better for you to send him away.'

'I cannot do that,' Elvira said. 'But I will make sure he doesn't hurt you. I will have a collar and a chain made for him.'

Arkady hated to wear the collar, and hated being chained up even more. But it was easier for Elvira to concentrate on Malvado's lessons without the dog to distract her.

Every evening, she asked him again, 'Shall I kiss you now?'

And every evening he replied, 'No. You do not love me enough yet.'

And so every day, Elvira listened more carefully, and tried harder to remember the things he taught her: the names of kings and queens and foreign lands; the stories of wars and curses and fights over succession. She was not very interested in wars, and she wished Malvado could think of different ways to woo her. She wished he would sing to her, or admire her hair, or let her tell him about her mother, whom she still missed so much.

But one night, when she caught his eyes watching her gravely while he spoke, she felt a spark of love ignite suddenly inside her. Dear Malvado, she thought. Of course she loved him! How could she not, when he had been so patient and so thoughtful with her?

'I must kiss you now!' she cried. 'Let me break your spell, Malvado!'

Before he could stop her she closed her eyes and bent down towards the cushion where Malvado was sitting. His skin felt cold and slimy under her lips, and for a moment she was terrified that the spark of love she had felt wasn't strong enough to destroy the witch's magic. But as she lifted her face from his head, she felt a great whooshing and swirling and swelling – and when she opened her eyes, a tall man was standing in the place where the toad had been.

'Well done, Elvira,' he said. 'You may be a stupid girl, but you have managed to kindle enough feeling in that gullible heart of yours to set me free.'

Elvira stared at him. He didn't look anything like she had expected. He was dressed in black robes, with a long, straggling beard and sharp eyes and a smile colder than the toad's skin.

'Hello, Malvado,' she said bravely. 'Hello, my prince.'

Malvado laughed. 'I am no prince,' he said. 'You should learn not to believe everything you are told. I am the sorceror Malvado, the sworn enemy of your father. It was I who sent the plague to your land. The witch who imprisoned me in that cursed amphibian body banished the plague at the same time. She thought she had vanquished me for good – but now that you have freed me, my conquest of your kingdom is assured.'

'No!' shouted Elvira. 'No, no!'

Elvira could hear something else now: the noise of Arkady barking frenziedly, and pulling wildly at his chain.

Malvado sneered. 'Your prince was here all the time,' he said. 'He set out to rescue you years ago, but on the way he was foolish enough to take pity on a talking toad who asked for directions to the nearest pond. Although the effort of it almost killed me, I mustered enough magic to turn him into a dog: a scruffy, ugly, fatuous dog, who could do no more than whine mournfully at his princess and sit by her side with his clumsy tail wagging.'

'I have always loved Arkady!' Elvira shouted. 'I love him more than I could ever have loved you, even if you had been a prince!'

Things happened very fast then. There was a crack of lightning, and Arkady appeared before her in the shining armour of a prince. With one slash of his sword he cut his chain loose, and with another he lunged at Malvado. But Malvado was too quick for him: he drew a wand from under his robe and shrieked a curse at Arkady. As Arkady fell, his sword was thrown into the air, and Elvira seized it and thrust it at Malvado. She felt the blade pierce his flesh and heard him cry out.

'No!' he shrieked. 'Ah, Elvira, you ungrateful girl!'

For the magic which had allowed Elvira to return Malvado to human form also gave her the power to kill him. Malvado crumpled before her, his eyes bulging just as they had when he was a toad. For a moment Elvira stood looking down at him, and in that moment she felt a morsel of pity, no greater than the morsel of love that had driven her to kiss him.

But Malvado had no pity in him, and certainly no love. In his dying seconds, he uttered another stream of cruel words, and as he breathed his last, Elvira fell to the ground beside Arkady.

And so the princess and her faithful prince died together, in the garden where they had spent so many happy hours together. But as the life drained from their human bodies, two beautiful trees sprang from the ground: a ravishing rose with flowers the same colour as Elvira's auburn hair, and a slender dogwood around which the rose twined itself lovingly.

When the king found out what had happened to his beloved daughter, his heart was broken, and he sent his cruel sister far away.

The plague never returned to that country. But every year the people still string up their bunting and bake their cakes and sweetmeats and dance in the streets to celebrate Elvira's birthday. And in the castle garden, the dogwood and the golden rose still hold each other close, with the skylarks nesting high in their branches.

The Magic Mirror

There was once a farmer whose fields were always greener and more productive than his neighbours'. People were jealous of him, but he would tell them: 'There is no secret to it. My crops grow strong and tall because they are lovingly tended. I love my wife and she loves me, and together we work hard in our fields so that whatever we plant will flourish.'

His neighbours grumbled, but they knew that he was telling the truth. They saw the farmer and his wife out in the fields from early in the morning until late in the evening, in rain and shine and thunderstorms. They saw them ploughing and planting and weeding, lifting their heads now and then to smile at each other. And the farmer was generous: when his neighbours didn't have enough food, he would always share some from his stores with anyone who needed it.

One spring, the farmer's wife gave birth to a little boy. They named him Silas, and they loved him even more than their fine green fields. He was a strong, healthy baby, and before long the wife was back in the fields with her husband. They took turns to carry their son on their backs, and while they worked they talked to him. They told him how to till the land and tend the crops, when to plant and when to harvest. 'When you grow up,' they told him, 'these fields will be yours.'

But before Silas was four years old, his mother was taken ill. For a long winter she languished in her bed, and by the spring she was dead. Life was never the same again for the farmer and his little son. The joy had gone from their hearts, and from their farm. Every year their fields were a little less green and their harvest was a little smaller.

And then came a year when nothing grew at all. Silas was full of despair.

'I must do something,' he told his father. 'I must go and look for work.'

And so he set out down the long road to the city. He walked all day, until his strong young legs could walk no further, and as the sun set he stopped at the edge of a village to eat the tiny parcel of food his father had packed for him. He was still hungry when he had finished, and his feet were sore, and now that the light was fading he could tell the night would be cold. I wish I had more food, he thought, and new boots so that my feet wouldn't hurt so much. I wish I had brought my winter coat to keep me warm at night.

There was a well nearby, and Silas left his pack under the tree where he had been sitting and went to fill up his flask with water. Beside the well there was something that he took at first for a pile of old clothes, but as he came closer he saw that it was an old man, sitting crumpled on the ground.

'Boy,' said the man. 'Will you fill my bottle with water? I am too weak to reach into the well.'

'Of course I will,' said Silas. 'Let me fill yours before I fill mine.'

The man handed him a glass bottle, and Silas looked at it in surprise. It was a curious and elegant shape, with words and pictures carved around it.

'What a beautiful bottle!' Silas said. He filled it from the well and handed it back to the old man, who drained the water from it in one gulp.

'Will you fill it again?' he asked. 'I am still thirsty.'

Silas was thirsty too, but he did as the man asked. When he had drained the second bottle of water, the old man asked him to fill it for a third time. But this time, when Silas held it out to him, he shook his head.

'You have been kind,' he said. 'You have filled my bottle three times before quenching your own thirst. This time you must drink from my bottle, and while you drink you may think of three wishes you would like me to grant.'

Silas smiled. He didn't believe for a moment that the old man could make wishes come true. But he tipped the bottle towards his lips and drank the cold water, and as it flowed through his body he felt things happening to him. A fine new pair of boots appeared on his feet, and his winter coat settled on his back, its pockets bulging with food.

Silas was astonished and delighted – but very quickly his mood changed to dismay.

'Wait,' he said, 'these are not the things I truly wish for!'

If he had known the old man really had the power to grant wishes, he would have thought more carefully. How could he have settled for boots and a coat and some food when he might have had anything he wanted?

The old man looked at him closely. 'You wished for these things. I told you to think of three wishes, and these are the things you thought of, are they not? Did you not believe I could grant your wishes?'

'I'm sorry,' said Silas. 'It's not that I'm not grateful. It's just – my father is starving, and his crops have failed. I should have thought of him.'

The old man nodded. 'I will give you one more wish,' he said. 'But this time, choose carefully.'

Silas shut his eyes and thought about his father. He thought about the stories his father told of the years when their farm was the envy of all their neighbours, and his proud claim that their crops grew so well because he and his wife loved each other so much – and because they tended their land with the same love. What he should wish for, Silas thought, was his mother – and as that thought settled in his mind, he felt a great surge of love and longing. He had grown up without a mother, but in that moment he could hear her voice singing to him and he could feel her arms around him, keeping him safe. They all needed her, he thought. He and his father and the farm.

The old man nodded. 'That is a very good choice,' he said. 'It is not in my power to bring your mother back to life, but from this day onwards you will be able to see her and talk to her. You will be able to draw strength again from her love.'

Before Silas could reply, the man touched the water bottle that was still in Silas's hand, and it turned at once into a mirror the same shape and size as the bottle, with the same ornate carvings around its frame.

'When the sun sets each day, take down the mirror and look into it,' the old man said. 'Your mother will be there, waiting for you.'

'Thank you,' Silas said.

'If you ever wish it, the mirror will turn back into a water bottle,' the old man said, 'and however much you drink from it, it will always be full of water.'

Silas laughed happily. 'I will never want water more than my mother,' he said.

'As you wish,' said the old man. 'But now you should rest. You have a long walk home tomorrow.'

Silas started at dawn, and he made good time in his new boots. By lunchtime he was home. His father was surprised to see him, and delighted when he emptied the food from his pockets on to the table. Together they ate the best meal they had had for months. When they had finished, Silas told his father about the old man by the well, and he took the magic mirror out of his coat.

'It can't be true,' his father said. 'It must be a trick. Perhaps we will go up in smoke.'

But as sunset approached, both father and son knew that it was worth the risk. They set the mirror on the table and sat down in front of it – and as the golden light of the setting sun fell through the kitchen window and touched the mirror, there she was: Silas's mother, as lovely and lively as she had been all those years before.

Silas and his father wept to see her, and she wept a little too when they told her what had happened to the farm.

'Did you think my love had gone?' she said. 'It is with you still:

with both of you. Together you have all the strength you need to grow crops as tall and strong as ever.'

Early the next morning, Silas and his father went out to the fields and started turning over the ground. When they had finished, they took the last of their seed and sowed it carefully, lovingly, on the bare earth. Every day, from then on, they worked hard in the fields, and every evening they sat in front of the mirror and reported on their day's labours. As the weeks passed, the crops started to grow. Through that long summer, their fields flourished, and every evening the farmer's wife, Silas's mother, praised their efforts.

Their harvest that year was almost as good as the ones before she had died.

'Next year will be even better,' she said. 'Look after the ground carefully through the winter, and save the best grains from the harvest to sow next spring.'

For seven years after that the farm flourished. As Silas grew taller and stronger, his father grew older and his strength began to fail – but every evening, talking to his wife, his face lit up again like a young man's.

Then one summer, a drought came. There was no rain for weeks, and then for months. The wells dried up, and even the rivers shrivelled into muddy rills. The crops began to wilt, then turned brown and crumbled to dust, and Silas's father fell ill and took to his bed. As Silas trickled the last drops from their water butts into his father's mouth, he looked down at him in desperation.

That evening, he spoke to his mother alone. His father had a high fever: Silas wasn't sure he would survive the night.

'It's time,' his mother said.

'Time for what?'

She smiled. 'Time to say goodbye,' she said. 'You need water more than you need me. Remember what the old man said? If you turn the mirror back into a water bottle it will never be empty.'

'And then can I turn it back into a mirror?' Silas asked, but his mother shook her head.

'Then I can't do it,' Silas said.

'You can,' his mother said, 'and you must. You have had everything you need from me. You will always have my love, Silas.'

Silas nodded slowly, tears running down his face. He knew she was right. He knew he had to save his father now.

'Goodbye, Mother,' he said. And as he spoke the last syllable, the mirror was gone and in its place was the curious bottle he had first seen all those years before, brimming with clear water.

Silas nursed his father back to health, and the drought passed. But the old man never recovered all his strength. He still drank each day from the glass bottle, but a year later he fell ill again.

'It is time,' he said then, just as his wife had done. 'The farm is yours now, Silas. Look after my fields. Love them and cherish them, and they will always feed you.'

Silas wept, but his father smiled at him.

'Don't weep for me,' he said. 'I am going to join your mother. I will be happy forever now.'

The winter that followed was hard for Silas. But the next spring, he fell in love with a young woman from the village. That summer, when anyone passed the farm, they could see Silas and his young bride out in the fields all day long, in rain and shine and thunderstorms. They saw them ploughing and planting and weeding, lifting their heads now and then to smile at each other.

To this day, Silas's farm has the greenest fields and the strongest crops of any in the land. And on a high shelf in the farmhouse stands the glass bottle with its ornate carvings, always full of water.

Acknowledgements

This book would not have been written without the bountiful support of my lovely husband, who is so well versed in the roles of house elf, therapist, personal chef and human thesaurus that I might be accused of taking him for granted – but I promise I never do. Special thanks too to Juno, who has lived through the process with us and never failed to make me laugh (or make me sweet treats when they were needed), and to Clemmy, Katie, Toby and Daphne, who have been constantly on tap through the family group chat and ready to provide the answer to pretty much anything.

Sam Fincher, plumber extraordinaire, provided invaluable insights into Ben's work, but is in no way responsible for any inaccuracies or infelicities in my representation of him. Among my writing friends, I'm hugely grateful to Catherine Coldstream and Julia Hollander for many 'working' lunches and feverishly productive writing retreats; to Julie Summers for moral support, tomato seedlings and delightful suppers; and to Vanessa O'Loughlin, who is such a generous supporter of so many writers' work. And I can't fail to mention the many friends and neighbours who make life better in so many ways, or the Bach Choir, which keeps me happy and sane.

Without Patrick Walsh and the team at Pew Literary, *The House at the Edge of the Woods* would never have got further than my laptop – and without Selina Walker, Rose Waddilove and the many, many people at Penguin Random House who have played a part, it would have been a much less good book. Thank you, thank you to all of them.

Bringing a book from manuscript to what you are reading is a team effort, and Penguin Random House would like to thank everyone at Century who helped to publish *The House at the Edge of the Woods*.

PUBLISHER
Selina Walker

EDITORIAL
Rose Waddilove
Charlotte Osment

PRODUCTION
Helen Wynn-Smith
Faye Collins
Annie Peacock
Elizabeth Moyes

UK SALES
Alice Gomer
Olivia Allen
Kirsten Greenwood
Jade Unwin
Evie Kettlewell

DESIGN
Ceara Elliot

INTERNATIONAL SALES
Richard Rowlands
Linda Viberg

PUBLICITY
Hana Sparkes

MARKETING
Isabella Levin

AUDIO
James Keyte
Meredith Benson